TARGET ON
HER BACK

JULIE MILLER

COLTON COWBOY
JEOPARDY

REGAN BLACK

MILLS & BOON

First Published in Great Britain 2020
by Mills & Boon, an imprint of HarperCollins*Publishers*
1 London Bridge Street, London, SE1 9GF

Target on Her Back © 2020 Julie Miller
Colton Cowboy Jeopardy © 2020 Harlequin Books S.A.

Special thanks and acknowledgement are given to Regan Black for her contribution to *The Coltons of Mustang Valley* series.

ISBN: 978-0-263-28028-9

0420

MIX
Paper from
responsible sources
FSC™ C007454

This book is produced from independently certified FSC™ paper to ensure responsible forest management.

For more information visit: www.harpercollins.co.uk/green

Printed and bound in Spain
by CPI, Barcelona

TARGET ON
HER BACK

JULIE MILLER

In memory of Maggie McGonagall Miller, the gentlest creature I have ever known. What a blessing it has been in our lives that you picked us to be your pack that day at the humane society. You were so loved, my sweet baby dog. I hope you have squirrels to chase, plenty of treats and a warm lap to snuggle in up in heaven.
I miss you.

Chapter One

"Let go of me." Professor Virginia Brennan tugged free of the older man's bruising grip. That only made him latch on with both hands.

"Where is Lombard?" The white-haired man's thick accent turned his *w* to a *v* and reminded her of Chekov from the *Star Trek* television show she loved to watch. Only this man was no teen heartthrob or outer space hero.

"I don't know, Dr. Zajac. Bullying me won't help." The chamber music playing in the background beneath the conversations around them sounded oddly discordant as Virginia "Gigi" Brennan found herself backed against the vestibule wall outside the Muehlebach Hotel's grand ballroom.

"You cannot hide him from me," her coworker at Williams University accused.

"I'm not." She shoved at his chest, silently blaming the couple that walked by for averting their heads from the esteemed researcher's harassment and doing nothing to intervene. But Evgeni had seen them, too, and—perhaps wanting to uphold his reputation with the donors who supported his joint research with Ian Lombard—he released her. Once Gigi slid beyond arm's reach, she gestured to the restroom hallway where she'd last seen her friend and mentor, Ian Lombard. "I saw you two arguing a few minutes ago. Now he's gone." She needed to find Ian herself, so she could leave this nightmare of noise and people at the university reception in downtown Kansas City and go home. Her face ached as she summoned one more PR-worthy smile. "I'm looking for Ian, too. I was really hoping you'd seen him."

Zajac's accent grew more guttural as his anger rose. "He fears me now and will not show his face." He rattled off something in rapid Lukin, speaking too quickly for her to grasp more than "years of research," "betrayal" and something about wrapping his hands around the man's neck.

"I don't know what that means," she said, trying to appease his temper. "Perhaps if you repeat it more slowly." As a visiting professor working on the research team she headed for Ian at Williams University, she knew it was her responsibility to maintain good working relationships with every member of Ian's staff. Evgeni Zajac and his department at their sister university in the tiny Eastern European country of Lukinburg provided the raw materials and several of the preliminary ideas that Ian's team developed into state-of-the-art technology. Keeping both ego-driven men happy was typically part of her job as the calm, quiet wunderkind at the WU School of Engineering and Technology. But she had problems of her own tonight. "I don't suppose you have twenty dollars I could borrow. I need—"

"Where is my Hana?" Evgeni dismissed her with a wave of his hand, spinning around to look for his wife, who also acted as his translator, and he stalked back into the reception room. He cursed his missing wife, Ian and what sounded like the entire North American continent. She had been lectured by temperamental colleagues before, but never in a foreign language. Considering she didn't want to be at this fund-raiser in the first place, and had stayed longer than Ian had promised she'd have to, Gigi figured she didn't need to chase after Dr. Zajac to offer an apology to mend obviously strained international relations.

Clutching her university ID from the lanyard hanging around her neck, she scanned the crowded ballroom for options. She supposed she could ask Gary Haack, another colleague with whom she worked closely on the research team, to loan her the money she'd need for cab fare back to the university where she'd left her wallet, phone and keys. Or maybe he'd call a car for her. How many times had he said he'd like to get closer to her? That she could ask him for anything? About as many times as he'd cornered her in her office or his, invading her personal space in the name of a work issue. She wasn't any good at flirting or being flirted with, so his repeated invitations to one event or another wound up making her feel suspicious rather than flattered. No. Not an option. Knowing Gary, there'd be strings attached to any favor she asked of him. Besides, she couldn't spot his blond head towering over the other guests at any of the catering tables or gathered around the various displays of inventions and technologies Ian, Evgeni and their research team had developed.

Venturing into the crowded room to ask anyone else for help made her almost physically ill. She'd come with Ian tonight, and now Ian was gone. Getting herself home was all on her shoulders now.

She slipped away from the party and retrieved the old ivory sweater she'd thrown on at the last minute from the coat check room. Sliding it on for warmth over the short sleeves of her black sequined dress, and hugging it around herself for the comfort of her late mother's memory since she'd knit it for her years ago, Gigi took the escalator up to the lobby. She paused at the bank of glass doors facing Wyandotte Street and exhaled a weary sigh.

Of course. It was raining. The sidewalk outside was

wet and shiny, reflecting the lights from traffic, the hotel and Municipal Plaza across the street. Even if the weather was nice and she wasn't a woman alone late at night, the university would be too far to walk from here, especially in the black high heels that pinched her toes.

Options, Gigi. Think of options. Going back to that crowd and begging someone for help wasn't one of them.

Thinking was what she excelled at when she wasn't overwhelmed by people and emotions, and when she saw the bright lights from the city bus letting out passengers at the corner of Twelfth Street and Wyandotte, she knew what to do.

Flipping over her university ID, she let out an audible breath. Her bus pass was still tucked inside the plastic sheath. Clutching the lanyard in her fist, she stepped out into the chill of the rainy autumn night. With her heels splashing over the pavement, she hurried across the street and knocked on the closing bus doors so she could climb in before it drove away.

Twenty minutes later, having used up every bit of extroverted energy her shy genes could muster, she was back on campus. She was tired, damp and cold. But she still wasn't getting home anytime soon.

She cleared her throat, giving the night security guard in the gray-and-black uniform another chance to wake up.

"Officer Galbreath?" she repeated, hugging her long cardigan over her dress. It was colder here inside the regulated air of the Williams University Technology Building than it had been outside, perhaps because her feet were still wet and squishing in her ruined shoes. "Jerome?"

Her only reply was a gravelly snore. The older gentleman with the mahogany skin and salt-and-pepper hair had dozed off at his desk in the lobby. Since she'd been absentminded enough to leave her university ID looped around her neck like a piece of jewelry, she had her own key card to enter the research lab on the second floor. But if Jerome Galbreath didn't log her in before she did so, she'd set off the after-hours security alarm the moment she opened the door.

The last thing she wanted was for campus security and the Kansas City police to swarm the building and question why she was breaking into the lab in this ridiculously short and soggy getup, long after classes had ended for the day and most of the campus had shut down for the weekend. Gigi hated swarms of anything—birds, bugs, people crowding around her, too many people talking at once.

Tonight's party had been pure torture. She'd done the job the university had expected of her, but now she needed solitude and silence to take the edge off her frayed nerves. That meant yoga pants or jammies, a cup of hot tea and a book or movie to immerse herself in at home.

Only, she couldn't get home.

She already felt like a dork for leaving her phone, keys and wallet in her backpack at work because she'd been so nervous about attending the hoity-toity reception at the Muehlebach Hotel. *Come to the party, Gigi,* Dr. Lombard had said. *Put on something pretty. Ride in the limo with me to the hotel and drink champagne. The university is buying. You deserve to have a little fun to celebrate our success. You do have a party dress, don't you?*

Um, no.

It wasn't until Dr. Lombard had said that he needed her to come along to explain the technicalities of their research to interested guests while he schmoozed the crowd of visiting Lukinburg dignitaries and donors who'd made generous contributions to the department that she'd agreed to go. He needed her expertise to make tonight a success.

That had always been her Kryptonite—someone needing her. Since most people, beyond her sister and a few close friends, barely noticed her shy, studious self, the idea of being important enough to be needed, to be necessary to another person, was as alluring as it was unfamiliar. She'd been suckered in by those words more than once in her life. As smart as she was, it was a lesson she should have learned by now.

A lesson that wouldn't leave her stranded in downtown Kansas City after dark.

She was more than eager to support Ian Lombard's cutting-edge research into new-market computer-component and power-consumption applications, and the Lukin investors were willing to fund that research because it gave them a market for the raw materials produced in their country. Gigi knew how to conduct herself in a classy manner at sedate university functions, how to smooth things over for her brilliant, but volatile boss. And although she'd gotten lost during Dr. Zajac's tirade, she even spoke a few words of Lukin, so she could communicate with their guests on a rudimentary level. She was proud of Dr. Lombard's work—her work, too, since she'd been his right hand for two years now. She'd taken over teaching one of his classes to free him up to concentrate on fast-tracking his research.

But celebrate? Schmooze? Dr. Gigi Brennan fit that role about as well as this fancy dress she'd borrowed from her younger, curvier sister fit her. Although Tammy had insisted that she couldn't go wrong with a little black dress, the outfit was too short to be comfortable and hung loose on Gigi's willowy frame.

Gigi's willingness to put on Tammy's dress and brave the reception had ended the moment she realized Dr. Lombard had left the party without her. He'd needed her, all right—to cover for his inexplicable absence, to represent the department while he went off and…what? Went home to get a full night's sleep? Skyped a phone call with his drama professor wife who was currently researching Henrik Ibsen in Scandinavia? Rendezvous in a hotel room upstairs with one of those dewy-eyed grad students he liked to flirt with while said wife was out of the country?

The why didn't matter. Gone was gone. Lombard had taken advantage of her inability to say no to him. She'd call her sister for a ride, but Tammy had been at a teachers' conference in Vegas this week and was staying a couple of extra days to have some fun. Gigi was on her own. Nothing new there. She should be used to that by now.

Gigi had made it back to the university where her car was parked.

But she wasn't going any farther without her keys.

And a sleeping security guard.

She was the responsible one. The family breadwinner who'd stepped up to take custody of her underage sister after their parents had died in a traffic accident. She kept food on the table and a roof over her and Tammy's heads.

So what if she got so caught up in her work some days that she lost track of the time?

So what if she babbled like an idiot or completely shut down when her nerves got the better of her?

She was the one with the Ph.D. she'd earned by her twenty-fourth birthday three years earlier.

She was the one who'd been selected to be a part of Dr. Lombard's team to find applications for his technology. Weaponry. Environmental sciences. Medical programs. Business efficiency models. There was a lot of money to be made in the practical applications of Lombard's research. Money meant not just an impressive paycheck for the duration of his funding, but also the prestige that would allow her to move to a bigger university, like Massachusetts Institute of Technology or Harvard, to pursue her own research, or at least to head up her own program here in Kansas City.

With a résumé like that, she should be able to get herself home.

Gigi adjusted her glasses on her nose and silently debated how difficult it would be to extract the computer tablet from beneath Jerome's folded arms on top of the desk where he slept. She quickly dismissed that idea because the guard wore a gun, and if she accidentally startled him awake, who knew how he'd react? For a split second, he might think she was stealing the tablet, or worse, attacking him, reacting before his thoughts cleared enough to recognize her.

So, she knocked on the counter above the desk. When he stirred, she reached over the counter to nudge his arm. "Jerome?"

She jumped back half a step when the guard's breathing stuttered. Flattening his palms atop the desk, he pushed himself up in his chair and blinked her into focus.

"Professor Brennan?" He picked up the nearly empty coffee mug on the desk beside him, frowning before he set it back down and pushed it away. "That didn't do me any good. Don't know why I'm dragging tonight. Looks like you got caught out in that rainstorm."

"I did. Thankfully, it didn't last long." She pushed a lock of wet auburn hair that stuck to her cheek up into what was left of the bun she wore at her nape. "I'll dry out soon enough."

He smiled up at her for a moment before squeezing his eyes shut and rubbing at his temple. "Can't seem to stay awake."

Gigi leaned against the counter, worried about the lines furrowed beside his eyes. "Are you feeling all right?"

"I've got a mother of a headache. Maybe I'm coming down with something."

Gigi's Ph.D. was in applied physics, not medicine, but even she could see that something was off about the man who'd worked the night shift here since retiring from KCPD, a few years even before she had joined the faculty. Jerome Galbreath didn't just fall asleep on the job. "I've got a couple of ibuprofens up in my office. Would that help?"

"Maybe. Thanks." Still seeming a little disoriented, Jerome inspected the imprint that the corner of his computer tablet had left on his hand before shaking off the drowsy fog. "How long was I out?"

"I've only been here a few minutes. Friday nights are pretty slow. I imagine it can get kind of boring."

He shook his head, disagreeing with her speculation. "I didn't just doze off. That was a deep sleep. Sorry about that." He punched the power button on the tablet and pulled up the personnel screen. A lot of expensive equipment and cutting-edge technology was housed in the lab where she worked on the second floor. Only a handful of professors and staff held key cards to access the faculty offices and lab itself, and the university kept close tabs on anyone who entered the building. Officer Galbreath rose to his feet and pushed the tablet across the countertop so she could sign in. Even as he rubbed his temple again, he offered her his usual smile. "You're here mighty late."

"I left my bag up in my office when I changed for the party." If Dr. Lombard hadn't been in such a hurry to put in an appearance at the reception, she might have remembered to borrow an evening purse from Tammy, too, and switch a few necessary items to it. Like car keys and her phone.

"Do you have your key card?"

Gigi pulled the purple-and-white Williams University

lanyard she wore from inside the front of her dress and held up the attached key card ID. "Right here."

"Doesn't exactly go with your outfit," Jerome teased.

"That's why I'm not the fashion icon of the family." She scrolled through the names on the screen to find her own but frowned when she saw the one that was still highlighted. "Is Dr. Lombard here?"

Surely, he wasn't here at this hour to work. Unless that argument she'd witnessed between Ian and Dr. Zajac had prompted him to come back to the lab to…what? Retrieve evidence to prove a theory or show proof of a patent? Correct a mistake in their findings or investigate a flaw in their product development?

The security guard took the tablet from her and frowned. "I must have forgotten to log him out when he left."

"But he was here?" Gigi clarified. "When?"

"He was in a meeting in his office when I came on duty at nine. There was a message on my desk saying he wasn't to be disturbed." He punched in a number on his phone before handing her a folded-up note. "I thought he had that reception with those foreign investors."

Gigi nodded, skimming the brief, typed missive. "I was there with him. For a while."

Jerome—
Private meeting in my office tonight.
No visitors. No calls.
I'll lock up.
Dr. Lombard

Private meeting? Tonight? When he should be out celebrating his success? And not leaving her stranded? She was Ian's right hand when it came to work. Why wouldn't she know about this meeting?

Maybe she should rethink the curvy young student theory. "You didn't see anyone with him, did you?" Although the sterile lab was hardly conducive to romance, Ian did have a leather couch in his office. "A woman, perhaps?"

"I didn't even see him. Probably my mistake, and he's long gone." Jerome grinched about not being old enough to nod off like he had and hung up the phone. "He's not answering in his office." Gigi went ahead and signed herself in and Jerome waved her around the counter and connected the chain from his desk to the outer wall to indicate that access to the building was blocked while he was away. "I'll walk up with you and make sure he's gone before I sign him out. It's past time for me to make rounds, anyway."

Jerome opened the elevator doors and ushered her inside. When the doors opened again onto the second floor, the hallway was dark except for the security lights casting a sickly yellowish glow across the white marble floor tiles. The entire wall across from them was devoted to the research lab and faculty offices behind a row of floor-to-ceiling windows framed by stainless steel and secured by key-card access locks. The impressive facade allowed students and visitors to peek inside without disturbing the pristine sterility of the workstations where Gigi and Ian, other university staff, visiting professors, and promising graduate students worked. The display of technology was also meant to inspire students in classrooms on this side of the hallway, as well as motivate visiting donors to give even more money to the university and its research-and-development programs.

But tonight, instead of inspiring or motivating or even feeling much like the familiar workplace she was used to, the darkened lab on the other side of the glass was filled with shadows. The vague outlines of tables and equipment took on menacing forms at night, like predators in a cave, lying in wait for their unsuspecting prey to wander inside to become dinner. All her imagination needed were a few blinking monitor lights to masquerade as eyes for the creatures, and the nightmare crawling over her skin and raising goose bumps would be complete.

Gigi startled at the brush of Jerome's hand against her arm. "Sorry."

She pushed aside his apology and stepped off the elevator. "My fault. I was letting my imagination get carried away with how creepy this place looks at night." She followed Jerome across the hall, pulling her key card from around her neck as he unhooked the flashlight from his belt and shone it through the glass.

"It's mighty dark in there," Jerome pointed out. "I can't tell if Dr. Lombard's office door is open from here, but there sure isn't any light coming from there."

Gigi swiped her card through the lock, but nothing happened. "That's strange." She thought again of the shadowy predators inside. "There aren't even any equipment lights glowing…" When her card failed to work a second time, she typed in her override code and opened the door. She paused, grabbing Jerome's arm as he entered ahead of her. This wasn't right. "There should be lights on. Monitors regulating electricity. Ongoing tests."

Jerome nodded and flipped the light switch beside the door. Nothing. He went to the nearest table and turned the manual switch on a lamp. No light. "Do you think we blew a fuse?"

She glanced up at him. "We don't use fuses anymore. The lab and research offices are on a self-contained, computer-regulated system."

His blank stare told her she'd missed the point. "Figure of speech, Professor."

"Oh. Right." Her trepidation turned to concern about the stability of the millions of dollars of sensitive equipment housed here. "The lab is on its own breaker box from the rest of the building, including security. A surge of some kind must have blown the entire circuitry. Otherwise, the backup protocols would have engaged." She shook her head. "Nothing's on in here."

"Take this." Jerome handed her his flashlight. "I've got a light on my phone. I'll go down to the basement and check the breakers. Will you be all right in here by yourself?"

Gigi nodded, turning the light to her closed office door near the front of the lab. "Everything I need should be in my backpack."

Jerome hesitated a moment, surveying the dark cavern around them, including Ian's closed door. "Apparently, Dr. Lombard did leave. Why wouldn't he check himself out?"

"Maybe he didn't want to wake you." Gigi offered him a silent apology. "You *were* sleeping on your tablet."

"I worked the night shift at KCPD for twenty years before I took this position. I have never fallen asleep on the job. Not like that." His eyes narrowed as he considered an idea. "Will you be able to find your way downstairs okay? Once I reboot the system, I want to go back to my desk and smell my coffee."

"Smell your coffee?" She swung her light right into his face. He squinted and put up his hand against the brightness before she quickly lowered the beam. "Sorry. Your headache."

"Exactly." He lowered his hand. "Call it an old policeman's hunch."

Gigi pretended she understood what he was talking

about, even as her brain started calculating possible explanations. "You go ahead. As soon as I get my bag and keys, I'm heading home."

"Okay." His face softened with a wide grin. "Be sure to check with me on your way out. I don't like losing track of people."

"I'll bring the ibuprofen down when I do." She turned to her office and took a couple of steps around a stainless steel table before her deductive mind finally got what he'd meant by his odd comment. "Wait. Do you think your coffee was drugged…?"

By the time she reached the hallway, Jerome had already disappeared into the elevator. Gigi shook her head, realizing that solving one mystery had led to another. "Why drug that sweet old man?"

Maybe she was too tired, too drained from all the social interaction of the evening to fully understand anything tonight. She turned the light to her office door and made her familiar way through the maze of equipment to unlock it and head inside. She instinctively flipped on the light switch inside the door, then silently chided her foolishness when nothing turned on. She retrieved her backpack from her desk before opening the center drawer and tucking the bottle of pills for Jerome into a side pocket. She swapped out the flashlight for the reassurance of her own phone in her hand and turned on the flashlight app. Then she looped the bag over one shoulder and headed back to the lab.

Metal clanged against metal and she froze. Had the shadowy predators awakened? "Stupid imagination," she muttered. She swept her light across the lab, although it wasn't bright enough to reach every corner. She'd heard one sharp clank, then nothing. Was someone here? "Jerome?" No way could he have gotten down to the basement and back so quickly. But was that…? She squeezed her eyes shut, as if that would sharpen her hearing. Was that someone breathing? Gasping? Her eyes popped open again. Now the only thing she heard was her pulse throbbing in her ears. She wasn't alone. "Ian? Are you here?"

She pulled her door shut and turned toward Ian's office at the back of the lab. She'd gone five steps when her hip smacked into the corner of a cart that had rolled out of place. Ignoring the stinging bruise that was already forming, she moved the cart back into its proper position and stepped around it. "Ian?"

Was that what she'd heard? The cart bumping against a table? She knew enough about physics—a lot about physics—to know that the cart hadn't just moved on its own. Had they had a break-in? Was that why someone would drug Jerome? Why the lights would be out? She quickened her steps, watchful for any other carts jumping out to attack her. There didn't seem to be anything missing. Although she could imagine Ian had brought his latest conquest here to his office, and they'd knocked into tables and equipment trying to get at each other, unable to keep their hands to themselves until they made it into the privacy of his office. At least, that's what she imagined a truly passionate encounter to be like. Losing track of space and time, knocking into things, laughing, touching, loving…

Gigi shook those longing thoughts out of her head and concentrated on the facts. A clandestine meeting wouldn't require flipping the circuit breaker—or drugging the security guard who had no reason to question Ian entering the building, with or without a guest.

"Ian? I'm sorry to interrupt your meeting, but if you're here, answer me."

Her shoe crunched over broken glass and she stopped.

Her blood chilled away that brief shot of annoyance and left fear in its wake. "Ian?"

Something was wrong. Ian might have a weakness for a pretty face, but his pride in his work, maintaining a state-of-the-art showplace and feeding his ego, took second place to nothing and no one. Something was very wrong. "Ian!"

She slid on something slippery and she grabbed a nearby table for balance. This was not good. She pulled her foot up from the goo she'd stepped in, hating the gross, sucking sound it made.

Righting herself against the table, she turned her light to the puddle of red on the floor. A soupy brown liquid coated the top of it. Was that a chemical spill? She couldn't identify the faint acrid smell that stung her nose. The lab had been in pristine condition when she'd left for the reception. Ian would never allow a mess like this. "Dr. Lombard? Are you in here?"

All at once, the lights kicked on, blinding her momentarily before she blinked her surroundings into focus. Now the damage was clear. She was walking over jagged shards of glass stained with… "Blood."

She gasped a fearful breath. "Oh, my God. Jerome!" She shouted an alarm for the security guard to return. "We had a break-in!"

As if she could yell loudly enough for him to hear her through steel beams and cinder blocks. Gigi didn't wait for the guard to come to her rescue. There'd been a struggle here. And someone was hurt.

"Dr. Lombard!"

For a split second she hoped that whoever belonged to this trail of blood had gotten himself to a hospital. But then she heard the sounds coming from Ian's office. Something falling to the floor. Groans. Curses. Another crash.

"Ian!" Gigi punched in 911 and skirted her way around the blood to reach Ian's office. "Ian? Are you here? Are you all right?"

He wasn't.

She shoved open the door, dropping her bag to the floor before she raced across the room and knelt beside her boss. "Oh, my God. What happened?"

Ignoring her attempt to get him to lie flat on the floor, he flung his arm up to pull a stack of books off his desk. He cried out when they hit his stomach and fell to the floor. A crumpled notepad dotted with blood lay on the floor next to him, the blood soaking into the paper and blotting out some of the numbers and symbols written there. He pushed away Gigi's hands and flopped what seemed to be his one functioning arm at the desk again, pulling more things onto himself and the floor.

"Ian, stop. Lie still." She pushed him onto his back, trying not to gag at the wounds puncturing his tuxedo shirt and turning the white pleats red. He was hurt badly, maybe dying. "What do you need?"

"Pen," he muttered, spitting blood when he made the *p* sound. "Find…finish…"

The dispatcher had answered her call and was talking to Gigi on the phone. But she ignored the questions and pulled down a pen from the top of his desk. She pressed it into his hand and tugged a velour throw blanket off the nearby couch, wadding it up to press it against the worst of his wounds. He was weak, but struggling with her, determined to scribble something on the paper beside him.

Gigi punched the speaker button on her phone and set it on the desk, freeing her hands to stanch his wounds. But there were so many. There was so much blood. "Ian? Stay with me."

"Ma'am?" The dispatcher's voice was louder now. "Tell me what's happening. Are you all right?"

Shoving at her glasses to keep them from falling off her nose, Gigi leaned over Ian. She shouted to the dispatcher. "I'm okay. My boss…" She swallowed her panic. She needed to make sense. "There's been a break-in at the Williams University Technology Lab. My boss, Ian Lombard, he's been stabbed. He's bleeding badly."

So much blood. She could see now that the pool of blood she'd stepped in earlier had become a trail of red dots across the carpet in here, and then a smear that led right to Ian's desk. He must have been attacked out in the lab, then made his way in here to call for help or to escape his killer or to… "Damn it, Ian, stop messing with that paper."

"I've dispatched an ambulance and the police to your location. Ma'am? I need your name. Can you tell me your name?"

"Virginia Brennan. My friends call me…" She stopped that useless sentence and wiped the perspiration from Ian's forehead before returning the pressure to his wounds. Not that she could cover them all. But she had to try. "Professor Virginia Brennan. I work with Dr. Lombard. Please hurry."

The blood was coating his lips now, trickling from his mouth as he tried to say something to her. "Safe…"

"Who did this to you?" Gigi tried to decipher his babble. At least he'd given up on writing his last will and testament or whatever note had been so important that he'd risked his life to put pen to paper instead of calling an ambulance himself. "He's been stabbed multiple times," she reported to the dispatcher. "Abdomen and chest. He's losing a lot of blood."

"Is the victim awake? Responsive?"

"Must finish…work…" he spat out. "Go…"

"I'm not going anywhere," she promised before answering the dispatcher. "He's conscious. But he's incoherent. Ian, I don't understand—"

With a strangled gasp, he grabbed a hank of her long hair and jerked her down to gasp in her ear. "Finish it."

"Finish what? What are you talking about? You're not finished."

He rolled his head from side to side. "Made deal… But I couldn't… So sorry…"

"Sorry for what? What deal?" His life was seeping through her fingers.

"My prize…" His rheumy eyes tried to focus. "Too damn…smart… Smarter…than me."

"Don't talk. Save your strength." She cursed the urge to cry and extricated his fingers from her hair to speak to the dispatcher. "There are too many wounds. I can't stop all the bleeding."

"I thought she…my own fault… You must…"

"An ambulance is on its way."

"Listen to me!" Fluid bubbled up from his lungs and Gigi's eyes burned with tears. Help wouldn't get here in time. Where was Jerome? Where was that stupid ambulance? "Take…" He wadded up the paper he'd scribbled all over and, with a monumental effort, dragged his hand onto his stomach, nudging it into her blood-stained fingers. "For you… Trust no one…" She glanced down at the words that were so important to him and saw nothing but random letters and numbers. "Finish…"

"Finish what?" Gigi whipped her gaze around the room, desperate for help. "Help me!"

"You'll…understand…"

"Understand what?" When he kept batting against her hand, she took the paper and stuffed it into the pocket of her sweater. But even in those few seconds that she'd eased the pressure on his wounds, his eyes drifted shut. "No! Ian!"

She patted his cheek, urging him to open his eyes again, mindless of the bloody fingerprints she left on his skin. "Stay with me."

But he was gone.

Ian Lombard was dead.

Gigi sat back on her heels, eyeing her soiled hands, feeling the tears burn down her cheeks. She heard someone hurrying through the lab behind her. Help. At last. "In here!" She turned her head, catching a shadowy movement from the corner of her eye. "Jerome—"

Pain exploded in her skull. Her glasses flew off and she crumpled to the floor beside the dead man. The room spun and blackness consumed her.

Chapter Two

"Whose honor were you defending this time?"

Detective Hudson Kramer touched his bruised knuckles to his lips, wiping away the blood that trickled down his unshaven chin, and gave his amused partner the stink eye. He stepped away from the two dazed men lying in a puddle on the asphalt. "Make yourself useful and get out your handcuffs."

At least Keir Watson had had the good grace to even the odds in this lame excuse for a back-alley brawl behind the Shamrock Bar where Hud had been plying his dubious charm on a pretty blonde. He'd had about twenty minutes of doing all right for a thirty-two-year-old whose only luck with women was the bad kind. Twenty minutes of thinking he wasn't going straight to the friend zone and that she might just say yes if he asked her out on a real date and kissed her good-night. Twenty minutes of sharing laughs and feeling like his luck just might be changing until Stinky Smith here and his wingman, I'm-With-Stupid Jones, decided that loud and drunk and hitting on anything with boobs was going to get them laid tonight.

Hud had been content to let the bartender handle the rowdy pair—a bar frequented by local cops rarely needed a bouncer on duty—until Smith and Jones had lurched over to his table, sat down on either side of Ricki and proceeded to horn in on the blonde and her drink. Hud had politely asked the two drunks to leave. But *polite* had no effect on their beer-soaked brains, and when one of them draped his arm around Ricki and her smile turned to a look of panic, Hud stepped up to get the job done.

"I identified myself as a cop," Hud assured his friend, hauling the guy who'd taken a swing at him to his feet. Although polar opposites in dress and demeanor, Keir Watson was as close to Hud as his own brother—the entire Watson clan made Hud feel like part of the family, especially now that his own siblings had found their hearts' desires away from Kansas City. So, he took great pleasure in flicking at the grime that dusted the damp lapel of Keir's preppie suit before pulling his own cuffs out of the back pocket of his jeans and slapping them on the bruiser with more muscles than brains. "I escorted these gentlemen out the back door, offered to call a cab for them, warned them I'd cite them for drunk and disorderly…" He cinched the cuff around Stinky's other wrist, securing them without being too tight. He looked up into Stinky's unfocused eyes, making sure the young man understood they were going for a walk. "Then this bozo thought taking a swing at me was a good idea."

Hud had stopped growing when he hit five foot eight. Despite his lack of height, a combination of martial arts and weight training often gave him an advantage over larger opponents in a fight. Besides, he didn't have to be as street smart as life and his years as a detective with KCPD made him in order to outwit these two.

"But you escorted them out of the bar because…?" Keir was still trying to push his buttons as he followed Hud with his prisoner. They escorted them to the end of the alley where a uniformed officer would meet them with a black-and-white to drive the two perps down to the precinct to sleep off their out-of-control drunkenness. "I know there's a woman involved."

"Give it a rest, Keir. Jesse the bartender cut them off, and they got a little surly. When I asked for their ID, they started to raise a ruckus. I was not counting on…" Hud bit back a curse when his prisoner weaved to the side, doubling over to retch behind a row of trash cans that had been knocked over in their scuffle. "You okay, bud? Feeling better?"

"Yeah," Stinky drawled. Feeling a touch more sober, he stopped and tried to take stock of his surroundings. "Where's Danny? He didn't make it with that blonde, did he?"

Danny must be the guy in the prophetic I'm With Stupid T-shirt. He perked up at the mention of his name. "What blonde? Did I get her number?"

Keir laughed. "I knew there'd be a blonde. Now this little fracas is starting to make sense." He grinned at Hud. "They said something crude. You took exception. When you asked them to leave, they didn't cooperate. So, you *encouraged* them to do so. Is that about right?"

Hudson grumbled a curse at just how well his partner knew him.

They cleared the alley and headed toward the circle of light beneath a lamppost to wait for the black-and-white to pull up. "What's your friend's name, Danny?" Keir asked.

"Kyle." Danny stumbled as he tried to turn and get a look at the detective in the suit and tie. "Who are you?"

"I'm the police, Danny. Detectives Watson and Kramer. Remember?" Keir's patience in explaining the situation to the two men who likely wouldn't remember much of this encounter made Hud shake his head. "You're both going to spend the night in jail. You understand that, right?"

"Am I drunk?" Kyle asked, staggering ahead of Hud.

"Yep," Hud assured him. When they reached the lamp-post, he turned the young hotshot so he could sit on the concrete barrier beside it. "You're going to be a little sore in the morning. I had to twist your arm and put you down on the ground to get you to stop trying to hit me."

"I hit you?"

"Lucky punch," Hud conceded.

"Did Danny hit you?"

"I doubt it," Keir answered, helping Danny sit before he fell. "He'll be a little sore, too. He tripped over the two of you and face-planted the asphalt before I could catch him."

Kyle appeared to be nodding off. Hud gently tapped his cheek to force his bleary eyes open. "You don't talk to a lady like that again. You don't touch her unless you have permission. You don't drink so much you can't even tell me your name. And you sure as hell don't get behind the wheel of a car when you're like this." Hud reached around Kyle and pulled his wallet from his jeans. "Let's try this one more time. I'm Detective Kramer, KCPD. I'm going to check your ID. You got any weapons, sharp objects, drugs on you?"

"I don't think so." Kyle answered while Hud read his name off his license. "Are you going to arrest me?"

"For being a dumb ass?" He tucked the billfold into Kyle's chest pocket as a pair of uniformed officers pulled up in their vehicle. "You're not worth the paperwork. Just be safe. And be smarter about how much you're drinking next time."

After the uniforms drove away with the two drunks, Keir stepped back into the end of the alley beside him. "So you got those two idiots safely out of the bar and off the streets. How'd you make out with the pretty blonde they were so rude to?"

Hud swore again. "Ricki. I left her alone." He checked

his watch as he retreated toward the Shamrock's back door. "I've been gone twenty-five minutes. You got this?"

He barely saw Keir's nod before he ran back inside the Shamrock. By the time he cleared the polished walnut bar with its green vinyl seats and zeroed in on the empty table where he'd left Ricki, there was no point in hurrying. The only thing he could cuddle up with there was his worn leather jacket. A quick scan of the remaining patrons at the tables and pool tables told him his "date" had left.

He turned to the bearded bartender in the leather vest, hoping Jesse Valentine would tell him she'd just stepped into the ladies' room. Jesse gave him an apologetic smirk. "Sorry, man. She got on her phone almost as soon as you went outside with the Blunder Twins. A guy showed up about five minutes ago. She left with him."

Propping his hands at his waist, Hud tipped his face to the tin-tiled ceiling and let the suckage of this particular Friday night wash over him. He'd often been the friend his sisters or another woman called for that safe ride home. The irony of being the man the woman no longer wanted to hang out with wasn't lost on him.

He startled at Keir's hand on his shoulder before his partner pulled him back to the bar. Keir asked for a glass of ice water. He dipped his handkerchief inside and handed it to Hud to press against his mouth. "Everything all right?"

"You know, I gave up the prime of my dating life to raise my younger brother and sisters." Hud perched on a stool and held the cold cloth to his split lip. "I don't regret it for one second. We needed each other after Mom and Dad died. I was going to keep the family together, no matter what. But now they've all got college degrees and careers. They're engaged or married and starting families, and I can't catch a break with a woman now that I'm available and ready for some action."

"Ready for some action? Seriously?" Keir pulled out the stool beside him but waved off Jesse's offer of his regular drink. "Please don't tell me that's a line you've used."

"Don't judge me."

"You've got no game, my friend."

"Tell me about it."

"Seriously, dude." Keir clapped him on the shoulder to take the sting out of his words. "If she stood you up while you were taking care of business, then she's not the one for you."

Small comfort. Lonesome was lonesome. And Hud had spent far too many nights on his own or with a woman who wasn't the one for him.

The fact that Keir had ventured out into the earlier rainstorm on their night off and wasn't drinking pricked at Hud's suspicions, giving him a respite from his pissy mood. It was no coincidence that his partner had come to the Shamrock looking for him. Something must be up at work, especially since he had a beautiful wife and baby girl waiting for him at home. Hud pulled out his wallet and asked Jesse how much he owed for the warm, half-drunk beers at his table.

"They're on the house," the bartender assured him, refusing his money. "Thanks for clearing out the riffraff."

There were any number of things he'd rather be doing tonight than working, and all of them had to do with a woman. But since there were none in his life, he turned his attention to his partner. If something was wrong with the family, Keir would have mentioned it right away. This was KCPD business. Hud pushed to his feet and pocketed Keir's soiled handkerchief before crossing the noisy bar to his table. "Why aren't you home with Kenna making goo-goo eyes at that new baby of yours? I know you didn't drop by just to back me up with Stupid and Stupider."

Keir followed. "That *new* baby is six months old and you haven't visited your goddaughter in two weeks, Uncle Hud."

His mood brightened by the mention of his goddaughter. Hud grinned as he tucked in his flannel shirt and adjusted the gun holstered on his belt. "Lilly's eyes still as blue as the sky?"

"Now that's the line you ought to use," Keir teased. "She's as beautiful as her mother. Just as headstrong, too."

Hud pictured Keir's wife, a former criminal defense attorney turned county prosecutor who enjoyed the well-earned professional nickname, The Terminator, and laughed. "I bet she is. Hey, if you and Kenna need a night out on your own, all you have to do is call Uncle Hud, and I'd be happy to come babysit that sweet little angel."

"I will take you up on that offer," Keir said. "But not tonight."

"I take it we caught a case?"

Keir nodded. "Murder. One of the professors over at Williams U was found dead in his lab. Multiple stab wounds. B shift is short staffed, and this is a high-profile enough victim that the captain wants us to get the investigation started ASAP."

"High profile?" Hud shrugged into his jacket, his personal life pushed aside at the urgency of those first few hours in a murder investigation.

"It might be related to that bombing we had downtown this past summer."

"When the Lukinburg royalty was in town?"

Keir nodded. "The professor's lab is funded by the Lukin government. Not sure if the two incidents are related, but Captain Hendricks wants us to check it out. You up to working on a Friday night?"

"Well, I'm not going home to snore in my recliner, watch TV and feel sorry for myself."

"Good man. I'll drive." Keir buttoned his jacket and headed for the door.

Hud tossed a tip on the table for the waitress and followed his partner out into the night. "Works for me."

FORENSIC EVIDENCE WAS in plentiful supply at the crime scene. But it was up to Hud, Keir and the crime lab to make sense of it.

While the medical examiner rolled the victim to the elevator in a body bag, Hud pulled a pair of disposable foot covers over his work boots and squatted down to inspect the broken glass and paperwork tossed around the pool of blood in Ian Lombard's office. Clearly, there'd been quite a fight in the lab—one that had probably started out there, then ended in the office. Judging by the blood trail, Lombard had been stabbed repeatedly before dragging himself back here.

But why? To reach the phone? There were plenty of bloody fingerprints and smears around the desk, but none on the phone itself. Even though there was no evidence that he'd made a call, Hud scribbled a reminder in his notebook to pull the local usage details on Lombard's office, home and cell numbers. If nothing else, an earlier call might give them a clue as to who he'd been meeting on campus after hours.

The man must have been expecting company, judging by the two untouched shot glasses and pricey bottle of rye whiskey sitting on the coffee table in front of the leather couch. The bottle still had a red wax seal over the lid, indicating Lombard and his guest hadn't gotten around to pouring drinks. Had his killer been here to make a business deal? Was someone offering money for or demanding results from his research? Murder was one way to resolve a disagreement in terms—or to ensure a deal before those terms could be changed.

And if the victim hadn't been trying to reach the phone to call for help, then what had he been after? Why not use the cell phone linked to his name to call 911? Why not crawl to the door and shout for the guard downstairs to help him? Or trip the security alarm? The guard had indicated that opening any of these doors without the right card swipe and passcode would trigger an alarm at the security desk and at the campus security office. And why hadn't the guard responded to a brawl of this magnitude in the first place? The guy would have to be deaf not to hear the shattering glass and shifting of furniture and equipment.

Hud studied a neat, rectangular void in the blood pool. On a hunch, he pulled his own cell phone from his pocket and held it over the empty spot, confirming his suspicions before snapping a picture.

Keir appeared in the doorway, pausing to pull on his own shoe covers. "Find something?"

"Lombard's cell phone is missing, right?"

His partner crossed the room. "The ME couldn't find it anywhere on him. Just his wallet, watch and his glasses case. He had a wad of cash on him, so I think we can rule out a robbery. Although, I don't know what half that equipment out there is for. Something could be missing. We'll need to talk to someone on his staff."

Hud pointed to the open safe and file cabinet in the corner. "Those drawers don't hold anything but personnel files and student records. The safe has been ransacked, but the perp left a box of rocks behind."

"A box of rocks?"

Hud had been skeptical, too, until he opened the container and read the packing slip inside. "*Gold* rocks. The university shipped it in from Lukinburg. Over twelve thousand dollars' worth. Apparently, there's some science-y thing they do with it."

Keir let out a low whistle. "So, we're not looking at a robbery. Still, either the perp knew the combination to that safe or Lombard opened it before he was killed."

"Or he was forced to open it. Maybe the perp didn't find what he wanted and lost his temper."

"Could this be industrial espionage?"

"Possibly. We'll need to check Lombard's computer, broaden our search for missing flash drives." Hud pushed to his feet. "Check out that void. It's the same size as my phone."

"You think the killer stole Lombard's phone? Would it have a big enough memory to store his research data?"

"I'm not tech savvy enough to know. But it could hold contact information that identifies the killer, or something else incriminating, like a picture or text." Stepping across the spot where Dr. Lombard had died, Hud pointed to a second, much smaller stain several feet from where the body had been found. "What do you make of that? I'm wondering if the killer got hurt, too. That happens a lot with stabbings. We might get DNA."

Keir checked his notes. "The security guard seems to think it's from the witness."

"We have a witness?" Hud's job just got simpler if they could get a description of what had happened or who the perp might be.

Keir's weary sigh blew the idea of *simpler* out of the water. Apparently, nothing was going to come easy for Hud tonight. "One of the lab staff found Lombard before he died. Called 911 and tried to administer first aid."

"Any dying declarations from the victim?"

"Haven't talked to her yet. The paramedics are checking her out. Blow to the head. She's lucky she's not dead, too, walking into the middle of a crime like that."

Her. She. Apprehension knotted in his gut. "My luck with women hasn't been stellar lately. Why don't you handle the witness interviews. I'll stay up here and see if I can find whatever was used as the murder weapon."

"Unless the killer took that with him, too."

Hud nodded at the possibility, if not probability, that he wouldn't find the weapon here. If the killer had been clearheaded enough to pick up the victim's cell phone, then he wouldn't forget to take the murder weapon. "Doesn't mean I'm not going to try."

Keir pocketed his notebook. "I need to finish up with Officer Galbreath. Have him run me through the security system. A lot of it's computerized, apparently. He showed me where he reset the breaker in the basement after the power outage."

"Give me a good gun and a guard dog any day over all that high-tech mumbo jumbo," Hud grumbled. "It's too easy to hack into or override a system and cover up any sign of what's been done. I hate all those nano-bits sneaking around behind my back."

"This *is* the school of technology," Keir reminded him with a teasing grin. "Not everybody's as old-fashioned as you are, my friend."

"Have I told you to bite me lately?"

"Not for an hour or so."

Hud made an exaggerated show of typing the reminder into his phone. "I'll add looking for a way to overload the circuitry while I'm up here."

"Maybe our witness can help with that. Besides giving us a rundown on anything that might be missing." Keir backed toward the hallway. "I can talk to her as soon as I'm done with Galbreath and the medics clear her." He hesitated a moment, wanting to say something more.

"What?"

"You know I was just giving you grief at the Shamrock earlier. Don't give up on the idea of finding the right woman. Other than Dad, you're the babysitter Kenna trusts most with Lilly. And look at Millie—she's practically adopted you because she thinks you're a prize." A married woman, a baby and Keir's stepgrandmother. Yeah, Hud had a real prowess with women, so long as they were taken, under the age of two or over seventy-five. "Don't let the fact that this witness is a woman get in your head. You won't screw anything up by talking to her."

"Not tonight." Hud combed his fingers through his hair, then shook it back into its spiky disarray. His heart and his ego had taken one too many hits lately to trust that he wouldn't scare off a fragile woman with the wrong word or stupid impulse. "I'll owe you a solid if you take this interview for me."

Keir considered the bargain for a moment, then nodded. "I'll ask one of the unis to hold her until I'm done with Galbreath. He's retired KCPD, so his testimony should be reliable. But…"

But was not an encouraging word. "But what?"

"Galbreath claims he might have been drugged. He insists that no one could have gotten in or out of Lombard's lab and office without a key card and passcode, even with the power off. I'll ask him to report to the crime lab for a blood draw. See if there's anything in his system."

Relieved to be focusing on the case and not his own shortcomings again, Hud exhaled a measured breath. "That would explain why he didn't see or hear anything. Lombard must have known his killer if he loaned him a key card or brought him in with him. Sounds like premeditation to me if the killer knew to take out the guard, and how to get around the security system." He surveyed the trashed lab, shaking his head. "This mess looks like a disagreement that got way out of hand, though. Impulsive, not planned."

"Maybe the guard's covering for falling asleep on the job. I'll press him on it, see if I can get him to admit anything." Keir paused in the doorway and turned. "You'll be okay on your own?"

Wasn't that the irony of the evening? Hud snickered a wry laugh and waved his partner out the door. "I'll manage."

"The ME will run a full autopsy, but he says the victim probably died from exsanguination, either from the multiple wounds, or one that nicked an artery or internal organ. He suspects we're looking for something long, sharp and jagged. Probably not an actual knife." Hud had suspected as much. He was looking for a weapon of opportunity. Unfortunately, the lab had plenty of possibilities. "Should I send the CSIs up?"

Hud nodded, already spotting something he wanted to investigate. "Yeah. We'll need a team to clear this place."

Keir left to meet up with the security guard who was waiting downstairs with the uniformed officers who'd cordoned off the building. Meanwhile, Hud squatted down to snap a picture of glass shards from several beakers and a door that had shattered when a stainless steel table had tipped over into the storage cabinet where they were shelved. If there was a longer piece, it might do as a murder weapon. He'd ask the lab techs to collect the glass and piece it back together to see if a big enough sliver was missing.

He moved on to a narrow tube of steel sticking out from beneath a metal cart. A Bunsen burner. It had a long cylindrical shape with a ridged rim at the top that could account for a jagged entry wound if the killer was strong enough to drive the blunt tip through the skin. The scattered drips of blood dotting the debris that had spilled out of the cabinet and off metal trays from the table were cast-off drops, not indicators that any of these items were the actual weapon. But there were dozens of possibilities littered throughout the lab. Scissors. Giant tweezers. Even some of the knobs on this equipment could be broken off and used to stab someone.

Hud was photographing the possibilities of a good, old-fashioned toolbox that lay open on the floor inside a storage closet when he heard someone softly clearing her throat at the open doorway.

"Good. I can use the backup," he answered. "All I'm doing is taking pictures. I haven't touched anything. I'll be done with my initial scan in a few minutes." He dropped to his knees to count the number of screwdrivers in the top tray of the toolbox. "The number-one thing we need to find is the murder weapon. You can start in the office."

"Okay," a soft voice answered. He heard tentative footsteps, as if the CSI was tiptoeing around the evidence scattered across the floor.

Okay? No warnings about detectives disturbing potential clues and giving orders? No complaints about already having to wait for the ME and how the clock was ticking away on their Friday night plans?

Hud turned his head toward the unexpected acquiescence in that one word.

From this vantage point near the floor, all he saw were a pair of killer black high-heeled pumps. He frowned. What crime-scene technician reported for duty dressed like that? Hud sat back on his heels. "Where are your booties?"

The sexy heels stopped. "Booties?"

With a tabletop of equipment and half the lab between

them, his view of the woman hadn't improved much. And yet, the scenery had improved in a way that stirred a heated interest in his blood.

Through the open space beneath the table, the high heels connected to bare legs that went up and up. He took in miles of creamy skin stretched tautly over strong calves. A sweet curve at the knee. His gaze traveled three or four inches higher until he finally ran into a hem of shimmery black material. For a man who was vertically challenged, he'd never had a problem admiring legs that were long and lean and...

There was a smear of blood on her left thigh. A circle of crimson darkened the sequins above the smear. The observation splashed cold water on the awareness sizzling through him. Blood on her skin, but no sign of a cut or scrape. Not her blood, he hoped. "Ma'am, do you have authorization to be in here?"

"The officer downstairs said the detectives wanted to talk to me."

"Ah, hell." Hud pocketed his phone and pushed to his feet. "Don't move."

His initial fascination with those sexy legs dampened with a tinge of concern and anger. This must be the witness, the woman who'd found Ian Lombard and tried to save him. Somehow, she'd missed connecting with Keir. As he rose, he finished his assessment of the woman's appearance. The cream-colored sweater she wore was stretched out of shape and spotted with more blood. The sweater was pulled tight over the flare of her hips. The front overlapped and was held in place by tightly crossed arms. The rolled-up cuffs were stained with blood, too. In her fingers, she clutched an ice pack.

His gaze finally reached a long strand of straight, brick red hair, caught in the clasp of her arms across her chest.

Then he saw the swanlike neck, the gently pointed chin, the glasses over dove-gray eyes and… Any lingering lust burned completely out of his system as recognition kicked in with a vengeance. He was embarrassed that he'd ogled her like that for even one moment. That he'd equated *sexy* with any part of her.

This woman was a nerdy mix of brains and class. She was awkwardly shy, too complicated for him to fully understand and not anybody he should be getting hot and bothered over. And she had absolutely no business showing up at his crime scene covered in blood.

"What the hell?" Gigi Brennan's was not the face he was expecting to see. "What are you doing here?"

Chapter Three

Even with the headache throbbing at her temples, Gigi recognized the square jaw dusted with golden-brown stubble and the abundant muscles that belonged to Detective Hudson Kramer. The charming remnants of the Ozark twang that colored his voice and his warm brown eyes had been the stuff of her limited fantasies for two years now. He'd been her first grown-up kiss and the last one that mattered since the fateful night when they'd first and last met.

The tiny snowflakes of light that danced through her vision, a by-product of the goose egg at the back of her head, painted the detective in a gauzy haze as he crossed the room and took her by the elbow to walk her into the hallway where the lights weren't quite as bright. Even if she didn't trust her vision, his firm grip and the scent and sound of warm, supple leather moving with every fluid step were firmly imprinted in her memories.

"Downstairs," he ordered, pulling her along beside him.

He escorted her all the way to the lobby where he halted beside Jerome's desk. He swung his gaze back and forth and muttered a curse, clearly looking for something he wasn't finding.

She scanned the lobby with him, taking in the uniformed officers and campus security on both sides of the floor-to-ceiling windows that framed the building's front doors. The ones inside were engaged with various conversations on their radios and with each other, while the officers outside were herding curious students and a growing group of reporters away from the building, ambulance and squad cars parked at the curb in front of the building.

"Did you lose someone?" she asked, her voice little more than a whisper.

But he'd heard her. "My partner."

He grumbled the words like another curse. Gigi was about to suggest she come back at a better time when a bright beam of light flashed in her eyes. Pain seared through her brain and she had to squeeze her eyes shut and turn away from the glare.

"Damn reporters. We don't even know what's going on yet, and they want the big story." Detective Kramer tightened his grip again and ushered her over to one of the small decorative trees in a giant pot in the corner of the lobby. "Sorry about that. You're the witness who found Lombard?"

"Yes." She was slightly breathless from the spike of pain through her eyes and her quick hike up and down the stairs. Or maybe slightly breathless was the way she always reacted when she thought of Hudson Kramer.

"Keir must still be downstairs with Galbreath." Detective Kramer scanned the lobby one more time before huffing a sigh and reaching inside his jacket to pull out the badge hanging from a chain around his neck. "Professor Brennan? I don't know if you remember me. I'm Detective Hudson Kramer." He held up the badge to identify himself as KCPD. "We met a while back at the Shamrock Bar. We played pool."

Gigi didn't need to see his badge, or the gun strapped to the belt of his jeans to remember the spiky brown hair and teasing smile. "I know who you are, Detective. You were interested in my sister, Tammy, that night. But she was hitting on the guy you were with, so you settled for spending the evening with me." She adjusted her glasses on the bridge of her nose, a long-ingrained habit that surfaced whenever she felt particularly self-conscious. She doubted he remembered that evening as clearly as she—few people ever obsessed over minutiae the way she did. "You were kind enough not to leave me stranded there when Tammy left with your friend. He was your partner, wasn't he?"

"Still is." That teasing smile appeared as the tension radiating from him eased. "Keir met the woman he wound up marrying that night…after he realized nothing was going to happen with your sister."

Since Tammy hadn't mentioned Keir Watson again, Gigi supposed her sister hadn't felt a spark of attraction, either. Not the way Gigi had been fascinated with this man. "Tammy said he was a gentleman. A change of pace from the men she usually dates. I'm glad things worked out for him. Sorry you didn't get a chance to hang out with her, that you got stuck with me."

"*Stuck* isn't the word I'd use. I didn't mind giving you a ride home." Once they got to her 1940s bungalow, he'd walked her to her front door and, after a brief hesitation, had muttered something like, *What the hell*, and leaned in to give her a good-night kiss.

His fingers had tunneled into her hair to hold her mouth close to his. His stubble had tickled her lips. His heat had warmed her mouth. His touch held a faintly possessive claim she'd never experienced before. She'd barely gotten past her startled response and parted her lips to kiss him back when his hips bumped against hers and her back was against the solid oak door. His tongue speared between her lips and rolled against hers. She'd tasted the tang of beer on his tongue and felt the unyielding impression of rough denim and hard muscles pressed against nearly every part of her. Her small breasts grew heavy with the friction of his chest brushing against them. She wanted to mimic everything his mouth was doing to hers, explore the silk of his hair and the sandpapery contrast of the stubble along his jaw. But just as she was discovering every taste, every texture, every masculine scent about the man, he was pulling away. He smiled, unclutched her fingers from the warm cotton of his shirt and politely bid her good-night. Even though she'd blown that kiss, Gigi could still recall the feel of his firm, warm lips demanding something from hers. She remembered how her body had tingled and desire had rushed straight to her head like a runaway train.

Apparently, trains hadn't crashed in any memorable way for Hudson, though. He probably didn't even remember that kiss. "You turned out to be quite the pool player. I enjoyed my evening."

Not enough to follow up and call her afterward. But then, no one ever did. Gigi dipped her chin and tucked a long, loose strand of hair behind her ear. The subtle touch was another trick she used to turn the focus of her thoughts to something she was far more comfortable with than hormones and emotions. "You showed me how to play, and I'm a fast learner. Pool is basic geometry and physics. Once you figure out the angle and how much you need to spin the ball, if at all, the shots were easy."

There it was—that blank stare that indicated she'd either said something the man didn't understand, or she'd bored him into losing interest in the conversation with her logic speak.

And there was the polite smile. Nice guys always smiled before leaving. The louts just rolled their eyes and walked away, or worse, made a joke about how she didn't make sense before they went and told their friends to steer clear of Professor Brainiac.

But the usual routine ended there, leaving *her* the confused one when Detective Kramer laughed. It was a rich, robust sound from deep in his chest. "Remind me to hire you as my secret weapon the next time some dumbass challenges me to a game. I'd stop losin' money." The laughter stopped as quickly as it had started, and Hudson peered through the lenses of her glasses, making her drop her gaze. "You got a good whack on your head, didn't you? The lights bothering you in here?"

She didn't realize she'd been squinting at him until he mentioned it. "A little."

"Come on. I was going to let Keir handle the interviews. But since he's busy, let's find someplace quiet to sit down and answer a few questions." His fingers folded more gently around her elbow to pull her into step beside him again. Hud notified one of the officers to give them some privacy, then pushed the front door open for her. After briefly sizing up the crowd of onlookers and press gathering beyond the yellow crime scene tape at the end of the front walk, he steered her over to a landscaped seating area. "It's wet out here. Do you mind?"

Right now, she'd go anywhere, as long as it was away from the lights and reporters and curious faculty and students. She shook her head.

With an assortment of shrubs and the trunk of a golden-leaved pin oak between them and the crowd, he led her to a metal bench. "You look like you're dead on your feet."

"Not as dead as Dr. Lombard."

He laughed again. "You're funny, Professor. Oh…" His smile flatlined. "You weren't making a joke. Sorry."

"That would be a humorous play on words," she admitted, hearing the phrasing a moment too late. "I suppose I was pointing out the obvious."

He pulled a blue bandanna from his back pocket and wiped the lingering water droplets off the metal plank before sitting down. "It's a little cold, but we'll warm it up soon enough."

Warm it up? Neurons must be misfiring in her brain. He surely didn't mean…that he would… Now? With her?

"You and Lombard were close?" he asked, patting the bench beside him.

Definitely a misfire. Gigi blinked the confusion from her panicked thoughts and sank onto the edge of the bench. The detective wanted to ask questions about Ian's murder, not exchange body heat. Maybe she *did* have a concussion that had rattled her brain.

Hudson leaned against the back of the bench, no doubt hoping his relaxed posture would encourage her to do the same.

But holding herself ramrod straight and hugging her sweater around her for warmth seemed to be the only things keeping her together tonight. She didn't think Hudson made her nervous so much as her reactions to him did. It was one thing to treasure a memory and spin a few fantasies about a man who was earthy and sexy and unlike the polished, intellectual egoists she usually spent time with. It was something else entirely to carry on a cogent conversation with the real man. Especially with her head throbbing and her emotions reeling from all she'd been through tonight.

"Ian was my boss. My mentor. A friend, too, I suppose. We made a good team. He had the ideas, and I had the patience to make them happen. I could pick up the errors in his formulas and rework the elements to complete prototypes of the technology he designed."

"He's the front man and you're the backup singer. But you need both to make the record happen."

"That analogy works. He gave me a break when some other universities wouldn't. Ian hired me to be the lead on his research team, coordinating with the visiting Lukin professor and managing the Williams U staff."

"You're kind of young for all that responsibility, aren't you?"

Gigi shrugged. She'd always been the youngest in almost every situation—school, research, learning about life. "I'm an overachiever. And I'm...smart."

"I remember that." His eyes crinkled with a smile. "When we first met you told me you'd already earned your Ph.D. That you might have earned it a year sooner if you hadn't taken several months off to take custody of your sister and handle the details of losing your parents. Reminded me of my situation growing up with my younger brother and sisters. You and I were both orphans suddenly saddled with a family to raise. Gave us something to talk about."

That was when she realized that she *was* talking to Hudson Kramer. About things other than work. Even though she'd been a dork about what drink to order and not knowing how to play pool, he'd made her feel like he understood what she meant when she rambled on or couldn't find the right words. The more time they'd spent together that night, the more she realized she wasn't completely tongue-tied with a man. She admired his commitment to his family and felt honored that he'd shared something so personal from his life. He'd made it easier for her to open up and share about hers.

Apparently, he still had a knack for getting her to open up.

"Teaching isn't really my forte. I didn't get a stellar

recommendation on my classroom performance from the school where I did my doctoral thesis. But I'm really good in the lab. Ian saw that, and he gave me the chance to work here on groundbreaking research, to get my name under his on a couple of papers we've published." Ian Lombard may have done more for her than she'd realized. "My teaching has improved with his coaching. I do better with the smaller classes here at Williams."

"You get nervous in front of a crowd?"

"I get nervous in front of anybody. But you already know that. That night at the Shamrock, you were hoping that Tammy wanted to pick *you* up. She's the social one. She's comfortable with friends or a room full of strangers." Gigi squeezed the mushy ice pack in her grip, almost surprised to find it still there. She slid a glance at Hudson, wondering if tonight was making any more sense for him than it was for her. "Did you know that research shows public speaking causes more stress for individuals than dealing with death or divorce?"

"I did not know that." Nor did he understand why she'd pointed out that fact to him—judging by the questioning arch of his right eyebrow. "Here." He plucked the ice pack from her fingers and reached behind her to find the knot in her scalp above the remnants of her bun and gently place it there. He guided her fingers up to hold it in place. "That's not doing any good in your lap." He leaned forward, bracing his elbows on his knees, possibly trying to make himself look smaller and less threatening? She might top him by an inch or two in height, but there was no way to diminish how the brown leather of his jacket stretched tautly across his broad shoulders and muscular arms and bulged over the gun strapped to his waist. His drawl might be charming, his eyes kindly indulgent, but physically, he was coiled dynamite. She was in the midst of analyzing why her pulse quickened at that metaphoric assessment when he turned his face to hers and said, "You're talking to me okay."

Startled to be caught staring at his masculine shape, Gigi snapped her gaze up to his. She looked away just as quickly, thrusting her free hand into the pocket of her sweater, curling her fingers into the thinning knots of wool—yet another trick to short-circuit her panicky thoughts and give her shy energy someplace to go. Now she could focus on the reason they were talking at all. "This conversation has a purpose. If I'm assigned a task, I will get it done. You need to know about Ian. What I saw in the lab. What I know of his timeline tonight. If I recognized the person who hit me. Details. I'm good with details."

"I'd like to know all of that if you're up to it." He pulled a notepad and pen from inside his jacket and flipped through several pages with scribbled words and a crude outline of the lab and Ian's office. "Tell me what happened tonight. Just as you remember it."

For several minutes, Hudson took notes while Gigi told him about the party and taking the bus back to campus, how she'd found Jerome asleep and thought that strange. She mentioned the suspicious power outage and how she'd discovered Ian in his office and tried to save him. Hudson continued to brace his elbows on his knees, leaning forward while she sat up straight beside him and talked to the back of his thick brown hair.

She was curious about the two lines he scratched beneath the words *Still Alive* before he asked, "Lombard told the security guard he was meeting someone here tonight. Do you know if it was a man or woman? There were two glasses set out on the table in his office."

Gigi mentally replayed the snapshots of everything that had passed by in a panicked blur earlier, stopping on the memory he wanted. "Cut-glass old-fashioned glasses. With a whiskey bottle. A brand I couldn't afford. Ian had expensive tastes."

Hudson was grinning when he turned his face to her. "You *do* notice details."

Was he making fun of her obsessive observational skills? "Isn't that what witnesses do?"

"Not necessarily." He sat up, angling his body toward hers. She jumped inside her skin when his knee brushed against hers, but quickly squelched the instinct to slide away from the warm denim. He probably hadn't even noticed the contact. And he certainly hadn't reacted as if they'd traded an electric shock the way she had. He'd think her rude. Or arrogant if he thought she was avoiding his touch. It wouldn't be the first time a man had misinterpreted her skittish reactions. "You'd be surprised how adrenaline, shock or whatever emotions they're feeling can affect how a person remembers what they've seen."

"Isn't what I'm saying accurate?" Maybe he did think something was off with her. He had to understand it was her social skills that went on the fritz around a man she was attracted to. But no one should question her intellect. "I don't usually make mistakes. Not with—"

"The details," he finished for her. He chuckled in his throat. "I trust your memory more than most, Professor. Now tell me, did Dr. Lombard leave the party early to meet somebody?"

"He didn't say anything to me. But…"

When she didn't complete the sentence, Hudson dipped his head to look up into her eyes. "But?"

Good grief. His eyes weren't just brown. They were flecked with honey and cinnamon and even a bit of mossy green. Hazel eyes. Why hadn't she noticed that before?

"Professor?"

Right. Gigi blinked away her fascination. This was not a scientific experiment on the intriguing variegations of iris color in the adult male. He was a detective and she was a witness. *Answer the question, already.* Gigi turned away slightly, breaking the innocent contact with his knee and gaze so she could focus. "Ian had an argument with one of the visiting professors, Evgeni Zajac from the University of Saint Feodor in Lukinburg. I don't know what it was about, other than Dr. Zajac accused Ian of something. Evgeni doesn't speak very good English, so I'm surprised it lasted as long as it did. I don't know where his translator, his wife Hana Nowak, was." She rubbed her fingers over the bruises Evgeni had left on her upper arms. "Evgeni thought Ian was hiding from him. Maybe their argument upset him, and that's why Ian forgot me."

"Forgot you?"

He asked her to spell Professor Zajac's name before she answered. "Ian gave me a ride to the reception. That's how he convinced me to go."

"By promising you wouldn't be alone with all those people."

Gigi nodded.

"And then he left without you. Hence, the bus." The dark eyebrow arched again. "Even I've had better dates. And that's saying something."

"It wasn't a date." She hastened to correct the detective's misconception of her relationship with her boss. "I wasn't his type."

The evocative eyebrow flattened with a frown. "Lombard had a type?"

With the ice pack mostly melted and her arm tiring from holding it in place, Gigi set it on the bench beside her and buried her cold fingers in the pocket of her sweater, flexing them around the cell phone she carried there. She felt guilty for even thinking ill of the dead. Although he'd never been anything but kind and supportive to her, Ian Lombard had had two major shortcomings—an ego that matched his IQ and a weakness for a pretty face.

But then Hudson touched his pen to the back of her knuckles through the knitted wool, stilling the outward manifestation of her internal debate. The touch startled her into looking into those eyes again. "Cold?" he asked. "Do we need to go back inside?"

She shook her head, wondering if he'd picked up on the way she touched her glasses or clothes or hair to break into her thoughts when she got stuck inside her head. "It's a habit. It calms me. I hate clothes that don't have any pockets."

"Me, too." With the barest hint of a smile crinkling the corners of his eyes, he said, "Tell me about Lombard's type, and how a leggy redhead like you doesn't qualify."

Leggy redhead? Was that a compliment? No. She tamped down that rush of anticipation that surged through her. It was a statement of fact. She did have long legs and auburn hair. But it was sweet that he'd noticed a couple of *details* about her, too. Hudson Kramer really was surprisingly easy to talk to.

"Dr. Lombard used to…" Was there any polite way to say this? "He's—was—a married man. But he had wandering eyes. He flirted with some of the students. They'd meet for…consultations…in his office. Sometimes, after hours."

"He liked them young."

"And blonde. And curvy. He even asked me about Tammy after she stopped by to take me to lunch on my birthday last year." That had been the first time she'd explained the ground rules of sexual harassment to Ian, and why their students and her sister were off-limits to him.

"That could make some enemies. Did it ever go be-yond flirting?"

"I couldn't say for sure," she confessed. "It never hap-pened with me. He said he valued me too much as his as-sistant." It had been one of those rare times when she'd been glad she was a shy, forgettable woman who didn't turn heads. "He's been reprimanded by the university. Threatened with a sexual harassment suit. I thought he'd stopped his philandering, though. I haven't heard any re-cent complaints from any of my students, or gossip from the faculty and staff."

"A guy who's a player is always going to be a player. But you don't know anyone who'd carry a grudge against him for that? An angry parent? Husband? Boyfriend? The victims themselves?"

Gigi shook her head. "His wife had threatened to di-vorce him. But they were going through marriage coun-seling. She's out of the country, anyway, so it couldn't have been her."

Detective Kramer grunted as if that didn't necessarily give the woman an alibi. "What's his wife's name?"

"Doris Lombard. She's a theater arts professor here. She's on sabbatical in Norway this semester."

"Let's say Zajac didn't follow your boss here to finish the argument, and there aren't any disgruntled students who'd take exception to being pawed by a man with au-thority over them like that." He flipped to a new page in his notebook. "Do you know if he was having problems with anyone else?"

"Like what?"

"Anything. Personal? Professional?"

She couldn't think of any specifics, but she knew Ian hadn't been universally liked. "There's always compe-tition in the academic world—for grant money, tenured positions, funding for programs. There are a lot of egos, too, that come into play when you're talking about that kind of money."

"What kind of money are we talking about?"

Gigi considered some of the numbers Ian had bragged about—numbers that seemed to have made his wife overlook those dalliances with younger women. "Thousands. Millions. Not just for the university, but for whoever holds the patents for various discoveries. Sometimes companies or alumni investors will pay a stipend for research or teaching programs above and beyond university funding."

"Did anybody think Lombard had stolen their patent? Or taken credit for research that wasn't his?"

Mentally running through a list of jealous coworkers and competitors, Gigi almost missed the squishing of dead leaves and wet mulch behind her. Before she could turn to see who was approaching, Hudson sprang to his feet. "Stop right there." He pulled back the front of his jacket, exposing his badge and resting his hand on the butt of his gun. "This is a crime scene and you're trespassing."

Gigi rose to her feet, recognizing the stink of too much cologne.

This was *not* what she needed tonight.

Chapter Four

"Gigi? Darling, I just heard. You poor thing." *Darling?* The tall man with wire-rimmed glasses and a neatly trimmed blond beard rushed up to Gigi and pulled her into his chest, hugging his arms around her. "I can't believe someone killed Ian. What is this world coming to?"

"Gary." Water dripped from his hair and ran down her neck as her cheek smushed against the scratchy tweed of his jacket. "I don't need a hug right now."

"I always said you needed to be running that program. You or me." Ignoring her protest, he shook his head spraying her with more droplets. "Ian was a front man—you were the workhorse who covered his ass more than once."

"Gary!"

She'd gotten one hand free to palm against his tweed lapel when a second, stronger hand did something to Gary's grip and pried her free.

Gigi stepped back to brush the moisture from her skin while Hudson's shoulder moved into the space between them. He flashed his badge. "Detective Hudson Kramer, KCPD. We're having a conversation here. Police business."

"Police?" Rubbing his wrist and looking confused, Gary glanced from the badge to Hud and over to Gigi. "Were you here when Ian was killed? Do you need me to call an attorney for you?"

"No—"

"They don't suspect you had anything to do with this, do they?"

"I don't think they—"

"We don't," Hudson stated emphatically. "She's a witness, not a suspect. I'm going to have to ask you to leave right now, sir."

"What happened?" Gary asked, deaf to both Detective Kramer's request and Gigi's distress.

The image of puncture wounds and shredded clothes and skin was branded on Gigi's brain. "He was stabbed. Several times."

"How awful." Gary's blue-eyed gaze darted down to her sweater as she rolled the stained cuffs back into place. "Oh, my God. Are you hurt?"

He stepped around Hud.

"It's not my blood."

His arms stretched out toward her.

She tried to retreat, but her legs hit the bench. "Don't—"

A wall of brown leather filled her vision as Hud once again inserted himself between Gigi and the man she'd spent far too many hours with in the lab. "Okay, pal. Next time I won't ask nicely. She said to back off."

"I work here. We're friends," Gary insisted, briefly tilting his gaze down to Hudson. "More than friends. Tell him, darling."

The endearment made her skin crawl. "Stop calling me that."

"We've gone out several times—"

"Once."

"What's your name, sir?" Hud asked.

"And whose fault is that?"

"Name."

The tall man's gaze darted back and forth, as if he didn't

quite understand why Hud kept interrupting him. "Gary Haack. *Professor* Gary Haack." He emphasized the title, just like he'd emphasized his family's money and all the things that made him a good catch on that *one date* when he'd taken her to dinner and the symphony. "I'm with the engineering department. I head up Lombard's research team. Along with Gigi," he added, either as an afterthought or a reason to explain his claim on her. "Tell him, darling."

"ID."

Gary's eyes landed squarely on Hudson now. He lifted his chin to an arrogant tilt. "I am not some common criminal. I'm here to support Miss Brennan."

"*Professor* Brennan," Hud corrected. "And she's not your darlin'." Gigi felt something warm inside her at the subtle defense of her honor and hard work. She'd gotten used to fending off Gary's attention all by herself. She'd gotten used to doing a lot of things on her own. Was it any wonder that she'd fashioned Hudson Kramer into some kind of champion after one evening of playing pool at a bar and one awkward yet memorable kiss? He was still waiting, still not giving a flying flip about Gary's claim that he had a right to be here. "ID."

Grumbling a protest, Gary pulled out his wallet and handed Hud his driver's license. "Here. But if you won't let me comfort her, you must at least let me do my job." Hud jotted down the information while somehow keeping a sharp eye on Gary who leaned to the side to address Gigi directly. "We need to get ahead of this and do damage control. Do the investors know yet? They know we can continue Ian's work without him, right?"

The investors were the last thing on her mind right now. Gigi hugged her arms in front of her, jarred by the abrupt change in topic. "I don't know. There are reporters here, but I don't think they've broadcast anything yet. Why aren't you still at the reception? And why is your hair wet, but not your clothes?" It had always been easier to analyze details than to process emotions for her.

"Reporters, right." Ignoring every question, Gary adjusted his glasses and smoothed his damp hair into place. "I'll make a statement to them. Represent the department since I'm sure you're not up for that. As for the reception, except for Ambassador Poveda, once Ian disappeared, Dr. Zajac and the rest of the Lukin representatives left." Gary paused with his hand on the knot of his tie. "Speaking of… Here comes Zajac now."

Sure enough, she spotted Evgeni Zajac's white hair, psychedelically tinted by the red-and-blue lights spinning on top of a police car parked at the curb. With his beautiful younger wife beside him, patiently translating whatever he was saying to the officer beside the police car, he gestured wildly, pointing to the building, then pointing to the crowd gathered behind the yellow crime scene tape, finally pointing to her. Once his dark eyes had zeroed in on her, he started walking toward them. He might be restricted from going inside the technology building, but there was nothing to stop him from crossing the lawn and speaking to her outside. "Gary! Gigi!"

Gigi closed her eyes against the dizzying discomfort that swept through her at the idea of facing more people. With the ground spinning beneath her feet, she grabbed on to the most solid thing she could find and ended up clutching a handful of soft, worn leather. When her fingertips dug into the muscle of Hudson Kramer's arm, she felt a warm hand covering hers. "You okay?"

She opened her eyes at the husky drawl to discover Hudson's golden eyes looking into hers. Before she could process the concern in those eyes, before she could explain the tightness in her stomach or even say she wasn't feeling well, Evgeni and his wife, Hana Nowak, joined them.

Dr. Zajac was the first to speak. "Can we get into the lab? Is our work safe?" He made no mention of, much less apologized for, the way he'd treated her at the reception. "Was any of our classified work taken or destroyed? The gold?"

"We don't know that yet," Gary answered. "Gigi was a witness—"

"A witness?" Hana Nowak's dark eyes, filled with pity, turned to her. Her accent was far less pronounced than her husband's. "You were there when Ian died?"

"—but I haven't been able to get two words in edgewise with her," Gary continued.

Evgeni demanded a translation from his wife.

"Hey!" Hud's voice topped them all. Gary, Hana and Dr. Zajac all snapped their attention to him. "This isn't a party. You all need to leave."

Hana was the first one to accede. "Of course. You have work to do." She tugged on her husband's arm. "Ev. Can't you see Gigi is in mourning? This is the time for sympathy, not work. I am so sorry, my dear." Hana leaned over the back of the bench to pull Gigi in for a hug. Although the position was awkward, the other woman's grief seemed genuine. Gigi wound her arms lightly around her and held on long enough to hear the sniffle of tears against her collarbone. "I know Ian was your dear friend. He was a great man. I am sorry for you," she added, blinking back tears as she pulled away. She reached into her husband's pocket for a handkerchief and dabbed at her nose.

"Thank you, Hana." The thirtysomething woman's black hair hung in a smooth, damp ponytail down her back. She must have been caught out in the rainstorm, too. Only, her wet hair looked sleek and shiny, like thin strands of polished obsidian, while Gigi's bun was a mess and her loose hair was frizzing with the humidity lingering in the air.

Hana linked her arm through her much older husband's. "Evgeni expresses his condolences, as well."

When she turned a reproving gaze up at him, he shrugged. "Of course. It is a great tragedy to lose a mind like Ian's." He turned to his wife and asked her something in Lukin.

Hana's eyes widened before she repeated it in English. "Has anyone notified Doris Lombard yet? Evgeni believes his wife should be the one handling the arrangements for Ian's funeral, and give permission before there is any kind of autopsy."

"A crime has been committed, ma'am," Hud explained. "Mrs. Lombard doesn't get to say whether there's an autopsy or not. The ME will handle it. And yes, Mrs. Lombard has been notified by the police. She's been informed of the suspicious circumstances and is making arrangements to get back to Kansas City."

"Poor Doris," Hana offered. Evgeni muttered something about Ian's shortcomings as a husband, and Hana yanked on his arm, her cheeks coloring with embarrassment. "It is not wise to speak ill of the dead." She apologized to the rest of them for whatever her husband continued to grumble about. "I am so sorry."

"You had no love for Ian Lombard?" Hud asked, finally returning Gary's license.

"None of us did," Gary answered. Dr. Zajac nodded his agreement. "Ian was a brilliant man, but he could be a jerk to work with." He pointed to Gigi. "Ask her. She cleaned up after him more than he deserved."

"Please don't say anything…like that…to the reporters," Gigi pleaded. "Ian was temperamental, but he was always good to me—like a father figure."

He rolled his eyes up to the stars with an impatient huff. "You were his prized possession. The academic whiz kid he discovered who made him look better than he was." Although his tone was filled with concern, Gary's choice of words made her uneasy. "Is that what you want me to tell the reporters? That you two were close?"

"I don't want you to mention me at all. And I don't want you to smear Ian's reputation. That would be a blot on the university. On the program. On all of us."

Evgeni muttered a phrase, which she'd learned was a Lukin curse.

"Ev!" Hana chided. "What Gigi is saying makes sense. We shouldn't be talking about Ian's indiscretions when we are on the verge of expanding your project's funding."

"*Our* project," Gary corrected. "We just lost one ego-maniac. I don't intend to let another take his place."

"Nobody's saying anything to any reporter until KCPD releases an official statement." Hud put an end to the conversation. "I need to finish interviewing Professor Brennan. Without any of you upsetting her." He pointed to the uniformed brunette standing just inside the main doors. "Y'all are going over to that officer and give her your names. Then you can wait inside the lobby. Since you knew the victim, my partner and I will want to ask you a few questions."

Evgeni cursed at the directive. "I will do no such thing. I did not leave my country to come here and be treated as a criminal. I will invoke diplomatic immunity."

"That's your call, sir. But I'm still gonna have to ask you to leave the crime scene."

Hana apologized for her husband's outburst and pulled him away from the bench. "Of course, Detective." The couple turned toward the parking lot. "Come, *dorogoy*. We will drive to the Lukinburg Embassy and inform them of what has happened. They will want to know about the tragedy of tonight's honored guest."

Just as the overwhelming tension in the air started to dissipate, Gary stepped closer, straightening to his full height, no doubt to assert his influence and take control of the conversation. "I'm not leaving Gigi." Ignoring Hud's instruction, Gary circled around the shorter man and reached for her. "She doesn't handle interpersonal—"

"Gary, don't."

"Now—" Hud stiff-armed Gary out of her personal space "—would be a good time to go."

"She needs me." When Gary reached for her again, Hud grabbed his outstretched fingers and spun him around, twisting his arm up behind his back.

"Final warning. Next time I arrest you for interfering with a police investigation."

Gary yelped in protest but didn't struggle. "I'll have your badge for this."

"Go ahead," Hud dared him. "Report me."

Gary looked down over the jut of his shoulder at Hud. He was half a foot taller than the detective who had him pinned, but Gigi had no doubt who would win if this escalated into a physical fight. And while the realization that Hud was defending her wishes warmed her with an unfamiliar thrill, there'd already been too much violence tonight. "Please do as he says."

After shooting her a look of hurt, Gary put up his free hand in surrender. "Very well. For you." Once Hud had released him, Gary straightened his jacket and rubbed his shoulder. "In case you didn't recognize it, I was trying to help you. I would think a familiar face would be welcome right about now." He shot an accusing glance at Hud. "You know she's not comfortable around a lot of people, right?"

"You included, apparently."

"How dare you." Gary's voice took on a harsh tone. "I am a respected member of this faculty—"

Hudson pulled out his handcuffs.

Gary held his ground. "I want to hear it from Gigi. I'm not abandoning her."

"Go," Gigi pleaded. Her nerves were frayed to the point that she couldn't hold Gary's probing gaze. "Please."

Hud's shoulders expanded with a deep, measured breath. "That means you're out of here."

Gary answered with a self-righteous snort. "I guess I'll go talk to that officer."

"I guess you will."

Seeming to understand that Hudson's words were an order, not a request, Gary headed the opposite direction in which Hana and Evgeni had disappeared. As he moved past Gigi, he held his thumb and pinkie up to his face and mouthed the words, "Call me."

Never. She would deal with all this by herself before she would agree to whatever obsessive strings Gary wanted to tie to her in exchange for his comfort and support.

"Interesting friends you've got there." After dismissing her coworkers from the conversation, Hud turned halfway to face her, and she discovered she still held a tight-fisted grip on the sleeve of his jacket. "You okay?"

As confused by the emotions clouding her thoughts as she was embarrassed at the liberty she'd taken by sinking her grip into him more than once, she released Hud's arm and the back of his jacket and collapsed onto the bench.

"Sorry," she apologized automatically. "I guess I kind of blanked out there for a few seconds. I didn't wrinkle your jacket, did I?"

"Impossible. This leather is as tough as I am." He replaced his cuffs in his pocket and sat on the bench beside her. "You didn't answer my question."

"Uh, huh." Aware that Hud had spoken, though not really hearing his response, she craned her neck over her shoulder, wondering what Gary was saying to the police officer inside the lobby, and why he had positioned himself so that he was facing Gigi through the window. Was that piercing blue gaze showing concern? Or some kind of creepy claim on her allegiance?

It must be after midnight by now. The temperature was dropping. She couldn't seem to hug herself tightly enough to stop shivering.

And then she felt the tip of a warm, calloused finger on the point of her chin. Hudson turned her face and focus back to him. "Eyes right here, G. They're not going to bother you anymore tonight."

He stroked his thumb beneath her chin, turning a very practical touch into something that felt like a caress. The tightness in her chest eased, and the cloudy air of malaise that had taken over her thoughts drifted away. She processed the husky timbre of his voice, and the odd choice of words that had pulled her back from her panicked reaction to that confrontation with Gary and the Zajacs. "G?"

He chuckled as he pulled his hand away. "It's half of Gigi. I'm lazy."

"Gigi is already short for my given name, Virginia."

"Then I'm really lazy."

The tension in her relaxed at his self-deprecating humor. "That's a goofy thing to say."

"Goofy enough to make you smile. I like this look better."

"Better than what?"

"Like you're scared of something." He glanced over at the front doors. "Or someone."

"Gary?" She slipped her coworker a glance, but he turned his back to her as soon as he realized he'd snagged Hud's attention, too. "I'm not afraid of him." She idly rubbed her arm where Evgeni had bruised her earlier. "Of any of them. I see them every day at work. I…trust them."

Even as the words left her mouth, she was revising her opinion. She'd trusted them all before tonight. Something had changed leading up to Ian's death. Egos. Secrets. Tempers. Money. Something she didn't yet understand.

Hudson looked as skeptical as she felt. "You didn't want Haack touching you. Intimating that you were more than friends. Or mentioning you to the press."

Gigi wasn't sure how to explain why she didn't want a handsome, accomplished man like Gary paying attention to her. She had next to no experience with men, but she'd like to think she could enjoy herself more with a man than the stilted conversations and end-of-the-night gropefest she'd endured on their date. "I don't mind working with him. He's good at his job. The students love him. He represents the engineering part of our technology development while I'm in charge of the physics. As the coassistant on Dr. Lombard's research project, there'd be no impropriety if I wanted to date him. We went out once. He's asked me out several times since, but…"

"But?"

"I don't want to."

"You don't want to go out with Haack?"

"I missed my whole teenage learning-about-boys-and-sex years because I was steamrolling my way through school at an accelerated rate. Then I was taking care of Tammy and now I work. I should be flattered that a man with Gary's reputation wants to have a relationship with me. But I can't tell if he really cares about me, or if I'm just the type of woman he thinks he *should* care about. I don't feel any chemistry. If I have to settle for that kind of spark-free relationship, then I will proudly wear my virgin hat until the day I die."

He laughed out loud at her answer. "Virginia Brennan, you are a unique woman. You tell it like it is, don't you."

Gigi had never thought about the sound of a man's laugh. But she liked the sound of Hudson Kramer's. It was musical, came from deep in his chest and was as genuine and easy to like as the man himself. The sound of it made her prickle with a magnetic energy, just as the tingling sensation where he'd caressed her skin earlier had. And how could his eyes pull off this gentle puppy-dog look and still have that sharp, wolflike directness that had chased Gary and the Zajacs away?

Oh, hell. This was no fantasy. She was attracted to the real man.

"G?"

Once she realized that he'd stopped laughing, she adjusted her glasses to mask the fact that she was staring. Assessing. Appreciating. Embarrassing herself with this silly crush. And had she just admitted she'd never slept with a man? Hudson's eyes were of no consequence to her. His laughter didn't mean he thought she was funny—he was simply making her feel comfortable enough with him so she could answer his questions. He probably had a hot date waiting for him once this interview was done. She reminded herself that there was nothing personally protective about dismissing Dr. Zajac and his wife or getting Gary Haack to leave her alone. It was pure practicality. Detective Kramer had a murder to investigate, and he didn't need any interruptions when he was interrogating a witness.

"I'm sorry. That knock on the head seems to be affecting my concentration. Normally, I'm not so easily distracted." That statement was true. Although, she typically didn't spend much time in the company of a man she found so…distracting. "Did you have more questions you wanted to ask?"

A frown tightened his mouth, as if he didn't like her response. "Just one. Did you see who hit you?"

"I would have told you right away if I'd seen the killer."

"I didn't ask about Lombard's killer."

"Isn't it the same person?"

"Not necessarily. Lombard was already dying when you found him. But you experienced your attack firsthand. Your perception will be different." Okay, so not everything about Hudson Kramer was charming. Or sexy. Or distracting. That biting tone was nothing but irritated detective. "What do you remember before you were knocked unconscious? You're the expert on details. Sounds? Smells? Anything you can think of might be a clue."

Gigi closed her eyes and dutifully replayed the blurry images from her memory, looking everywhere except at the dead man beneath her hands. There'd been a glimpse of movement in the corner of her vision. "Black."

"He was a black man?"

"No. I don't know. I never saw a face. I was down on the floor with Ian. I never had a chance to look up." The sounds of Ian's labored breathing and her own frantic gasps gave way to charging footsteps. "I heard the crunch of glass first."

"There was a lot of broken glass at the crime scene. Your attacker probably couldn't avoid walking over it. And then?"

"Then I saw black. Rushing at me. Closing in all around me, it seemed. Just an impression before pain exploded in the back of my skull. Black shoes? Pants? A shadow?"

She shook her head, knowing the vague description wasn't much help. "My glasses flew off and I must have passed out. Nothing was clear."

"Did you smell anything?"

Something pungent. Woodsy. Chemical? Cologne? Gigi's eyes popped open. "Alcohol."

"Medicinal? Something from the lab or cleaning crew?"

Gigi shook her head. "The kind you drink."

"There was a whiskey bottle in Lombard's office. But it was full, unopened."

"But I can still smell it." She raised the rolled-up cuff of her sweater to her nose and breathed in. "It's on me. It's in the blood that's on me."

"The murder weapon had a sharp, cylindrical shape." He wrote something in his notes and circled it three times.

"Like the neck of a broken whiskey bottle. Someone must have replaced the bottle and taken the broken one with him."

Hudson grinned, creating a flash of white in the middle of his stubbled face. "You *are* good at details."

He tucked his notebook and pen inside his jacket. The interview must be over.

"Was I helpful?"

"You did great, G." He held his hand out to her, forcing Gigi to unlock her crossed arms to take it. His grip was warm. Firm. Gentle. He released her the moment she stood. "I think you've answered enough questions for one night. We're done. Unless you think of something else that might help, or you remember any dying declarations Lombard might have said."

"Like *So-and-so killed me*?"

He grinned. "I've never been that lucky. You got someone to drive you home?" He tilted his head toward the building, indicating that Gary was watching them again.

"Besides Mr. I-Got-No-Clue-About-Personal-Boundaries over there? Or Dr. Foreign Fury and his put-upon wife?"

She shook her head, unable to hide her smile at his spot-on descriptions. "I'm the one others call for that sort of thing. Designated driver for girls' night out. Getting stranded on the road. I'm usually available and willing to help."

"Watching someone who was an important part of your life die is a lot harder to deal with than helping a friend who has a flat tire. If it hasn't hit you yet, it will." She stiffened at the unexpected touch of his hand at the small of her back as he turned her toward the sidewalk. "What about your sister?"

"She's out of town. I'll be fine, Hudson…" She stopped and faced him, needing to break even that polite, impersonal contact in order to remind herself that there was nothing happening between them here, at least not on his part. "I mean Detective Kramer."

"Hudson or Hud is fine." She didn't understand how he could be friendly one moment and frowning at her the next. "You have a head injury. I'll borrow my partner's Camaro and drive you home."

So she could relive that awkward good-night kiss from two years earlier? No thanks. "The paramedic cleared me. The bleeding stopped and I don't need stitches. My pupils reacted the way they're supposed to. She told me to watch for signs of a concussion. I'm to go to the ER right away if I feel dizzy and nauseous or my headache and vision get worse."

"None of that sounds good. Let me get Keir's keys."

"That isn't necessary." This time she reached for him when he started for the building. For a split second she wondered if holding on to the man himself would be as addictive as snatching up a handful of worn leather. "My car is here. My things are in my backpack in the lobby. One of the officers wanted to look through it before removing it from the crime scene. My keys are there. As soon as I get it back, I can drive myself. I'll be fine."

"You'd better be." He winked, and a blanket of warmth fell over her at the friendly gesture and teasing tone. Fantasy or not, Hudson Kramer really was a nice guy. How could she not smile when he was so kind to her? "Let me run in and get your bag."

She was still smiling when he returned, looping the strap of her backpack over her shoulder. "Professor Haack lawyered up the moment my partner started asking questions, so we had to let him go. He said he'd come down to the precinct office tomorrow to give us an interview. In the meantime, if he gives you any more trouble over this, you give me a call, okay?"

Tempting as it might be to let Hud form a line of defense between her and the unpleasantries of her world, Gigi knew she had to rely on her own strength. She unhooked her keys and lifted her hand in a slight wave as she backed toward the parking lot. "Thank you. For everything tonight. Please catch whoever did this to Ian."

"I will."

She hesitated when he fell into step beside her. "I said you didn't need to—"

"Don't finish that sentence. You're not walking to your car by yourself at night. Especially with all you've been through."

Perhaps thinking she'd argue further, his hand settled at the small of her back, guiding her toward the parking lot. Although she didn't want to make anything too personal of his chivalry, Gigi was nonetheless relieved to have the safe escort to her car. After all, there was a murderer loose on campus, and he might just think she'd seen something incriminating. Or, without KCPD around to run interference, Gary or Dr. Zajac might chase after her for a private conversation. Plus, Hud was right. Eventually, the grief of watching her mentor die in such a violent fashion was going to catch up to her. And there really was a calming sense of protection in Hud's armed, muscular presence beside her. No one could blame her if she shortened her stride just a fraction to lean into the sheltering warmth of his touch.

Once they reached her car, Hud pulled away to hold the door while she climbed in behind the wheel. "I'll call you tomorrow to make sure you're okay. My partner and I will probably have some follow-up questions for you then. You might remember something important after the shock wears off and you've had a chance to rest up."

That sense of someone giving a damn about her well-being faded. Hudson Kramer was a kind man, yes, but he was more worried about solving Ian's murder than he was learning there was no one in her life to take care of her. She started the engine and reached for the door handle. "Good night, Detective."

He moved into the vee between the door and frame of the car and leaned in. "I thought we were going with Hud."

Suddenly, the late hour and roller-coaster ride of emotions she'd been on this evening hit her. Tears stung her eyes and she reached up beneath her glasses to wipe them away. She wasn't lying when she explained away her stilted good-night. "I think I've handled all the stress I can tonight. I'm really tired. I just want to go home."

He studied her for a moment before he straightened away from the door. "Okay, G." He closed it while Gigi started the engine. "Works for me."

Her innate curiosity about his reaction, and confusion

with clever, slangy banter forced her to roll down the window. "What works for you?"

He grinned, as if her question amused him. "You going straight home and getting some rest sounds like a smart plan to me."

"What I said works for you because you approve of my plan?"

"I guess." He shrugged. "It's just a thing I say. A way to agree with someone and let 'em know I like what they said. It was good to see you again. I wish it had been under better circumstances."

"Me, too."

He stepped back as she shifted the car into Reverse. "Good night, G."

"Good night, Hud."

Gigi backed out and turned her car toward the exit. She studied him in the rearview mirror until he turned away and headed back into the building to continue his investigation.

Hudson Kramer was physical and outgoing, while she was intellectual and too introverted for her own good. There was absolutely no spot on their personality vertices where their x and y axes intersected. Yet despite their differences, he'd been kind to her. He was patient with her awkwardness and didn't make her feel like five feet nine inches of weird, gawky misfit the way most men did. Who was she kidding? She made herself feel that way. Counseling in high school, assertiveness training during her graduate coursework and repeated social advice from Ian and her younger sister hadn't done much to make her comfortable in her own skin. They'd only given her strategies to cope with her shyness and social anxiety.

Work made her feel comfortable. Losing herself in the puzzle of an ongoing project. She could manage the day-today basics of raising her sister and earning her degrees and holding down a job. She ran her research team efficiently and earned a healthy salary that allowed her to not only buy a home in a nice neighborhood but remodel it to suit her own tastes. One-on-one, she could talk with the most influential of people when it came to her science. But social interactions? Parties? Men she was attracted to? Forget about kisses no one else remembered. She might as well dress in camouflage and disappear behind a potted plant.

Chapter Five

Gigi's trip home took her ten minutes longer than usual because of the perennial road construction in the city narrowing busy streets to a single lane or requiring a detour. And when she'd turned off Rockhill Road to drive over to Main, she'd been certain that someone was following her. For a few brief moments she'd felt a happy warmth and then a pang of guilt, thinking Hudson Kramer was making sure she got safely home.

But then she remembered he'd said something about borrowing his partner's Camaro to drive her home, and this vehicle had too high a profile to be any kind of muscle car. Not that she was an expert on cars, but she'd guess that was an SUV or extended-cab pickup truck looming in her rearview mirror. Her grip on the steering wheel tightened with every turn the dark vehicle made with her, even speeding up to get through a yellow light behind her.

But when she turned into the historic bungalow area north of the Nelson-Atkins Museum of Art, the vehicle drove on past. She exhaled a breath she didn't realize she'd been holding and felt the last dregs of her energy waning along with her paranoia.

Driving almost by rote now, she followed the curve around Gillham Park to the row of craftsman-style bungalows where she lived. Seeing the cars parked along the curb on either side of the street was nothing new, since the houses were close together, and driveways were a relatively new update that only a few homes, like her own, had. The street meant home and the sanctuary that called to her as stress, anxiety and grief robbed her of energy and left her with a bone-numbing fatigue.

She kept having to restart the mental checklist of everything she'd need to do in the upcoming days. Take inventory of the lab and Ian's office—had anything been stolen? Was there equipment that needed to be replaced or repaired? Gary Haack had been right about one thing—the Lukin investors would need to be notified. But first she would bring her team together tomorrow, to fill them in on Ian's death. She'd need to fill out and sign a police report, so that meant a trip downtown. She'd have to set up a meeting with the dean to talk about continuing Ian's research. Did she include Dr. Zajac in that meeting? Gary? Who was responsible for cleaning up the mess in the lab? And what else could she remember that would help Hud and his partner find Ian's killer? There had to be something more useful than the smell of whiskey and a swirl of black—

"What the…?" She stomped on the brake and jerked to a halt as a black SUV swung out of her driveway, nearly clipping the front fender of her car. She honked her horn, but the warning sound was drowned out by the spinning of tires screaming to find traction on the pavement. For a split second, she relived the attack at the lab as the black vehicle lurched forward and barreled toward her. Before she could do more than glimpse the shadowy form of the driver through the windshield, the SUV ripped off her sideview mirror, scraped across the driver's-side doors and raced on to the next intersection, tires squealing around the corner before the SUV even switched on its headlights. "Stop! You… Idiot!"

Gigi's heart pounded against her rib cage, her breaths coming in shallow, panicked gasps. Her thoughts instantly went back to the vehicle that had followed her through downtown. But that had been a mistake, right? That vehicle had driven on. It couldn't have doubled back someplace and beaten her home. Could it?

Where had that SUV come from? With all the vehicles parked along the curb, she hadn't seen it backing out. Had she dozed off behind the wheel? Gotten too caught up in her thoughts to notice someone turning around in her driveway? She did have one of the few homes on the block with a driveway, so that explanation made sense. Still, the timing of the accident was unsettling. And the driver hadn't stopped, so she certainly wasn't getting anyone else's insurance to pay for her busted mirror.

For about two seconds, she considered turning around and following the SUV to at least get a license plate. But the roar of its engine faded into the night, and she doubted she'd be able to catch up to him.

Instead, she rubbed at the sore spot on her chest where the seat belt had yanked her back against the seat, and forced herself to take a deep breath, vowing to check every door and window of the house and garage to make sure she hadn't had a break-in. With her senses reawakened like a jolt from a crash cart, she eased up on the brake and pulled into her driveway.

Her headlights flashed across the back of Tammy's yellow Volkswagen. Could that be an explanation for the car that had hit hers? Gigi had driven Tammy to the airport on Wednesday. But with her car still parked here, could one of the men she dated have thought her sister was at home for a late-night rendezvous? But what man wouldn't call or text first? Someone drunk? Obsessive? Someone she probably didn't want her sister dating. Gigi found herself wishing she *had* interrupted an impromptu booty call, and that her sister was home. She could use a friendly face to-night. And a hug.

Gigi pulled up behind the VW, then unlocked her white-knuckle grip around the steering wheel and opened the door. She lifted the mirror that was dangling from a few wires and shook her head at the missing paint and dented metal. Although she was an expert in several technologies, car repairs were not in her wheelhouse. She'd have to add a visit to her insurance man and the service department at the car dealership to her list of things to get done.

"Virginia? Is that you?" The light went on at the porch next door and a feathery voice called to her across the yard. Gigi looked over the roof of her car to see her next-door neighbor Kelly Allan step outside in her chenille bathrobe. The older woman cradled her Pomeranian in her arms and hastened down the front steps as quickly as her arthritic knees would allow. "My goodness. Are you all right? I saw everything if you need a witness. You're lucky that car didn't kill you. I'm just glad Izzy had already finished her outing." She looked to the intersection where the dark vehicle had disappeared. "It's not safe for man or beast in this neighborhood, anymore."

Wisps of the woman's gray hair caught the light from her porch and framed her head like a silvery halo. But Gigi suspected there was nothing angelic or chance about this late-night meeting. Miss Allan set her tiny puff of a dog on the grass and crossed the yard while Gigi locked her car and dutifully circled around it to greet her elderly neigh-bor. "I hope the noise didn't frighten you. I didn't see him until he was right on me. He should have had his lights on. Of course, it's after midnight. The driver probably wasn't expecting any traffic. I'm sure we're fine now," she reassured the frail woman. "What are you doing up so late?"

Her neighbor tugged on the leash she held in her hand. "Potty training the new puppy. When Izzy says she has to go, we go."

Gigi eyed the pampered Pomeranian who hadn't been a puppy for a couple of years now. She was pawing through the red leaves that had fallen from her neighbor's dogwood tree, no doubt on the trail of a squirrel or other small rodent. Knowing Miss Allan's eccentricities, the late-night walk in her lavender robe had more to do with her hobby of spying on the neighbors than it did with walking her dog. "You probably shouldn't be outside alone at this time of night."

"You're telling me. This used to be a nice neighborhood when my parents built this house." She fluttered her manicured fingers in the air. "Now we've got strange cars parking here in the middle of the night. Or driving slowly around the block, like they're checking our houses to see which one would be easiest to break in to and rob." She softened her shrill voice to a whisper. "I thought he must be one of Tammy's young beaux, sneaking out of the house before you got home. I realize she's a grown-up now, but it still must be awkward to have your big sister interrupt when you're entertaining a young gentleman."

"Tammy's out of town, Miss Allan." That vague sense of alarm that had gone dormant since her interview with Hud resurrected itself. She glanced back at her own well-lit porch but saw nothing out of place. "You said *sneaking out of the house*. Did you see him inside my place?" Did she need to call 911?

Instead of explaining her cryptic comments, Miss Allan hugged the gold fur ball to her chest. Her eyes had narrowed to study Gigi's ragged appearance. "Are you all right, dear? You look a bit rattled. Why are you all dressed up? Did you have a date?"

Goose bumps prickled Gigi's skin as she looked up and down the street for any sign that could explain away this uncomfortable feeling of being the object of unwanted attention. It was the same sense of creepy she'd felt when Gary had spied on the last of her interview with Hud. Could he have gotten here before her? Did she even know what kind of car Gary drove? "Miss Allan, was the driver parked in my driveway or just turning around?"

"Did he dump you?" The older woman went on as if Gigi hadn't spoken. "Men these days don't appreciate a quiet girl like you."

The woman was lonely and making conversation. Gigi typically indulged her because she understood that kind of isolation. But if she couldn't get the information that would ease her own concern, then she wanted to go inside and check the house for herself, call the police again if necessary, then get into a hot shower and sleep for about ten hours. She retreated to her car, moving toward the steps of the stone porch. "It wasn't a date. I had a work thing this evening. If you'll excuse me, I really want to see if my house is okay."

She stopped when she realized her neighbor was following her.

"You work too much, Virginia. I bet men would ask you out if you did something with your hair. And wore clothes that show your cleavage." Miss Allan gasped an apology before resting her hand on Gigi's arm and tilting her face up to hers. "I'm so sorry, dear. I didn't mean to point out any inadequacies. You know, you can buy a bra that has gel in the cups. That'll give you a little more oomph upstairs. Men like that."

If her boss hadn't been murdered and her car wasn't

wrecked, then getting dating advice from her eighty-five-year-old neighbor was a strong indicator that Gigi's night couldn't get any worse.

"Thank you for watching the place, Miss Allan." Gigi's patience for small talk had zeroed out, along with her self-esteem and flagging energy. She'd had one too many shocks tonight to handle anything but solitude right now. "You don't want Izzy to catch a chill in this night air. Good night."

If Miss Allan wanted to say anything more, Gigi wasn't waiting around to hear it. "Good night, dear."

Since nothing seemed to be disturbed on the front porch, Gigi slipped inside, turning the dead bolt behind her and heading past her bedroom and living room at the front of the house. In the kitchen, she spared a moment to peek through the curtains of the side window to make sure Miss Allan and Izzy got safely inside their house before she flipped on the light and took off her shoes. Her toes throbbed with thanks at being released from their high-heeled prison, although she shivered at the cold tiles beneath the soles of her feet. Then again, maybe it wasn't the floor that chilled her.

She set her backpack on the peninsula counter and made sure the dead bolt was still in place on the back door before moving through the rest of the house, including Tammy's loft-bedroom suite. Although she found a torn screen in the laundry room, no one seemed to have gotten in. The television was still in the living room, her computer and Tammy's gaming and music systems were still in their bedrooms. If there had been an attempted break-in, then maybe Miss Allan's watchful eyes or Gigi's late arrival had scared him away before he could take anything.

She was safe. Alone, but safe. And alone was better than having an intruder to keep her company, right? Alone was better than facing reporters or being bullied by Evgeni Zajac or *darling*ed by Gary Haack.

With her naked toes protesting the chill of the wood-and-tile floors, she returned to the kitchen and picked up the teakettle on the stove. A hot cup of tea might chase this frosty mood away. She'd get the water started, then take a quick shower and change into her pajamas.

She was leaning against the edge of the copper farm sink, filling the kettle under the faucet when she noticed the blood that was still on her hands. A mix of disgust and grief squeezed in her chest and she set the kettle aside to thrust her fingers beneath the water instead. Pumping a palmful of soap from the dispenser beside the sink, she lathered up her hands until she could no longer see the skin. Although a crime-scene technician had scraped beneath her nails and the paramedic had given her a disinfectant wipe to wash up at the ambulance, there was still evidence of Ian's last moments staining her fingers. Increasing the water's temperature, she rubbed at her cuticles and scraped the bristles of the cleaning brush she used on the dishes beneath her nails.

She rinsed and soaped again and again until her hands blurred in front of her eyes. Gigi had lost people she cared about before—most notably her parents who'd died in a car wreck. Her father had perished instantly, and her mother had held on for two more days in the hospital until she, too, had succumbed to her injuries. At that time, she'd had a master's thesis she needed to finish so she could get a job to support herself and her younger sister. There had been funeral arrangements to make, insurance to deal with. She'd shut down her emotions then because it had been the only way she could get through it all. She'd become strong because she had to be. Tammy had needed her. No one else was going to take care of them.

But she was so damn tired of being sensible and strong and dealing with the trials life threw into her path again and again. Just because she *could* deal didn't mean she always wanted to be the one who had to.

If it hasn't hit you yet, it will. Hud had been right.

Logically, she knew the shock was wearing off, and irrational thoughts were sneaking past her broken defenses. The blankness that had gotten her through tonight was crumbling away, allowing the grief, helplessness and rage to bombard her emotional barriers. She tried to focus on some of the good that had happened tonight, like the hug from Hana Nowak, her neighbor's concern, Hudson Kramer putting up a wall of muscle between her and Gary's unwanted touch, walking her to her car like a gentleman or calling her by that silly nickname, G. But she couldn't recall the warmth of Hud's hand at her back or feel the softness of his jacket clutched in her fingers or hear the deep timbre of his laughter soothing her senses. She was alone. She was frightened. She was lost. And it seemed no amount of logical thinking or silly fantasy could give her the comfort she needed.

Shutting off the water, Gigi sank to the floor and let the tears come. More than the physical trauma of being attacked, the emotional trauma of all she'd dealt with tonight washed over her in waves.

Ian Lombard had looked out for her. He'd hired her for a job she loved, advised her when she struggled with her teaching. *You're my prize, Gigi,* he'd told her after the first time the university had honored Ian and his team for their groundbreaking work. He'd meant something to her, and he'd died beneath her hands.

He'd argued a lot, too. With his wife. His staff. University officials. Yes, he'd abandoned her tonight at the reception, but he'd never turned those volatile words on her.

She remembered Ian gasping for breath to speak to her as blood gurgled in his throat. *My prize....smarter than me.* He'd valued her in ways that few people did.

Her body went limp and her sinuses burned. Tears rolled down her cheeks, singeing her skin and fogging up her glasses.

She sat there on the floor in front of the sink, her knees hugged to her chest, quietly crying until her cheeks felt chapped and her nose ran. She sat there until the tears ran out and there was no emotion left. She was exhausted. Her eyes felt gritty. But she could think. A little.

First of all, she needed a tissue. She could stand up and reach the paper towels. But her legs felt as weak as her brain. How many times had she hidden a tissue into the pockets of her sweater, to give her something to work between her fingers, dispelling the nervous energy she felt when she got self-conscious in front of a lecture hall or conference table? Pretending the blood stains weren't there, marring the sweater her mother had knitted for her years ago, she reached into her left pocket. There was her phone. She reached into the right pocket. There was a tissue. But her victory was short-lived.

Feeling a tinge of panic, she dug through both pockets again.

She was missing something.

The note. Ian's note.

The scrap of paper he'd been so desperate for her to take.

Find... Finish it.

"Finish what?" she murmured, grabbing the edge of the sink and pulling herself to her feet.

She stumbled over to the counter and rummaged through her backpack, unzipping each pocket before dumping out everything but her laptop. What had she done with that note? It had been Ian's last gift to her, and she'd lost it.

Or maybe it had been Ian's last cry for help. *Finish it.*

"He was giving me a message." One that only her brain could understand and figure out.

A clue to his killer? A motive?

Gigi checked her discarded shoes, unrolled the cuffs of her sweater for any sign of the crumpled note. She tried to recall the symbols she'd seen on that paper. *A. U. N. O. 3.* Ian often encoded his notes to keep curious eyes from copying his work until he was ready to reveal it. But would a dying man waste his final moments writing in code? She shook her head. Not random letters. Not even code. Au. "Gold." NO_3. "Nitrate. Gold nitrate." It was a scientific formula. Similar to one they'd been developing for a small-size, large-capacity power cell to drive industrial computers, one that could also be adapted to other uses in the medical and military fields. Only, they hadn't been able to shrink the capacitor to their target size yet and still maintain the control function they wanted. The formula Ian had given her had been slightly different. And definitely incomplete. *Finish it.*

She'd have to remember the rest of the formula or develop it herself if she couldn't find that piece of paper.

She paused a moment in her frantic search. The new formula—the new device—would be worth millions to anyone who wanted to revolutionize the computer industry. Maybe even more to the person who could weaponize their design and sell it on the black market.

Motive. Millions, if not billions, of motives for killing a man.

"Where is that damn paper?" She unzipped the cosmetics bag where she carried some medications, lip balm and a compact. She opened the compact. She looked in the bottle of ibuprofen, even though she knew she hadn't stashed Ian's note in either location. She unzipped her bill-fold, checked the cash there, sorted through her debit and credit cards and ID. "What…?" She pulled her driver's license from behind her bank card. "Why are you here?"

She slipped her license back into the see-through pocket where she normally kept it. The punch cards she kept for gasoline and a campus coffee shop were in the wrong pocket, too. Hud had said the police had searched her bag before she left the university. Would they rearrange the contents inside?

Or had someone else searched through her backpack?

That chill crept up her spine with renewed strength as she backed away from her things on the counter. She threaded her fingers through her hair, even relishing the slight tug of pain at the back of her scalp. "What is happening to me?"

Whoever had searched her bag, read her license, would know her address. If that person wanted Ian's formula, and thought she had it—if that person had taken the note, but realized it was unfinished work and believed she could complete the formula—if that person thought she understood their motive for killing Ian…

Trust no one, Ian had warned her.

Gigi quickly stuffed everything back into her backpack and closed it. There were too many reasons for someone to search her house, to follow her home—too many reasons why she might be the key to solving Ian's murder.

She bypassed her black heels and slipped her feet into the grass-stained tennis shoes she wore when she worked in the yard and headed out the door to her car. She started the engine and saw the light in Miss Allan's bedroom come on. She'd come home late, been nearly run down, and now she was leaving again in the middle of the night. She was really giving her neighbor some juicy gossip to obsess over.

But she needed to talk to Hud. She needed to tell him what was happening.

He wanted details? She had plenty of them to share.

And he would listen. Even if he thought she was nuts, he would still listen.

He was a good man. He might even be her friend.

Forget that he'd been her fantasy for two years.

The most important detail to her right now was that Hudson Kramer made her feel safe.

Chapter Six

Tuning out the familiar buzz of noise around him in the precinct offices, Hudson stared at the sketch of the Lombard crime scene he'd made in his notebook, wondering what was wrong with this picture. The first forty-eight hours were crucial to a murder investigation, and he was burning through that time without anything but a suspected murder weapon he couldn't find to show for it.

What was wrong with this picture was that Virginia Brennan was smack-dab in the middle of it. He couldn't imagine anyone less suited for the violence of that crime scene or less equipped to understand the secrets and motives that would lead someone to commit murder. She was too shy to deal with the ensuing chaos, too traumatized by the loss of her boss and friend to cope with the wham-bam push to move as quickly as possible to find answers and arrest a suspect.

What was wrong with *him* was that he kept thinking about the statuesque redhead with the big, soulful eyes instead of concentrating on the clues that wouldn't fit together in any sensible way. Some pointed to premeditation while others indicated a crime of opportunity spurred by anger. Too many suspects had motive for killing Lombard. And while Keir was tracking down which of those suspects would have also had the opportunity to be at the tech lab with Dr. Lombard, there was no way to eliminate any of them until other pieces started falling into place.

Gigi had no business being this close to a murder investigation.

And he had no business resurrecting that ill-advised attraction he'd put out of his mind these past two years. The quiet, complicated professor couldn't be more wrong for a streetwise smart-ass like him. Or maybe he was having trouble accepting that he was wrong for her. It would be his dumb luck to fall for someone he couldn't have. She was class and culture and cutting-edge science, and he was…not.

Buzzing his lips with a regretful sigh, Hud glanced up from his desk in the bullpen at the Fourth Precinct office. With most of B shift out on patrol, there were only the desk sergeant near the elevators and a handful of detectives and uniformed officers scattered throughout their cubicles on the main floor. The offices of the precinct captain and other command ranks were dark and locked up and would probably stay that way until Monday morning. Most of the men and women on duty were typing up reports or shootin' the breeze around cubicle walls, or in the break room drinking coffee and eating the night shift's equivalent of an afternoon snack. A few, like his partner at the desk across from his, were fixated on computer screens as they tracked down leads on cases.

Although he had a working knowledge of computers, Hud tended to go old school, writing down his observations and insights on an investigation by hand rather than texting notes to his computer. He liked the visceral feel of putting pen to paper. There was something about the tactile experience that flowed up his arm and triggered the thought processes in his brain.

Only, tonight, his brain was misfiring. Instead of piecing together details on the murder, the only thing he could see when he tapped his pen against the paper was a waterfall of long auburn hair and dove-gray eyes that had shown him panic, sadness and, if he wasn't mistaken, heat when he'd caught her staring at him on the bench outside the Williams University Technology Building.

Damn. Had he really forgotten that whole sexy librarian vibe Gigi Brennan had charmed him with two years ago when he'd rescued her from being abandoned at the Shamrock Bar? It wasn't like she had a killer rack or was a cute kind of pretty like her sister or even had an easy-to-hang-with personality.

Maybe it was because she wasn't like any woman he'd met that she'd made such an impression on him.

She'd been so serious about learning the rules of playing pool, so curious why he'd chosen a bottled beer over the draft his partner had. She'd explained the advantages and disadvantages of the fluorescent lighting above the pool table and expounded on why men were more drawn to her gregarious sister than to a shy, self-avowed nerd like her. And then she'd leaned over the corner of the table with her bottom bobbing in the air beside him to get a different angle on an impossible shot, and all the blood in his bemused brain had rushed straight to his groin. She'd also earned his undying admiration when her last striped ball had caromed off two sides and sunk into the corner pocket.

Her victorious smile that night—because she'd mastered the skill, not because she'd defeated him—had hit him with the same surprising force as the way she'd smiled tonight after he'd gotten rid of her pesky coworkers and first called her G. Making Gigi Brennan smile made him feel good, made him feel like an able-bodied man instead of a second-string sidekick to men who topped six feet and knew how to charm the ladies.

There was something adorable about the way she peeked over her glasses to make eye contact when they were close. And those legs—long and lean, nicely curved—man, they went on forever. The sequins and bulky sweater hadn't been the right look for her, but he'd love to see her in a slinky pencil skirt that stopped right above the dimple in her right knee, like she'd worn that night at the bar. Along with a button-up blouse that he could unbutton. Or a shapeless white lab coat with some lacy lingerie on underneath it. He had a feeling that Gigi was full of surprises beneath that introverted exterior.

Surprises like the way she'd thrown herself into that kiss two years ago.

Hud absentmindedly flipped through the pages in his notebook, seeing images from the past rather than what was right in front of him. His blood simmered as his thoughts fully engaged on the wrong topic. He'd been a little taken aback by Gigi's eager response to his goodnight kiss at the end of that weird, unplanned date night. The heady rush of being desired had fueled his ego and soothed something needy buried deep inside him. That was so not a kiss between casual acquaintances or even friends. Gigi's grabby hands and welcoming passion had fueled something else inside him, too.

For about twenty seconds, he'd savored everything the woman was willing to give him. Had urged her to give even more. And she had. Her inexperienced mouth had been hot and sweet, and oh, so ready to learn. Her hands had traveled over his face and shoulders, pinching the skin underneath as she dragged herself closer, as if she couldn't get enough of the taste and feel of him.

It was that twenty-first second when he'd come to his senses and remembered he was supposed to be her safe escort home, not some sex-starved wingman who'd take advantage of her awkward innocence.

It was about twenty-five seconds into saying good-night when he reminded himself that university professor Virginia Brennan—the shy intellectual with the conservative clothes and social naivete—was way out of his league for a working-class Joe like him. She was big-city born and raised while he was half hillbilly from the Ozarks. She had multiple college degrees, and had mentioned scholarships and early graduations, while he'd enlisted in the police academy to get a job to support his siblings. He had to work his way through night school to earn his degree and finally make detective three years after the other members of his academy class had.

Gigi was interesting, a puzzle of contradictions he didn't understand. She was unintentionally funny and vulnerable in a way she probably didn't even realize, which, of course, triggered every overprotective bone in his body. Plus, he figured he'd have to be about twice as smart as he was to be half as smart as her. There were lowlifes on the streets in No-Man's-Land he had more in common with.

And yet she'd turned that polite kiss into something heated and raw and...

With his feverish frustration and useless fantasies about to blow out his ears, Hud pocketed his notebook and rolled his chair away from his desk. He shrugged into his jacket and tapped the desktop to get Keir's attention. "Hey. I'm going to take a short drive to clear my head. You want anything while I'm out?"

Keir looked up from the ME's preliminary report he'd been studying. "I'm good." He pointed to the data on his computer screen. "You were right about the whiskey bottle. Niall said he found alcohol in several of the wound tracts."

Keir's ME brother hadn't wasted any time getting them

the information they needed to confirm Hud's suspicions. "Great. The only bottle on the scene was sealed and clean. I guess that means doing some Dumpster diving to find a broken bottle. Shouldn't be too many of those around the city."

Keir laughed at the snark that colored Hud's voice. "Hey, it's your lead. *You* get to dive in."

Hud's mood lightened a little bit at his friend's teasing. "Whatever happened to teamwork?"

Waving his hand in front of himself, Keir pointed out his spit-and-polish perfection. "Suit and tie." Then he pointed to Hud. "Hillbilly chic…" His gaze narrowed and moved past Hud. "What's she doing here?"

Hud turned, fully expecting to see Keir's wife, or possibly Keir's sister or stepgrandmother, showing up with some kind of family emergency. Instead, he saw Gigi Brennan at the sergeant's desk, signing a clipboard and looping a visitor's badge around her neck. She still wore the same sequins-and-sweater look from earlier, although she'd traded in her heels for a normal pair of tennis shoes. Had his wandering thoughts somehow conjured her here?

"Close your mouth, Kramer," Keir advised him, rising to his feet. "You finished the interview, right?"

Hud's surprise was quickly replaced with a wary feeling that raised the hairs on the back of his neck. "I took her statement and sent her home." Had that pig Professor Haack forced his company on her again? The urgency in her movements clearly indicated something was wrong. "She shouldn't be here."

"She's making a beeline right to you, buddy."

Hud waved off the desk sergeant who had picked up the phone to alert him to her arrival and moved forward as Gigi zigzagged her way through the desks. Without those high heels, he could look her straight in the eye—

hers were red-rimmed, determined and focused squarely on him. "G? What are you doing here?"

"Did you find a note at the crime scene?" She started talking before she stopped in front of him. "It would have been on Ian's university letterhead. Handwritten. Crumpled up. Stained with his blood."

"What are you talking about?"

Her words spewed out in a panicked rush. "I remembered something. Key evidence, I think. Except I lost it. Or someone took it from me. Ian *did* say something important to me before he—" her gaze darted past him to Keir "—before he…died." She turned to the break room, then to her right, seeing the uniformed officers and other detectives pause their conversations and lift their focuses from their computers. He could see her mentally counting all the faces staring curiously at them. Her hands tightened around the straps of her backpack and her words faltered. "Um… I… Why are there so many people here? It's the middle of the night."

He probably shouldn't remind her that this was light in terms of personnel. "KC's a big city. The police work around the clock. Somebody's always on duty. Friday nights keep us especially busy."

She touched the temples of her glasses as if they needed adjusting. Nervous habit? Or coping mechanism? "Why are they looking at me?"

"Don't pay any attention to those yahoos. We don't get a lot of visitors this time of night who aren't in handcuffs." He didn't want to mention that the dried blood on her sweater might have some of them concerned about needing their help. He tried to ease some of the tension tightening her posture with another joke. "And the only time a lady stops by to see me is when my sisters are in town."

"You don't have a girlfriend?"

"Not at the moment. Not for a long time."

"Why not?"

"Good question." Women got what they needed from him, and then they set him aside and moved on. He guessed she wasn't really looking for his dating history, though. Gigi's nerves had kicked in and her brain had shut down. "Hey." Let his coworkers start the inevitable gossip. Gigi was upset, and she'd come to him for help. A damsel in distress had always been his Achilles' heel. Hud slid his fingers along the line of her jaw, cupping the side of her face. When she startled, he anchored his fingertips at the nape of her neck before she could pull away. Her hand came up to wind around his wrist, but her attention had shifted out of her head and back to him. Damn if that wasn't another thing he liked about her—her instinct to reach out to him and hold on. He stroked his thumb across her cheek, noting the pink irritation around her eyes. "You've been crying. Are you feeling okay? Any symptoms of a concussion?"

She shook her head. "Physically, I'll be fine. But you were right. You said the shock would wear off and the grief would hit me, and it did."

"I'm sorry, G."

She released him as suddenly as she'd latched on to tug up the hem of her sweater and pull out a wad of tissues that she waved in front of him. "But I'm glad I had that crying jag because I was looking for these when I remembered the note."

"The one you lost at the crime scene?"

"The one that Ian gave me."

"Lombard gave you a note?"

"Before he died." She stuffed the tissues back into her pocket. "He couldn't really talk, so he wrote it down. He was adamant that I take it. I tucked it into my sweater and now it's gone. I don't know if I lost it or if it was stolen. Somebody rifled through my bag. Maybe the killer was looking for it. I know the police searched it. That's why I hoped you had it?"

Hud shook his head. He didn't have three college degrees, but he wasn't stupid. Still, this conversation wasn't making much sense. He took Gigi by the elbow and turned toward the meeting rooms lining the walls at the far side of the bullpen. "Let's go someplace a little more private. Then you can start at the beginning."

"I'll bring you two some coffee," Keir offered, trading a nod with Hud as they walked past. His partner obviously shared his concerns about this late-night visit. He wasn't sure what key piece of evidence Gigi thought she'd had. But the fact that she was now missing it had her worried. And that worried him.

Hud opened the door to the first empty room and led Gigi to a chair at the head of the table. He crossed to the window to glare at the nosy officers who'd moved to keep him and Gigi in their line of sight before pulling the blinds shut on the *Hudson-Kramer's-with-a-woman?* shock on their faces. "I said to call me if you remembered anything else about Lombard's murder. I could have looked up what we've catalogued from the crime scene so far for you. You didn't need to come downtown in the middle of the night like this."

"I didn't have your number," Gigi answered. "Besides, there was that SUV that spooked me, so I just wanted to get out of the house."

His hand fisted around the cord. "What SUV?"

"The one that sideswiped my car. One that possibly followed me home."

"Someone hit your car?" He spun around. She'd already taken one blow to the head. "Were you hurt? Who followed you?"

"I don't think so. He was backing out of my driveway—"

"He was at your house?" Hud pulled out his cell phone to put in a call to Patrol. "Did you get a plate number?"

"It was too dark, and he was going too fast. He didn't have his lights on. He was probably just turning around. Not all the houses on my street have driveways."

"Can you describe the car? The driver?"

"Black? An SUV. The car had tinted windows. I could barely make out the outline of a driver and then he was gone." She raked her fingers into her hair to push it off her face, wincing when she must have tugged against the goose egg on her scalp. "I thought he'd broken in, but I think he just vandalized my screen. And I don't see how someone following me could possibly get to my house before me."

The list continued and he was getting pissed—at whoever was terrorizing this woman tonight. He didn't for one damn minute think she was crazy or that this had anything to do with the blow to her head. He pulled a chair down to the corner of the table and sat right in front of her. "Let me get this straight—a car ran into you? You should have called me right then. Or 911. You were followed from the campus? You think someone tried to break in—"

"I couldn't find any broken locks or windows to confirm that theory."

"—went through your bag and stole Lombard's note out of your pocket? Damn it, G. A man was murdered. You were assaulted. Stuff like that isn't supposed to happen to a woman like you."

He couldn't tell if it was his harsh tone, spelling out the accusations she'd listed or the fact he was sitting close enough to inhale the alcohol and disinfectant and something fainter that was soft like vanilla clinging to her clothes and skin that widened her eyes and made her fall silent. She stuck her hands into her pockets and leaned back in her chair. Away from him.

Oh, hell. The last thing he needed was for her to be afraid of him. "I'm sorry. I didn't mean to…"

His apology drifted off when her gaze darted to the whiteboard on the wall and she pushed to her feet. She picked up a marker and started writing—symbols, numbers, letters that didn't form words—while she spoke. "Whoever attacked me must have overheard what Ian was saying to me, and wanted that information for himself."

"What are you doing?" he asked, wondering if this was another shy person thing to keep her hands busy so talking or being alone with him wouldn't make her so nervous.

"Writing down everything I remember from Ian's note."

Hud rose more slowly and circled the table, not wanting to frighten her into shutting down again. Pushing a chair aside, he leaned his hips back against the table and folded his arms over his chest. "You think that note is the reason Lombard was killed?"

"Possibly." She erased two numbers with the side of her hand, then wrote them again, reversing the order. Wow. All those letters and math-looking symbols meant nothing to him. But apparently it was a language in which Gigi was fluent. She stepped back for a moment to survey the board before pointing to the top line of her work. "This is part of a formula."

"For something your lab was working on?"

"For something revolutionary if it's what I think it is."

"Is it worth a lot of money?"

Despite her obvious fatigue, her whole body hummed with energy as she analyzed what she'd written. He knew a handful of scary-smart people—and then there was whatever was going on inside Gigi's head. Like an athlete who was in the zone and running the perfect race, it was kind of hot to see the wheels churning inside her brain and feel the intelligence radiating out of every pore. "Potentially. If the equation was completed. A prototype would have to be built. We have the materials at the lab. If the design works, it could be worth a fortune."

"A prototype for what?"

She spun around to face him, her soft eyes sparkling with a silvery gleam. Oh, yeah. Brainpower was definitely hot. "Think of the biggest computers in the world—that run multinational corporations or communication networks." She waved her arms in a big circle. "Computers that fill warehouses and underground bunkers and need their own power plant to run them." She tugged on his wrist to uncross his arms, then placed the marker in his hand. "Then shrink it down to fit in the palm of your hand."

He looked at the board. "That's what all that is? A computer?"

"The power cell to run one. Ian must have cracked the code. But I can't tell if he didn't finish the equation— or he just didn't finish writing it down before he died." He wondered if she even knew her fingers had remained wrapped around his over the marker and that she'd given him a subtle squeeze before she pulled away to examine the whiteboard again. "I don't know what this line of numbers means. Phone number? Bank account? Maybe he encrypted a message to me."

"While he was dying?" In Hud's experience, people who were dying took the time to share hopes or regrets, not play scrambled communication games.

"Ian could be a little paranoid. I got pretty good at deciphering his notes." She visibly shivered and hugged her arms around herself again. "Except, I have no idea what it means."

"Could it be a password?" Hud suggested, trying to come up with a more practical explanation. "If it's a phone number, it would have to be a foreign country exchange." When she glanced back at him, he winked. *I know a couple of things, too, sweetheart.* "Too many numbers to be local."

"Dr. Zajac and his wife are from Lukinburg. They travel back and forth between our countries a couple of times a month."

"And you told me Lombard's wife is studying abroad this semester."

Gigi nodded. The silvery light that had brightened her eyes a few moments earlier was fading. "Do you think he wanted me to call Doris? Tell his wife he loved her? Or apologize for his past mistakes? I'm not good at stuff like that."

"I can plug in the numbers and run a quick search. See if a phone number pops up." He copied down everything she had written in his notebook. Wait. *Part of a formula?* "This isn't complete?" His instincts going on high alert, he pushed away from the table. Following her across town? Hitting her car? No way was any of that random. "Maybe the killer thinks you know something he couldn't get from Lombard and now he's after you."

"After me?"

He rubbed his hand up and down her arm, alarmed by the trembling he felt there. That rush of energy that had propelled her to the whiteboard was rapidly dissipating. She was going to crash soon. Crash hard. "Look, I don't mean to scare you, but—"

"No. That makes sense." She sank into the closest chair. "Ian said I was smarter than he was—he knew I could fig-ure this out. He wanted me to complete his work one last time. If I had access to his notes, I could decipher them. I know how his mind worked. I could probably do it without his notes. If I had a few days."

"Would anyone else be able to finish the formula and build a prototype?"

"Possibly Dr. Zajac."

"The foreign professor who likes to argue?"

She nodded.

"What about his wife?"

"Hana?" Gigi shook her head. "She's a translator. Her only knowledge of physics and engineering would come from observation. She transcribes his notes, sits in on staff meetings. She's familiar with the jargon, but I doubt she could apply what she's learned into a device that could actually work." Her lips tightened with a frown. "If he had the equation in front of him, Gary could build the prototype."

He tried not to grin at the venom behind her tone. He wondered what Haack had done to Gigi to make her have such a low opinion of the guy. But when he saw her shiver, any idea of being amused vanished. Hud shrugged off his jacket and draped it around her shoulders. Kneeling in front of her, he pulled the jacket together in front of her slim body and continued to rub his hands up and down her arms, willing his body heat to keep her going a little while longer.

"Hang in there, G. We'll figure this out." He glanced up at the board and shrugged. "Well, you'll figure *that* out. I'll take care of the bad guys."

"Like a team? Brains and Brawn?"

"Yeah. I'll be the muscle head. Probably work out better for us both that way." When even that self-deprecating joke didn't earn a smile, he caught a lock of long, auburn hair that had fallen in front of her glasses and brushed it back behind her ear. It was as smooth and silky to the touch as he remembered from that night he'd sunk his fingers into her hair and kissed her. The tactile memory triggered a visceral response deep in his gut, heating his blood even as he felt her chilled skin beneath his fingertips. He cupped his hand against the side of her neck, wishing he had the right to pull her into his arms and show her how that brawny strength could shield her and support her through the physical, mental and emotional turmoil she'd been through. "You've had a long night. You should be home soaking in a hot bath or sleeping by now."

"I don't like baths. It takes too long to fill the tub, and my skin gets pruney. A shower is much more efficient."

Not helping with the errant hormones. The pruney comment made him notice her skin. It'd be a shame to do anything that might mar that smooth, creamy expanse. Despite her dark red hair, there was nary a freckle he could see across her cheeks or long neck. That alabaster skin was unblemished all the way down to…

He thanked the fates for the soft knock at the door and pushed to his feet to see Keir enter. His partner handed Hud a cup of coffee and set another, along with a handful of sugars and creamers, on the table in front of Gigi. "I brewed a fresh pot. Wasn't sure how you take yours."

Unaware of the questioning look Keir gave Hud as he took in the leather jacket around her shoulders and his rapid retreat from the witness he was supposed to be interrogating, Gigi pried the lid off her coffee cup and dumped in two creamers. "Usually I drink tea, but I need something stronger to keep me going tonight. Thank you."

"My pleasure." Keir pulled back the front of his jacket to prop his hands on his hips as he studied the writing that filled the whiteboard. "What's this? Are we having science class?"

Hud drank a sip of the potent brew to tamp down those crazy flashes of desire Gigi stirred in him and think like a detective again. "It could be the reason Lombard was killed."

"What's it mean?" Keir asked.

"It means whoever builds what this formula has designed can make a powerful weapon that could be controlled remotely, or bring down a satellite or communication grid from their basement, or run an entire hospital from the back of a truck, making the owner an awful lot of money—legitimately. Even more on the black market." He glanced over at Gigi, huddling in his jacket and warming her fingers around the coffee cup. "Is that about right?"

She nodded. "You're a good listener." She lifted her gaze to Keir. "Of course, our lab wasn't designing the minicapacitor for criminal applications, but that's motive, isn't it?"

"That's a hell of a lot of motive," Keir agreed.

The more important piece of information Hud had gotten tonight was that Gigi was in danger. "Lombard gave this information to Professor Brennan, and now it's missing. She was assaulted at the crime scene. Somebody rammed her car tonight. And she believes someone followed her home and was casing her house." He slid his notebook across the table to Keir. "Her address is in here. Send a black-and-white over there to keep an eye on the place until I can get there. I'm driving Gigi home."

"You are?" She tilted her chin to him. "What about my car? I'll be stranded again."

"But you won't be alone." Hud closed the lid on his disposable cup, prepared for any argument she might give him on this. "Right now, you need sleep. Monday, we're going to take pictures of the damage to your car, file a police report and send it to your insurance. I've got a shop guy who works on my truck. We'll take your car to him once we've got the paperwork done."

"I have to go to the lab tomorrow—later this morning, I guess—to inventory supplies and equipment, meet with the research team." She braced her hand on the tabletop and stood. "You're giving up your time to chauffeur me around? What about your investigation?"

"You *are* the investigation." Not that he thought she had the strength to protest much, but he wasn't going to argue with her on this. He turned back to Keir. "It's not much to go on, but I also want you to put out an APB for a black SUV with tinted windows. The paint job will probably be scratched up from hitting Gigi's car."

"I'm on it." Keir snapped a picture of the address with his phone, backing Hud's plan without question. He returned the notebook and took several pictures of the whiteboard. "I'll copy these into our case file while you head on out. The lab said they'd get me some preliminary results yet tonight. I'll keep you posted."

"I recommend we keep Gigi's name out of the press for now. Although, the killer may already have a bead on her as the key to all this." He waved his hand toward the whiteboard.

"Agreed. If you need anything else, let me know. I could send my brother or sister over to help keep watch if you need to sleep."

Keir's oldest brother and younger sister were both detectives. His middle brother worked at the crime lab and was probably finishing up the autopsy on Ian Lombard right now. "Thanks. I'll be okay tonight. I may need someone to spell me later."

"One of us will be there," Keir promised.

Hud held out his hand to Gigi and waited for her to circle around the table to join him. "Shall we?"

When she tried to return his jacket, he held it so that she could slide her arms into the sleeves instead. The fact that she didn't protest him railroading her into leaving with him was a sign of how exhausted she must be.

Keir stopped Hud on the way out. "Professor, you mind giving me a minute with my partner?"

"It's Gigi." She offered him a weary smile. "And no. I'll find a restroom and meet you out here."

Hud gave her directions to the closest facility and watched her until she disappeared inside. Once they were alone, he faced his partner. "All right. Let's hear the lecture."

Keir didn't waste any time getting to the concern that had been stamped on his face. "What are you doing, Hud? There's no protection order on this case. You didn't even want to take lead with this witness. Now you're spending the night at her house? Promising her 24/7 security? Captain Hendricks wants us to solve a homicide, not babysit a woman who's gotten under your skin. We haven't even been on this case twenty-four hours."

"I've known her for two years. She needs me."

"She needs a friend."

No doubt. With Gigi's social anxiety and her sister out of town, there probably weren't many people she'd call on at a time like this. "Well, then that's what I'll be. She's alone and she's scared, and I don't think she gets people. She'd be easy to hurt. Easy for our perp to victimize and take advantage of. Until we arrest a suspect, this guy's going to keep coming after whatever is locked up inside that brain of hers."

"She's not the one I'm worried about." Keir's mouth twisted with concern. "I've seen you do this a hundred times. Running in to save the day. Giving up a little piece of your heart because a woman needs you. How many pieces you got left?"

"Enough to get G through this. Enough to keep her safe." Hud raked all ten fingers through his hair and muttered a curse. His partner knew him better than any other man on the planet. Keir wasn't the only detective to see the pattern repeating itself. "Look, I know I've had nothin' but bad luck with the ladies. Maybe it's time to give up on the idea of forever. But I won't give up on right now. And right now, Virginia Brennan needs me."

"She needs a cop."

"I *am* a cop."

Keir considered his argument for a moment, then nodded. "And a damn good one." He reached out to shake Hud's hand and squeeze his shoulder. "However this plays out, I've got your back, partner."

Hud nodded. "Works for me."

Chapter Seven

Hud snapped one last picture of the window into Gigi's laundry room before the uniformed officer beside him propped a piece of plywood over the cut screen. "I appreciate the help."

"Not a problem, sir." He radioed his partner, who'd stayed inside the house with Gigi while they'd swept the yard and surrounding area. "We'll cruise by the place again before our shift is done in the morning," he added before striding away.

"Thanks." Hud debated whether or not he should tell Gigi about the pry marks that bent the strike plate on her back door. If the perp had used something heavy enough to leave those marks, then he'd probably only been seconds away from switching tactics and breaking through the window to get inside. And if he'd been inside already when Gigi got home… Hud had seen too much to not be able to imagine how a lone woman discovering an intruder with a crowbar and a cutting blade might end up.

He rolled his neck and reached up to massage the tension gathering beneath his collar. What had stopped the perp from the easy break-in in the first place? Someone willing to commit murder wouldn't hesitate to break a window. The juxtaposition of crime elements here was just as perplexing as the clues from the scene of Lombard's murder.

How much did he share with her about his investigation? Hud wanted Gigi to be aware of the danger she was facing, but with sunrise coming in a couple of hours, he didn't want to upset her so much that she couldn't grab a little sleep before she called her staff in for an emergency meeting, and they looked through Lombard's files and computer.

The perceptive squint behind her glasses when she opened the door rendered his internal debate moot. "Tell me what you found."

Hud scraped his palm across the stubble of his jaw and offered her a wry grin. "There's no sugarcoatin' anything with you, is there."

"I need to understand everything that's happening to me. I don't function well when my mind's a jumble."

She locked the door before heading into her kitchen. The entire room smelled like potent coffee and something spicy, but it couldn't mask the scent of warm vanilla that emanated from her damp hair and skin after her shower. She'd coiled that brick-colored hair on top of her head and wore flannel pajama pants, bright green socks and a gray hoodie over a T-shirt. She should have looked frumpy, or like a teenage girl in that shapeless getup. Instead, all he saw was *sexy librarian* with those loose tendrils falling from her upswept hair clinging to her long neck, and that sweet, heart-shaped butt framed in faded plaid flannel.

Although he'd told her she should go to bed while he checked her security, she'd insisted that she wanted to stay up long enough to wash her sweater and wrap it in a towel to let it dry. Although he got the feeling that she was normally fine on her own, and would appreciate a quiet house, he couldn't blame her for not wanting to be alone until her boss's killer was caught. Or, judging by the legal pad loaded with equations and scribbles she'd left sitting on the countertop by her mug of tea, she didn't intend to rest until she completed Lombard's formula.

"Hud?"

The moment his gaze focused on hers, she adjusted her glasses in that habitual gesture, waiting for his answer. He hung his jacket on the back of a chair and adjusted his gun on his belt. "You did have a visitor. Somebody was looking for a way into your house. Either the locks were solid enough to thwart him or he got interrupted before he could get in. Officer Cho and I patched it up."

"When we first moved here, I was a child. It wasn't the best neighborhood, but it was close to my advanced prep school. Dad installed steel-framed windows and steel doors with dead bolts. We never had a break-in growing up." She filled a plate with crudités and cookies. "Plus, Miss Allan next door has insomnia and likes to keep an eye on the neighborhood. She was up when I got home. Maybe he saw her at her window. Or turning on her lights was enough to chase him off."

"Possibly." He was glad to see an empty plate on the countertop peninsula, indicating that she'd eaten a snack to sustain her. He pulled out a stool there and sat down. "I don't subscribe to coincidence enough to believe it was a random break-in attempt. Whoever was here will be back with better tools. Or he'll find another way to get to you."

"Because he thinks I have the rest of Ian's formula?"

He nodded to the yellow legal pad. "Or he thinks he can convince you to complete the work for him."

She set the plate in front of him, giving him the choice of a healthy or sugary snack. "How would they convince me? Bribery? I don't need the money. They won't kill me because what they need is inside my brain."

"You saw what they did to Lombard. There are ways to bend you to someone's will. Torture? Blackmail? Threatening your sister?" She was right. There was no point in sugarcoating the truth. He needed Gigi to remain vigilant about her safety. "And I'd hate to think what might happen once he gets what he wants from you. This isn't the kind of guy who'd leave a witness behind."

Her skin blanched. "I'll call Tammy and see if she can stay in Vegas for a couple more days."

"If she needs to come back for work, tell her to stay with a friend. She should be made aware of the situation. But it's easier to keep an eye on one of you than it is two."

Her fingers danced across the countertop to rest on the legal pad. "What do I do in the meantime? Besides solve the most important equation of my life."

He reached across the countertop to cover her hand with his, stopping the subtle drumming. He shouldn't make too much of this Gigi-whisperer superpower he'd discovered, but she seemed to center herself at his touch. When she turned her fingers into his palm, he had no problem holding on. "You pour me a cup of that coffee. You stay aware of your surroundings and know that I'll be close by."

Her lips softened with the hint of a smile before she pulled away to retrieve a mug from the cabinet. "I made myself a cup of tea. But I brewed coffee for Officer Cutler while she was here. I didn't know what you like to drink. Besides beer. I don't have any of that. Sorry."

He plucked a baby carrot from the plate she'd put in front of him and popped it into his mouth. "Technically, I'm on the clock, so I couldn't have a brewski, anyway."

"Do you want me to make you a sandwich?"

"Black coffee will do me just fine."

After setting a mug of the steaming brew in front of him, she set her tea in the microwave to warm it up before coming over to stand on the opposite side of the peninsula. "Sorry you got stuck with me. Again. You're a good sport to put up with my eccentricities."

He took a bite of one of the cookies, then paused a moment to savor the molasses, sugar and cinnamon before he polished it off and reached for another. "Good sport, nothin'. These are damn good." Her eyes widened at his, er, enthusiasm. "Sorry. I should have put that a better way. My mama, rest her soul, wasn't around long enough to teach me not to be a potty mouth. You made these?"

She hid a blush that warmed her creamy skin behind her mug and a long drink. "Mom was the knitter. I like to bake when I get stressed."

This woman could bake on top of being Einstein-level smart and all sorts of distracting? He'd never expected that heaven would wear horn-rimmed glasses, make him apologize for cursing and bake like his grandmother. Keir was right. He'd already lost a piece of his heart. "I've never regretted spending time with you, G."

The blush intensified before she turned away to clean the kitchen. Mixing bowls in the dishwasher. Wiping down countertops. Moving the plastic container stacked with cookies over to the peninsula where he sat. "Does that mean you're staying?"

"At least 'til I finish my coffee." Since reaching for Gigi to find out if her lips were as kissable as he remembered would be a monumental mistake in terms of professional ethics, he reached for the cookie container instead. "And a couple more of these. Or until you're ready to go to bed."

The beaters she was rinsing clattered into the sink. "Bed?"

"To sleep, G." That breathless gasp of anticipation stirred a response behind the zipper of his jeans. She'd made that same husky sound when he'd said something about heating up the bench on campus earlier that night. If he had a better read on women, he might think she was interested in him for more than protection or friendship. But he was probably just shocking her with the double entendre she read into his words. "You'll sleep inside," he reminded her, "and I'll be out in my truck."

"Of course. We could both use some rest before going into the lab." Her movements seemed jerky now, more hurried as she finished putting the kitchen to rights. "I'll be done in a few minutes. Then you can leave."

"I didn't mean…" Great. Now he'd hurt her feelings. "I'll stay as long as you want me to."

"No." She waved aside his apology without looking at him. "You have a job to do. You don't need to babysit me. The house is secure now, so I'll be fine. Brains and brawn, remember? You have bad guys to catch. I have numbers to decode—"

"G." He stood and circled around the peninsula. "Maybe we should talk about what's happening here."

"What's happening?" She stuffed the beaters into the dishwasher and closed the door. "Nothing's happening."

"How much experience do you have with men?" She groaned and walked away before he could reach her. "I think you might have a little crush on me, and it's making you nervous."

"I haven't had a crush on anyone since I was fourteen and graduating high school. I'm a grown woman now."

"I know it." He caught her hand and pulled her around to face him, hoping he could break this panicked embarrassment that made her flee from him. "Believe me, Ms. Legs, I know." At least she was listening to him now. Her gaze darted across his face, trying to read his expression. He rubbed the pad of his thumb across the back of her knuckles, telling her in every way he could that she could relax around him. Her sensitivity or self-consciousness or whatever that outburst had been seemed to calm with every stroke. "Maybe I've got a little crush on you, too. I think we've got sort of a sexy professor/naughty student thing goin' on between us."

Her eyes narrowed with a quizzical frown. "That's a thing?"

"Yeah." He moved half a step closer. "I'd say it's definitely a thing."

Her fingers trembled beneath his. "Like Ian and his students?"

"No." Nothing like a reminder of the sexual-harassment accusations against her late boss to throw cold water on whatever was happening here. Hud stiffened and pulled away.

But her fingers turned to clench tightly around his. "Because you're a grown-up, too? And I don't have any power over you?"

Oh, she had some kind of power over him, all right. Maybe it was a fascination with someone who was so different from him. Or her social innocence—that seemed to trigger all kinds of alpha-male response in him with the urge to shield and support her. Or maybe it was the fact that she was just as isolated and too long without a meaningful relationship as he was that made him sense the kindred longing simmering between them. It made no sense how much he liked this woman, how much he wanted to protect her, how much he wanted to kiss her right now to see if that spark of attraction they'd felt two years ago had been a fluke—or if they hadn't given themselves enough of a chance to see what could happen between them.

Hud was reaching for the tendril of hair that had gotten caught behind the earpiece of her glasses when his phone dinged in his pocket. He muttered a curse when he heard another ding, indicating a long text. He let Gigi go to pull out his cell. *Next to no luck with the ladies.* He should get a T-shirt to commemorate his lousy timing.

"I'd better take this." She wasted no time in hugging her arms around her waist and retreating a step while Hud read the text messages from Keir. "We got one test result back from the lab. On your friend the security guard. Keir says there was enough Phenergan in his system to knock out a man twice his size."

"Poor Jerome."

Hud read aloud as he typed his response to Keir. "And Phenergan would be? How easy—"

"It's a superdose antihistamine," Gigi answered before he could finish the text. "It's also used as a sleep aid or treatment for nausea—especially travelers who are prone to motion sickness." Hud looked up at her, dumbfounded by the factoids cataloged inside that brain of hers. She shrugged. "Physics and engineering aren't the only sciences I've studied."

"Okay, Professor Smarty-Pants, do you know if that's an over-the-counter drug?"

"I'm pretty sure it's prescription only, Detective Lame-Nickname." He gave her credit for handing the teasing right back at him. "Is that important?"

Resilient wasn't a tough enough word to describe this woman's strength. "We can track any suspects who have access to that prescription." He typed the information to Keir and sent it.

"Will Jerome be okay?"

"The report from the hospital said he's resting comfortably. His wife is with him." He waited for Keir's thumbs-up emoji and then pocketed his phone. "Somebody definitely wanted him out of the way."

"Ian's killer?"

"Most likely." He shrugged on his jacket. Keir's text had been the reminder he needed to focus on the case, and not the redhead stuck in the middle of it. He wasn't the guy to teach Gigi about man-woman relationships, anyway. "I think we've done enough investigating for now. If we don't get a little shut-eye, neither one of us will be worth anything later today."

"Okay."

"Walk me out?" He took her hand, not wanting her to feel like he was leaving because of her. "I want to hear the dead bolt locking into place behind me." Some of the tension in him eased when she fell into step beside him. "Remember, you've got my number in your phone now. Call or text if you see or hear anything suspicious. Or if you remember anything you think might help the investigation." He didn't let go until they reached the front door. She unlocked it and pulled it open. The light from the porch lamp washed over them with an eerie yellow glow. He stepped outside but turned to reassure her. "Everything has been checked and rechecked. You're secure in your own home. I'll be out front, making sure everything's settled in the neighborhood. I'll drive you to the lab later this morning. You don't leave this house unless I'm with you. You don't let anybody in but me."

"Got it. Prisoner in my own home. Wait for you. Try not to be scared."

She rattled off the list by rote and Hud laughed. "I don't know when you're trying to be funny, or when you're dead serious. But you sure make me pay attention when you have something to say."

"Do you remember kissing me two years ago?" she asked out of the blue, surprising him as if she'd read the inappropriate thoughts on his mind earlier tonight.

No sense denying it. He trailed his gaze around the

rectangle that framed her. "Right here in this doorway. Under this porch light. For a first kiss, I'm afraid I wasn't much of a gentleman."

"I've never forgotten it. Or you."

He swallowed hard at the earnest confession. Didn't that beat all? Had a woman ever said anything so good for his ego? But he'd paid the price far too many times for being the right man at the right time, and not the right man for the long term, to let the thrill of having made an impression on the brainy professor go to his head. He chuckled instead. "In a good way, I hope?"

Gigi looked stricken at the idea she might have insulted him. "Of course. You generated an exponential amount of body heat. You made me feel delicate and feminine. For a few seconds, I wasn't that weird, gangly kid surrounded by a bunch of grown-ups who knew more about life than I ever would. You kissed me like I was a woman. It was exciting and seductive and when I leaned into you, you didn't budge. That kind of strength is—" she lowered her chin and peeked over her glasses "—sexy." She whispered the last word as if they were sharing a secret—or that she'd never said the word to a man before. Hell's bells. Every muscle in his body tightened with that one husky word.

So much for not letting this woman go to his head. She played havoc with his good intentions. He wanted to take her in his arms and get this itch for her out of his system. "You thought all that while I was kissing you?"

"I'm always thinking. Except when I'm sleeping, of course. And even then, sometimes…" She adjusted her glasses on the bridge of her nose. No wonder she needed those little circuit-breaker touches to give her brain a rest. She was a whole new level of complicated he'd never dealt with in a woman. "I only wish I'd done a better job on my end. I wasn't very experienced. I'm still not—"

Hud pressed two fingers over her lips to silence her. "Easy, G. I'll have you know that I stewed over that kiss for a long time afterward, too."

Her eyes widened before she pulled back from his touch. "Because you felt guilty about giving in to social convention when you weren't really feeling it?"

Um, no. He didn't think he'd ever used the phrase *social convention*, much less worried about what anyone else might say when a woman was willing, and he wanted to kiss her. Gigi's emotional honesty required no less from him. "Because I wanted more. You were eager and hot, and it caught me off guard how much I wanted you. So, I backed off."

She dipped her hands into the pockets of her hoodie, looking all starchy and scientific as she considered his response.

"You thought I was hot?" Funny, what details registered with her.

Hud grinned. "You're not fishing for compliments, are you?"

She shook her head as though she had to move that notion aside to evaluate later. "Then why did you stop? I was into it. I was into you."

"I could tell. And believe me, that is all kinds of temptation to a man." He braced his forearm on the door frame beside her and leaned in, wanting to keep this conversation private from any curious neighbors. "I'm one of the good guys, though, remember? You said so yourself. I didn't want to take advantage of your situation that night. We'd just met, and it wasn't even a real date. And I could tell you're not a casual-fling kind of gal."

"I'm not. At least, I don't think I am. Although I've never had a fling. Or even really dated anyone seriously..."

Her cheeks warmed with an adorable shade of pink. "I'm totally not cool admitting that, am I?"

"I hear enough lies in my line of work that your honesty is refreshing." He touched her hair, finally allowing himself the opportunity to relearn its smooth texture as he pulled that wayward strand away from her glasses. He studied its burgundy fire between his fingers before tucking it behind her ear and letting go. He stepped back, needing the late-night air to move between them to cool his skin and the impulses firing inside him. "They say that opposites attract, and yeah, I'm attracted to you. Something might have happened that night if you'd invited me in. But I didn't want you or me to have any regrets. Ultimately, you got to have something in common to make a relationship work." He pointed to her, then tapped his thumb against his chest. "High society—working class. Brains—brawn. Lady—potty mouth."

She mimicked his pointing, understanding his reasoning even if she struggled to make sense of the desire she felt. "Outgoing—introvert. Experienced—not." She retreated a step and hugged the edge of the door. "So, we have no common ground on which to base a relationship. And you didn't think I would go for a one-night stand. That's why you ended the kiss. That's why you didn't call."

"My gut said it was the right thing to do." Had she missed the whole point of his not-having-anything-in-common speech? "I'm the guy from the pool hall, G. I don't get invited to fancy receptions at the Muehlebach like you do. The only letters after my name are KCPD. I didn't think you'd say yes if I asked you out."

"For the record, I would have. I suppose if I'd been more assertive, *I* could have called *you*. Tammy's always telling me to take charge and go after what I want. I've just never applied that philosophy outside the classroom or the lab."

She offered him a rueful smile. "And now we have Ian's murder to focus on. What might have been, huh?"

"Yep. The opportunity was there, and we missed it. Just my kind of luck." In two years, nothing had changed. If he didn't walk away now, he never would. "I promise, this missed chance between us won't affect my commitment to this investigation or to keeping you safe."

"I believe you."

Maybe there was hope of salvaging a friendship yet. "Good night, G."

He reached the edge of the porch before he felt a tug on the sleeve on his jacket. When he turned, Gigi's fingers slid along his jaw to pull his mouth to hers. Her soft lips molded to his, branding him with her surprising heat. Her kiss was sweet and chaste and brave for this woman, and Hud couldn't help but respond to her touch, to the fingers fisting in his jacket and scudding across the stubble of his beard to sink into his hair.

He settled his hands at her hips, sliding beneath her hoodie to find the slim nip of her waist. The tips of his fingers brushed against a strip of soft, warm skin between her top and pants, and the discovery triggered a satisfied growl in his throat. He held himself in check for as long as he could, savoring the tender, closemouthed kisses. Her arms drifted around his neck, her fingers clutching his scalp, tickling the nape of his neck, pulling herself closer until her long thighs butted against his. His arms moved with the same leisurely exploration around her waist until he palmed the smooth skin of her back with one hand and squeezed a handful of that decadent bottom with the other.

Gigi's sexy purr of frustration called to Hud like a siren. She wanted more and so did he. He lapped up her surrendering sigh and took over the kiss. He teased the seam of her mouth with his tongue, and when her lips parted, he drew her full bottom lip between his. He breathed in her warm vanilla scent and tasted the spice that lingered on her tongue when he thrust inside to claim her mouth.

He was good at noticing the details, too. Details were hot. Soft skin and silky hair beneath his fingers. The sweet taste of molasses cookies and eager woman against his mouth. The firm poke of a responsive breast beading against his chest as she pushed aside his jacket to get closer. Despite his best intentions, if Gigi wanted to make out on her front porch, then by damn, he was going to give the woman what she wanted.

They kissed and kissed, little pecks and longer drags, and Hud learned that slow and sweet was as heady as any fast-and-furious romp. The thickness pulsing behind his zipper wanted to take this lip-lock to a more private place where he could strip off these shapeless clothes and see just how far she wanted to take this kissing experiment. Her living room couch. Her bed. Hell, he could make do with the rug in the foyer so long as she wrapped those gorgeous legs around him and let him show her just how seriously mind-blowing this kind of chemistry lesson could be.

But, before his common sense could kick in and overrule his throbbing staff, Gigi pulled away. He hated to think that unsatisfied groan had come from his own throat. But since he doubted she'd ever initiated a kiss, he wasn't going to scare her away by demanding anything more.

Easing the tightness of his hold on her, he straightened her pajamas to cover her skin and rested his forehead against hers. Her glasses had fogged up to the point he couldn't see her eyes, so he studied her pink, swollen lips and the slightly abraded skin around her beautiful mouth. "Damn, woman. I'm not complaining, but what was that about?"

"Me going after what I want. In case I have to wait

another two years for my next kiss." Her breath gusted through her nose. He was secretly pleased to discover she was struggling just as hard to get her breathing back to a normal rhythm as he was. He hadn't disappointed her. She sure as hell hadn't disappointed him. She studied her fingers as they smoothed the front of his shirts and straightened the collar of his jacket. Their busyness stopped and she tilted her gaze above her glasses to him. "You don't always have to be a good guy with me. Not if you don't want to be. I feel a connection, Hud. I wish you… I want you to…"

"To what?"

She curled her fingers into her palms and pulled away entirely. "I'll stop talking now. I've said more words to you tonight than I did to anyone else the entire week." She tugged off her glasses and pulled the hem of her T-shirt from under her hoodie to wipe them clean. "It's weird how I can talk to you. That doesn't usually happen outside work. I feel safe with you. I'm sure this is annoying. I have so many thoughts in my head, my words can't seem to keep up. Sometimes, it's easier just to shut up until I think of the right thing to say."

Uh-uh. She wasn't apologizing for wanting him. Or kissing him. Or admitting she was as much out of her depth with this attraction as he was. Hud tunneled his fingers into her hair, framing her face, moving in close enough for her to see him. "Don't you ever be afraid to say anything to me."

She evaluated him intently before smiling. "Thank you for not rolling your eyes when I explain things."

"Huh?"

"Trust me, it's a thing. Good night, Hud." She put her glasses back on and retreated into the house. "I'll see you in a few hours."

He inhaled a deep breath of autumn air. "Works for me."

He waited for her to lock the door before jabbing his fingers into his hair and facing the street. There wasn't a stitch of movement on the block. Parked cars. Dark houses. Was it paranoid to think this stretch of urban reclamation was too quiet? He climbed inside his truck and pulled out his cell to text his photos and observations to Keir at precinct headquarters.

Then he set his phone on the dash and leaned back against the headrest. Protection duty he could handle. But, hell. What was he supposed to do with that dump of information Gigi had just laid on him? She felt a connection. She wanted him to be a bad boy with her. She'd been thinking about kissing him for two years and couldn't wait a moment longer to kiss him again. She appreciated his strength and thought he was sexy.

There was nothing wrong with any of that. Especially when he felt a connection, too. His blood still simmered with the sweet fire of that kiss and the need in those curious, grabby hands. She was innocent and hot and his for the taking.

So why was he hesitating to embrace these feelings he had for her?

By the time he'd completed his next security sweep, he knew the answer.

He didn't want to get his heart broken again.

He didn't want to help Gigi discover the woman she could be—the sexy, funny, smart, caring woman he already knew she was—and then lose her to another man. He didn't want to be the supportive friend, the safety net, and then be set aside when she no longer needed him.

He'd been lucky enough to awaken something in her, something stunted by the awkwardness of being a mental prodigy and her natural shyness. Like him, she'd become the parent to her younger sibling, putting Tammy's needs before her own while relationship opportunities passed her by. Now, Professor Virginia Brennan, Ph.D., was a free woman, established in her career. She was grown-up and aware of her desires. He was the nice guy she'd targeted for her attention.

But Hud didn't want to be the next scientific experiment in Gigi's life. The way she threw herself into a kiss, he had no doubt she'd be all kinds of amazing in the bedroom. And as complicated as her thought processes might be, he liked having a conversation with her. She didn't lie or put on airs. She made him laugh and baked like his Ozark grandma. But once she gained the confidence she needed to pursue a relationship, then what?

She'd leave *nice* and *safe* in the dust and find herself a man like Gary Haack or Ian Lombard, someone well educated and well-off, a man who she'd have a lot more in common with than a couple of passionate kisses.

Chapter Eight

A loud bang from the neighbor's backyard jolted Hud's attention away from the update he'd been texting Keir. He saved the message to Draft and quietly slipped out of his truck. Gigi's front door was still locked, her windows closed, curtains drawn. Except for a dim glow seeping through the blinds of her bedroom window, she'd turned everything else off in the house and gone to bed. Some fine protector he was. What had he missed?

He tuned his ear to the creak of wood and panting breaths. Someone was running through the neighbor's backyard.

Wrapping his hand around the butt of his sidearm, Hud crossed the side yard to flatten himself against the gray siding. "KCPD!" he warned, hearing the crunch of footsteps in the leaves. "Step out and identify yourself."

"Izzy! Come back here." A quavering woman's voice shouted before a small dog popped around the corner of the house, dragging a leash behind it. The woman, wearing a gray tracksuit that matched the color of her hair, limped around the corner a moment after. Although Hud hadn't pulled his weapon, the older woman put her hands up. "Don't shoot. Stop her! Please!"

Hud stomped on the leash as the dog darted past him. After the sudden tug that flipped her over, the Pomeranian pounced to her feet with a high-pitched bark. But the moment Hud knelt and held out his fist for the dog to sniff, the puffball nuzzled his fingers. "Easy there, Tiger." After receiving a friendly lick, he scooped the dog up in one hand and handed her over to the woman. "Are you all right, ma'am? Are you hurt?"

"I bumped my hip on the deck railing when I tried to catch her. I'm too ornery to actually be hurt."

Relieved by the false alarm, Hud covered his gun and grinned at the reunion. "Is she an escape artist?"

"I'll say." The reprimand carried little weight as the woman hugged the dog to her chest. Then she extended an arthritic hand. "Kelly Allan. I'm Gigi's neighbor. This is Izzy."

Hud gently took her hand. "Detective Hudson Kramer."

"Usually, we don't go out for another hour, but something had her attention. She was scratching at the back door and shot out before I had a good hold on her leash."

"You heard something? Wait here." Instantly on guard, Hud pulled out his flashlight and moved around the woman to look through her backyard. A possum waddled along the back fence before disappearing beneath her utility shed. Birds chirped while nocturnal critters scuttled away before daybreak. Maybe he had nothing to worry about. The prowler who'd tried to break into Gigi's house hadn't returned.

Or maybe he had.

Hud hoisted himself up over the back fence to check the easement that ran behind the row of houses. Tire tracks. No leaves had gathered in them, so they had to be fairly fresh. He found them again in the mud behind Gigi's house. Still, there was no way to tell if the mud had been disturbed just a few minutes ago or late last night. He turned the flashlight and looked all the way up and down the empty gravel alley. Why did it feel like something sinister was surrounding Gigi Brennan? He was missing something important here but couldn't see it. Just in case, he snapped a picture of the tread marks with his phone. If he could match them up with a particular model of SUV tires, he'd update the BOLO on the car that had sideswiped Gigi's.

By the time he got back to the neighbor lady, neither she nor Izzy seemed alarmed by any sign of an intruder. He'd trust the dog on that one. "I don't see anything right now, ma'am. Looks like you've got a possum under your shed, though."

"That's Old Sam. As long as he eats the ticks and bugs in my yard, he can live there. Besides, he gives Izzy something to sniff around for." She squeezed her thin lips into a frown. "This was something else. Izzy doesn't pick up Old Sam's scent until she's out in the yard."

"Maybe your dog heard me," Hud suggested. "I was doing a security sweep around Gigi's place a few minutes ago. Someone tried to break into the professor's house last night."

"I know."

Of course, she did. His gun and badge, and the squad car from earlier, would be hard to miss. He rested his fingers against the older woman's fragile elbow and escorted her to her back deck. "Then you know it might be safer if you wait until daylight to take Izzy for that walk."

Miss Allan's blue eyes sparkled with something other than moonlight as she smiled up at Hud. "Are you Gigi's new beau? Well, not that she had an old one, but are you?"

Had she seen that kiss on Gigi's front porch? When she winked at him, Hud knew that she had. While he appreciated that Gigi had a friend looking out for her, he also hated that his lack of willpower might stir what he suspected was a pretty healthy rumor mill at Gigi's expense.

"I'm actually here to protect Professor Brennan. She's a witness to a crime I'm investigating."

The older woman stroked the dog's ears and winked. "I've never seen a police officer conduct an investigation like that."

Well, hell. Was he blushing? He doubted a sudden heatwave had blown through before dawn. "You don't miss a trick, do you."

"Not often. I know something's going on at the Brennan house. It's always quiet when Tammy's away. It hasn't been quiet tonight."

If Miss Allan had eyes on the neighbors, then she might be able to answer some questions. "Did you see anyone around Gigi's house earlier? Besides me and the uniformed officers, of course."

"I saw that man getting into his car. He nearly ran Gigi down."

Hud pulled out his notebook. "He was driving pretty fast, huh?"

"He wasn't driving. He got into the passenger side."

That could explain some of the discrepancies of the crimes surrounding Gigi. Having two perps, one impulsive, the other calculating; one unafraid of violence and the other with an aversion to it, explained a lot. "Could you describe the car that ran into Gigi's?"

"Black SUV, tinted windows. The man who got in was bigger than the driver, although I didn't see anyone's face. They wore stocking masks."

He jotted that down. "Are you sure?"

She tapped her cheek. "Cataract surgery. I've got good eyesight again."

No wonder she liked to spy on the neighborhood.

"You're proving to be a very helpful witness, Miss Allan."

"It's nice of you to say so." At Hud's insistence, she

turned and carried Izzy up onto the deck. "I can tell by your accent and your manners that you're a Southern boy."

"As far south as Lake Taneycomo. Ozarks born and raised."

She paused when she reached the screen door. "What on earth would make you leave that beautiful part of the state and come up here?"

"My parents died. I was twenty years old and needed a job I could support my younger brother and sisters with. It was either the police or the military, and I wanted to be at home to keep my siblings together."

"Admirable. I dated a young man like you once. A Marine." Her sharp eyes dimmed, and she took on a wistful tone. "He was killed in Korea back in 1951."

"I'm sorry."

"I'm sorry, too. Ed was a good man. I would have married him if he'd come home to me." When she sniffed back her tears, Hud offered her the bandanna from his back pocket. "You're a good man, too. You take care of our Gigi, all right? I can tell she likes you."

"Yes, ma'am. I'll keep her safe."

She opened the door, but stopped, her sad expression abruptly changing. "And you should go ahead and have sex with her. I'm sure she'd like the idea if you asked— she might not think of it on her own. I swear sometimes that girl can't get out of her own head." She pushed the bandanna into his hand and squeezed his fingers. "It's those quiet ones you have to watch out for. Hidden passion. Every. Time."

Another heat wave washed over him. While he was a little embarrassed by the octogenarian's lack of a filter, he was also suddenly struck by the image of Gigi's long legs wrapped around his waist and her eyes darkening with desire while he explored every inch of that soft, creamy skin and buried himself inside her. Ah, hell. He seriously needed some sleep to dispel that fantasy. Or maybe he'd better just get back to work.

Miss Allan was safely on her side of the screen door now. Hud backed away. "I will, um, take that advice under consideration."

He had a feeling Kelly Allan had been a handful long before she'd lost her Marine in the Korean Conflict. And she knew it, judging by the smile she gave him. "Aren't you going to ask me how I know she likes you?"

All right. He'd bite. "How? Because you saw her kiss me?"

"Because she invited you inside." She set the dog down and shooed it into the kitchen. "Other than workmen and Tammy's beaux, there hasn't been a man in that house since their father died." She latched the screen door. "Good night, Detective."

"Good night, ma'am."

The light came on in the front room of Kelly Allan's house, and Hud supposed she was watching to see if he was going to take her up on that sex-with-his-witness advice. He grinned and offered her a salute. He'd be out of a job if every citizen was as vigilantly aware of the world around them as Miss Allan was.

He turned his attention back to the soft glow of light through Gigi's window. He knew it was her bedroom from the security sweep he'd done inside the house earlier. He imagined her in bed with that legal pad, puzzling over the numbers in Ian Lombard's formula. He hoped exhaustion had claimed her, and she was finally getting the rest she needed.

Although he hated the circumstances, Hud liked watching over her. He knew it went back to his penchant for rescuing damsels in distress, for wanting someone to need him now that his younger brother and sisters no longer did. He liked knowing he could help, that she trusted him enough to ask for his help. He liked being close to Gigi, period. Nothing long-term was going to come of this bond forming between them. If he remembered that, maybe he could come out of this second-chance encounter with Gigi Brennan unscathed.

Settling in behind the wheel of his truck, he finished his report to Keir, adding Miss Allan's observations about the car and two intruders. As soon as he hit Send, his phone dinged with an incoming text alert.

He sat up straight when he saw Gigi's name. Had he missed something suspicious while he'd been chasing a possum and getting schooled on how to manage his love life?

His alarm eased into amusement. Kelly Allan wasn't the only woman who liked to spy out her window.

What did Miss Allan say to you?

Hud typed his response.

She could tell I was from the Ozarks. Said I remind her of an old boyfriend.

He hit Send and waited.

She didn't embarrass you, did she? She gives advice freely.

He absolutely would not mention the sex comment. Gigi had reached out to him again—invited him into her world, as the nosy neighbor had claimed. He hadn't been a part of anything but work for a long time. Even a text conversation with the auburn-haired professor made him feel the connection building between them.

She said there were two people in the car that hit you. I've got Keir tracking it.

Two people tried to break in?

Gigi appreciated knowing the facts, but he didn't want to scare her.

I'm not going anywhere.

Her reply was quick.

You don't have to sit in your truck all night.

Yeah, I do.

Why?

Was she worried about the intruders returning? Or asking why he cared enough to be here?

She likes you, Miss Allan had said.

Differences aside, impossible future notwithstanding, the feeling was mutual.

Because nobody gets to scare you, hurt you or make you feel unsafe in your own home. And I want to be first in line to ask you out for coffee when you wake up in the morning.

BREAKFAST QUALIFIED AS a date, right? Even drive-through coffee on the way to Williams University?

Gigi rolled onto her side and punched her pillow up to support her neck. She was going on twenty-four hours without sleep. She should be dead to the world right now. But between nightmares of Ian's pale lips gurgling up blood, and random numbers floating through her brain, trying to gel into equations, falling into a restful slumber had proved elusive.

Hudson was close by, keeping an eye on her home. While part of her relaxed in the security of his strong presence, another part of her hummed with anticipation. Hud wanted to take her out. She hadn't scared him off with that impulsive kiss or any one of her erudite ramblings and incidents of social klutziness.

Was this how Tammy felt when a man asked her out? Smiling so much her face hurt? Worried about what to wear, what to say? Anxious like a child about to embark on an amusement park ride, yet eager for the roller coaster to start?

She had no illusions about being easy for a man to want to spend time with. But she had hopes.

Hudson Kramer made her feel hopeful.

It might only be coffee. But to Gigi, it was everything.

She burrowed her cheek against the cool percale and closed her eyes, savoring the unfamiliar anticipation, waiting for her alarm to go off at eight.

Next thing she knew, the alarm startled her from a deep, blank sleep.

She rolled onto her back, refusing to open her eyes against the morning sun that would be peeking in around the edges of her bedroom window. A moment later, she slit open one eye and frowned. Where was the sunlight? She glanced at the clock. Huh? She'd only been asleep for twenty minutes. That music wasn't from her alarm clock. It was her phone.

With a bam, bam, bam of surprise, awareness and worry, she pushed aside the covers and reached for her phone on the bedside table. She squinted a number she didn't recognize into focus and swiped the green arrow to answer the call.

"Hello?"

There were a dozen plausible explanations for a call before 7:00 a.m. on a Saturday morning. A wrong number. A concerned colleague who'd just heard about Ian's murder. Tammy finally getting her messages and calling from her Vegas hotel room to see if she was all right.

But Gigi listened to the measured, even breathing on the other end of the line and knew this call was none of those things. The anticipation that she'd fallen asleep to darkened with foreboding.

"Professor Brennan?" The breathing gave way to a hollow, mechanically distorted voice. Easy enough to achieve with a telephone app. There was no way to tell who was calling. "I want what Lombard gave you."

The note. An invisible fist tightened around her heart and lungs. Gigi swung her legs off the side of the bed and turned on the lamp, scrambling to find her glasses. *Don't focus on the fear. Think, G. The police need you to find answers. You need to listen to this call.* "You already have it. You stole it out of my pocket."

"You know it's not the entire formula," the hollow voice continued. "I need the rest. I want you to get it for me."

This was Ian's killer. The man who'd attacked her. The man who'd stolen the information Ian had entrusted to her and who had tried to break into her home to steal the rest.

She needed Hud. KCPD could trace this number. He could touch her hand and dispel the fear that overwhelmed her. But she couldn't call for help or text him an SOS without ending this call. Searching for another idea, she pushed to her bare feet and hurried around the bed to the front window. She pulled open the curtains and snapped the window blind, sending it spinning around the top. Hud's truck was just parked in her driveway, just as he'd promised. But his chin was down to his chest, his face impossible to read in the predawn shadows. Was he hurt? Asleep? Looking down at his phone? Gigi knocked on her window, pressed her phone against the glass and pointed to it, willing him to look up and see her.

But he was too far away to hear, too engrossed in something else to see.

If he wouldn't come to her, then she needed to get to him.

"What if I say no?" she challenged, turning toward the hallway. "You killed a man. I'm not going to reward you for that."

The hushed breathing was almost more unsettling than the cartoonish voice.

"Your choice." The hallway floor was cold beneath her feet as she ran to the front door. "I can make life very painful for you. I can end it entirely."

"End…?" She skidded to a stop. Her pulse thundered in her ears. Her breath came in quick, deep gasps. "Who is this? What do you want from me?"

"Don't play dumb, Virginia. It doesn't become you. I already killed Lombard for cheating me out of our bargain. I assume you'll be more cooperative."

His logic was flawed. "You won't kill me. You could have killed me at the lab, but you didn't. You need me alive."

"There are other ways I can hurt you. Ian's obsession with you was…misguided. I want to knock you down from your golden perch. Pluck every feather off you. Carve you into tender little fillets until you are screaming the information I need." The caller paused to let that image sink in, to let her understand that needing her and not harming her weren't mutually exclusive. "The same could happen to your sister, your boyfriend."

"My boyfriend?" Hud. He thought…? He'd been watching her closely enough that he'd seen the two of them together. Everyone who was important to her was in danger.

"Fail to cooperate and I'll kill them both and make you watch. You're good at watching the people you care about die."

Her skin crawled with the knowledge that this man had touched her things, touched her, while she'd been unconscious. But what he promised if she didn't do what he demanded was so much worse. "That's all I had of Ian's formula, I swear. I can't give you what I don't have."

A sharp knock drummed at her front door. Her startled gasp caught in her throat. He was here. The threat was here.

The voice droned on in her ear. "You know Ian's work better than anyone. You're the only one who can get me what I want. Their lives are on you."

"G! Are you all right? Open the door!"

Hud! He'd gotten her signal. Her toes seemed to stick to the floor when she tried to go to him. She stumbled, braced her hand against the wall to steady herself.

"Deliver Lombard's formula and the prototype to this address." While he rattled off an address in the industrial area off Front Street, she forced her stiff legs to move toward the door. "Write it down." She didn't need to. She wouldn't forget. Another curse of her complex mind. "Repeat it to me." She did. "I want that formula Monday morning at six."

The knock on her door became a pounding fist. "It's Hud. What the hell is going on?"

"What if I need more time?" She reached for the door. "That's less than forty-eight hours."

"This isn't a negotiation. And don't double-cross me like Lombard did. We'll be watching."

"We?" The slip of the tongue jarred her.

"Open the damn door or I'll break it down." A heavy thump rammed the door, rattling the front of the house. Had he thrown his shoulder against it? "G!"

"I'm here." Her voice shook as badly as her fingers as she grabbed the knob on the dead bolt and turned it. The door swung open and Hud rushed inside, pushing her away from the opening and kicking it shut behind him. He held his gun down at his side. His chest expanded with a deep breath. His eyes—searching, intense—locked onto hers for a split second before he snatched the phone from her ear.

"This is KCPD. Identify…" She heard a click disconnecting the call before Hud even spoke. Hud looked at the phone, looked at her. "Talk to me right now."

Gigi hugged her arms around her middle. "He killed Ian. He said I was the only one who could… He wants me to… It took Ian years to develop those components and come up with workable designs, and I have forty-eight hours." She couldn't get warm again. She couldn't stop shaking. "He left me alive to…to finish Ian's work."

"Come here." Hud's arm snaked around her shoulders, pulling her to his chest. He holstered his weapon, stuffed her phone into his jacket and reset the dead bolt before wrapping both arms around her and sealing her against his abundant strength. "I got you."

She tucked her face against the juncture of his shoulder and neck and slid her arms beneath his jacket to anchor herself to his heat. He held her tight, his hand in her hair, his cheek rough against hers. He held her until she stopped shaking, until the rhythm of her breathing calmed and synced with his. She absorbed the scent of leather and the salt on his skin. She immersed herself in the healing power of being held, sheltered, surrounded by Hudson Kramer.

When she finally could release a breath that didn't burn through her chest, she eased her grip on him, although she was reluctant to pull away. His lips pressed against her forehead, and again at her temple. "I need to go to work, G," he whispered, before pressing a third kiss to her lips and unwinding himself from her arms. Hud shrugged off his jacket and had her slip her arms inside the sleeves before moving her away from the door. He nodded to the afghan draped over the back of the couch. "You want to sit and get warm? Or stay with me?"

She latched both her hands around his.

He nodded. With his hand firmly grasping hers, he led her through the house to check every lock on every door and window, ending up in her bedroom. He closed the blinds she'd opened to signal him and then pulled out his phone to call his partner and report on the situation. "I'm sure it's a burner phone, but track the number, just in case. And I want a record of every incoming call she gets here and at the university. I need a fresh set of eyes sittin' outside Professor Brennan's house, too," he told Keir. "We're runnin' on fumes here." Gigi pulled on a pair of socks while he talked, then straightened the quilt and sat on the edge of her bed while Hud and his partner made arrangements for tapping her phone and setting up round-the-clock coverage for her between Keir and his law-enforcement family. "Works for me." Hud glanced at Gigi and winked before answering his partner's question. "She's strong. She'll be fine." The fact that Hud believed that about her made Gigi believe it herself. She sat up a little straighter inside the leather jacket that engulfed her and nodded. "Shoot me a text. I'll be inside when you get here."

After he hung up, he pulled over a chair from her desk and set it down in front of her. He sat facing her, tugging her hands from inside the sleeves of his jacket to warm them between his in his lap. The calloused stroke of his hands around hers shot tendrils of heat through her skin and into her blood, sending his warmth throughout her body. "Good. They're not ice-cold anymore." His eyes that had glowed like a predatory wolf's when he'd first barged in to protect her had softened like a puppy dog's now that he knew she was safe and he'd taken steps to move his investigation forward. "I saw the lights going on, the blinds going up. It got my attention."

Every caress of his thumbs across the backs of her knuckles seemed to ease a little more of the tension inside her. "I couldn't think of how else I could without hanging up the phone. I tried to get to you. But then he said…"

"Tell me exactly what he said."

Gigi recounted everything from the heavy breathing to the less than forty-eight-hour deadline he'd given her to deliver Ian's work. She wasn't sure if it was intentional, but when Hud released her to write the information in his notebook, his knee shifted to touch hers, maintaining a constant contact she found both calming and intimate, like a secret shared between them. His knee remained there, warming a lucky spot of skin through denim and flannel as he copied down the address the caller had given her.

"There're nothing but warehouses and train tracks in that part of the city."

Hud tucked away his notepad. "We'll scout the location and set up a net to capture this perp when you make the drop. You won't be alone."

In the short time they'd been together, she was learning to read the nuances of Hud's expression. He didn't just mean Monday morning at the drop-off. He wouldn't be leaving her to face any of this on her own. Detective Brawn would keep her grounded, keep the fear at bay, so she could handle the brains part of this investigation. "After the staff meeting, I'll get on Ian's computer to see if I can locate the right file. I know a few places he'd hide things like a flash drive he didn't want anyone else to get their hands on."

"Maybe something there can tell us who he was meeting with last night. Or we can uncover if he's been doing nonuniversity business on the side."

Reluctantly, she pulled her knee away and leaned over to the bedside table to pick up the legal pad and study the equation. Her math was good. She'd already filled in some of the gaps and could project the outcome of the equation. But without knowing what result Ian was working toward, and how this breakthrough differed from the other research they'd been doing, she'd be making an educated guess. The application might not work with the minicapacitor's design if she didn't get it right. "What if I'm not smart enough to do this?"

Hud reached across the gap between them, gently cupping her cheek and jaw. "I don't know anybody smarter than you."

While she appreciated the bolster of support, designing and building a working prototype would be challenging to complete in forty-eight hours, even under ideal circumstances. A dead mentor and the threat to hurt her or someone she loved were hardly ideal working conditions. "What if I can't figure it out before Monday?"

Hud dragged his hand down her arm to recapture her fingers. "It doesn't matter. They're not gettin' what they want. All we need is something plausible enough for them to take the bait. I'm not letting them get away with murder, assault, attempted burglary—and whatever else I decide to charge them with."

"He said he'll be watching me. Won't he know if I make something up? Also," she confessed, "I'm not very good at making stuff up."

Although he chuckled, the laughter never reached his eyes. "Juries love a clear motive. So yeah, it would be nice to have the formula and designs so we can clearly identify why your boss was killed. Especially if we can put a dollar value on what the killer wanted from him."

"And now me."

He plucked the legal pad from her lap and studied her math and drawings. Then he shook his head and set it back on the nightstand before reclaiming both her hands. "We're going to find out who these people are long before they get their prize, whether it's the real thing or a ruse."

"He…they…threatened to kill Tammy. And you. And to…" She swallowed a hard knot of fear at the disturbing images the caller had described. "He sounded like he'd enjoy hurting me if I don't cooperate. Like he was hoping I would fight back. Just so he could—"

Hud swore before she could finish that sentence. "Get out of your head, G. Listen to me." Before she could read his intent, he'd scooped her up off the bed and pulled her onto his lap. His fingers feathered into her hair to tilt her head against his shoulder. Gigi grabbed a handful of his shirt and snuggled in as he anchored her between his arms and thighs. "I can take care of myself." His arms trembled around her, as if he was having a hard time stopping himself from squeezing her too tightly. "I'll have Keir put Tammy into protective custody when she gets into town. Nobody is going to hurt you. Not while I'm around."

"You're staying?"

"This bed looks like it sleeps two."

Gigi pushed away to look him in the eye. "You said we had nothing in common."

"You're afraid, and I don't like it. That's enough, isn't it?"

"That's not a logical syllogism."

"I don't know what that means. But I do know we both need sleep, even a couple hours of it, if we're going to solve this case and arrest these bastards." He stood with her in his arms, carrying her as if she was a dainty scrap of a woman, instead of someone who topped him by an inch or more. She felt the flex of his muscles, tightening to support her, then relaxing as he laid her gently on the bed. Perhaps she should be afraid of strength that could snap her like a dried-up twig. But there was no fear with Hud—nervous anticipation, yes, but never fear. Despite fatigue and worry, there was a thrill that quickened her pulse every time he touched her. Parts of her seemed to heat up and melt with every caress or kiss.

Hud's broad shoulders and stubbled jaw couldn't be more masculine. She wondered...she wished... Her poorly timed yawn confirmed that nothing other than sleep was going to happen here over the next hour. Just as well.

"You're good at taking care of people, Hud." She shrugged out of his jacket, instantly missing the scent and heat that had surrounded her. But when he sat on the edge of the bed beside her, she didn't miss it quite so much. "I remember when we played pool that night, you said you'd raised your brother and sisters. You gave up your home and moved to Kansas City so they wouldn't be separated into foster homes. They were lucky to have you. I'm lucky to have you, too. For as long as you're willing to stay."

"I'm not going anywhere." He unhooked his belt and set it, along with his gun and badge, on the nightstand beside her things. "Outside is too far away for me to know you're safe—hell, the next room is too far away—to know that that low-life coward isn't hurting you physically, or doing something to screw with that big, beautiful brain of yours."

Gigi looked up into his rugged face, into his kind eyes, and realized she'd never had a man carry her to bed before, not since she was a little girl and she'd fallen asleep studying or watching a movie, and her father had carried her in. The essence of security was similar, but there was little else that felt the same as Hud's promise to be here with her. These feelings of desire and trust were as overwhelming as they were unfamiliar. And yet, she couldn't imagine anything that felt more right, more inevitable than giving herself to Hudson Kramer.

But not now. Now, she needed something else from the man. She patted the quilt beside her. "Will you hold me?"

"Yeah. I'd like that." He sat in the chair to untie his boots, and then he was leaning over her. He removed her glasses and set them on the bedside table before pulling back the quilt. "Get under the covers. I'll sleep on top." Gigi scooted beneath the quilt, bracing herself as the mattress dipped with Hud's weight. He gathered her against his chest when she rolled over to face him and bring his handsome eyes and the dimple beside his mouth into focus. "This better?"

Nestling into the heat of his body, Gigi splayed her fingers over the reassuring beat of his heart. "Much. Is this okay for you?"

"Yes, Professor." He kissed her forehead, then nestled his chin at the crown of her hair. "Now go to sleep. We've got a whole hour before we have to get up."

Although desperate for a nap, her body hummed with a nervous energy. Her gaze shifted to the top button on his flannel shirt, and her fingers followed. The waffled material of his undershirt was soft, the buttons hard, the

crisp curls of chest hair peeking through the veed neck-
line somewhere in between. His skin leaped beneath the
brush of her fingertips, like an electrical pulse had zapped
from her touch.

He caught her hand against his chest, stilling her curious exploration. "Talk to me, G."

There had been an underlying train of thought she
hadn't acknowledged. But now she did. "What if he calls
again? He said he'd be watching me, so I can't cheat him
out of what he wants."

His right hand traced leisurely circles against her back.
"From here on out, you don't answer your phone without
me listening in. He's not going to terrorize you anymore.
I want him to deal with me."

"Won't that just make him angry?"

"He doesn't know angry until he sees me pissed off."
Even in that lazy drawl of his, even in that hushed tone,
she heard the vehemence of his promise. "That's what will
happen if he threatens you again."

Emotions swelled inside Gigi that logic couldn't process, and shyness and self-preservation could no longer
contain. She pushed herself up on her elbow and pulled
his mouth up to hers in an impulsive kiss.

She knew something better than satisfaction when
his hand cupped the back of her head and his lips moved
against hers. She was aware of her breasts pillowing
against his chest, his hand settling at the curve of her hip,
that husky growl rumbling in his throat, and far too many
barriers of covers and clothing between them before she
pulled away.

She rode the rise and fall of his chest before he tucked
her back against his side. "Not that I'm complaining, but
what was that for?"

"I don't always express what I'm thinking and feeling

in a way that others understand. But that way seems to work for you and me."

"I think I get the message, Professor." She felt him smile against her forehead before he kissed her there. "You're welcome."

Chapter Nine

By noon on Saturday, Hud realized he was well and truly screwed in the self-preservation department.

Now that the CSIs had cleared the scene at Williams University, Hud stood in the doorway to Ian Lombard's office, watching a team of graduate students clean up the lab and inventory what the KCPD criminologists had left behind, while Gigi sat at her late boss's desk, searching through his computer for any leads on Lombard's unfinished formula. Thanks to the glass windows in each of the offices, he could monitor all the activity in the technology lab from this vantage point.

Keir sat in Evgeni Zajac's office with Hana Nowak and an international-law attorney from the Lukinburg embassy, trying his hand at getting the visiting professor to share his insights about the victim and his alibi for the time of Lombard's murder. The old grouch had plenty of accusations about Ian Lombard—from hogging the spotlight at last night's reception to hitting on his raven-haired wife—but no real leads beyond admitting he'd argued with Lombard at the reception about whose name should be at the top of the paper they were presenting back in Lukinburg. Since they'd worked as a team to develop the capacitor design, in his home country where he was a revered scholar, his status should be reflected in the presentation. Was a coworker he believed had taken credit for what was rightfully his enough motive for murder?

As for Zajac's alibi? His wife corroborated his claim that they'd left the reception and were driving home when they'd gotten the call about Lombard's death and had headed to the university instead. Beyond that, Hana Nowak wasn't saying much. She wore dark glasses, complained of a headache and was letting the attorney do most of the translating for her husband.

Although Keir had peeked behind Hana's glasses and said he'd seen no signs of abuse or even the tears she'd been crying last night, Hud had already moved Dr. White Hair to the top of his suspect list. He'd caught Gigi wincing when she'd slung her backpack over her shoulder that morning. She'd dismissed his concern that she was feeling an aftereffect from her assault, but, with a little prodding, had reluctantly shown him the bruises Zajac had left on her arm at the reception.

Hud had wanted to arrest the man then and there, but Gigi and Keir both had reminded him of the bigger prize they were after—Lombard's killer. A man with that big of an ego, that much of a temper, was the kind of man who'd get into a fight with a rival, trash a lab and stab his opponent with the most convenient weapon available. But would Zajac have the patience and forethought to drug a security guard?

Zajac wasn't the only research team member who didn't seem to see Lombard's death as a loss. The day after his boss's murder, everything was business as usual for Gary Haack. The bearded blond man had shown up for the eleven o'clock emergency staff meeting with the dean and department chair in his neatly pressed suit and tie, and had taken charge of cleaning up the lab.

He'd tried to take charge of the meeting before that, too,

interrupting Gigi's response to a question about Lombard's current workload. Haack strode to the front of the table and draped his arm around Gigi's shoulders in a show of solidarity, giving an eloquent speech about staying the course and carrying on their research because huge discoveries were within their grasp. Gigi had visibly squirmed.

Hud had been ready to march across the room, break Haack's arm and remind the self-important stooge that Gigi was the one who'd called the dean to set up this meeting. But even as Hud acknowledged Keir's warning nudge to suppress his instinct to rescue her, Gigi touched her glasses and scooted away from the tall man's grasp. She circled around the conference table, burying her hands deep in the pockets of her white lab coat. He suspected those hidden hands were twirling a pen or shredding a tissue, but outwardly, she was calm, well-spoken, professional. Today was about supporting each other, she'd said. Making sure the entire faculty, staff and student body felt safe at Williams. She thanked the dean for making counselors from the student health department available to anyone who needed to talk. Today was about rebuilding the sanctity of the lab and remembering the good things they could about Ian Lombard. The dean and a few of the staff shared stories about Lombard's impact on their lives. Hud recognized the tactic for what it was. She didn't necessarily want to be in the spotlight, but she was still controlling the meeting.

When Gigi had looked to him, he'd winked and grinned with pride. Who understood interpersonal relationships now, Haack?

Now with his stomach rumbling for the lunch they'd missed, Hud crossed his arms over his chest and leaned against the doorjamb. Could there be anyone else with a motive to kill Lombard beyond these people here? The first forty-eight hours of an investigation were all about find-ing leads and closing in on a definitive suspect so KCPD could wrap up the case before the press tainted the facts and the perp had time to go underground and disappear. He and Keir had plenty of suspects and motives, but almost twenty-four hours in and they weren't anywhere close to making an arrest. And, with the threats to Gigi, the perp was the one calling the shots.

Could the killer really be someone this close to her?

While Zajac circled the wagons to protect himself and his wife from any sort of accusation, Haack had asserted his authority by supervising the grad students in the lab. Every now and then Haack's gaze darted over to Gigi, perhaps curious about what she was looking for in Lom-bard's office—or maybe worrying that she was stepping into Lombard's position. He somehow doubted that Haack would accept Gigi's authority over him.

Maybe he should move Haack ahead of Zajac on his suspect list.

Hud's fingers itched in a closed fist as he recalled the tall man's proprietary claim on Gigi, when clearly, what-ever he thought was happening between them wasn't mu-tual. Maybe Haack's interest in Gigi had more to do with control than attraction. If Gary couldn't get ahead of her academically and professionally, then he'd undermine her personally—keep her stuck in her shy shell, make her de-pendent on him. Hud didn't have a good read on the engi-neering professor yet, other than the smell of money and a long streak of entitlement running through his veins. Hud's instincts said Haack was a man with a hidden agenda. Now whether that agenda was to take over Lombard's research project, world domination or simply getting into Gigi's pants, Hud didn't know. But he didn't trust the guy.

Still, Lombard's unsolved murder wasn't what had him

in such a mood this afternoon. Hud could credit his rest-less impatience with this murder investigation with the nearsighted redhead in the office behind him.

He'd slept aroused for an hour while Gigi snored softly in his arms. The woman liked to touch and explore with her hands, but that was nothing compared to the way she snuggled up against him, demanding every inch of body-to-body contact he could give with layers of clothing and a fluffy quilt between them. He wondered if she'd been as painfully aware as he was of how her thigh had wedged between his legs, unconsciously cupping his groin and making him wish there weren't ten layers of cloth be-tween them, ensuring that he couldn't get to Gigi's body, no matter how badly that most male part of his anatomy wanted to. Maybe she spent so much time inside her head that her body felt neglected, or maybe she'd never had the opportunity to explore and embrace the differences be-tween her soft, lithe body and a harder son-of-a-gun like him before. Maybe she'd been so afraid, so alone, that the only way she could relax enough to sleep was to feel him pressed tightly against her, surrounding her, promising to keep the unseen enemy at bay.

His emotional survival had gone right out the window when he saw that frightened look on Gigi's face as she held the phone to her ear, a look put there by whatever vile things that pervert had said to her. Good luck. Bad luck. No luck with women. It didn't matter. Gigi had wormed her way inside his head and his heart. Walking away from her before he got burned was no longer an option. She needed him. Yeah, she needed the kind of protection a cop could provide. But he couldn't stand back and let any other man or woman with a badge take the lead on this case.

Gigi Brennan needed *him*. To touch her. To hold her. To hear the pleas for help and insightful revelations mixed up with all her big words and awkward ramblings. She needed him to help her feel safe enough to explore her desires and understand her feelings.

And he needed her to... Hell. He needed her to need him, to see him as her hero, to want him for the man he was. He'd had two whole years and half a weekend to decide that his feelings for Gigi were real.

It might not last. She might wake up one day and realize that he wasn't the only man ogling those gorgeous legs, or who appreciated that sexy intelligence and was charmed by her shy vulnerability. For now, for the duration of this investigation—until the killers were caught and the threat to her had ended—Hud was in this relationship. They'd missed their chance to connect two years ago. And most of the impediments that could keep the two of them from lasting as a couple were still there.

But for forty-eight hours, at least, this woman had his heart. She'd have his gun and his badge—and his life— if she needed it.

After Monday morning, the need would be gone. Reality would creep in and push them apart. A killer would be behind bars, he hoped, she'd feel safe and he'd be sent back into the friend zone, relegated to sidekick status again. After this case was closed, it would be up to Gigi to decide if they had any chance at a future. With his luck—

"Hud?"

Thank God he didn't have to finish that thought.

Turning from his observation position, he frowned at the shadows that looked like bruises under her eyes. She'd been working too long at this, but with the time crunch hanging over her head, he doubted he could convince her to take a break. Instead, he circled the desk to look over her shoulder at the computer screen. He saw rows and rows of numbers with dates and time stamps. A log of some kind. "What did you find?"

"Nothing about the formula. But I did find this."

"What am I looking at?"

This morning, she'd twisted her hair up into a bun at the back of her head after putting on black pants and a blouse to come to the lab. She pulled out a pen she'd tucked beneath her hair clip and used it to point out items on the screen. "These are our power-consumption records. Because of heightened security and the sensitive nature of some of the compounds and equipment we work with, the lab is on its own power grid. When we're all here working, of course, we need more power. But when we're gone for the night, the lab is on a cycle that reduces power. There's enough to maintain the security locks and protect ongoing experiments."

"You said the power was out when you found Lombard. The guard had to reboot the system."

Gigi nodded and pointed to line number twenty-seven. "Someone accessed the power grid Thursday night to alter the consumption cycle."

Hud gripped the back of her chair, not yet understanding the point she was making. "Lombard was killed Friday night."

She scrolled down the page and pointed to nine o'clock Friday night. "Somebody programmed the blackout. Right from this computer. A complete system shutdown. I got here about ten p.m. Jerome was already asleep at his desk."

Hud straightened. "The blackout would take lab security off-line?"

She nodded. "Any entries or exits from the lab couldn't be tracked. No key cards or codes would be recorded. No cameras would be working. Whoever Ian was meeting wouldn't show up in any records."

"His killer could have been lying in wait for him. With the lab dark, he'd never see the attack coming. Maybe the plan was to lure your boss into a trap and force him to give them the formula."

"I have one question."

"Only one?" He had nothing but questions. A couple of concrete answers would go a long way toward solving this murder and ending the threats against Gigi.

"Why would Ian come into the lab if the power was off?" She logged out and shut down the computer. "This place was his baby. If he thought something was wrong, he'd have called the campus police. He'd have turned the power back on himself to protect his work."

Hud had an idea about that, although he wasn't sure Gigi would like it. "You said your boss was a player. If the right temptation came along, promised something he couldn't resist, mightn't he set up a clandestine rendezvous that couldn't be traced? That wouldn't get back to his wife?"

She surveyed the room, her gaze finally landing on the whiskey bottle and glasses still sitting on their tray on the coffee table in front of the couch. "That would explain the two glasses. He was coming here to meet a woman. He left me at the reception to deal with Evgeni while he…" Her breath seeped out on a disappointed sigh. "Ian left a note for Jerome saying he had a meeting and didn't want to be disturbed. Then he powered down the lab to hide his comings and goings and enjoyed a drink and an argument that got way out of hand. But how does date night gone bad have anything to do with the formula? And who doctored Jerome's coffee?"

He moved his hand to squeeze her shoulder. "The woman set him up. Preyed on his weakness. Promised him a few favors in exchange for a look at his work. We think she had a partner, so it could have been an elaborate setup to force your boss to turn over his formula." Gigi's gaze followed his when he looked through the windows to the other people moving throughout the lab and faculty offices. "Any candidates out there for our mystery woman?"

"He liked them blonde and curvy." Her voice was barely a whisper. "One of the grad students?"

"Does it have to be a blonde?" He spotted Zajac and his wife leaving the lab while Keir finished up a conversation with their attorney. "Hana Nowak seemed genuinely upset about Ian's death."

"If they were having an affair, I didn't know about it. Of course, I don't pick up on those kinds of cues between people. But if Evgeni found out, that could explain his temper lately." Gigi shook her head. "For the brains of this operation, I'm not being very helpful, am I. I can't find any notes about the new capacitor design anywhere. Encrypted or not, if Ian was hiding the formula here, it's gone."

"The killer wouldn't still be coming after you if he had it."

"Still doesn't make me feel very useful. Can I get out of here now?" Although the crime lab had taken the rug where Ian Lombard had bled out and died, along with several other items, there were still plenty of memories in this room to haunt Gigi. "I need to take a break."

"You're doin' great, G." Hud pulled her to her feet. "Just a few more things we need to wrap up here. Then I'll treat you to an early dinner."

"Our second date." All the reasons why they couldn't have a lasting relationship faded into little blips of white noise when she smiled at him like that.

But the moment they stepped out of Lombard's office, Gary Haack was there, blocking Gigi's path. "Do you have a minute?"

Hud slipped his hand to the small of Gigi's back and pulled her to one side. "No, she doesn't."

Gary shifted to stop them from crossing the lab, holding his hands up in surrender. His apologetic smile looked friendly enough, but Hud didn't trust it. "Look, Detective, I know you and I got off on the wrong foot. I didn't realize the two of you were an item when I tried to step in and help last night. I guess it wasn't meant to be."

"Gary… We work well together. Why can't you be satisfied—"

He cut off Gigi's protest before it could gather any steam. "On paper, you and I would make an unstoppable team. Like Pierre and Marie Curie or the Mosers. But I see now you want something different. I know when to make a graceful retreat."

Like hell he did. What game was he playing now?

"Different?" Gigi echoed, turning to Hud. "I'm a normal…" She tilted her gaze up to Haack. "How is what I want different…?"

"You got a point, Stringbean?" Hud prodded. He understood the snide put-down in Haack's surrender speech was meant for him, even if Gigi didn't.

"Wow. I haven't heard that one since high school," the taller man deadpanned. "Did you come up with that all by yourself?"

"Would you two stop," Gigi chided. "I'm helping the police with their investigation. What's the issue? Can it wait?"

"Not if we want to get this inventory done before your friends leave." Gary smoothed the lapels of his spotless white lab coat as he included Hud in his answer. "It's a lab question that has nothing to do with your case, Detective. It will only take a couple of minutes."

If Hud didn't need that inventory to determine what,

if anything, had been taken from the lab, he'd have shuffled Gigi as far away from Professor Fancy Pants as he
could. But that was his personal aversion to the man talking. He and Keir *did* need the inventory for potential evidence. Plus, he wasn't about to undermine Gigi's authority
here. If she was the expert Haack needed to consult, then
she needed to do her job. Hud met Haack's arrogant gaze
straight on as he removed his hand from Gigi's back. "Go
do your thing, G. I'll wait for you in your office."

"The VPAL needs to be repaired. But we also talked
about replacing it at our last budget meeting. If you'd give
me your two cents…"

Haack cupped Gigi's elbow and the two professors
walked over to inspect a piece of machinery. Hud's fingers curled into a fist down at his side. "I'd like to give
him my two cents."

Keir ended his conversation with the Zajacs' attorney
and joined Hud, nodding down at the fist beside his thigh.
"Not getting along with the locals?"

Hud flexed his fingers, forcing them to relax. "Can I
make a guy a suspect because he's a smug bastard who's
playin' G for a reason I haven't figured out yet?"

"Well, it won't hold up in court, but I understand."

His partner's comment diverted Hud's attention. Of
course, Keir would understand this deep-seated suspicion
and worry. He'd met his wife shortly after she'd been bru-
tally assaulted. Back then, every man his wife knew had
been a suspect in Keir's book. Plain and simple, personal
feelings complicated an investigation.

Gigi rejoined them as the two men traded a fist bump,
and the three of them went into her office. "Did you two
uncover something to celebrate?"

It was impossible to explain the bond two long-time

partners like he and Keir shared. "Nah. We're just a couple of bros who are preternaturally joined at the hip."

An eyebrow arched above her glasses. "Preternaturally?"

"Despite what Haack says, I know what a few big words mean."

"I wasn't implying that you didn't," she answered, upset that she might have insulted him.

"No worries, G." He cupped the side of her jaw and made sure she saw the humor in his eyes. "I'm teasing. Your friend Haack puts me in a mood."

"He puts me in a mood, too." She reached up to rub her hand up and down his forearm before breaking contact to pull her backpack out of her desk. "That interruption was just him getting me alone for a few minutes. He wants me to support his application to head up the research team now that Ian's gone. He said he's more leadership material than I am—that I'm a good worker bee he wants to keep on the team."

"Worker bee? He said that?" Hud followed her while Keir closed the door for privacy. "I hope you told him to stuff it. You ran that meeting this morning like you owned the place."

"I was a nervous wreck."

"It didn't show. You handled it because you had to do it."

He saw the brief flash of a smile before she shrugged out of her lab coat. "Thanks. I told him I didn't want to talk to the department chair about that yet. We haven't even had Ian's funeral. And with this forty-eight-hour deadline hanging over my head…" She shook her head as she pulled out the ivory sweater she'd washed last night. She fingered one of the stains that had faded to a blush pink. That had been Lombard's blood, and whatever comfort the hand-knitted garment had given her in the past was gone now. Instead of putting it on, she stuffed it inside her backpack. "I can't even think about what happens beyond Monday morning."

Hud pulled his leather jacket off the back of her chair and draped it around her shoulders, squeezing her upper arms to remind her there were other places she could find the solace she craved. "Deep breaths, G. We'll get through this one day at a time—one minute at a time if we have to."

Keir joined them on the opposite side of the desk, keeping them on task. "Did you check your office?"

Gigi nodded, stepping away from Hud's grasp to sink into her chair and open the top drawers to reveal the mess inside. "Someone's been through it. Things are out of place. Just like my backpack and billfold were. Your lab people dusted for prints but didn't find any but mine."

"Just like everywhere else. Whoever was here wore gloves. Anything missing?" Hud asked.

She shook her head. "It's creepy to know that someone has touched all my stuff, maybe even while I was on the floor, unconscious."

Gigi's obvious discomfort doubled Hud's desire to get her out of here. But there was still work to do before they could take the break she desperately needed. He turned to his partner. "Did you complete the background check on Haack? We know he comes from old money. Please tell me he got disinherited or has a gambling or drug issue."

"Sorry. His financials look solid. If he's hurting for money, there's no record of it."

Gigi slid her arms inside the sleeves of his jacket and hugged it around herself. "Gary might kill Ian out of jealousy, but why threaten me to produce the rest of Ian's formula? We could just work on it together at the lab."

"Who'd get credit for the invention?" Hud asked. "Whose name would be on the patent?"

"Both of ours. And I'd insist on including Ian, since he developed the idea first."

Keir shared Hud's bad vibe on Gary Haack. "A man with his ego might not want to share the glory."

Hud agreed. "And if he's working with a partner, as we suspect, the partner could be the one who needs the money from the sale."

Keir had another idea. "The partner could be holding something over his head, too. Forcing him to be the accomplice."

"*If* Gary's the one behind this," Gigi clarified. "He could just be a class A jerk."

"That's a given." Hud conceded his theories were all speculation thus far. "Guess I can't arrest a man because I don't like him putting his hands all over you."

Soft gray eyes shot up to meet his gaze. "Teasing?"

"No."

A blush colored her pale cheeks as she quickly ducked her head and went back to straightening her desk. Yep. *Smooth move, Kramer.* That had just come out as possessively caveman as it sounded. He glanced over to see Keir's amused look that said he knew just how far and how fast he'd fallen for Gigi.

Determined to stave off another lecture on the ill-advised impulses of his love life, Hud turned their focus back to the investigation. "Your blackmailer has to be someone with access to you here. Besides Haack, we've got Zajac." He turned to Keir. "What did you find out from him?"

"Directly? Not much. Either he thinks we're suspicious of him, or he's truly hiding something." With a wink that told Hud he understood the diversion for what it was, Keir pulled his cell phone from his jacket and scrolled through his texts. "I reached out to Carly Petrovic." Carly was a former undercover officer Hud and Keir had provided backup for on a couple of cases. On one of her assignments, she'd helped protect a bona fide prince, and now she was married to the manager of IT security at the Lukinburg embassy. "Her husband put out some feelers for us. He says there's chatter about some Lukin dissidents—a new mob descended from the previous regime—who are trying to reassert their power. The dissidents are trying to arm themselves to carry out a terrorist attack. A couple of their suspects have applied for visas to come into the US."

Gigi stood beside Hud. "Homeland Security won't let them into the country, will they?"

Keir shrugged. "Captain Hendricks is notifying local and state authorities. If the Lukin government doesn't lose track of them, and they aren't traveling under false documents, we should be able to prevent them from coming to Kansas City."

Hud had a lot of experience reading his partner's expressions. And the one he wore now didn't inspire him with confidence. "But the Lukins have already lost track of their suspects, haven't they?"

Keir nodded and typed in a text. "They're off-the-grid. Carly and her husband are doing everything they can to track them down, whether they're still in Europe or here in the States. I can find out if one of them is a blonde."

Hud felt the brush of Gigi's fingers against the back of his hand. He would never deny her when she was brave enough to reach out to him, and quickly linked his fingers with hers. "Could Dr. Zajac and his wife have a connection with the Lukin dissidents?"

Keir eyed the clasp of their hands. "The professor adamantly denies supporting anyone from the old Lukin regime. The new government gave him freedom to pursue his own research, and he's grateful for the opportunity. That's about all his attorney would let him say."

"What about Hana? She has connections to Lukinburg, too. Could she be working with the dissidents?"

"She didn't say much. Kept complaining about her headache. Said she hasn't felt well since stepping off the elevator. Motion sickness, I guess. I imagine being married to that blowhard doesn't help." Keir swiped aside his texting and punched in a number. "I'll ask Carly's husband to dig a little deeper into Hana's background, see what he can find out."

Keir put the phone to his ear and left just as Gigi's phone chimed from the pocket of her backpack.

Her hand went cold within his grasp. "Do I have to answer it? What if it's him?"

The hollow voice that had threatened everything she cared about.

Hud pulled her phone from its pocket and set it on the desk without releasing her hand. Pulling out his own phone, he punched in a number to request a trace on the incoming call. "Put it on speakerphone. I'll be right here."

Nodding, Gigi answered the call. Her voice was quiet, cautious. "Hello?"

"Virginia?" a woman's voice answered in a clear, unaltered tone. "Is that you?"

"Yes?"

The noise in the background—indistinct conversations, a loudspeaker, traffic noises—indicated the woman was calling from a public place. "Oh, thank goodness I reached you. This is Doris Lombard."

"Doris?" Gigi's tone lost that breathy suspicion and she released Hud's hand as compassion overrode her fear. False alarm. Hud deleted the text and tucked his phone back into his pocket. "Sorry, I was expecting someone else. How are you holding up? Are you on your way back to Kansas City?"

"I'm here. At the airport." The roar of a plane taking

off in the distance confirmed her location. "Is there any way you can come pick me up? Ian dropped me off back in July, so I don't have my car. And I've been too upset by everything that I forgot to hire a car. It's rush hour and it'll take forever to catch a cab home. Would you mind? I've been surrounded by strangers for hours. I'd appreciate seeing a friendly face."

Gigi shook her head before she answered. "Oh, Doris. I'm so sorry. I can't. My car is in the shop. I had…" She glanced over at Hud, searching for the words to downplay everything that had happened for the grieving widow. "I had an accident."

"Oh, my goodness. Are you all right?"

"I'm fine. I'll be fine." She energized her tone again. "You're the one I'm worried about. I was there when Ian died. I tried to save him. I'm so sorry I couldn't."

"Don't you worry about that. I'm glad he had a friend with him at the end. That means a lot to me." They heard the warning siren of a luggage carousel about to turn on. "Is there another time when you and I can talk? I was making plans on the flight, and I was thinking—if you'd be willing… Not everyone was a fan of Ian's—would you give the eulogy at Ian's service? I know he'd love it if his prize protégé said something kind about him."

"Eulogy? In front of everyone?" Hud watched the color draining from Gigi's face and pulled out the chair for her to sit down. "Will it be a big service?"

"I imagine. Colleagues from the university. Students. Of course, family and friends." Hud sensed the numbers growing exponentially in Gigi's head and squeezed her shoulder to stop her from imagining the worst. "We'll talk about it soon. All right?"

"All right. Soon. Again, I'm so sorry about the ride. Do you want me to ask someone else to pick you up?"

"No. I'll suck it up and deal with the cab line. I just thought we could kill two birds with one stone. I'll call you later. Goodbye, Virginia."

"Bye."

Gigi stared at her phone for several seconds after ending the call. While this hadn't quite escalated into a panic attack, Hud needed her to do him and KCPD a big favor. He knelt beside her, gently brushing aside a lock of fiery hair. "My truck is parked right out front."

She knew exactly what he was asking and shook her head. "I don't want to talk about Ian's funeral. I don't know how to help her with her grief. And I really don't want to stand up in front of a huge crowd and deliver a eulogy."

"You could do it if you had to, G. From what I've seen, you can do anything you put your mind to. But right now, I need you to call her back. We *want* to drive Mrs. Lombard home."

"We do?"

"You're not finding anything here. The next logical place where Lombard might hide something is at his house." He glanced through the windows into the lab to see Gary Haack quickly adjusting his glasses and turning away from spying on them. "Besides, I wouldn't mind puttin' a little extra distance between you and these suspects."

Gigi swiveled her chair toward Hud, searching for something in his eyes. "You think Doris would let us look around?"

He rose to press a soft kiss to her lips. He'd meant to encourage her, but her fingers settled against his jaw, and her tender, eager response soothed a raw spot inside him before he pulled away. "I know it's asking you to step out of your comfort zone, but I need you to ask her."

His lips tingled as she trailed her fingertips across the line of his mouth. Then, she lifted her shoulders and turned back to the desk. "I'll call her back, tell her we're on our way."

Chapter Ten

Gigi climbed down from the back seat of Hud's truck while he retrieved Doris Lombard's rolling carry-on bag. She would have waited to climb the pillared front porch with him, but the older blonde woman linked her arm through Gigi's and pulled her into step beside her to enter the stately white home.

Although there were clearly staff or at least a regular cleaning crew taking care of the two-story Colonial, based on its home-magazine-worthy decor and dust-free surfaces, there was no one here to welcome the mistress of the house. Doris had shed tears on the drive from the airport and shared her plans for her husband's service once the medical examiner's office released Ian's body from the lab. But as soon as she pushed open the front door, Doris heaved a relaxing breath and smiled.

She led them into a study where bookshelves framed a painted brick fireplace. "You can toss your jackets here."

Doris unbuttoned the jacket of her taupe suit and laid it across the back of the first of two black leather sofas. Gigi had been to the home a couple of times before and recognized this room as Ian's home office. Anticipation buzzed thought her veins. This would be the spot to find something that could help her crack the meaning behind

Ian's cryptic notes. "Can I get you anything?" Doris asked, heading to the liquor cabinet behind the desk.

"No, thank you." Gigi shivered inside Hud's leather jacket, while he'd pulled a black KCPD windbreaker to put on from the back of his truck. But Doris seemed unaffected by the autumn chill in the air. Maybe she'd adapted to the cooler temperatures in Scandinavia, and a brisk evening in Missouri felt balmy by comparison. "How was the weather over in Norway?" she asked. Maybe she was the only one sensitive to the cooler temps. Or maybe her curious mind couldn't help but get distracted by things that didn't seem to fit. "Is it cold there?"

"Very. They get their winter much sooner than we do here."

"And yet you have no coat." Gigi eyed the sleek silver carry-on as Hud set it down and joined them in the study. The small suitcase was the only luggage they'd retrieved from the airport. "I doubt anything substantial would fit into your bag."

"Gracious." Doris looked down at her silk blouse and skirt. "I must have left it on the plane. I was so upset about Ian, I just wanted to get home." Her eyes crinkled up and she sniffled.

Gigi was no good at understanding people's emotions. She'd let a potential puzzle get in the way of her compassion. She quickly pulled out a tissue for the other woman. "I'm sorry. Here."

"Thank you." The blonde woman dabbed at her nose before raising her steely blue gaze to Hud. "Detective, is it possible for me to see him? When will he be released to the funeral home?"

Hud pulled out his cell phone. "I'll call the ME's office and find out where they are in the process."

"Thank you." While he stepped into the foyer to make

his call, Doris opened the liquor cabinet, inspected the display of bottles and then selected one. She held up the bottle of Irish whiskey for Gigi to see and then set out three glasses. "This was his favorite. Would you join me in a toast?"

"No, thank you."

"Detective?"

"I'm on duty, ma'am." Hud smiled an apology and returned to his call.

"Then I'll do this on my own." Doris poured herself a shot and raised her glass to the portrait over the mantel. "To Ian. You weren't a great husband. But for thirty years, you were mine." She downed the amber liquid in one smooth swallow before closing her eyes and hugging the empty glass to her chest. Gigi's head was bowed in respect to the private moment when the glass clinked against the tray in the liquor cabinet, startling her. The moment of reverence ended as Doris crossed the room. "Now. What is it you wanted me to show you?"

Though not exactly the way Gigi expected a widow to grieve, she knew every individual had his or her own process to deal with the loss. She unfolded a slip of paper where she'd written down the numbers Ian had given her and handed it to Doris. "Do these numbers mean anything to you?"

Doris pulled her glasses from her purse and read over them. "The first six match the combination to Ian's safe. But there are too many other numbers here. I don't know what they are. Unless..." Infused with a sudden energy, she went to a smaller painting hanging on the wall and pulled it open like a door to reveal a safe. She turned the combination dial and lifted the handle to open it. "Maybe that old goat was thinking about me at the end, after all." She sorted through a stack of plastic folders inside, pulling out different ones to compare numbers. With each comparison, her shoulders sagged a little more. Eventually, she replaced the entire stack and turned a sad smile to Gigi. "It's not the insurance policies or investment portfolios." She studied the paper one more time before handing it back to Gigi. "I'm stumped. How did you get these numbers?"

Gigi slipped the paper into her pocket. "Ian gave them to me. But he never said what they were. Do you know why he would do that?"

"Maybe he thought I wouldn't remember the combination. The rest I can't explain." Doris glanced at the contents of the safe again. "Do you want to look?"

The older woman stepped back as Gigi peeked into the cube-shaped recess in the wall. Besides the legal documents Doris had mentioned, there were embossed leather jewelry cases and a semiautomatic handgun with a lock wedged into the trigger. Although the weapon gave her some pause, Gigi's pulse rate kicked up a notch at the ten flash drives stored in a clear plastic box. "What are those?"

Doris pulled out the rectangular box. "Papers Ian wrote. His notes on various projects. I confess, even if I could open the files, I wouldn't understand the science. He shared my love for the theater—we used to have season tickets to the Kauffman Center. But I never quite understood his obsession with math and tinkering. Here." She handed Gigi the box. "Maybe they'll mean something to you. Or they'll be useful to the lab."

"Are you sure?" She cradled the plastic between her hands, already calculating what the documentation inside could mean. "I don't have a warrant to take them."

Doris patted Gigi's hand and smiled. "It's a gift. He'd want you to have them. He often spoke of you as though you were his scientific muse. Perhaps even a daughter. We never had children, you know."

"Thank you, Doris. He meant a lot to me, too." She leaned in to hug the older woman, as grateful for the gift as she was anxious to find out if it could help her solve the riddle of Ian's formula. "I'm honored to have them."

"If there's a Nobel Prize in there, you let me know." Gigi couldn't tell if that was a soft laugh or another sniffle as Doris pulled away. Her gaze was trained beyond Gigi's shoulder. "Your detective friend is waiting for you. You'd better go. I have phone calls to make."

"Will you be all right here by yourself?"

"I won't be alone for long. My attorney will be stopping by soon. Thank you." Doris pulled Gigi in for another quick hug before leading her to the front door. "For everything."

When they met up in the foyer, Hud relayed the information Doris needed from the ME's office and escorted Gigi out to the truck. She was so excited to dive into this new possibility that Hud had to quicken his pace to keep up with her long strides. "What's that?"

"Answers, I hope." As soon as she was seated inside, Gigi opened the box and studied the labels on each flash drive. She didn't need the paper to compare it to, but she pulled it out to make her point to Hud the moment he closed the driver's-side door behind him. "If the first numbers are the combination to the safe, then the next one could be…" She pulled out the one that matched. "Hopefully, the rest of those numbers can get me into whatever files are on this."

"Look at you goin' all Nancy Drew on me." He started the engine while she buckled in. "Interesting catch about the coat, too. While I was on the phone with Niall, I snuck a peek inside the hall closet."

"And?"

"There were three women's coats hanging there. She must own stock in the coat market if she has another she can afford to leave on a plane." He drove around the circular driveway and pulled into the street.

"Is that important?"

"What does your gut tell you? You noticed it for a reason."

Not that she trusted her gut, but the incongruence did bother her. "We need to call the airline to find out if her coat is in the lost and found. Or if she was even on that plane."

Hud tapped the side of his nose in a universal sign that she'd gotten it right.

"But why? Surely, you don't suspect her. Doris seemed genuinely upset."

"So did Hana Nowak. So did you." He looked at her across the cab of the truck. "There's only one of you I trust has told me the truth about everything."

"Me, right?"

His laughter filled up the truck and Gigi smiled.

But the respite was brief. Before Hud could dial Keir's number, her own phone rang. The urge to laugh vanished and fear chilled her blood. "What if it's him?"

Hud turned off onto a side street and parked against the curb. "Put it on speaker."

She pulled her phone from her backpack and answered. "This is Professor Brennan."

Hud reached across the console to squeeze Gigi's hand as she recoiled from the low, ominous breathing that answered. With his free hand, he texted Keir to trace the incoming call.

"Did you find what I needed?" the weird, distorted voice asked.

"Not yet." Hud silently signaled for her to keep the conversation going. "I'm working on it. I might have a new lead. But it will take time to decipher—"

"Time is a luxury you don't have, Virginia." With each beat of silence that passed, the tension inside Gigi knotted tighter and tighter. "I know Lombard's widow gave you something. Is it my formula?"

"How did you know…?"

Hudson swore. The artificial voice laughed. "I hear your boyfriend is with you."

Hud unholstered his gun and texted the word *BOLO* to Keir Watson—be on the lookout for. The creep must have followed them, could be following them right now. He said he'd be watching. Hud pushed open his door and checked up and down the street.

The laughter ended abruptly. "He can look, but he won't find me. He won't be able to protect you or the people you love. As a matter of fact, I have eyes on your sister right now. Looks like she had a fun trip to Vegas."

Gigi's terror erupted in a burst of anger. "You stay away from her! I'm working as hard as I can. You'll have Ian's formula. Monday morning at six, just like you said."

Hud climbed back in as soon as he heard the threat and dialed his partner. He wasn't wasting time on a text.

"Don't disappoint me," the voice warned.

"I won't. I promise. Just leave Tammy alone."

But the line had already gone silent.

"Hud?" Her hands were shaking too badly to keep hold of her phone. "He's going to hurt her."

Hud shifted his truck into Drive and spoke the moment Keir picked up. "Gigi just got another call from the perp."

"We're tracking it."

"Where is Tammy Brennan?"

"The officer I assigned to her is with her at Gigi's house right now. She's picking up clothes and toiletries."

"Secure her in the house," Hud ordered. "Perp said he had eyes on her."

"I'll alert Officer Logan and send backup."

"How can he know we were just at Doris Lombard's *and* have eyes on my house?"

"Two perps, remember? Hell. Between the two of them, they've probably seen every move we've made." Hud reached beneath his seat and pulled out a magnetic portable siren. He stuck it on top of the truck and turned on the lights and the shrill alarm, picking up speed with every passing block as they raced across the city. "Hold on."

She nodded.

"Get out of your head, G," he warned. "Don't you be thinkin' the worst."

"How can I not? I have to work a scientific miracle or else he'll hurt her."

"Reach inside my jacket pocket," he instructed, nodding toward the leather jacket she still wore. "My pen and notebook are in there. Keep your hands busy. Keep your mind focused."

She thrust her hands inside the deep pockets and curled her fingers around the items there. It was a ridiculous exercise, under the circumstances, but it worked. Hud's scent, something to focus on, the fact that he'd listened and observed and remembered what helped her cope with the panic worked.

"You with me?" he asked, never taking his eyes off the road.

"I'm okay," she answered. And she meant it.

They were sailing through a red light on Brush Creek Parkway when Keir called back. "I'm en route to Gigi's house now. Logan has it locked down tight. You were right. Gigi's caller used a burner phone. Looks like it was turned off immediately after the call so we couldn't pinpoint an exact location. But I can narrow it down and tell you what cell tower it pinged off."

"And?" Hud cursed when he didn't get an instant response. "Where did it come from?"

"Gigi's neighborhood."

Chapter Eleven

Gigi raced up the steps to her front porch. She barely had the key inserted into the lock when the door swung open. "Tam…"

She retreated a step as a twentysomething black man in a KCPD uniform filled the doorway. "Are you Gigi Brennan, ma'am?"

"Yes." Her feet danced with panic after hearing those threats. But his raised hand stopped her from sliding past him to get inside. "Who are you? Where's my sister?"

"Officer Albert Logan." She felt Hud at her back as the tall, muscular officer included them both in his warning. "I'm sorry. I need to see your identification."

"This is my house. Tammy?" She patted her pockets. Of course, her billfold wasn't there. "My backpack is in the truck."

"Easy, G." Hud caught her before she could dash to the truck where they'd parked at the curb and turned her to the front door. He flashed his badge to the young officer. "Detective Kramer. I've got lead on this case. Keir Watson is my partner. Glad to see you're doing your job, but I need her inside and out of sight ASAP."

"Is that Gigi, Al?" She heard a familiar voice shouting from upstairs.

Albert Logan's stern expression relaxed into a smile.

"He said you were the only cop I could let in besides him." He stepped back and held the door open. "Sorry for the delay, ma'am. She's upstairs."

Gigi bolted up the stairs to her sister's bedroom suite. "Tammy?"

"Right here, you big worrywart." Tammy met her in her doorway, her strawberry-blond hair pulled back into a ponytail, her beautiful smile fixed firmly in place.

Gigi swallowed her up in a tight hug. "Are you all right? What are you doing here? You're supposed to be in protective custody."

"I need clothes." Tammy squeezed her right back. "Al picked me up at the airport and is going to drive me to a safe house." As she pulled away, Tammy's blue gaze shifted to Hud who'd followed her up the stairs. Since Gigi had gotten all the shy genes in the family, Tammy extended her hand and offered him a smile. "So, who's this bad boy you brought with you? I'm Tammy Brennan. We've met before, haven't we?"

Hud smiled back. "Hudson Kramer, KCPD. You have a good memory. The Shamrock Bar, a couple years back. You bought my partner and me a drink. Your sister tagged along and kicked my ass playin' pool."

Tammy's mouth rounded with a big O before she pointed to him and whispered, "He's the guy?"

"The guy?" Hud echoed.

Gigi shushed her sister's excitement. She'd mentioned her crush on Hud a time or two over the years, but she didn't realize how much Tammy had actually listened.

Tammy propped her hands at the waist of her snug jeans and beamed a smile at Hud. "This *is* an interesting development. That explains the gym bag with a change of men's clothes in the downstairs bathroom."

Gigi reached back to take Hud's hand. "Sorry about that. She doesn't have a filter."

"Nosy much?" Hud teased, linking his fingers with hers and not looking one bit self-conscious about the innuendos Tammy had thrown his way.

Tammy hugged Gigi to her side. "Hey, she's not the only Brennan with a curious mind. I'm just the extroverted version."

"I can see that." And just like that, Hud shifted from teasing charmer into cop mode. "You haven't noticed anyone following you? Received any threats?"

Tammy released Gigi and crossed to the open suitcase lying on the bed. "Your partner asked me the same questions. No and no. Then he said Gigi was in danger and introduced me to Al. Said he was going to be my shadow for a while. Between your messages and calls from Detective Watson, I'm happy to have the company." She paused in the middle of rolling up a pair of slacks. "You're keeping my big sister safe?"

"I'm doing my best." Hud's hand squeezed around Gigi's, silently making sure she was all right before excusing himself from the conversation. "I'll leave you two to finish packing. I'll be downstairs getting a sitrep from Officer Logan."

"Tell Al I'll only be a few more minutes." Tammy tossed her pants into the suitcase and followed him out the door to watch him go down the stairs. "Nice butt."

"Tammy!"

"Oh, relax. I'm happy for you." Tammy strolled back into the room to resume her packing. "It's about time my big sister found a guy to shack up with."

Gigi's thoughts short-circuited. "We are not shacking… We're working together on a police investigation. Brains and brawn."

"He's definitely got the brawny part down." She stuffed socks into her running shoes and added them to her suitcase. "I wonder if he'd make a good big brother."

"He would. He has three younger siblings. His parents died and he raised them just like I… Oh. You." The recitation of Hud's history ended when she saw the cheese-eating grin on her sister's face. "Give me a break, okay. This relationship stuff isn't anything I've ever studied in a classroom."

Tammy waved off the reprimanding tone and closed her suitcase. "You don't learn this kind of stuff from a book. You learn it by living it. Although, this murder/blackmail scenario isn't exactly the meet-cute I'd go for."

"Meet-cute?"

"My point is, if you like Hud and he likes you, then go for it. After all you've given up in your life—for your studies, for me—nobody deserves a happily-ever-after more."

"I don't know if this is long-term. This situation has thrown us together and intensified things. I like him. And I think he kind of likes me."

Tammy carried her suitcase to the doorway and glanced down the stairs. "Oh, sweetie, he likes you a lot. He barely took his eyes off you until he left the room. And even then, he didn't want to go."

Was that true? Did Hud watch her the way she sometimes watched him? She touched the temple of her glasses. "He's protective of me."

"Another reason I like him." Tammy took her hand and sat on the bench at the foot of her bed, pulling Gigi down beside her. "I know I'm not the best person to give relationship advice, but I do know you. I've never known anyone who was more of a one-man kind of woman than you are. I know how hard trust is for you, how hard it is for you to come out of your shell and embrace your emotions. You've already let Detective Kramer in. I saw you reach for him instead of sticking your hands into your pockets and dealing with all this chaos on your own. He's your one."

Her sister's earnest blue eyes saw things more clearly than Gigi had. A one-man kind of woman. That made sense with her aversion to Gary. He wasn't the one. Hudson Kramer was that man. He always had been. All the logic in the world couldn't explain it, but she was in love with Hud.

"Look at the annoying little sister being the smart one for a change." Gigi was a little uncomfortable with both this role reversal and the acceptance of her feelings for Hud. "What do I do about it?"

"What do you want to do?"

"I want to be with him. In every way."

Tammy slid her arm around Gigi's waist and led her into the bathroom. "Okay, then. I have two bits of advice. One, I know you're not on the pill. Even though I am, I keep a box of condoms in here beside the sink." She opened the drawer and set the box in Gigi's hand. "You're the one who taught me to be safe. Help yourself."

"I don't need that kind of advice. I know how things work." She stuffed the box back into its drawer and closed it. "What's number two?"

"In my experience, men can be pretty thickheaded. You have to tell them plain and simple exactly what you want and how you feel. Can you have that kind of conversation with him?"

"I think so."

"Wow. He really is the one." Tammy stretched up to give Gigi a big hug. "You'll be a rock star with this guy—I can tell."

Hud called from the bottom of the stairs. "Time to go, ladies. Officer Logan is waiting out front."

Reluctantly, Gigi pulled away. "I wish I could be the

big sister who gives you this kind of advice, instead of the other way around."

"No worries. We both have our skill sets. If you weren't as practical and driven as you are, I wouldn't have a college degree or a career. I might not even have a roof over my head. You don't have to gossip or be girly-girl with me. You were there for me, Gigi. You provided for me. You gave me a safe, solid foundation so I could go out and be the wild-and-crazy girl that I am. You took care of me and made us a family. That's how I know you love me."

"I do." They traded another quick hug. "The idea of this man hurting you… I want you to be safe, okay?"

"Don't worry about me. I think Al looks pretty capable if anybody gets too close." She shrugged into her jacket, picked up her purse and suitcase, and headed downstairs. "I love you, too. Now, wrap up this whole murder-crime thingy, get your man and call me when you have time to bake some cookies and stay up late and talk. I'm dying to tell you about my adventure in Vegas."

Gigi followed Tammy to the porch where Hud was waiting for them. Officer Logan picked up Tammy's suitcase and carried it to his squad car at the end of the driveway, where he popped the trunk to stow it inside. "Am I going to like this story?"

"Probably not. But I won four hundred dollars and the guy was cute."

"You're hopeless."

Tammy trotted down the steps, walking past her yellow Volkswagen on her way to the squad car. "I'd like to think I'm hopeful—"

Boom.

One second, she was smiling, the next, Tammy was flying through the air as her car exploded. A wave of heat collided with Gigi. She hit the painted white planks of the porch hard, knocking the breath from her lungs. Hud landed beside her, then rolled on top of her, shielding her with his body as fire, metal and glass rained down around them. Whatever he shouted in her ear, she couldn't hear.

She could only hold on and pray her sister wasn't dead.

GIGI PACED THE CORRIDOR outside Tammy's room at Saint Luke's Hospital. The hour was late, and Tammy needed her rest, but Gigi wanted to hear one more report from the doctor checking on her and tell Tammy she loved her again before saying good-night.

Keir Watson and his wife, Kenna, had stopped by the house to get Gigi a pair of jeans, a blouse and a sweater to change into. They'd brought Hud clean clothes as well, along with a preliminary report from the crime-scene technicians and the grim news that Tammy's car had been remotely detonated by a cell phone wired into the explosives.

A neat trick any engineer or physicist could put together.

She knew at least two men with a beef against Ian Lombard who could pull that off. There were also Lukin dissidents and terrorists and drug smugglers all over the world who'd be willing to plant a bomb in exchange for Ian's formula and the potential weapons and industrial machinery that could be made from it.

The blast could have been the result of random timing. But she believed, and Hud agreed, that whoever had dialed that number had been watching the house, timing it perfectly to injure Tammy and terrorize Gigi. A few seconds sooner, and Tammy might have been killed. A few seconds later, Tammy would have been gone and Gigi wouldn't have witnessed the explosion and the damage done to her own sense of security.

Gigi reached the end of the corridor, turned and paced back past Hud and Keir and Kenna, each of them on their phones, working some angle on the investigation with the crime lab, the KCPD patrol division and the district attorney's office. She walked toward Tammy's room and the grim expression of the uniformed guard standing watch outside her door. Albert Logan's squad car had protected him from the blast. But it couldn't protect him from the guilt he must be feeling—the same guilt Gigi felt. That bomb could have been placed there at any time over the past twenty-four hours. Maybe that was even part of what the two intruders had been up to the night before. As Gigi walked by, she reached out and squeezed Albert's forearm. His dark hand covered hers for a moment.

"Not your fault," she whispered, and kept walking.

"Yours either, ma'am." She nodded her thanks but wondered if Albert believed it any more than she did.

The momentary deafness caused by the concussive blast had faded away, but there still seemed to be a shroud covering her brain, preventing clear thought from coming through. None of her own scrapes and cuts were serious, but she still felt off-kilter.

Tammy had been the closest to the exploding car, but she'd been far enough away that none of her injuries were life-threatening. Still, with a broken arm, a bruised kidney and multiple lacerations, the doctors wanted to keep her in the hospital overnight for observation and rest. Life-threatening or not, Tammy's injuries filled Gigi with fear and ignited an anger that needed a place to channel before she started screaming or broke down into tears.

That's why when her phone rang and she recognized the number, she answered before Hud could stop her. "What do you want?" she demanded, hitting the speaker button as Hud abruptly ended his call and ushered her into the empty room across the hall. "I'm doing what you asked. You didn't have to hurt my sister."

"That could have been you."

"You're not motivating me. You're pissing me off." Gigi heard herself shouting but couldn't seem to rein in her emotions.

The hollow voice laughed. "The great Virginia Brennan does have a trigger, after all. Can I tell you how satisfying it is to hear you lose it?"

"Who is this? Gary? Evgeni? I won't give you what you want."

Hud's golden eyes locked onto hers, warning her she was pushing the caller too far. Or maybe wondering if she really was losing it.

The caller refused to answer her accusations. Instead, he filled the small hospital room with the insidious sound of that mechanically distorted breathing. Then he calmly reminded her that he was the one controlling her life. "Let me tell you how angry I'll be if you don't give me what I want. I can get to your sister in the hospital. A simple injection, and she could have an embolism in her lung or heart. She could suffocate under a pillow or receive the wrong medication."

"You son of a bitch."

"Language, Virginia. No more noble defiance. You bring me what I want, or Tammy dies."

"I'll be there. But if you threaten my family again…"

The click of his disconnect felt like a slap in the face. The anger and frustration grew too strong for her to control and she cocked her arm back, ready to sling her phone across the room.

But a saner figure caught her wrist, plucked her phone from her grip and pulled her tight against his chest. "I've got you, G. You have the right to be angry. You're exhausted. It's okay to be afraid." She pounded her fist against Hud's shoulder until the tears came. And when the emotional outburst had run its course, his cool lips grazed her forehead. "You with me?"

She nodded. Then she cupped his stubbled jaw and looked into those green-gold eyes to read the steady reassurance there. "I freaked out on you again, didn't I."

His smile didn't quite reach his eyes. "I bet you do that to all the guys."

She laughed as he meant her to, but wasn't quite feeling the humor, either. She brushed her lips against his and hugged him again. "You're an anchor for me. I don't think I could get through these forty-eight hours without you."

"Yep, I always wanted to be the heavy chunk of iron hanging around some woman's neck."

She went stiff in his arms. "I'm sorry. That doesn't sound like a compliment. But to me, it was."

"It's okay, G." His words took on a bittersweet tone as he pulled away. But he wrapped his hand around hers and they walked into the hallway together. "The doctor should be done by now. Let's say good-night to Tammy and get you home for a decent night's sleep. That hour we got this morning won't cut it. You're workin' a miracle tomorrow, remember?"

"No pressure, huh?"

After the doctor's reassurance that rest and follow-up visits with the specialists who'd worked on her were the only medicine Tammy needed, the sisters traded hugs and said good-night.

Despite the cuts and bruises on her face, Tammy smiled as she lay back on her pillow. "You go get these guys, sis. And, Hud? Take care of her."

"I will," Hud promised, giving her free hand a squeeze. "Rest up, kiddo. We'll check in on you tomorrow before you're taken to the safe house."

While Gigi dimmed the lights and closed the door,

Hud took Albert Logan aside and pointed his finger in the young officer's face. "You do not leave your post unless this man—" he pointed to Keir "—or someone he introduces to you personally relieves you. No one goes into that room except for medical professionals, and then you go in with them. Tammy is not to be left alone. Understood?"

"She won't be."

"Good man." After a friendly smack on the shoulder, he turned to Keir. "You got this?"

Keir nodded. "We'll keep her safe, Gigi, I promise."

"Thank you, Keir." Hud wasn't the only man she was learning to trust. Gigi held out her hand and felt herself being pulled in for a brotherly hug.

"You keep an eye on this tough guy, okay? I'll handle the rest."

"I'll do my best."

When the hug ended, Hud slipped her backpack onto her shoulder and took her hand to lead her to the elevators and down to the parking garage.

Once they were inside his truck and the heater was running, Hud turned to her. The yellowish lights of the garage cast an unnatural glow across the rugged angles of his face. But his golden eyes were tender, familiar. "What do you need tonight? Food? Rest?"

Gigi leaned back against the headrest, wishing that climbing over the center console and cuddling in Hud's lap was an option. She exhaled a deep breath and felt weariness consume her. "I need to think. I'll figure out the damn formula. But not if I can't…think…because my brain is overloaded with this helplessness and anger."

He reached across the cab to tuck a strand of hair behind her ear. "You are anything but helpless. Everything's in motion from our end. We'll have officers undercover in the Front Street area early Monday morning, and a SWAT team on standby. And I will be right there with you."

She turned her cheek into his lingering hand. "I don't want anyone else to get hurt."

"Not gonna happen, G. The trap will be set. We'll get this guy and his accomplice." He reversed out of the parking space and followed the arrows up to the street-level exit. They merged with the lights and traffic of Saturday night on the Plaza before he suddenly grinned and filled the cab of the truck with his infectious energy. "You said you need time and space to think."

"Uh-huh."

"Home or office?"

What was going on in that handsome head of his?

"Where would you feel more comfortable?"

It was hard not to smile when he seemed so delighted with whatever he was planning. "Home, I guess, considering everyone I work with is a suspect."

"Burgers or pizza?"

Her stomach rumbled at the mention of food, reminding her they hadn't eaten since they'd shared coffee and doughnuts that morning. "Pizza."

"Sleep or sex?"

The choice shocked her. Excited her. "Could I have both?"

They pulled up to a stoplight and Hud leaned across the console to press a quick, hard kiss to her lips. "Now you're thinkin'."

She leaned back in her seat as the light turned green. "Wait. You were just trying to distract me, weren't you? Get me out of my head?"

He chuckled. "You feel better, don't you?"

Deflated to learn this was some kind of game, yet

strangely energized by the fun banter and possibilities, Gigi swatted his arm. "You stink, Hudson Kramer."

He caught her hand before she could pull away and brought it to his lips to kiss her knuckles. The scrape of his beard tickled her skin, but his promise seeped in and warmed her from head to toe. "It'll happen, G. I wouldn't offer if I wasn't serious. I want it, too."

She was a quick study. She could play the game, too. "So, you're saying you want sleep?"

"Dr. Brennan—if you weren't such a complete brainiac detached from your emotions and too shy to spit out a complete coherent sentence when you get nervous, I'd think you were flirtin' with me."

She weighed the accurate, yet faintly disparaging words against his sly tone. "Teasing?"

He winked.

She'd never flirted with a man before, had she? It was fun to see the pink coloring his cheeks. "Well, I do have three college degrees, so you know I like learning new things. My research tells me that you'd be an excellent teacher."

His answering groan might well be the sexiest sound she'd ever heard him make. "You sure it's me you want?"

She didn't have to think about it, and she was no longer afraid to admit it. "I've never thought about it being anyone else but you."

The traffic thinned out and he pumped on the accelerator. "Pizza first."

"Because I'm going to need my strength?"

He laughed out loud. "No. I think I am."

GIGI PUT AWAY three slices of a hamburger-and-mushroom pizza and two molasses cookies before she picked up the remote and paused the movie she and Hud were watching. With her long legs stretched to the coffee table in front of them, and an afghan covering her from shoulder to stockinged toe, Hud had hoped she'd fall asleep. Then he could safely put her to bed and grab that cold shower he'd been thinking about ever since she'd called his bluff and said yes to having sex with him. He didn't think he'd ever wanted a thing as badly as he wanted to feel Gigi fly apart in his arms as they explored the chemistry that no textbook could fully teach her.

But tonight wasn't about him. None of this weekend was about him and what he wanted. His official job was to unmask a pair of killers and keep KCPD's greatest asset for getting the job done safe. His unofficial job was to listen and comfort or prod or protect or be whatever Gigi needed so she could complete Lombard's formula and bait the trap to arrest them.

"Tammy said I needed to tell you exactly what I want."

Not the opening to a conversation that he'd expected. But he was learning that Gigi's complex brain sometimes took the scenic route to get to the point she wanted to make. He picked up another cookie from the plate on the coffee table and leaned back against the opposite corner of the sofa to munch on the decadent treat. "You're taking relationship advice from Tammy? The woman who picks up guys in bars and comes home with secrets from a teachers' conference in Las Vegas?"

"Yes." She curled her legs beneath her and turned to face him. "Growing up, I wasn't the normal one, Hud. Tammy could always make friends and interact with people. She's learned a lot more about relationships and human nature than I ever have. She's like you. She has instincts about people, and embraces her feelings about them." She tapped the side of her head. "I have to logically figure everything out."

Hud swallowed his cookie and turned off the TV. Apparently, sleep and a cold shower weren't going to happen. "Then talk to me. Let's figure this out together. What did Tammy want you to tell me?"

"Someone just tried to kill her. You and I might not live past Monday morning. My whole life has been put on hold while I earn degrees and bury my parents and raise my sister. Even if I'd had a normal life, I've been too introverted and too intellectual to get out of my head and be brave about going after what I want."

Hud mirrored her position on the couch. With his gun and badge on the coffee table beside the cookies, he gave himself permission to answer as a man, not a cop. "There's nobody braver than you, G. You lead a research team and teach a lecture hall full of students, even though it's a challenge for you. A coward would have folded at the first sign of trouble with your boss's murder. You came to me—at the crime scene, at the police station—to help find his killer. You kissed me when I was too stubborn, too afraid to risk feeling something for a woman again. Don't you ever tell me you're not brave."

He waited for her to touch her glasses to settle whatever nerves she was feeling. But her hands remained clasped on top of the afghan in her lap. "Then…if I said I wanted you to make love to me tonight…you'd be okay with that?"

"Don't want to die a virgin, hmm?" He waved aside that comment, regretting the words the moment they left his mouth. "Sorry. Bad joke. Those are my defenses talking." If she could be brave enough to share what she was feeling, then he owed it to her to do the same. He slid across the couch until he could touch the soft skin of her cheek and run his fingers through the auburn silk of her hair. He found the clip at the back of her head and unhooked it, letting that long waterfall of hair tumble through his fingers. "I'd be very okay with that."

He knew he had a history of being quick to give his heart to a woman who needed him. But this felt different. Never in a million years would he have thought a woman like Gigi and he could work. But tonight, he felt like all the missteps with other women, all the lousy timing and bad luck, all those trips to the friend zone had simply prepared him for this one woman. He desperately needed to get everything right this time. The thought of another man touching her the way she'd just asked him to made him a little crazy. He wanted every first touch, every first anything with her. He'd become the Gigi-whisperer, yeah. But she'd done something for him, too. Gigi had gotten under his skin, gotten into his head, gotten into his heart. Meeting her was the best kind of luck a man could have.

Gigi made him feel like he was enough.

He tugged on the back of her neck. "Come here."

When he fell back onto the couch and she landed on top of him and kissed him, he knew he was more than enough. Her legs tangled with his and her long hair fell around his face and shoulders. Her fingers curled into his shirt, digging into the skin underneath. His hands found a palmful of her bottom and the back of her head to align her body and mouth with his. Her small breasts beaded against his chest as her lips parted over his, and their tongues danced together.

His body was primed, and the woman was willing. She tasted of cookies and smelled like his favorite pizza. He released her only long enough to pull the bulky afghan from in between them, and then he was back, tugging her blouse loose and then sliding his hands against cool skin, stroking up along her back before dipping beneath the waist of her jeans and panties. Still, he needed more.

He sat up, spilling Gigi into his lap, freeing his hands to push the sweater she wore off her shoulders. The blouse came next. If she wanted to wrap herself in something, it was going to be him.

Hud sampled his way over the point of her chin, down the long column of her neck. He pressed a kiss to the soft swell of skin above her white satin bra and then dipped his head to take the nipple into his mouth, wetting her through the material, loving how she squirmed in his lap and then raked her fingers into his hair to hold his mouth against the straining tip while she whispered his name.

Then Gigi pulled his mouth back to hers, demanding a kiss while her fingers fumbled with his belt buckle. "Hud…" she whispered against his mouth, tugging on his shirt. "I can't get…" She slipped her hands beneath his shirt, the needy caress of skin upon skin making him shudder. "I want…"

"Me, too."

Moments later, they were naked in her bed. Hud rolled on a condom and pushed inside her, holding himself still as she adjusted to the feel of him filling her. He'd made her writhe with his hands and his mouth. But she'd insisted it wasn't enough, that she needed him, needed all of him. Her little cry of pain when he entered her nearly stopped him. But she buried her face against his shoulder and breathed such a warm, satisfied sigh against his skin that he swelled inside her.

Then she lay back against the pillow, her mussed-up hair falling in a halo around her head. With her glasses on the bedside table, it was easy to see the desire darkening her eyes. "I want more."

She was definitely a fast learner. That siren call was irresistible.

"Like this?" Bracing himself on his elbows above her,

he pulled gently out of her, then pressed inside again, her slick walls taking him in, easing the friction as he moved faster and faster, and grew harder and harder with every thrust.

"I know the basics." Her voice was a breathless gasp against his ear. There was nothing basic about the way she made him feel. She hugged him around the neck, skimmed her hands over his shoulders and back, nipped at his chin and jaw and earlobe until his heart pounded in his chest and every nerve ending primed him for release. "But isn't there something I can do for you? How can I make it better?"

"You can't, G. This is about as mind-blowing as it gets." Her hips squirmed beneath him and he knew she was about to come. He squeezed his eyes shut, determined to make this last, determined to make this good for her.

She grabbed his face, turning his gaze down to hers. "What do you want me to do?"

"It's a fantasy of mine. I shouldn't. Not your first time."

"What? Tell me." She lifted her head and kissed him squarely on the mouth. "Tell me."

"Wrap your legs around me. Stretch yourself open. Hold me with your…body." He gulped in the middle of that sentence because she did exactly that. He slipped in a fraction deeper and nearly lost it then as her body gripped his.

"Like this?"

"Yeah… Just like…" Her heels linked behind him, pulling herself into his helpless thrust. "Gorgeous…legs…"

"Can't you talk…either? That feels…" She raised her hips to meet the next plunge.

He quickened the pace. Her body shook. Her fingers dug into his skin as her back arched. "Let it happen, honey. Let it happen."

He buried his face against her neck and she shuddered all around him, crying out his name.

He followed after, losing himself in the pleasure and warmth and welcome that was G.

After fetching a washcloth to clean them both, and retrieving his gun to set it within arm's reach on the bedside table, Hud climbed beneath the covers and spooned his naked body behind hers. He smoothed her hair away from the dampness at the nape of her neck and kissed her there. "You okay?"

She seemed boneless and completely spent. "I've never been this okay in my life."

He chuckled, then had to put a firm hand on her hip to stop her from rubbing her bottom against him. Whether she was simply trying to find a comfortable position to sleep, or he'd awakened the irresistible tigress in her, they both needed time to rest before they tried this combustible chemistry experiment again. "Easy, G. You may be a little sore for a while. I'm guessing you've used some muscles you never have before."

Her fingers moved tentatively along his forearm around her waist. "What about you? Was I all right? Did you enjoy it, too?"

"I don't think *all right* is big enough for what I'm feeling. What are some big words you know? Marvelous? Stupendous? Horny as hell and ready for more?"

"I'm serious, Hud." She gave him a playful elbow to the gut for teasing her as his list continued.

"Sated? Superlative? Splendiferous?"

"Perfect."

Chapter Twelve

Hud tried hard not to feel cast aside when he woke up to find the bed empty and cool beside him.

Maybe last night had just been about a woman wanting to get her virginity card off the table, and he'd been the guy she trusted enough to give herself to. Or maybe last night had been the ultimate Gigi-whisperer exercise. If a touch could distract her from her thoughts, a kiss could center her, then making love with all that incredible, full-body contact must have cleared her brain to come up with the next Nobel Prize for Physics.

Could he have been wrong about her? Maybe she *was* the kind of woman to take what she needed from him, then back off from any relationship blossoming between them. And maybe this had nothing to do with him at all. When he pulled on his jeans and followed the smell of coffee and bacon to the kitchen where she was sitting cross-legged in a chair at the table, poring over her laptop, he reminded himself that she was a unique human being, far more comfortable with those brainy calculations he didn't understand than with her emotions. And with a deadline barreling down on her in fewer than twenty-four hours, he couldn't blame her for wanting to get an early start.

"Morning." Still, when her only response to his greeting was a nod and a point toward the scones sitting on a platter on top of the stove, it was difficult to believe that last night had meant the same thing to Gigi that it did to him.

He spotted the box of flash drives on the table beside her and told himself that the woman had her priorities straight. Instead of assessing his wounded ego, he popped a slice of crispy bacon into his mouth and carried the teakettle over to top off Gigi's mug.

She barely looked away from the screen to drop the tea bag and strainer back into her mug. "Thanks."

Communication. That was a good sign, right?

"Did you find anything?" he asked.

She picked up the nearly used-up legal pad she'd been writing on and flipped to a new page to jot down a series of numbers and symbols. "I got the flash drive to open."

At least one mystery had been solved. "The string of numbers was the combination to his safe, the label on the flash drive—"

"And the encryption code." Just like two nights ago at the precinct, she was obsessed with writing and drawing and scratching out and writing again.

He'd better leave her to her work. After all, she was the brains of this operation. He couldn't help her with any of that. He carried the kettle back to the stove, poured himself a mug of coffee and devoured a buttery lemon scone that pricked his taste buds and melted down his throat. Wow. In so many ways, Gigi really was the woman of his dreams.

But right now, she didn't need him. Reminding himself that there was work he could be doing, too, he grabbed another scone and headed to the bathroom to run hot water for a shower and a shave.

Fifteen minutes later, he stepped out of the shower, wrapped a towel around his waist and realized he wasn't alone. Gigi stood inside the bathroom door, curling her toes in the throw rug there. For a split second, excitement surged through his veins. Had she come to join him?

But then he saw her arms locked around her waist in a tight hug, and a different kind of heat put him on full alert. Something was majorly wrong. Had she gotten another phone call from that terrorizing thug? From the hospital? Was there someone breaking in? Just how long would it take him to get his gun from the bedroom next door?

Then she touched her glasses and her eyes zeroed in on his. "It won't work."

Hud was already crossing the room. He squeezed his hands around her shoulders, reassuring himself that she wasn't hurt or in any immediate danger.

She was upset about something, though. He could feel her trembling. If he wasn't still soaking wet, he'd pull her into his arms. "What are you talking about?"

"Ian's formula. It won't work."

Hud retreated a step. Not the bad news he'd expected. "How do you know?"

"Because I'm really smart."

That was a given. "I mean, what's wrong with it?"

"His equations don't balance. I found a mistake. His heat ratio is off." Her gaze swept across his chest and down to the edge of the towel below his belly button before she averted her head to face the toilet. "I have to go to the lab."

"Not a problem. I'll be ready in ten minutes and can take you there."

When he reached around her to open the door, she stopped him with a palm against his chest. He felt that touch like a brand and wondered if her fingers had been singed by the same heat he felt. "And I'll need you to put on a shirt because I can't think when you're naked like this."

At last. This was the woman hidden inside Professor Brennan that he'd needed to see this morning. No longer caring if he dripped on her, Hud leaned in to seal his lips to hers in a gentle kiss. "Imagine how I felt last night when I got to see and touch all of you."

Her fingers tested the smooth skin of his jaw after his shave in the shower. "I don't know how to deal with the morning after—what I'm supposed to say or do. Tammy didn't tell me and I didn't think to ask. But it was wonderful and thank you and I'd do it again and—"

"It's okay, G." He pressed a finger to her lips and smiled. "We'll figure us out later. Right now, I need to get you to the lab."

HUD WATCHED GIGI do her thing in the lab. With spare parts cannibalized from other devices, a mix of compounds from a storage cabinet, wires and microchips and commands typed into her laptop, Gigi had accomplished in three hours what a top-of-the-line mechanic could do to his truck in an entire week.

Even though Hud stood at the entryway to the lab, several feet from the table where Gigi was building her high-tech contraption, to keep an eye out for any unexpected visitors, she'd insisted he put on a pair of safety goggles. Now he was glad he had.

"Firing up the mobile power bank," she announced, pushing a button on her computer. At first nothing happened. Then the capacitor started to hum. She disconnected her computer and set it on a nearby table, allowing Lombard's design to generate its own power. He followed the connecting cords to the hot plate with a large glass beaker filled with water sitting on top of it, a centrifuge and an old computer she said no one would miss if this didn't work out. "I gave it a series of simple commands to complete on each piece of equipment."

A circuit she'd plugged into the tablet-sized device

started to glow. Red at first, then gold as it released chimeras of heat into the air. The color flowed along a series of wires and microchips she'd embedded in a viscous gel. "Should it be doing that?" he asked.

The device vibrated enough to dance across the table. The gel melted into a puddle of goo as the circuit burned white-hot and the water inside the beaker boiled with an instant fury before it bubbled over the top and the glass shattered.

"G!" She was already backing away when he ran to pull her to safety.

The fried circuit erupted with a tiny flame that had fizzled out by the time Hud could grab the fire extinguisher to smother the burned-out device.

Gigi stared at the foam-covered mess for several seconds before she turned to her laptop and typed in some pertinent information. "Enough spark to light a cigarette, but not enough power to run a portable generator or guide a missile or even turn on my toaster. It never got past the first command before it burned itself out."

"Your boss's design is an epic fail."

"This is twice the size of what Ian designed, and it couldn't handle the power output. No way could this be miniaturized and get any usable results."

Hud pushed his goggles up on top of his head and nodded his agreement. "This is why someone killed him?"

"It's a great idea. But I can't imagine Ian being so far off in his calculations." Gigi linked her fingers with his and leaned against his arm. But then he felt her stiffen against his side. "Once Ian's killers realize this isn't worth the cost of the parts, what will they do to Tammy? To you? To me?"

He pressed a kiss to her temple, trying to soften the harsh reality of his words. "I don't imagine these people are going to say, *Nice try*, and go away."

"What if Ian told them it didn't work? Maybe that's why they killed him. And now they're coming after me because they think I can fix it."

Her eyes were distorted by the safety goggles when he turned to face her. He pulled them off her face and tucked them into the chest pocket of her lab coat. "Nobody's coming after you. You give them something tomorrow morning. Anything that looks convincing. And we'll arrest them. Once we know exactly who's behind this, we'll be able to poke holes in their story. By the time they figure out the formula doesn't work, they'll be fingerprinted and stuck in a jail cell." He touched his finger to the point of her chin. "Can you put together something like that?"

Gigi nodded.

His phone buzzed in his pocket. "It's Keir. I need to update him on where we are with this. Clean up what you need to, and let's get out of here."

Hud strode back to her office to answer his partner's call. He gave him the news about the failed experiment, and the fake version of Lombard's formula and design they were going to pass off to Lombard's killers and Gigi's blackmailers early tomorrow morning.

He watched Gigi through the glass windows as she put together another gadget that she could pass off as Ian's invention. After sticking that into her backpack, she wiped down the salvageable equipment and swept the rest into the trash. Then, almost as though she couldn't help herself, she pulled up a stool and sat at the table with her legal pad and started sketching something on the paper. She'd once told him that she was always thinking—with the one notable exception she'd confessed in the bathroom that morning. She was elegant and mesmerizing and powerful in her element. And yet she was vulnerable and brave—

"Earth to Kramer." Hud swore as he realized his distracted silence had left himself wide-open for the question he knew was coming. "I'll take that as a definite yes to falling for the damsel in distress?"

This wasn't like getting stood up by the woman whose honor he was defending in the alley behind a bar. "This is different, Keir. Even if nothing comes of this connection, I'm scared to death something's going to happen to her."

"But Hudson Kramer doesn't give up. You know she needs you right now."

What was that woman up to? Gigi was up again, pulling items out of cabinets, piecing something together he couldn't see from this angle. "I know."

"You love her."

"Gigi's waking up to her feelings and desires. I just happen to be the guy who's around to take advantage of that."

"Take advantage?" Concern crept into his partner's tone.

"Those aren't the right words. I'm lucky enough to be in the right place at the right time to reap the rewards. I'm her friend. But she's let me become more. She needs me to be more."

"You *do* love her."

Hud wasn't willing to admit that out loud. Somehow, saying the words made his feelings for Gigi that much more real. Saying the words would set him up for a world of hurt that he wasn't sure he could recover from when Gigi didn't need him anymore. "We have to keep her alive tomorrow when we make that delivery, Keir. Now get out of my head and get back to work."

AFTER VISITING TAMMY at the hospital and ensuring she would be fine recovering at the safe house, Gigi and Hud had driven home.

Who knew a man with such a strong German surname

could put together a delicious pasta and salad for dinner?
Although she appreciated his efforts to take care of her
and keep her distracted from her worries about the looming six o'clock deadline, Gigi had picked at her salad and
pasta Bolognese. They'd cleaned the kitchen together and
cuddled on the couch to watch the end of the movie they'd
cut short the night before. If these were normal circumstances, she would have considered this the perfect date
night—like the ones she used to imagine but had never
gotten to experience.

But these weren't normal circumstances. And no amount
of action, snappy dialogue and a hint of romance could
make her forget that. Although she relished the warmth
of Hud's body snugging her to his side, she'd missed the
movie's climactic rescue from the flooded building after
a devastating earthquake.

"What'd you think?" Hud asked, trying to make conversation because he was probably worried about her.

"It was…fine."

"Fine?" He pressed a kiss to her temple. "Talk to me,
G. I don't mind that you're quiet. But this is too quiet."

She was physically exhausted and emotionally drained.
But her thoughts kept coming back to one thing. "I don't
like being bait."

He lifted her onto his lap and tightened his arms around
her. "I don't like it, either. But—"

"It's our only shot at getting these guys—I know." Gigi
nestled her head against his shoulder. "Capturing the suspects in the act of acquiring the information they killed
Ian for is the best way to connect them to his murder."

Hud nodded. "Right now, the evidence is all circumstan-
tial. We can't get warrants to pursue specific leads until we
can name a prime suspect. Then we can break their alibi

for the time of the murder, search for weapons that match the wound and nail down the investigation."

"I know I'll be wired for sound and wearing a locator beacon in case we get separated. You and the rest of KCPD will be able to keep tabs on me. I say the code word and Keir and all your buddies will charge in to save me." She fingered the tiny button on Hud's collar. "I appreciate the logic and organization of all that. But I'm still scared."

He caught her hand and stilled its nervous twitching against his chest. "That means you're human. Being scared is what keeps your senses sharp. It's what helps you survive."

He didn't understand. "Yes, I'm worried about the danger tomorrow—the violence surrounding these two people is…cold… They seem to…enjoy it."

"But?"

Gigi wound her arm around his waist and hugged her thanks for his patience and perception with her. He *did* understand that there was more going on inside her head than fearing the danger of this operation. "I'm scared to find out who these people are. It has to be someone close to me, someone I work with—someone I trust."

"And you're wondering what other mistakes you've made about people. Who else wants to hurt you? Or use you?"

She nodded. "I thought I was making progress. But I really don't understand people at all. How am I supposed to trust my instincts about who's good and who's not when I wasn't smart enough to see the threat that was around me?"

"You know you can trust me. Right?"

She nodded. But then she found herself wondering if even that was a mistake. This man had her heart. She'd given him her body and bared her insecurities to him. But was she mistaking desire and empathy for love? Every newfound instinct said Hudson Kramer was the man for her. She didn't believe he'd harm her in any way, or that he could be a part of Ian's murder. He'd been with her during the phone calls, after all. But Ian's killer *did* have a partner.

Gigi shifted uncomfortably in Hud's lap. No. Hud wasn't a killer. He was a cop. They were partners. He was the brawn to her brains.

But the seed of doubt had been planted. Even if he wasn't part of the murder and blackmail, what if he was simply getting close to her, using her, for his investigation? What if she was as wrong about Hud as she'd been about Gary or Evgeni, Hana, or whoever was responsible for Ian's death?

"You know, I can almost hear the wheels turning when you get stuck inside your head like this." Hud gently stroked her back, stirring her from her thoughts.

Gigi squeezed her eyes shut. *Head or heart?* Which one did she trust? One had never failed her. It warned her to be cautious. The other required a huge leap of faith. *Head or heart?*

"Did you fall asleep?"

When his arms changed position, and she felt him move as though he was going to pick her up, Gigi scooted off his lap. "I don't think I can sleep tonight."

She stood so abruptly that he reached out to steady her and rose beside her. "You going to explain what's going on? Look, nothing has to happen tonight if you don't want it to." He glanced down at the sofa. "I can bunk out here if you'd be more comfortable on your own."

She needed to do something. She needed to busy her hands so she could get these horrible thoughts about the man she loved out of her head. "Do you like cobbler?" Gigi dashed to the kitchen and opened the pantry door. "I've got apples or a can of cherry pie filling."

"You're going to make me fat if you keep baking me all these goodies." He followed her into the kitchen, his eyes narrowed with a look that said he knew there was more than a sudden craving for something sweet going on here. "If you need something to take your mind off tomorrow morning, I do love cherry cobbler."

She hated this. She hated that she'd even considered doubting Hud in the first place. She hated that her logic had silenced what her heart was telling her. She'd always embraced her intellect, but now she hated it.

Suddenly, tomorrow morning didn't seem to be the most pressing problem she had.

And then she knew the answer. She knew how to regain her trust in her feelings. She spun around, stopping Hud in the middle of the kitchen. "I know how to solve Ian's formula. I can make it work." She unzipped her backpack and took out the mock-up of Ian's capacitor and set it on the table. "With a few adjustments, this will run half a city block. Do you want me to write the specifics down for you? I've even drawn a rudimentary design so you can replicate it. It would be worth millions of dollars to anyone who builds it and owns the patents."

His eyes sparked with anger, then grew surprisingly sad. "You *don't* trust me. After all we've been through…" He scraped his palm across his cheeks and jaw and muttered a curse. "No. I do not want the damn formula. I don't want you to give me anything. I am not the bad guy here."

She just offered him what the blackmailer wanted on a silver platter and he'd refused it. "Surely you can see the logic in my suspicion. You're in the perfect position to betray me. I've been blindly depending on you and falling in love, and I thought—"

"Falling in love?" He laughed, and it wasn't that sexy, manly sound she found so charming. That laugh grated with pain. "You think too damn much. Nobody's falling in love here."

"I was scared. You'd be the perfect infiltrator, the perfect weapon to use against me. You've been with me for the past forty-eight hours, going every place I go, watching everything I do. Once the idea got into my head, I had to ask." She tapped the side of her head. "I had to know up here. I'm sorry. You know I don't understand how people work."

"I thought you understood *me*. Thought you trusted me. That I'm here to protect you. That I…feel…for you. That I would never hurt you. I thought we were a team." He nodded toward the ingredients she'd set on the counter. "Go make your cobbler. This kitchen is no different than your lab—piecing together machinery, cooking up projects. Thinking about big ideas instead of dealing with real people because that's easy for you. Put your trust in your experiments, your equations, your mixing bowls. That's all you need—ideas and things. Stupid me. I was dumb enough to actually believe you needed me."

"You're not stupid. I never said—"

"It's time for me to check the perimeter of the house." He strode down the hallway. "Lock the door behind me."

"Hud." She'd hurt him by doubting him for even a moment, hurt him badly. There was no coming back from this mistake. There was no solution she could figure out on a whiteboard or her computer. "I'm sorry. I'm tired and I'm scared, and I don't know how to handle…us."

But he was out the door, walking to the front sidewalk, looking up and down the street. He walked to the fence and followed it until he disappeared by the back alley.

She was sprinkling the streusel topping on top of the cherries and cake when she heard Hud's familiar knock at the front door. She slid the baking dish into the oven and hurried to the door to let him in.

"Everything's secure. I'm going to sack out on the couch for a couple hours before we have to get to the drop-off. I'll call Keir to keep an eye on the house while I'm asleep." Once she realized that was all the conversation she was going to get tonight, she returned to the kitchen to clean up her mess. She startled when she heard his voice from the kitchen table behind her. "Have you written down the formula anywhere? Is it on a flash drive or in a file folder?"

He held the capacitor in his hand, the design that re-created Ian's failed model from this afternoon. With his arms folded across his chest, and his muscles straining against the cotton of his shirt, he made a deceptively large figure in her kitchen. The anger was gone, but the tough guy was still there. This was Hud the detective, the man who'd promised to catch a killer and keep her safe.

"I sketched some of the details on my notepad. But most of it's still in my head."

"Keep it there." He handed her the capacitor. "You're sure this thing doesn't work?"

"It'll overheat and burn up just like the one I made this afternoon."

"Good. I don't want that formula getting into the wrong hands. As long as it only exists in that crazy headspace of yours, there's no reason for them to hurt you. The minute those details are in a form they have access to, you become expendable."

Details. She couldn't help it. With the way her brain was hardwired, she just couldn't help it.

Gigi ran to the sink. She set the capacitor on the counter beside it and pushed aside the curtain to look across the driveway to the house next door. "The details aren't right."

"With your formula?"

Her brain had skipped beyond that, putting together a puzzle she hadn't realized was bugging her until this very moment. "Outside."

Hud joined her at the window, peering out into the darkness. "Did you see someone?"

That was the problem. "Miss Allan. Look at how quiet her house is." His posture bristled with wariness. His instincts were telling him something was off, too. "I come home late. She's out her door in the middle of the night in her pajamas to check on me. Her dog barks and she's out before dawn to see a possum and meet the cute new guy next door. But a car blows up in the driveway—an ambulance, the police and the KCFD come—and she doesn't even turn on a light?" Gigi hugged her arms around her waist. "Said cute guy just walked through her side yard, and—"

"I get it." Hud looped his badge around his neck and headed to the front door.

Gigi hurried after him.

"Lock the door behind me." Hud paused to squeeze her shoulder. Reassurance? A reminder to heed his instructions? "Put your shoes on. Keep your phone in your hand in case something's wrong and we need to make a quick escape. I'll check on her."

She grabbed the sleeve of his flannel shirt when he stepped out on the porch. "Are we okay?"

"Not now, Gigi." He shrugged off her grip.

Gigi. Not G. Not the silly abbreviation that sounded like *darling* or *honey* or *sweetheart* to her. They were so not okay.

It hurt to see him walking away into the shadows—to see him distancing himself when they'd gotten so close. She was the stupid one. She'd chosen her head over her heart, and that decision might well have cost her any chance she had with Hud. Her heart was paying for that mistake.

She stepped away from the door and hurried to the side window to watch Hud knock on Kelly Allan's front door. No porch light came on. No light at her bedroom window. Gigi's heart sank with a kind of dread she was becoming far too familiar with.

When Hud jogged down the front steps and hurried around to the deck behind Miss Allan's house, Gigi grabbed her tennis shoes and backpack and ran back to the kitchen to watch until Hud disappeared behind the corner of her house. She put her shoes on and stuffed the listening equipment inside her bag along with Ian's flash drive and a printout of his notes. She'd be ready to go the moment Hud told her to.

She pushed aside the curtain to watch her neighbor's house.

Why weren't any lights coming on?

She squeezed the phone in her hand. Why wasn't Hud calling?

Two bright flashes suddenly lit up the black windows of Miss Allan's kitchen. A split second later, she heard the *pop, pop* of two gunshots.

"Hud!"

A third flash revealed the silhouette of a figure with an outstretched arm, aiming at the back door. It was only a momentary glimpse, but the flare at the end of the barrel and the muffled pop of gunfire were unmistakable.

"No!" Her breath locked up in her chest. Terror squeezed her heart.

She dropped the curtain and turned away from the window. What should she do? *Think!*

She was desperate to go over there. Hud said to stay put. But he needed her. He could be hurt. Dying.

Her thumb automatically tapped 911.

Obey his orders? Take a chance?

Stick with the plan and catch a killer? Go to the man she loved?

A rapid knocking on her back door jolted her from her thoughts and she screamed.

Gigi glanced toward the front of the house and frowned. Hud always used the front door because the back door had been tampered with and was jammed shut. But the back door was closer to Miss Allan's house. If he was hurt… if he'd come to her for help… What if the shooter was in pursuit?

The harsh knock banged again.

When had she become a screamer?

Oh, hell. "Hud?"

She ran to the door. Unlatched the dead bolt. Unlocked the knob. She pulled with all her strength, jimmying the spindle from the twisted strike plate.

The moment it started to give, it took a hard shove from the other side and the door swung open.

Gigi stared into the barrel of a gun.

Chapter Thirteen

Gigi retreated as the curvy figure, dressed in black, with a black stocking mask hiding the woman's face and hair, walked in, pointing the gun squarely at Gigi's heart.

"Stop." Even slightly winded, Gigi knew that voice. "Did you call the police?"

Had she completed the call? Was anybody listening in? She'd been so worried about Hud.

When she glanced down to see, the woman ripped Gigi's cell from her hand and threw it to the floor, crushing the screen beneath the heel of her boot before kicking it away.

"Why are you doing this, Doris?"

"Because you and your boyfriend have a trap planned for us. Who knew you had a backbone and wouldn't do as you were told? Change of plans. I'm not feeling six a.m. anymore. We're meeting right now." When Gigi continued backing away from the gun, Doris Lombard's arm snaked out to grab her, crushing five bruises into Gigi's upper arm, and a sixth one against her breast as she shoved the barrel of the gun into her chest. "Where is the formula?"

"There." She nodded toward the peninsula counter, not wanting to take her eyes off the gun or Doris's cold blue eyes. "In my backpack. Where's Hud? Is he dead?"

"My partner is dealing with him. I can handle you all

by myself." Doris pinned her against the counter with her gun while she pulled the backpack toward her and unzipped it. "Did you make the corrections?"

Gigi wasn't surprised to hear the question. "You knew it wouldn't work. You gave me Ian's notes so I could fix the equation. So you could build a working capacitor and sell it or the plans to someone on the black market."

"Damn cop caught a piece of me." A second, taller figure, also dressed in black from head to toe, pushed his way in through the back door. He was tall, panting hard, clasping a gloved hand over his left shoulder, and annoyingly familiar. "Did you get it?"

Doris picked up the backpack. "She says it's in here."

"What did you do to Hud, Gary?" Gigi demanded.

Gary Haack glared down at her through the holes in his stocking mask. He tucked the gun he carried into his belt before turning over her backpack and dumping the contents onto the counter beside her. "Being too smart will get you killed this time, Professor Know-It-All."

"I don't have to be smart," she argued. "I could smell your noxious cologne all the way across the room."

Doris's gun pressed hard enough for Gigi to flinch. "She knows who we are. I told you we'd have to kill them both."

Tears stung Gigi's eyes. She blinked them away to keep her enemies in sight. "Hud is dead?"

"Two bullets will do that to a man," Gary joked. "He went down hard after that second shot." When he saw the tear trailing down her cheek, he reached over and traced it with his gloved fingertip. "Ahh, isn't that sweet. I thought maybe you didn't like men since you kept turning me down. But you really care about that cop." Gigi shied away from his repulsive caress. But she didn't get far because she bumped into Doris's gun on the other side.

The older blonde had peeled off her mask, giving Gigi

a clear look at the displeasure curling her lips. "I'm going to hate killing you, Virginia. You were the only woman I ever trusted with Ian. I'll do you a favor and make it quick."

"Easy, babe," Gary warned. "You got a taste for blood when Ian backed out of our deal." Since his identity was no longer a secret, either, and they didn't intend to leave her alive to tell anyone, Gary pushed his stocking mask up onto his forehead. With one arm hanging uselessly down at his side, he reached for the bag he carried on his back, grimacing as he set it on the counter beside Gigi. He pulled out a small laptop and opened it. "We have to make sure she fixed the errors that Ian refused to. Let me have a look."

Was Gary smart enough to see the discrepancies in Ian's formula? Would fooling him by changing numbers and variables buy her a few more minutes of life? Was there any way she could escape these two greedy, vindictive murderers and make her way over to Miss Allan's house to see if Hud was still alive? To see if she could save him? If there was any chance she could tell him how grateful she was to him for coming into her life and teaching her about love?

"What about Miss Allan? Did you kill her, too?"

"Shut up," Gary muttered, rummaging through her things until he found the flash drive from Ian's safe. "Is this the formula?"

Gigi nodded.

"Which one?"

She gave him the file number and encryption code she'd added this afternoon at the lab. While he waited for the file to load, he picked up one of her notepads and skimmed through the diagrams she'd drawn. Hud had been right. The real formula would be in Gary's and Doris's hands right now if she'd written it down. But would Gary recognize the fake? Her glasses were fogging up with the heat of her tears, but she left them in place to mask the uncertainty in her eyes.

He tossed the pad aside as the file came up and he scrolled through it. "Oh, Gigi, Gigi, Gigi."

You know you can't play me like this. Where is the real formula?

She held her breath, expecting to hear the words, but they never came. Instead, he shut down the laptop and pocketed the drive. "Miss Allan invited us into her house and served us iced tea yesterday when we told her we were friends of yours and were concerned for your safety. Didn't recognize me from Friday night. Then that yappy dog of hers decided he didn't like me and wouldn't shut up. Made her suspicious. She tried to fight with me when I refused to leave. When I shoved her away, she hit her head on the counter."

A little more hope squeezed out of Gigi's heart. "You could have called an ambulance."

"Oh, wise up." He slung the bag over his shoulder. "Do you know how much the Lukin dissidents will pay for this? How much I can make once I put my name on the design and sell it? There's too much money at stake here—too much satisfaction at besting you and Lombard both—for me to have any regrets now."

"So you killed Ian for the money and professional jealousy. And you...?" She turned to Doris.

The older woman was getting antsy about chitchatting, but she seemed pleased to share her motive for murder. "All those years Ian cheated on me, and that rat threatened to divorce me when he discovered my affair with Gary. Told me he'd rather destroy his formula than make the millions he promised so that I couldn't get a dime of it." Doris's nostrils flared as she drew in a breath, savoring it as if she was inhaling an intoxicating memory. "I stabbed him again and again, once for every woman I knew about."

Gigi supposed she should feel affronted that Gary had continually hit on her and even talked marriage while he was bedding his boss's wife. But frankly, she was glad she'd paid attention to the icky vibe she got off him and had steered clear of that relationship. Or maybe she should be sickened by Doris's lust for violent revenge.

Instead, she was focusing on the details. Analyzing the room and slyly studying the nuances of her captors, wondering if she had any chance of living through this, of seeing her sister again, of telling the police everything they'd just confessed to her. She wanted to go to Hud's funeral, to honor him, to thank him. She wanted to celebrate Kelly Allan's life, and Ian Lombard's. "How are you going to explain away all the dead bodies?"

"Why you, my dear." Gary packed up her notepads with his laptop and pulled his gun from his belt. "Brilliant scientist. Embarrassing social skills. Hold her," he said to Doris. The blonde moved her gun to Gigi's temple and grabbed her right wrist, forcing her arm up. Gary shoved his gun—the gun he'd used to shoot Hud—into her hand. Doris squeezed Gigi's fingers around the grip, leaving a set of fingerprints on it, before Gary pulled the gun away. He shoved her belongings into her backpack, along with the gun. "It will be easy to paint a picture of you cracking under the pressure to compete and achieve."

"I'm working with the police. They'll know that's a lie."

"Will they?" Doris joined the conversation. "Who did Ian trust with his secrets? Who took his formula and designs from the safe at my house?"

"Who left the Lukin reception early to meet Ian in his office?" Gary taunted. "I followed you out of the hotel. Would have offered you a lift, but I had other plans."

"That's not what happened. He left to meet with…" She looked at Doris's smiling face. "You."

"You were right, darling," Doris cooed, reaching up to brush a lock of hair off Gary's forehead, all without moving the gun aimed at Gigi's head. "She *is* a smart girl."

"You came back from your trip early," Gigi surmised. "Arranged some kind of late-night rendezvous with your husband. You both like the same whiskey. I bet you brought your own bottle. Drugged Jerome with your motion-sickness medication so he'd be passed out when the power went off in the lab." She glanced up at Gary, feeling her tears drying up and a whole lot of anger taking their place. Interesting how embracing her emotions could clear her head of debilitating thoughts and allow the details she needed to see to come into focus. "Nice job with that. Sneaking into Ian's office and programming the blackout."

"Your word against ours. And you'll be dead. The dissidents weren't happy you reneged on your deal with them."

The timer dinged on the oven, diverting Doris's and Gary's attention momentarily. "My cobbler is done." She touched the barrel of Doris's gun and nudged it aside. There were three college professors in this room, but only one of them was truly observant. "If you don't mind, I'd like to take it out of the oven. I'd hate for the house to burn down. It will be the only thing I have to leave my sister after I'm gone."

Gigi stepped away from the two of them. She needed to do this quickly before either of them got past the non sequitur of baking dessert when they'd been talking murder.

Keeping her back to Doris and Gary, she reached across the counter to pick up her oven mitts. As she pulled them on, she picked up the faulty capacitor and opened the oven door. She set the device inside, pulled out the baking dish and cranked the heat as high as it would go.

"What are you doing?" Doris reacted first. She grabbed a hunk of Gigi's hair and pulled her backward.

Gigi kept hold of the hot baking dish and swung around, smashing it in Doris's face. The glass shattered and the hot filling bubbled onto her skin and she recoiled, screaming.

"Doris!"

The ruthless blonde dropped her gun as she sank to her knees, cradling her burnt, battered face and moaning. Gigi snatched the mixing bowl off the counter and hurled it at Gary, forcing him to duck while she dived after Doris's gun.

But she'd miscalculated Gary's reach and her own clumsiness in shedding the oven mitts to pick up the weapon. He grabbed her by the neck and hauled her to her feet, kicking Doris's gun beyond her reach as he lifted her onto her toes.

"You think you're so damn clever?"

Gigi clawed at his hand, gasping for air, feeling the bones in her neck contract. He threw her against the stove, never loosing his one-handed grip on her—jarring her body, reminding her of the oven's rising heat.

"You don't get to win this time," he spat in her face, hurling her into the cabinets, cracking her elbow against the countertop and knocking utensils and measuring cups to the floor. She punched at the wound on his shoulder, but she was losing strength, losing consciousness. He slammed her onto the countertop, using his superior height to put even more pressure on her neck. She twisted, kicked. But her eyes were drifting out of focus. She opened her mouth, but no air seeped through his crushing grip. "Ian treated you like a goddess. Like you were the only one of us who mattered. His prize. I hate everything about you."

"Get your damn hands off her."

Hud's deep, drawling voice was pure predator.

His appearance at the back door was an unwelcome

surprise to Gary. His stranglehold on her neck loosened. Air rushed into Gigi's lungs as joy rushed into her heart.

"Hud?" she croaked, her throat raw, her world spinning.

Gary turned as five feet eight inches of coiled dynamite launched himself. Hud hit the bigger man square in the stomach, folding him in half and knocking him off his feet. The two men landed hard. Her ears filled with thuds of fists against bone and grunts for breath and curses of pain.

"Hud?" Her body was bruised, every breath a raspy scratch through her throat. But oxygen was filling her lungs and her strength was returning. "Thank God... Not dead..."

Gary kicked Hud off him and Hud tripped over Doris's huddled form as she tried to crawl away from the fight. Then Gary was on top of him, hitting him in the gut.

"Hud!"

He howled in pain. Her relief at seeing him alive quickly waned when she saw the blood soaking his shirt and rolling down the side of his face. She swung her legs off the counter, wobbling when her feet hit the floor. *Two bullets will do that to a man.* The man she loved had been shot twice and left for dead. But he wasn't dead. Hudson Kramer was strong. He was a fighter. He was a miracle. He'd saved her life, just like he promised.

He was on top of Gary now, his meaty fist breaking Gary's glasses with one blow. But he was so pale. So hurt.

He needed her help. Where was Hud's gun? Doris's gun? Gary's?

Her bag. It had been knocked to the floor in her struggle with Gary. But if she could reach it... She shoved Doris out of the way and...froze.

Her nose stung with the acrid smell of burning chemicals. Oh, hell. The oven. They needed to be on the other side of that peninsula. Now. "Hud!"

Doris staggered to her feet, holding the edge of the sink so she could stand.

Gigi spotted the white-hot glow through the oven door. "Hud!" She grabbed him by the shirt collar and dragged him off Gary. She pushed him toward the kitchen table and dove on top of him, crashing to the floor behind stools and cabinets. She wrapped her arms around his shoulders and rolled away from the open part of the kitchen as the oven exploded.

There was a whoosh like a freight train flying past and a horrible shriek. Glass shattered and shards of metal bit through wood cabinets.

"I've got you," she whispered against his ear as shrapnel rained down around them.

When the last of the debris had settled, Gigi pushed herself off Hud's chest. She heard moaning from the other side of the peninsula. People needed medical attention. She had to find a phone and call for help.

She realized that Hud's hands had latched on to her waist, holding on to her as tightly as she'd held on to him. His golden eyes searched her face with a fierce expression she didn't quite comprehend. "You...one piece?"

She nodded.

He was breathing irregularly, and she could feel the warmth of his blood soaking into her clothes from his wound. She was so afraid he was dying. She was so grateful he'd come back to her. There were far too many words that needed to be said.

So, she lowered her head and kissed him.

Then she pushed to her feet to see the damage that she'd done. Hud caught her hand and she helped him to his feet. "Need my gun." Between her and the counter, he braced himself and followed her around the peninsula. "Pretty boy took it off me."

"It's in my bag." She stooped down to retrieve it. "How badly are you hurt?"

"Not so bad I can't do my job." Hud checked the weapon before snapping it in the holster on his belt. "Help me with pretty boy."

Doris, who'd been hit by the oven door when it blasted off, was out cold. Hud picked up her weapon and tucked it into the back of his belt. Gary moaned from shrapnel cuts and his shoulder wound as Hud pulled his arms behind his back and cuffed him.

Then Hud sat, leaning back against her gouged and broken cabinets while Gigi grabbed two towels to stanch his wounds. He grimaced as she applied pressure to the hole in his side and the graze at the side of his head. His breathing was still off, his skin dotted with clammy perspiration. But his eyes locked on to hers as he took over holding the towel to his head wound. He nodded toward the oven. "What the hell was that?"

"Physics."

With his free hand, he pulled her to him to plant a hard, fast kiss to her lips. "Bless that beautiful brain of yours."

Gigi breathed a sigh of relief when she heard the first siren. It grew louder as the sounds of other emergency vehicles joined it.

"I called Keir before I stumbled over here. Cavalry's coming." He touched a finger to the point of her chin, asking for attention to his words, not his wounds. "What happened earlier. I overreacted. With my track record… We'll figure it out."

Hope blossomed with that promise. "I'm good at figuring out problems."

"Yes, you are."

"I'm sorry I doubted you. I was afraid I'd never get the chance to tell you I was wrong. I never meant to hurt you." Her sinuses burned as she held back tears. She was a one-man woman, and she'd nearly lost her chance with this brave wonderful man. "Gary said you were dead."

"Yeah. Well, thank God he's as bad a shot as he is boyfriend material." He glanced toward the graze that had mowed through his spiky hair. "This supposed kill shot was like a blow to the head. Knocked me out for a few minutes."

"Welcome to the concussion club."

He started to laugh but cursed instead. "Don't be tellin' jokes, G. I think this one—" he touched the towel she held at his waist "—is going to need some surgery."

She burst into tears.

"Hey." He caught the first tear with the pad of his thumb and wiped it away. He caught the next one, and the next as her glasses fogged up and the tears rolled freely down her cheeks. "What's this?"

"You called me G."

AT 6:01 A.M. the next day, Gigi knocked on the door to Hud's room at Saint Luke's Hospital.

Doris Lombard was under close guard in the ICU. Gary Haack had been stitched up and locked away in a holding cell until his arraignment. Tammy was at home with an off-duty Albert Logan, dog sitting Izzy, who was missing her late owner. Gigi's injuries were minor, although she felt beat-up and had been instructed to keep talking to a minimum until her throat had healed. She'd written a long statement about everything Gary and Doris had confessed and explained why she'd set off a makeshift bomb in her kitchen.

Then Keir had driven her back to the hospital himself, kissed her cheek and wished her luck.

Luck?

You're the first woman Hud's been with who I think is worthy of him. He loves you, Gigi. Go get him.

This was the going and getting.

Only, she wasn't exactly sure how she was supposed to do this.

"Come in."

Hud was awake. She'd been hoping she could watch him sleep for a while. Give herself more time to think.

"G, I know it's you. Keir texted me." He chuckled softly. "And you're the only one who'd hesitate to come see me." She stepped around the curtain and caught her breath as she found him sitting up against a stack of pillows on the bed. He needed a shave, but, other than the bruising around his left eye, the healthy color of his skin had returned. He had a bandage on his head, an IV in his hand and a blue hospital gown stretched tautly across his shoulders and chest. "I'm sorry I ever gave you reason to."

Head or heart?

Gigi's pulse quickened, but she knew the answer.

He'd come through surgery just fine, had received a blood transfusion and antibiotics and was expected to make a full recovery. Still, she wasn't sure if she could touch him yet, if she *should* touch him.

She stuck her hands in the pockets of her sweater, instead. "I've been thinking about us."

"Uh-oh."

She moved closer as the words tumbled out. "We don't need to have a lot in common to have a relationship. We complement each other. We balance each other's strengths. And when it comes right down to it, we do have some very important things in common—we're both good at our jobs, we love our families. Damn it, Hud, you wear your heart on your sleeve and I want to protect that. I didn't even understand what my heart was feeling until you showed me. And I…"

He pulled her hand from her pocket, and the familiar touch sent a tiny jolt of electricity through her, shorting out her nerves and leaving her with the clarity she needed to make sense.

Gigi turned her fingers into his palm, linking them together. "I'm sorry I ever doubted you, even for a moment. I don't want you just to make me feel safe. I want you to make me laugh. I want you to eat my cookies and bring me out of my shell and listen when I don't make sense to anybody else. I want you to help me understand my strength and believe in your own and never doubt that brains and brawn make an unbeatable team. I want you to kiss me every day and burn up my sheets at night. Or in the morning or whenever you decide you can't keep your hands off me. Because I want to put my hands on you, too. I want you to love me… Because I love you."

Hud tugged her onto the bed and pulled Gigi into his arms. "Works for me."

* * * * *

COLTON COWBOY JEOPARDY

REGAN BLACK

With special thanks to all of the authors in *The Coltons of Mustang Valley* world. It was an honor and delight to take this journey with you.

Chapter One

"Pick up, pick up," she chanted under her breath while the phone continued to ring, unanswered. Today was supposed to mark the start of her new career as Mia Graves, real-estate agent. Instead of an easy-breezy morning preparing her first listing, she'd been plunged into a nightmare. They hadn't covered anything like this in her classes or on the state exam.

Her palms were slick on the steering wheel and she kept checking her rearview mirror as she drove back into Mustang Valley proper. She didn't think she was being followed. At least she didn't see any familiar vehicles back there. Yet. Her stomach cramped. This could *not* be happening.

The call went to voice mail and she used the hands-free option to end the call. Before she could redial, an incoming call came through. As she recognized the number, another surge of panic chilled her skin. She declined the call and tried the babysitter again.

At last Tamara picked up. "It's Mia," she said, unable to suppress the quake in her voice. "I'll be there in five minutes. Please have Silas ready to go."

Please let Silas still be there. Surely, Tamara wouldn't have let him go home with anyone else.

"Of course. I just put him down for a nap."

My son is safe.

"The first morning away is always the biggest hurdle," Tamara continued in her unflappable way. "Are you okay, Mia?"

"Yes. Yes, I'm fine." With Tamara's soothing voice filling the car, she reclaimed a measure of her composure. Tamara and Mia's mother Dalinda had been as close as sisters, and Mia had always called her Aunt Tammie. When she'd felt overwhelmed and uncertain about childcare options for her new baby boy, Tamara had volunteered to help.

"Just frazzled. A friend invited me to lunch and if it goes well, I might just land a new client," she improvised. "That brings the tally to two."

"How exciting!"

"Yes," Mia agreed, checking her rearview mirror once more. "My friend specifically asked me to bring the baby along."

"Well, he's better than a business card, isn't he?" Tamara chuckled. "I have his things all set for you."

"You're a dream, Aunt Tammie. Thank you."

"Don't be silly. You're more than welcome to leave that angel with me anytime. Will I get to spoil him silly tomorrow, too?"

"I'll, ah, be working from home tomorrow," she said. Tamara knew her well enough to see right through a blatant lie. She would work from home, just as soon as she figured out where home would be for the next several days. "See you in a minute," she said, ending the call quickly.

Becoming an independent real-estate agent was supposed to be the ideal, no-brainer and no-limit career decision. She and her father had discussed several options before she'd started her classes. Establishing a base close to home would be better than the extensive travel demanded by her previous work as the manager of her ex-husband's charitable foundation. Setting her own hours gave her the most flexibility as a single mother and she'd happily daydreamed about days when her son could join her on occasional appointments.

Tears stung Mia's eyes as a foreign, desperate fear chased her to Tamara's neighborhood. Until today, she would have summed up her eight weeks of motherhood as pure joy offset by exhaustion and sharp spikes of worry. What she'd discovered today and the potential fallout reclassified those worries as trivial.

Today had been a test run for her. Her first hours apart from Silas since giving birth should have been a bit of an emotional challenge, not a harrowing ordeal. Resentment shot through her that once again her stepmother, Regina Graves, had ruined a good thing and thrown her life into turmoil.

Mia pulled into the drive and parked the car. Although her heart raced with urgency, she flipped down the visor and checked her reflection in the mirror. If anyone thought to ask Tamara about Mia's appearance and demeanor today, she wanted her aunt to report that she'd been calm and steady. Unfortunately, she was pale and a bit wild-eyed. Understandable after the vile threats Regina had made against her child, but it would cause Tamara worry and raise questions she couldn't begin to answer.

Reaching into her purse for her cosmetics bag, she applied a bit of highlighter at the corners of her eyes and a fresh layer of lip gloss. Maybe Tamara would blame the obvious signs of anxiety on her first day away from her baby boy.

She stepped out of the car and walked up the path to the front door. Tamara threw open the door, and seeing that loving, vibrant face almost brought Mia to her knees. She steeled herself. Silas needed her to be strong. Stronger than the threats aimed at him. His arrival had turned the past two months into the best two months of her life. She wouldn't relinquish that without a fight, no matter what her stepmother tried to do.

"Oh, my girl." Tamara pulled her into a hug. "The first time out is the worst."

"It is." Mia let herself rest for just a moment on that sturdy shoulder, soaking up the heartfelt support. Who knew how long it would be before she'd have anyone's support again?

Tamara beamed and released her so Mia could come inside. "At least your first client is a pleasure, right? It was so good of your father to let you list and sell his house in the country." She studied Mia closely. "Did going there today stir up memories? Your mother loved that house."

"She did," Mia agreed. "All good memories," she added because it was expected. And until an hour ago, it was true. All the memories of the country house had been wonderful, from her early childhood to weekends with girlfriends and, eventually, holiday gatherings as a married woman.

"I'd love to stay and tell you everything about this morning," she said. "But I need to be on time for that lunch meeting." She picked up the diaper bag Tamara had set in the foyer. "Thank you again."

"Everything is right there," Tamara said. "I'll go tuck him into his car seat."

"I'll come along," she murmured, gently closing the door. No sense making it easy if Regina had followed her.

Tamara smiled indulgently. "Ah, little mother. Nothing will do but to see him with your own eyes."

She nodded, her lips clamped together too tightly to speak as she followed the older woman down the hallway.

Tamara urged her to go on into the bedroom first. There in the portable crib, her tiny son slept, a vision of contentment. She watched his chest rise and fall and silently vowed to make sure he stayed safe. She stroked his soft cheek, followed the whorl of his curly dark hair as she listened to his soft breath. Lifting him gently, she snuggled him close before she buckled him into the car seat. He stretched his legs but didn't wake.

Mia wanted to take the portable crib, but doing so would raise more questions and concerns. She'd make do or buy a new one at some point. She picked up Silas and reached for the diaper bag, but Tamara insisted on carrying it to the car for her. Mia swallowed the protest. If Regina or anyone else had caught up with her, it would be better to have another witness to any trouble.

"Thank you again," Mia said at the car. After securing the seat, she closed the door and gave Tamara one more hug, praying it wouldn't be the last.

With Silas snoozing in the back seat, she had a renewed sense of calm as she drove away. From the moment the pregnancy test showed positive, her life had come into crystal clear focus. Her son was her singular priority and she wouldn't allow anyone or anything to hurt him, no matter what changes or precautions were required. She'd divorced, moved and launched herself into a new career. During her last trimester, she'd survived the helplessness and terror of the earthquake that rocked Mustang Valley. Her commitment wouldn't falter now.

Breathing easier as she left the neighborhood without another incident or threatening call, she turned her mind to logistics. Since she was currently staying at her father's house, she couldn't go home and she didn't dare call or drop in on him. Norton Graves had a mile-wide blind spot when it came to his second wife. He would never believe that Regina had threatened violence against his daughter and grandson.

Where did that leave her? She needed clothing for her and Silas, as well as cash and baby supplies. And then she needed a place to lie low while she decided what to do with the incriminating secrets she'd uncovered today.

She reached for the radio, turning on a soothing station for the baby. A few minutes later, an incoming call interrupted the music. The caller ID announced her father's name. Wary about what Regina might have told him, she used the button on the steering wheel to answer.

"Hi, sweetie," he said, sounding as jovial as ever. Maybe Regina hadn't filled his head with more lies yet. "How did it go at the house?"

"Great," she replied brightly. "Tamara said Silas was an angel." There, she hadn't lied to her dad.

"I had no doubts. How are you feeling? Your mother found it hard to leave you the first few times."

"I survived." Another truth. "It was an experience," she said. "Knowing he was with Tamara helped."

Her father chortled. "Tamara was the one who watched you for us so Dalinda and I could have a nice dinner."

"Life just keeps circling, doesn't it?" Her father rarely spoke about her mother, and never when Regina was within earshot. This was her chance to tell him what she'd seen, even if she couldn't show him the video yet, before her stepmother twisted the story against her.

"That it does." He cleared his throat. "One second. Come in. Mia? Regina's here. I'm putting you on speaker."

"Hello, Mia! How are you and the baby?"

She winced at her stepmother's overbright greeting. "Doing great, thanks." Her window of opportunity had slammed shut.

"We're both eager to hear when you'll get the listing up," her dad said.

Her father always knew how to pile on the pressure, but when it came to work, she normally thrived. He'd entrusted her with the sale of the country house—probably because Regina wanted to buy something bigger and newer—and she wouldn't let him down. "I'm not sure when the listing will go live," she said. Although she hated lying to him, it was the best of her options. "I might actually have a private buyer interested in the property."

"Already?"

"Might," she repeated. Taking a page from Regina's book, she put a sharp sparkle into her voice. "I mentioned the property to a few friends and apparently the word is out."

"That's fantastic news. For both of us. All of us," he amended quickly. "You should see the smile on my bride's face."

Bride, shark—when referring to her stepmother, the words were interchangeable in Mia's mind. "Super. I'll keep you posted," she promised. "Love you."

She ended the call and a rush of angry tears spilled down her cheeks. Would it ever be safe to see her father again?

Jarvis Colton adjusted the angle of his hat against the afternoon sunshine flooding the Rattlesnake Ridge Ranch. He'd been riding fence all day on the Triple R, a task that was often met with little enthusiasm.

Jarvis loved it. No one was more shocked by that revelation than him. He'd left a career as a management consultant—the suits, air-conditioned offices, deals over drinks and conference calls—to come out here and be a cowboy. A dark T-shirt, jeans, boots and his horse completed his new workplace uniform.

His brother and sister, Spencer and Isabella, still scolded him about this decision and he wished he could find the words to make them understand. If they ever joined him for moments like this, they might get it. As triplets, they were close, and when life had thrown them one challenge after another, Spencer and Bella were the only people he really trusted.

His siblings labeled his professional detour an emotional crisis and blamed his choice to store his belongings and walk away from a great condo and a lucrative career on bitterness and fantasy. They weren't entirely wrong. He could almost imagine that Spencer, a sergeant with the Mustang Valley Police Department, was expecting him to sabotage the ranch owned by Payne Colton, a man who had practically refused to claim any blood ties to the triplets. The next generation of Coltons—Payne's children—was closer to Jarvis and his siblings.

Jarvis couldn't deny the temptation. Payne, in addition to building the Triple R into one of the most prosperous cattle ranches in Arizona, also served as chairman of the board for Colton Oil. The family patriarch was charismatic and tough, and had ensured that his children would prosper for generations to come, while Jarvis and his siblings had been effectively cut out of the Colton family tree.

But when Jarvis traded his suits and office for barns and fields and long, hard-labor days, he'd done it with the sole intention of finding proof that the Triple R rightfully belonged to the triplets. At least the section of acreage he was crossing now.

Granted, the ranch foreman, Payne's son Asher Colton, didn't know Jarvis's motives, but he'd hired him, anyway. Jarvis had been pleasantly surprised to find his cousin was a fair boss and didn't treat him with any of Payne's dismissiveness or negligent animosity.

Working out here, Jarvis had soon discovered what his life had been missing. Cause and effect. Effort and reward. In business, his decisions didn't always yield an immediate result. While he knew the value of patience, he enjoyed the relatively quick confirmation of making decisions out here. There were short-term goals and long-range plans, but the day-to-day work made a clear and obvious impact.

And once the daily work was complete, Jarvis used his personal time to search for confirmation of the story their grandfather, Isaiah Colton, had told him when it had been just the two of them out fishing. Jarvis had never forgotten how special and important he'd felt when his granddad made him promise not to tell a soul, not even his siblings. According to Isaiah, back in the 1800s, the Triple R had been stolen from their branch of the Colton family tree, forever changing the family fortunes. Five years ago, just before he died, Isaiah had brought it up again, claiming the proof of that treachery was buried out here on the ranch.

Jarvis couldn't let the idea go. Especially not after the recent uproar within the Colton Oil side of the family. If there was any truth that Payne's oldest son, Ace, had been switched at birth, maybe Isaiah's story wasn't so far-fetched. So Jarvis gladly rode fences, not just for the protection of the cattle and preservation of the operation, but for himself, scoping out likely places to prove his grandfather had it right after all.

Based on everything he'd heard and his research into the history of Mustang Valley, he'd mentally earmarked this particular area. Now, finished with the official task of repairing any weak or broken fencing, he rode toward the place he wanted to dig. As he followed an overgrown trail, anticipation zipped through his bloodstream. Assuming Payne woke from his coma, Jarvis imagined the expression on Payne's face in court, hearing his precious land belonged to Jarvis, Spencer and Bella, and that he wasn't the wealthiest landowner in Mustang Valley anymore. How many times had Payne ignored their existence, claiming they shared a last name by accident rather than any true family connection?

If Isaiah was right, the change might shake up things in Mustang Valley more than the earthquake had a few months back. Of course, it was a long shot and a crazy notion, and it was unlikely such a scene would ever happen. But it was fun to think about. What if he actually found a deed or some other evidence his grandfather was sure had been buried out here generations ago?

Dropping out of the saddle, he gathered the reins in one hand and walked closer to where he wanted to dig today. Since setting himself on this path, he'd spent hours researching newspaper articles and photographs from four generations ago up through present day. With a landscape as picturesque as the Triple R and all the publicity surrounding Payne and his family lately, photographers were out here all the time.

He marked his position using a variation of a geocaching app on his cell phone and then started digging. Within minutes he was sweating through his shirt. Expecting anything less in Arizona this time of year would be foolish. Still, he didn't miss the cool air of a climate-controlled office. This effort, for the ranch, for his grandfather's pride, felt empowering and right, whether or not he found anything.

That was the piece no one else understood. Just looking for the truth filled him with a sense of purpose and honor. Isaiah, for all his faults, had been good to the three of them, and just about the only person in town who attempted to love them after their parents died. Due to Isaiah's well-known drinking habit, family court shuffled them off to the care of their bitter old Aunt Amelia. He owed Isaiah for trying to give them a foundation, a sense of their roots in the midst of grief and upheaval.

He pushed his hat back and wiped his brow, then cut into the earth again. A metal detector would make the job easier, but a shovel didn't need an explanation. As he used his foot for more pressure, the shovel squeaked. He thought he'd hit something. He paused, wiggling the shovel out and back in again. Silence this time. By touch, there was nothing but the hard-packed Arizona soil. He waited, listening again for the sound. When it came, he swore it sounded like a baby crying.

Raised in town, Jarvis hadn't worked the land his entire life. Over the past year he'd learned a great deal about the various wild animals and habitats in the area. Seemed early in the day for a coyote, but he supposed a mockingbird might manage that sound. He looked to his horse as the next rising cry carried on the air. The gelding merely flicked his ears, either at the high-pitched sound or a fly buzzing too close.

The sound faded and Jarvis resumed his digging. Whatever was making that sound, he couldn't waste this window of opportunity chasing it down. Unlike life in the office setting, he had to search when he had the chance. Work on a ranch could be calm one day and chaos the next. Personally, he enjoyed the unpredictability, the variety, even the long hours. As one of the hands, he might ride fence today and work on repairs around the property for the next month.

When it was clear the metal box his grandfather described wasn't in this hole, Jarvis made a note and started filling it in. With the sun sinking toward the horizon, he'd about given up on this location when he heard the sound again.

This time he was certain that wasn't a random animal. Not even mockingbirds could sustain that long, unhappy wail. If he had to guess, he'd say it was a baby, but what in the world would a baby be doing all the way out here? He tied the shovel to the pack behind his saddle and swung up onto his horse. Moving slowly, he followed the sound.

As he closed in on the sound, he couldn't reconcile the crying with the remote and rugged terrain, and yet it was the only logical conclusion. The pitiful wails drew him farther along the old trail to one of the warming huts built generations ago so cowboys could take shelter from bitter, cold weather.

"Hello?" Jarvis called out. The crying sound came again. "Everyone okay?" The last thing he wanted was to walk into trouble. He hopped out of the saddle, looping the reins around the lower branch of a tree that crowded the small rustic cabin. He was close enough now to hear someone trying to hush the baby, to no avail. "Do you need—"

"Stay back!"

He heeded the warning, stopping short as a woman stepped out of the hut. She held a sturdy stick like she was a major-league batter ready to hit a home run, using his head as the baseball. In the shadows behind her, a tiny child with big lungs wailed miserably from a carrier of some sort.

Jarvis held up his hands. "Take it easy." He used the tone he'd learned worked best with spooked horses. "How can I help?"

"You can't." She stepped forward, her grip tight on that stick. "Get out of here."

"I'm no threat." She was tall with gorgeous, light

brown skin, generous curves and defensiveness oozing from every pore, with or without the threat of violence. "I'm only here because of the crying. It's not a
sound we hear out this way."

"We?" Her dark eyes went wide and her gaze skit-
tered across the area behind him. "Who is with you?"

"No one. No one," he assured her. "Just me and my
horse." He held his hands out from his sides, palms
open. Something worse than the fear of being caught
squatting on Colton land had her wild-eyed. "I'm a
hand here at the Triple R. Did you know you were on a
working ranch? I was riding by, checking fences. How
did you find this place?"

She shook her head, stick still held high, the baby
still protesting.

"Show me some ID," she demanded.

"Okay, sure. Should've thought of that." He reached
for his back pocket with slow, deliberate motions. "Just
reaching for my wallet." He held it out and inched forward.

"Stay back!" He froze. "Toss it to me."

He obeyed and the square of leather landed close
to her feet. "Do you need some cash? Help yourself."

She glared at him, dark eyebrows snapping together.
"I don't need your money."

Great, now he'd insulted the woman holding the
weapon. What else was he supposed to think? Who
would bring a baby out here if they could afford better options?

He took a visual inventory while she flipped through
his wallet. Her dark hair was pulled up high in a messy
knot, a testament to the heat, he figured. She wore a
dress in sunset hues that hugged her lavish curves, the

soft fabric flowing over her body. Her face looked familiar, but he couldn't place her. She wasn't a woman he would've forgotten if they had met before.

"How about you put the stick down and take care of the baby? Is it a boy or a girl?"

"Boy." Her gaze darted between his identification to his face a time or two. "Jarvis Colton? This says you live here in town."

"Yes."

Her brow pleated over her straight nose. "I've never heard of you."

Why would she? No one had heard of Jarvis or his siblings. They'd never run in the same social circles as their wealthier cousins.

"If you're really one of the Coltons, why are you all the way out here riding fences?"

The judgment was loud and clear as her gaze skated over him. "It's my job. If we don't keep up with the maintenance, the cattle tend to wander off." Did she need to see the dirt under his fingernails or the calluses on his palms? He struggled to keep his cool. This woman was frightened. Though the tone was similar, she wasn't his sister, lecturing him on giving up his "silly cowboy quest."

No, this woman made him feel like stepping up, the proverbial hero riding to the rescue on a white stallion to protect her from the world.

The outrageous fantasy rocked him. First, the horse with him today was Duke, an average, hardworking chestnut gelding. Plus, Jarvis wasn't built for that kind of heroism. The only family he needed or wanted were his brother and sister. He took a step closer, despite his certainty that she would knock his head off if given the chance.

"I'm no threat," he promised. "Why not get him settled down and then we can talk. I can keep watch for you."

She opened her mouth just as the baby's cry changed, going from that high-pitched squeal to a wet gulp. She immediately dropped the stick and his wallet to tend to the child.

Jarvis picked up the discarded items, pocketing his wallet and leaning her stick against the open door of the small cabin. He hovered in the doorway, to keep watch and prevent scaring her further.

Her touch calmed the baby straightaway and the maternal, soothing croons lifted faded memories to the top of his mind. It had been years since he'd thought about his mother's warm voice and gentle hands. The soup and crackers and comic books she'd brought to him when he had a cold or sore throat.

"Your son?" he asked unnecessarily.

"Yes." She angled away from him, and a moment later the only sound in the cabin was the baby's muted suckling.

Jarvis studied every inch of the cabin, keeping his gaze well away from the nursing mother. It was so intimate and strange and he was intruding, an interloper of the worst kind. Leaving wasn't an option, though it was clear she'd rather he disappear. She and her son were vulnerable out here. He couldn't walk away without doing something.

"You know my name," he said. "Will you tell me yours?"

"Mia," she said. "This is Silas. He just turned two months old."

She shot him a cool glance over her shoulder and he remembered where he'd seen her. Magazines, catalogs and the stunning swimsuit editions. The first time he'd seen her in one of those, she'd posed near a rocky out-cropping with her hair loose around her shoulders and her showstopping curves showcased in a coral bikini. Water swirled around her knees and beaded on that marvelously smooth skin. His gaze skimmed over her body, filling in details he remembered. Was the tattoo on her left hip real or had it been added in postproduction for that last commercial she'd done?

Mia Graves. Local girl turned modeling superstar. Why was she out here in the middle of nowhere? Her father, Norton Graves, was a high-profile investment banker. Anyone doing business in the region had passing knowledge of the man. "You're Norton's daughter."

"I am."

Whoa. He jerked his thoughts back into line. "Do you need me to call—"

"No." The baby whimpered at her sharp tone and she twisted slowly side to side, patting him gently, murmuring apologies. "I don't need anything," she insisted. "Not from you or him, or anyone else." There was steel underscoring her words. "Some privacy here is all I need."

"You can't stay here." He should've phrased that better, but this wasn't any kind of place for a mother and infant.

"I know I'm trespassing," she said. "Please, it won't be for long. I can write a check or make a donation or something."

"But—"

"Please," she interrupted. "Do you have to report

me? I'm not hurting anything. I just need another day or two to figure out my next step."

It didn't take a genius to know she was holding back. No one, not even a ranch hand, would consider this hut habitable for more than a few hours. "How long have you been here?"

"Overnight." She shifted the baby, resting him on her shoulder and patting his back. "I didn't plan this."

"Obviously. What happened?" His thoughts were whirling. Was this a custody thing? He'd noticed the headlines from his sister's reports in the *Mustang Valley Gabber* about Mia's recent divorce. If she was in trouble, why wasn't her dad helping out? According to his limited knowledge, Norton valued his family and treasured his only daughter.

She rolled her eyes. "What will it take?" she asked.

"Take?"

"To keep you quiet," she said. "I can—"

He cut her off this time. "Don't finish that sentence." If she wanted to bribe him, he didn't want to hear it. "I don't need your money, either." He didn't want to dwell on what else she might be desperate enough to offer. "What kind of trouble are you in? How did you even get here?"

"I drove," she replied. "My trouble isn't your problem. I didn't think anyone would find me out here."

"You weren't wrong."

"Just lucky you happened along?"

"Well, yeah," he replied. That was how he saw it. The hut was just that. An unfinished, bare-minimum structure that hadn't been maintained or updated in years. There was no running water or even a bed. It was a glorified firepit. "I can help you."

He was already making a mental list of what he

might pull together to make her more comfortable until he could convince her to move someplace more secure.

"Thanks, but no thanks. We're fine right here, unless you plan to report me." She turned her back to him again as she continued to nurse the baby.

"I won't report you." Her skepticism didn't bother him half as much as her location. "But this isn't adequate," he insisted. "You can't take care of a newborn here." He didn't have any real experience with mothers or babies, but this couldn't possibly be the right environment. Mia Graves had been raised with the best of everything money could buy. How she'd successfully managed one night here baffled him.

He saw a grocery bag in the corner, next to a stylish tote overflowing with what appeared to be baby paraphernalia. "There are guest rooms at the ranch. I can make arrangements and you can clean up and rest."

"Wow." Her gaze was flat, annoyed. "Way to make a woman feel special."

She was a wall of stubbornness. "That's not what I meant. You look great."

One eyebrow arched in challenge.

Fine, he'd spell it out. "You don't have a bed. No real bathroom. That one chair is better used as firewood. Should I go on?"

"Please, just *go*."

He crossed his arms. He'd match her stubborn streak. "I'll let you stay, if you tell me what kind of trouble you're in."

"What you don't know can't hurt you," she said with a slow shake of her head.

Oh, she was completely wrong about that, but this was about her. Her and the baby. *Baby*, a voice shouted in his head, lest he forget that gorgeous women were for dating only. Babies came with relationships and starred in family photos on holiday cards. He wasn't cut out for *any* of that.

"What I don't know can absolutely be a threat to this ranch. It'd be good to have some advance warning if a furious husband is on the way."

"Allow me to clear that up." Her voice snapped like a whip. "Neither my *ex*-husband nor my father will be storming your ranch in pursuit of me."

Your ranch. He knew the words meant nothing to her, but they sent a pleasant sensation coursing through him. If he found the proof Isaiah told him about, it might very well become his ranch. He and Spencer and Bella would own the Triple R. Wouldn't that be a kick?

"What is that face about?" She circled a finger in the air around her own face.

"Nothing important." He wasn't about to let her shift the focus of this conversation. "Lover? Real mother of the baby? Who are you hiding from?"

Her gaze lit with fury. "Silas is *my* baby. I'm the one nursing him. Or did you miss that detail?"

He hadn't missed anything. In college, he'd been infatuated with Mia Graves, model. Everything from her sly and sultry expressions to her wide, gregarious smile captivated his imagination. Her meteoric rise had set the advertising and marketing world on fire. More than one of his professors had made them study either her career or the brands she represented.

"Okay," he allowed. "That was ridiculous. So clear it up for me. I can't protect you or the ranch without information."

It was hard for people to understand just how much territory was out here, how much ground the crew had to cover. "If you found a way to sneak in, someone else could do the same." He didn't want to think about coming back to check on her and finding a tragedy. On the flip side, he didn't want some crazed person destroying the ranch in an effort to find *her*.

"I'm here because this is the last place anyone will look for me. Can't we just leave it at that?"

"Afraid not." He couldn't allow her to stay here at all. Infatuation or sympathy aside, his responsibility was to the ranch.

"Why should I trust you to do the right thing?"

"Do you have a choice?" Her gaze dropped to the scarred plank floor and he felt like a jerk. "You don't have to tell me everything," he added quietly. "You aren't hurting anyone out here and no one needs to use this place. But you're isolated. I'd rather not come back to find someone hurt you."

"I really can't tell you anything."

"If not your dad or your ex, what other man has the resources to drive you to this?"

Her shoulders hunched and she cuddled her son closer as her bravado vanished. "Not a man," she said. "A woman. A woman with influence and access to far more resources than she deserves."

Chapter Two

Frustrated, Mia looked to the doorway and the stick she'd thought to use against Jarvis Colton, Triple R ranch hand. He hadn't tossed the stick aside or out of her reach; he'd placed it inside the open door. He looked like he'd walked straight off the set of a modern cowboy photo shoot. He might resemble a model, the type of man she used to deal with on a daily basis, but he wasn't. She had to remember he was a stranger and posed a very real danger to her plan.

Plan. What she had in mind so far barely qualified as an actionable concept. And now there was a witness to her current incompetence. She wanted to pull at her hair, this entire mess was so embarrassing. She tucked Silas back into his car seat so she wouldn't upset him if she got emotional again. And she didn't want to be at a disadvantage if Jarvis tried to force her out of the tiny cabin.

He had a powerful build and the dark T-shirt he wore revealed strong, sculpted arms. She wasn't exactly a lightweight, but he posed a clear risk, physically and logistically. When she'd started modeling, her agent had suggested she study self-defense. The skills she'd learned hadn't been tested in years and she'd prefer not to test them now.

"Mia."

The kindness in his voice nearly reduced her to tears. It wasn't fair that this chance encounter should make her feel less alone. Since escaping yesterday, Regina had sent her one threat after another. She'd sent pictures from Tamara's neighborhood as well as the courtyard in front of her ex-husband's condo. A night of worry and nightmares interrupted by her restless son hadn't helped Mia figure anything out. Unfortunately, Jarvis was right about this place. She didn't see good sleep coming anytime soon and Silas needed her at her best.

"I didn't know I was on the Triple R," she said. She caught herself working the gold band she wore on her thumb as her weary brain tried to get ahead of this stalemate with Jarvis so she could return her focus to the stalemate with Regina. "I thought I'd found an old hunting cabin."

"You basically did."

"Well, the good news is my problems shouldn't find me here."

He removed his hat and raked his fingers through his dark hair. "Let me get you to a better location," he said. "Somewhere up-to-date and safe."

He had no idea how much the idea tempted her. "There's no such thing as safe right now," she said. "My stepmother, Regina, is gunning for me." She glanced at her phone, resting at the top of Silas's diaper bag. Thank goodness the woman didn't have real guns. "This spot is only safe *because* it's run-down."

Jarvis frowned. "She thinks I'm too spoiled to rough it to this degree."

"You're not."

"No," she replied, though it hadn't really been a question. "We've never gotten along. The Graves family is a walking cliché. We have the trophy wife and the bitter, resentful daughter of a wealthy father determined to overlook any unpleasantness in favor of building his business."

While she vented, he'd stepped close enough that she couldn't ignore the scent of sunshine on his skin. This place might suit her and the baby temporarily, but he took up more than his share of the space.

"What happened?"

"What didn't?" She spared him the gory details of years of bickering and snide remarks and cut straight to the current issue. "Being newly divorced by the end of my first trimester, I talked with my dad about career options. Real estate felt like the right fit, so I took the classes. When I passed my state exam, he offered to let me handle the sale of his country house once I was ready to get back to work."

"Your stepmother doesn't want to sell the place?"

"I have no idea what she wants aside from wanting me out of Dad's life." Mia was too tired for this. "The house is an asset. If Dad's selling it, he'll buy her something better." Mia pushed at her heavy hair. Why couldn't this have gone down during cooler weather instead of this presummer heat wave? She wanted to change her clothes and freshen up, but she couldn't do any of that with an audience.

"Tell me what I'm missing," Jarvis prompted.

She reached for her bottle of water and drank deeply

while she debated how much to share. She wanted to believe the sincere concern in his gaze, but in her experience, voicing anything negative about Regina blew up in her face. "Yesterday I learned Regina has been using the country house for an affair. Probably not her first," she added. Her father was several years older than her stepmother, but not by so much that he couldn't claim they were happily married. It made her stomach pitch. "My marriage wasn't perfect, but we were loyal to each other," she muttered more to herself than the cowboy waiting for the rest of the story. "Long story short, I inadvertently caught her and her boyfriend in the act when I was there taking video for the online listing."

"Let me guess—you told your dad and now they're both mad at you."

"I wish it was that simple. I will tell him," she said. As soon as she figured out how. "As it stands, I can't tell anyone. Yet." She was so ashamed at how poorly she'd handled the moment. "If there was a chance to press an advantage, I missed it," she confessed.

In his car seat, Silas gurgled and kicked his feet. She'd let him down and now she was backed into a corner. "The man she was with saw me first. He thought I was there at her request."

She caught the wince on Jarvis's face, assumed her expression at the time had mirrored his. "Agreed." The *ew* factor had been off the charts. "So there I am, video rolling while my stepmother and a much younger hottie are all over each other. Naked, in case there was any doubt about their intentions."

Her son yawned, and love, protective and fierce, surged through her. She would find a way to get past this nonsense and give him the stable life she'd planned so carefully. "I ran out of the house and headed straight for Dad's office. Then the first call came through. Regina offered me money."

"Which you don't need," Jarvis said.

The quip made her smile. "Correct, but Regina goes for the easy out first. Every single time. I stopped answering her calls, determined to reach my father before she did. Then he called. Naturally, I picked up. Before I could say a word, he asked if I'd meet him and Regina for lunch to celebrate my first day. He said it was her idea and I knew I'd been outmaneuvered."

"How so?"

She stared at him. It was such a challenge to admit that the mistakes she'd made as a heartbroken teenager were still impacting her life today. "If I told him what I saw without any proof, he'd only be disappointed and lecture me about being too old for games."

"You're serious."

The way Jarvis studied her, she felt more exposed than she had on lingerie shoots, and more regret and shame than she'd ever felt as a kid when communication had completely broken down. "I did try to break them up. After they married, I put zero effort toward a smooth transition."

"What kind of effort did your stepmother make?"

No one, not even her husband, had ever asked that. To be fair, she'd been out on her own for years before she'd met and married Roderick Hodges. From the start, her ex had more important things on his agenda than delving deep into the rocky parts of her childhood. She'd happily left the house and those years behind. Until she'd accepted her father's invitation to move back in.

"That's all water under the bridge these days. Things are civil now. Or they were. I asked for a rain check on lunch, disappointing my father in the process, but I wasn't sitting through a meal in a public place while she gloated about getting away with it."

"What changed?"

"She threatened Silas," Mia said. Just thinking about that phone call and the text messages that followed brought angry tears to her eyes.

"What?" He frowned as if he'd misunderstood.

"You heard me. She told me that if I tattled on her to Dad or the police, my baby wouldn't wake up from his nap. Her words." It was too fresh, the fear too close to the surface. She swiped at the tear that spilled down her cheek, then hugged herself because she was too distraught to hug her baby. "I wanted to call the police, but what could I say? It would be her word against mine and my father sides with her." Every time. She brushed away another tear. "So I ran," she said in a whisper.

Jarvis swore.

Silas turned toward his voice and Mia bit back a request for him to watch his language. Her son was way too new and still far too young for it to make any difference.

"Of course you ran," he said, "But here?"

"Regina has always seen me as prissy and spoiled. Entitled, because Dad and I were so close. As if that was abnormal after Mom died." Mia deliberately unclenched her jaw at the memory of those old insults spoken when her father was out of earshot. "Despite everything I've done on my own in my career, she'd never expect me to hide out alone, definitely not in anything less than a five-star hotel."

Mia would love to hide with Tamara, where her son would have the best backup. But her mother's friend would be one more pressure point Regina could use against Mia. And while a resort vacation sounded perfect, she didn't have enough cash for that and using a credit card made it too easy for Regina to track her down.

"What about a guest room down at the house?" Jarvis suggested. "The place is massive, and almost no one would know. Everyone's distracted with Payne's recovery."

She shook her head. "I've been to the main house," she said. "As Mrs. Norton Graves, Regina runs in the same circles as the Coltons. She might be there right now, pretending to comfort Genevieve. She and Selina Barnes, Payne's second wife, are friendly competitors in all things of wealth and privilege." She smiled down at her son. "You've heard him cry. If we're within earshot of anyone, we'll be discovered within a day."

"But you'd be safe." He moved closer, filling the small cabin even more. "There's a chef and housekeeping. Hotel amenities without a credit card trail. You'd be able to care for him and yourself properly."

"Properly?" She bristled. How dare this cowboy come in and question her ability to care for her son? "Out. We are not your problem." Her primary concern was whether or not he would become a problem for her. "All you have to do is forget you saw me."

"As if." He folded his arms over his chest.

Unless she went on the attack, there would be no budging him. She looked around and started to gather the items she'd brought in from her car, stuffing them into the diaper bag. Within a minute she could be out of here. But where could she stay without drawing notice?

"Mia, stop. Let's assume you are out of her reach here. Have you sent the video to your father?"

She wanted to snap at him, this stranger who thought he knew her and was so sure he had all the answers. "Please leave me alone." Contrary to Regina's belief, Mia didn't beg anyone for anything. "I don't need you to solve this. I just need you to go."

"I could take the video to the police for you."

"Infidelity and sleeping around isn't exactly a criminal offense." Mia tugged at her hair. "She has the upper hand right now," she added, her chest tight. "Just, just look." She pulled out her phone and pulled up the text messages.

Having memorized the entire string of threats and pictures, she watched Jarvis's face as he scrolled through. He stopped, eyes narrowed, and she assumed he'd found the first set of pictures.

First, at the restaurant her father had suggested for lunch, Regina was pouring red wine into two glasses, her showy wedding set obvious. The next picture was a sickeningly sweet selfie of Regina and Norton, cheek to cheek, glasses touching.

The text that followed posed a question regarding Norton's medications and alcohol consumption.

"Is there an interaction risk?" Jarvis's query confirmed her assessment of where he was in the sequence of messages.

"Upper hand," she repeated. "There is a risk, but it's low. She wouldn't put an outright death threat against him in writing."

He swore again, this time under his breath. "She certainly didn't hesitate to threaten your son via text."

"No, she didn't. Knowing her, that means she has a plan to cover her tracks if it comes up."

"So what's *your* plan? You can't hide here forever."

She didn't appreciate the challenge in his tone as he returned her phone. "Of course not." She needed space to breathe and think and come up with a way to expose the woman who had, as of today, effectively shoved her out of the life she'd known. "I'll think of something."

She would find a way once she was sure her father and son wouldn't pay the price. Her father had been her rock, her idol throughout her life. She hadn't agreed with him on everything, particularly not his latest marriage, but they'd found a way to maintain their relationship. They weren't as close as they'd once been, but close enough. For years, Regina had been undermining that relationship. Jealousy, selfishness… Her reasons didn't matter. Mia knew she was wallowing out here, but she felt entitled to the time. Silas was safe. She could manage out here for a few days while she made up her mind how far and how soon to push back.

"If you could ignore us for a couple of days, I'll be out of your hair."

He stared at her for a long moment, then his gaze dropped to her son before cruising over the cramped cabin. "I can't ignore you." He settled his hat on his head. "I'll pick up some supplies for you."

"That's not—"

His mouth flattened and a sharp head shake cut her off. "It's necessary." He walked to the door. "No one will know you're here."

"Thank you."

He paused, halfway out the door. "My brother is a sergeant with the police department. If you decide you want his help, you'll get it."

"My pride isn't worth risking my father's life," she replied.

His eyebrows flexed over those warm brown eyes again. "You really think she'd do it? Kill Norton?"

"No doubt in my mind. She's gotten her way from the moment she married my dad, probably years before that, too."

"All right. Relax. I'll be back with some gear to make this doable."

"Thanks," she called after him.

There was no point wondering what lies Regina was spreading about why Mia didn't make it home last night. Her father hadn't called to check in, so she knew it had to be bad. And there was no point involving anyone, not even a police officer, until she could be sure the truth would be seen *and* believed.

Only when Regina was effectively discredited could Mia come out of hiding.

When the sounds of the horse had faded, she cuddled Silas until he fell asleep. Confident he was safe and content, she ducked out to the car she'd hidden in the brush to take care of herself. She shouldn't trust Jarvis so easily, but something in his gaze put her at ease. Not when he'd looked at her as if they'd met before; they hadn't. She would've remembered a man with that perfect combination of hard body and kind eyes. No, it had been the way he'd looked at her son after she'd told him about Regina's threat.

He might be the first person to immediately take her side on the whole "wicked stepmother" situation.

Not that she'd broadcast her frustrations everywhere. That would have backfired more than the occasional comments she made about Regina's spending habits.

Even her husband had encouraged her to ignore Regina's antics. A sickening thought occurred to her. What if Regina had seduced him, too? The highly unlikely but not impossible scenario was completely irrelevant now. She and Roderick were through and she was better for it. The divorce settlement had been generous and swift since he preferred to pay one lump sum to get rid of the child he never intended to meet and the wife who'd let him down.

She had a knack for disappointing the men she cared about most. That trend would stop now, with Silas. Nothing would keep her from being the mother he needed.

The real-estate endeavor wasn't precisely necessary right now, but she'd hoped to put the bulk of the divorce settlement into long-term investments. And despite loving motherhood—and Silas—more each and every day, her mind had been ready for a challenge.

Well, she had it now, didn't she?

She cleaned herself up a bit and finally changed into clean shorts and a soft tunic top that were better suited to the rustic conditions. There was a spark of hope that she'd get through this, and the only cause was Jarvis. How curious that one awkward and unsettling encounter with a handsome cowboy could make her feel a thousand times better during the lowest moment of her life.

She'd know soon enough if she'd made a mistake by trusting him, and while Silas napped, she set things up for a quick escape if it proved necessary.

JARVIS HOPED LIKE hell she'd still be there when he got back. His search for Isaiah's proof forgotten for tonight, he rode hard back to the stables and bunkhouse where he'd been living since Asher hired him.

His mental list of the things Mia would need to make her stay easier kept growing. Although *easier* would only be a marginal improvement. She needed running water, a real bathroom, a refrigerator. He couldn't make any of those things happen at the warming hut. She needed a lot more than she'd decided to settle for, he thought as the Colton mansion near the main entrance of the Rattlesnake Ridge Ranch came into view.

Her stepmother's ugly threats trailed after him as he rode straight up to the stable. It was a cruel person who threatened to kill an infant. He just couldn't wrap his head around how anyone could say such a thing. Not even Aunt Amelia, who'd reluctantly taken them in when their parents died, had been that cold.

No mother should have to hear that. He didn't care for the idea of Mia dealing with the threat on her own. The idea of bunking out there with her flitted through his head and he dismissed it quickly. While being in close proximity to the beautiful woman who had fascinated him through college appealed, he worried that standing guard for her would draw unwanted attention to her location.

Normally, he would personally tend to his horse's care after a long workday, but this evening, he handed the reins to one of the other men on duty. "He's had a full day," Jarvis said, scratching Duke's ears. "If we have any apples, he's earned it."

"Sure thing," Jimmy said. "Got a hot date?"

Jarvis laughed at the joke. He'd gained a reputation

for being the one cowboy every girl in town wanted to flirt with when they went out. Not that he hooked up often. Usually, he danced, made a few women smile and headed back to his room alone. He'd tried to tell the others that a good sense of humor was the key, but they refused to believe him.

"Got a call for a last-minute supply run for morning. You need anything while I'm going?"

Jimmy shook his head. "Not this time around."

"All right. I'll be back in an hour or so." Add another hour or so for getting the supplies into Mia's hands, but he kept that detail to himself. "Thanks again for the assist with Duke."

Jarvis picked up his truck and left the ranch through the service gate. He could get most of the supplies Mia needed at the feedstore that was conveniently located between the ranch and Mustang Valley. No chance he'd bump into Regina or anyone who ran in the same circles as Selina and his Colton Oil cousins there.

With a case of bottled water, a battery-operated lantern and a couple of blankets in the cart, he stopped to compare sleeping bags. He chose one that included a ground tarp and an inflatable pillow. He turned down the next aisle and decided a camouflage net might do a better job of hiding her car from view. Waiting to check out, he added a selection of meal bars. A nursing mother needed to eat more and more often. At least, that was what he'd learned from caring for the livestock on the ranch. Probably better if he didn't tell her that was his theory.

Not perfect, but easier, he thought as he loaded the purchases into his truck. A few small comforts should help her relax and rest. Maybe then she would be thinking clearly enough to make a better long-term plan.

As he pulled out of the parking lot, he finally gave in and called his brother. "Hey, Spencer," he said as his brother answered. "I have a hypothetical question."

"If it's about getting your career back on track, shoot."

Jarvis was more than a little bit tired of the refrain. "No. I, um, well I overheard a threat," he said. "A death threat," he clarified. "If I gave you the details, would the police department do anything about it?"

"Seriously?"

"Yes," Jarvis said through gritted teeth. "At what point do you investigate that kind of thing?"

He heard his brother sigh, could picture him rolling his eyes. "Hell, Jarvis. There are too many unknowns in your hypothetical."

"Come on, Spencer." Nervous, Jarvis adjusted the air vents to blow all the cool, air-conditioned air at him. He didn't know Mia well, but if first impressions could be trusted, she'd be furious that he'd made this call. "What evidence or complaint would you need to take action if someone threatened to kill another person?"

"We can't take action before a crime occurs. Depending on the facts and situation, we might do some surveillance. Most people don't go from zero to killer in one fast leap. We'd look for other signs of smaller trouble. Who are you worried about?"

Surveillance wouldn't work in this situation. There was no way to keep an official eye on Mia and her son without her noticing. "All right. That is helpful." Except it wasn't.

He suddenly understood why Asher didn't want to

use his father as bait to draw out the person who'd shot Payne several months ago. He wouldn't feel right putting Mia in a killer's crosshairs and he'd just met her. Not to mention she would never take that kind of chance with her son.

"All right," he said again.

"Are you in trouble?" Spencer asked.

It felt like it, though the trouble he sensed didn't fall into a category his brother could deal with as a cop. "No one's threatening me," Jarvis replied. "I'm thinking it'll blow over soon enough. If it doesn't, I'll let you know."

"Do that."

"Is it a crime to have an extramarital affair?"

"What the hell is going on with you?"

"Just answer the question," Jarvis snapped. "Please."

"Well, yes, technically it is a crime in the state of Arizona. We don't make a habit out of hauling in offenders or tossing them in jail. We typically let the divorce lawyers deal with that stuff."

"Good to know." So Mia was wrong about that; Regina's affair was a criminal offense. "I'll see you soon," Jarvis said, ending the call before his brother could ask more questions.

He hit a drive-through and downed a burger and fries, his mind set on finding a way to help her. He'd hope that if his sister was in trouble, someone would go the extra mile for her. And the baby. He couldn't get the little guy out of his mind. The kid was so tiny. Vulnerable. Completely defenseless if someone wanted to make sure he didn't wake up from a nap. Whether or not Regina really did intend to commit murder, Mia believed she was capable of doing so and that was all that mattered right now.

He considered calling Spencer back, but his brother would need solid evidence, not a chain of text messages. Jarvis didn't care about the video proving Regina was unfaithful; he was more concerned with her threats to harm Silas and Norton.

Jarvis didn't usually worry over the welfare of anyone other than his siblings. He sure wasn't the ride-to-the-rescue type, yet here he was, charging in to help Mia. She was on his family's land, whether or not his grandfather's story held up. And if trouble followed her, he had to be ready for it.

Instead of driving up through the service entrance used by the Triple R crew and support staff, he circled around, looking for the road she must have taken to get to that warming hut. This end of the property wasn't neglected, but it wasn't well used right now, either. Mia had made a smart choice with her hiding spot, though she couldn't stay indefinitely.

The light was all but gone, the first stars winking into view overhead, when he found where she'd turned off the paved road and onto Triple R land. The access road was only a single lane wide. Not a high-traffic area, even when they were grazing herds up this way.

He still didn't understand how or why Mia even knew to come out here or that the shelter would be available. One of several questions he hoped to ask without spooking her when he dropped off these supplies.

His truck lumbered over the bumpy road, rutted from the last time they'd had serious rain. When his headlights flashed off the window of her car nestled into a dip in the landscape, he breathed a sigh of relief. She'd stayed. That small act of trust filled him up, smoothing out the parched sections of his soul he largely ignored.

He turned off his lights as he came around to the front of the weathered shelter and then cut the engine. His heart sped up, anticipating another view of her lush curves and sultry gaze. Not that she aimed that specific gaze his way in an inviting manner, but it was enough to remember it was possible. And yeah, certain parts of him were really into the idea of winning one of those famously seductive looks from her.

He left the cab and moved around the front end of the truck to open the passenger door and take out the gear and groceries. "It's Jarvis," he called softly so his voice wouldn't carry too far. "You can put down the stick."

He heard movement and a low exhale. Relief? Disappointment? A soft light flicked on inside the hut and Mia stepped out, her body a mouthwateringly curvy silhouette.

She'd changed from the dress to form-fitting shorts and a loose shirt. But the sneakers on her feet told a tale. She was ready to run at a moment's notice.

"How's the little guy?" he asked, hoping to put her at ease.

"Snoozing again." Her raspy voice and half smile made him wonder if he'd woken her up. "Come in," she said. "I didn't expect you to come back."

Best not to take that personally. She was clearly rattled and convinced that those dearest to her were in danger. "If my sister was in trouble, I'd hope someone would have the decency to help her." Did that sound as sappy to her as it did to him? "I brought bottled water, too," he said, setting the supplies in his arms down on the worn floor. "Give me just a second."

Walking back in with a pack of diapers stacked on top of the water bottles and the strap of the sleeping bag hooked around one finger, he saw her swiping a tear from her cheek.

"What is it? Did I get the wrong flavors?"

Those dark eyebrows flexed into a frown. "No, the snacks are perfect. Thanks."

"Good." He winked at her. "I should have asked. Are you allergic to anything?"

"No." Her mouth twitched.

"Great." He smiled. "You said you were stocked, but I hear there's no such thing as too many diapers."

She rubbed her arms as if chasing away a chill. "I wasn't aware the Triple R had a day care."

"Not exactly." He rocked back on his heels and shoved his hands into his pockets. If there was a protocol for helping a woman on the run survive an insufficient hideout, he didn't know it. "My boss has a baby under a year old and his fiancée has a day care center. I've picked up a few things."

She yawned, and though she tried to hide it, he could see weariness embarrassed her. "Go ahead and roll out the sleeping bag," he suggested.

"You're not leaving?" she asked in a rush. "You can't stay."

Again, he refused to be offended. "I won't stay unless you ask," he said. "I have a camouflage net for your car. Just another precaution," he assured her. "Once that's in place, I'll be out of your hair." For tonight.

She nodded and set to work on the sleeping bag. He

dragged his eyes away from the enticing view of her long legs and curvy hips, away from the temptation to soothe or distract her. They didn't know each other, and while she'd trusted him with her story, he hadn't actually verified it. More than that, he'd set himself a task out here that was better done without an audience.

Working in the dark, he added the netting to the scrubby brush she'd used to hide her car. He could come back in the morning to make sure it was all intact and effective. She might think she was alone out here, but she wasn't. Not while he was on the property. She'd just have to get used to it.

Walking inside again, she had the lantern he'd purchased set up in a corner, giving off better light than the small flashlight she'd been using. The sleeping bag was unrolled, right next to the baby seat. "All set?"

"Yes, thanks."

"Is your cell phone charged?"

Another slight frown marred her brow. "It is. I've been running the car for a few minutes at a time."

Too primitive, he thought darkly. "Add my number to your contacts."

"That's really not necessary," she said, shying away from him.

"I can be here faster than any first responders because I know where I'm going. Do you have any kind of protection?" He eyed the stick near the doorway. "Besides the bat?"

She had the grace to smile. "Would it ease your mind to know I was the top hitter in softball three seasons running in high school?"

Squinting, he patted a hand around his neck. "Not much, no."

She laughed lightly. "Thanks for everything, Jarvis. Please don't worry. I've taken self-defense classes, too. We'll be out of your hair tomorrow. The day after at the latest."

"Don't leave without letting me know where you're headed," he pressed. "You said it yourself, your stepmom is resourceful."

"I think it's best if I reach out and offer to sign a nondisclosure agreement or something. There has to be a way to draw that up. To reassure her."

Or something? He didn't think a piece of paper would stop someone devious enough and mean enough to threaten a baby. "What if I found you a better place to hide?" Why couldn't his brain remember that her problems weren't his? The sooner she was off the ranch the better.

"We've talked about this," she said. "I can't go anywhere near the Colton house."

"I know." He took a step forward and drew up short. This was so strange, fighting himself to keep his distance. "There are two bunkhouses that we use now instead of this place if we have herds out this way. They aren't in use now," he added hastily. "No need for them really this time of year. But they're updated with power, freshwater wells and septic systems. You'd be more comfortable."

He'd be more comfortable. The bunkhouse he had in mind was farther off the beaten path of Triple R acreage. And if he loaned her his truck, no one would suspect a thing.

"Won't people notice the bunkhouse is in use?"

"People really don't come out here if the herds are grazing elsewhere," he assured her. He was willing her to take him up on the offer. "If anyone does notice, they'll assume it's a grad student taking soil samples."

"That happens often?"

"Not often. I've just heard others mention it. Seriously, it would be a better solution for you."

"Why does my solution matter so much to you?"

Seriously? Shouldn't it matter to anyone with common decency? A new mother and infant should *not* be in such primitive conditions. "It's a brother complex," he hedged. It had to be a sibling thing, because Jarvis didn't do involvement, romantic interest or relationships. Those ended badly.

Her gaze narrowed. "What did you do? Did you tell someone about me hiding here?"

"No." His denial didn't help matters at all. Her fingers curled into fists and her eyes blazed. If she had the stick, he'd be on the floor by now. "I haven't done anything to expose you, Mia. I just called my brother."

She muttered an oath under her breath and then bit down hard on her lower lip. "Let me guess—whiny stepdaughters can't file complaints with the police."

Granted, they'd only had two conversations, but he hadn't heard her whine once. "I was asking about how death threats might be reported." Damn it. Her brown eyes narrowed and her lips firmed. He kept saying the wrong thing. She was clearly ready to bolt. And then what? If she'd thought she was safe here, he needed to make sure she was safe here. "And adultery is a crime in Arizona," he added.

"Good grief." She rubbed her temples. "That's probably an accusation that carries more weight when the injured party files the complaint, not the stepdaughter of the unfaithful partner. Forget about me, Jarvis. I'll just go."

"Stay." His primary goal was to help her feel secure. Even here. He stepped forward and caught her hands, holding them loosely between their bodies. He rushed to full alert at the contact. Her skin was silky under his rough thumbs. He didn't crowd her, but he felt her pulse racing under his fingertips. "I'm saying this all wrong and I'm sorry for making you worry. I was trying to be transparent and reassure you."

She stared at her wrists, caged by his fingers. "That failed. Not that I want to be left in the dark, either. I've had enough surprise attacks for a lifetime."

"Noted. On both counts." A ghost of an amused smile slipped across her lips. "No one knows anything about you here. No one will. Not from me," he vowed.

"What about the rest of the crew?"

He'd manipulated the weekly schedule of responsibilities to accommodate his search. In his view, this was a happy coincidence, with her crisis and his search intersecting. "Won't be a problem. I'm the only one who is scheduled to be out this way."

She gently extricated herself from his grasp. "Okay."

He immediately missed the warmth of her skin. The wall she built between them was practically visible and plastered with no-trespassing warnings.

"I'd still prefer you move to the bunkhouse. Tomorrow," he added when she started to argue. The baby stirred, because of the conversation or because he had some other issue, Jarvis didn't know.

Mia sighed, scooping up her son before he could really work himself into a crying jag. She was lovely with or without the baby in her arms. That was one more strange new awareness in a day filled with oddities. Watching her struck a chord deep in his chest and resonated through his system. He'd developed a crush on her when she was modeling everything from swimsuits to eyeliner. Watching her devotion as a mother was like opening a safe expecting cash and finding a stash of priceless gems. This side of her was so unexpected, this facet of her beauty so raw and unpolished and alluring. Since when did he find mothers *alluring*?

He wasn't that kind of guy. He'd never wanted the hearth-and-home deal. Losing his parents was proof that life was too fragile and the world too fickle. Better to have some fun and move on before the good stuff got ripped away, leaving bloody knuckles, bruises and painful scars behind.

"Jarvis?"

She'd caught him staring like an idiot. "I'll, um, I'll keep watch tonight so you can rest easy." The statement made, it felt exactly right. How else would he make sure she didn't disappear without a trace? It was the practical thing to do, he argued with the voice in his head accusing him of being hopelessly infatuated.

"Stop it." She shook her head. "That will only draw more attention."

"From who? Nothing but coyotes and owls out here when the cattle are elsewhere."

Her lush lips twisted to one side. "I don't have much to fear from an owl, and a coyote has no reason to wander close enough to trouble me. Go home and get your own rest. I hear cowboys have to get up early."

"Just like mothers and models," he said. She rolled her eyes. "I live on the ranch," he added, hooking his thumbs in his pockets. "Call me if a coyote gets out of line."

"I promise."

Her smile was relaxed, natural, and the sparkle was back in her eye rather than frustration and fear. Promising he'd be back in the morning, he walked out of the warming hut and climbed into his truck. But he didn't go all the way back to the ranch. Instead, he retreated only so far as the service road and parked. Now he was effectively blocking anyone trying to take an established road toward her hiding place. It also meant he was less than a minute away if she *did* need him tonight.

As he adjusted the seat to get comfortable, he wondered which outcome would make him happier—an undisturbed night or one in which she called him for help. *What was wrong with him?* He didn't wish trouble on her or the baby. She'd been through too much already.

His brother would chide him for not verifying her story before siding with her. His sister would accuse him of being more interested in her face than her predicament. Although his siblings knew him best, neither of them would be entirely correct about this. Oh, he was plenty attracted to Mia and he hadn't vetted her claim with a source beyond her cell phone.

But he was running on his instincts and her reputation. That was more than enough to justify a few bucks in supplies and spending the night in his truck under the expansive sky.

Just as he was settling in, lightning slashed across the sky and a deep rumble of thunder chased it. So much for stretching out in the bed of his truck. Knowing rain was imminent, he cracked the windows and braced himself for a cramped and uncomfortable night.

Chapter Three

The sudden storm lashed at the warming hut and lightning revealed all of the gaps in the aged and weary structure. Mia rarely wallowed in regret. She'd invested years of effort and tears learning how to accept her strengths and her weaknesses equally. Right now, she wished she'd accepted Jarvis's generosity rather than resisting him due to her innate stubbornness and the fear Regina had planted in her heart.

Silas was restless, too, and she blamed either the weather or her own edgy energy. The combination definitely wasn't helping matters. She fed him, rocked him and changed him. She bundled him snug in a blanket and when that failed, she tried letting him rest in only his diaper.

Nothing worked. Her eyes were bleary and she was well beyond frazzled as she dealt with her son. In the parenting classes, they'd warned her there would come a time when nothing soothed the baby and she would want to pull out her hair. Like all the other parents in the room, Mia had chuckled nervously, not believing things would get bad enough to sap her patience and make her short-tempered with her child.

She believed it now.

If she'd thought consoling him had been a challenge when Jarvis found them, this was a whole new level of agony. Standing here when she had zero help nearby was a lousy time for a revelation. There was no one to trade off with, no option to walk away and take a breather, as the instructor had recommended.

"I'm trying, baby," she murmured, pacing as far from Silas as possible. "What is it you need?" She didn't want to let him work up another good cry. Not that she thought anyone would hear him over this storm.

Sitting on the sleeping bag, her legs crossed, she swayed gently side to side and watched his little face pinch, his body coiled for his next hearty wail. A good mother would be impressed by her son's lung capacity. Mia, feeling like a failure in every aspect of life, burst into tears herself.

"Oh, I'm sorry, baby. What was I thinking?" She tucked Silas into the security of his car seat and paced the three strides to the door of the hut. Swiping at her cheeks, she tried to pull herself away from the brink of a self-destructive meltdown. Nothing would improve if they were both sobbing.

How was it her father had been such an amazing single parent and role model after her mother had died? His commitment, patience and love had given her a solid foundation of confidence and self-worth, despite the grief and loss they were both coping with. He'd filled in and worked around that missing piece of her heart.

And then that foundation had been ripped away, thanks to Regina. The woman had entered their lives in a whirl of affection and companionship, things her father sorely missed after years as a widower. In short order, Regina began suggesting that Mia's resistance to a new mother figure proved she needed less attention from Norton and more independence. And Norton had fallen for it. Despite her stepmother's antics and efforts to drive them apart, her father's courageous example in the years prior had inspired Mia to raise her son alone.

It had been the right decision, the only logical solution, even knowing her husband wouldn't tolerate such a tectonic shift in their marriage dynamic.

On the other side of the weathered door, she could hear the wind changing and another swath of rain battering the hut. A leak in the roof splatted on one end of the sleeping bag Jarvis had delivered. She hurried to move things around the small space, while Silas continued to cry.

Steeling herself, she opened a bottle of water and indulged in a brief fantasy about ear plugs. As if she'd ever use them to blot out her son. She reminded herself that this was a moment, not forever. Her baby was safe even if he was currently unhappy. And she was a single parent by choice.

Roderick had been quick to remind her they'd agreed not to have children in order to better focus on their respective careers and the things they wanted to accomplish in the world. Of course, she hadn't gotten pregnant on her own; she'd been consistent and careful about preventive measures, and yet, by some miracle, she'd conceived. In her mind it was meant to be. Roderick saw it as a betrayal.

She'd been proud to leave modeling behind to be the wife and partner of a tech mogul with strong philanthropic values. They'd traveled, joined humanitarian projects around the world and she'd launched and managed his charitable foundation. They'd been happy and close and in love. Or so she'd thought. Why was she so easy to discard?

The better question was why she was rehashing all of this now. Her husband had stepped out of her life, or, more accurately, pushed her out of his with aloof efficiency. It was done. He'd run the numbers and pro-jections of parenthood expenses, including college, against his anticipated income and basically written her a check to cover that amount. No one could fault him for shirking his responsibility. Though Silas would never know his father, she was sure it was better than growing up around a parent who would ignore him.

"Not my first hard day," she reminded herself. "Won't be the last." The only good news, she thought as she adjusted her belongings again to avoid another leak, was that Jarvis had left.

She couldn't imagine how crowded it would feel in here with him. His presence overpowered every-thing, including her good sense. The instant attrac-tion had surprised her, once the distress of being found had worn off. Her pulse had fluttered and the ripple of temptation over her skin had scared her almost as much as the instinctive urge to trust him.

Mia hadn't trusted anyone other than herself in quite some time. She loved her father but questioned his decisions, which typically revolved around Regina's preferences. Although she'd accepted his feedback and advice about her new career options, going into real estate felt pretty foolish while she was hiding out in a leaky warming hut.

Had Regina set her up from the start? Was the scene

at the country house an elaborate scheme to permanently force her out of her father's life?

The answer couldn't be yes. But Regina did gain from the stunt, which made her speculation seem more plausible than paranoid. With Mia gone, Regina would now be the sole woman in Norton's life. Mia was no longer there to defend herself from any of Regina's lies or to protect her father from his wife's lavish spending habits.

She shoved her hands into her hair, pulling out the tie and finger combing the long, thick waves back from her face. Clearly, the stress and lack of sleep were catching up to her. Regina was cunning, to be sure, but from day one she had avoided any action that could possibly cast her in a negative light. Why would she put her status as Mrs. Norton Graves at risk by having an affair?

Mia should have the upper hand, with the incriminating video saved on her phone as well as backed up to a secure cloud storage. But all the advantages in the world were useless while Regina had the leverage.

Half of the leverage, she thought, picking up Silas again. Her sweet boy was still crying, but she was calm enough to make another attempt to soothe him. She sat in the lone chair, which she considered a testament to good craftsmanship rather than too brittle to be useful, and rested Silas on her chest, heart to heart, hoping he'd calm down.

These parenting challenges would only become more complex as her son grew. Someday, she hoped to find someone willing to become her partner in this adventure so she wouldn't go through every day alone.

Those days were light-years away at the moment,

but they could happen. She sang softly to Silas, stroking his dark, baby-soft curls while her mind drifted between the past and the future. Lasting love was more than fairy tale or fantasy. Motherhood confirmed that for her every day. Even the strident moments of motherhood underscored that soul-deep truth.

There *was* someone out there for her. A man who would treasure her for more than her connections. For more than the status of dating a former model. Someone who wanted to be both partner and father.

"We'll find the right someone," she whispered into Silas's hair. It was the same promise she made to him every day, in one way or another.

The roof sprang another leak and water dripped down, plinking on the floor close to the door. As much as she didn't want to move from this rustic little pocket of safety, the storm had made Jarvis's point. She didn't yet have a viable plan that would protect her father while she exposed Regina's infidelity. Until she had that plan, she needed a better place to hide.

"Momma will figure it out," she soothed as Silas's cries finally abated on a shuddering breath. "We'll go home. We'll be a family, just you and me." She'd figure out a career, with or without her father's support if necessary.

She just had to keep her son and father safe long enough to see that dream fulfilled.

Jarvis was up with the sun, grateful the rain had blown over. Less grateful for the stuffy cab of the truck and the kink in his neck. Other than the storm, there hadn't been any trouble through the night, which gave him confidence that Mia would be all right out here today.

From this vantage point, he had to work to separate her car from the rolling hills and scrubby grasses and he knew exactly where to look. He should go on to work, trusting her to stay put and stay hidden. Instead, he started the engine and drove back to the hut to check on her and Silas.

Before he was out of the truck, the cabin door opened just a smidgen as Mia confirmed it was him. Her caution only slammed home exactly how nervous she was about her situation. Then she stepped out into the morning sunshine, the baby in her arms, and he thought she was prettier than a sunrise.

"Good morning," he said. He noticed the circles under her eyes and the tension pinching the corners of her mouth. He was almost afraid to ask, "How did it go last night?"

"The rain made your point about the accommodations," she replied. "There are a few leaks in the roof here."

"A few?" He stepped back and eyed the shed-style slope. "We really should just knock this thing down." He knew he should've insisted on moving her yesterday. "We don't keep up with the huts," he said. "I'm sorry."

"It's not your fault I can be too stubborn for my own good," she said, smothering a yawn. "Does the offer of moving still stand?"

The guilt in her voice, in her tired eyes, punched him in the heart. Just when he thought life had drummed out all the soft spots. "I can move you right now," he said.

"Oh?" Her eyebrows flexed into a frown. "Don't you need to get to work?"

"Not as much as you need reliable shelter. Come on. I'll help you load up."

"Jarvis, I can wait until…" Her voice trailed off, exhaustion clearly interfering with whatever she'd meant to say.

"Now is just fine, Mia. Let me help." He closed the distance, guiding her gently back into the little hut to help her pack. She didn't resist or give him any attitude and somehow that lack of fight worried him more.

Inside, he cringed. Signs of roof leaks were everywhere, her supplies clustered in the dry spots. The roof had apparently let in more rain than it kept out last night.

"What if you're late to work?" she asked.

"Don't worry about me. It's not like I'd pin the blame on you," he teased, rolling up the sleeping bag. "Did you get any rest last night?"

"A little." She tucked the baby into his seat, rolling her eyes when he started to fuss.

"Is he okay?"

"Just grumpy. I think the storm was unsettling."

"Makes sense," Jarvis said, though he had no idea if it did or not. "There's a shower at the bunkhouse I mentioned." He'd make sure it was operational before he drove in. "And hot water."

"Really?"

He smothered a laugh at the eagerness in her voice. "Really."

"You'll have to tell me who I owe for the utility expenses. When I'm gone, I can send money back."

Not this again. He stood, the sleeping bag under his arm. "Let's wait and sort it out once you've had some sleep."

"Right." She buckled the baby into his car seat and wrestled to zip the diaper bag closed. "I should only need a few more days. A couple of people owe me favors. It's possible one of them will let my dad know what's going on without hurting him too much."

"There's no rush this time of year, I promise."

She started for her car, but he loaded up his truck instead. "If you can deal with being isolated until the end of the day, I'd rather you didn't move your car."

"Why? I'm not sure I'm comfortable with that," she said. "If something happens to the baby."

"You'll call me," he said. She frowned. He was running on instinct, unable to verbalize why her leaning on him was a positive thing for both of them.

"Without a car I'll feel trapped."

Right now she looked too exhausted to feel much of anything else. He hated to spell it out for her. "If someone does think to look for you here and they managed to find your car, it will look abandoned."

"How does that help me?"

He stowed her things in the truck bed while she got the car seat in place. Did she even realize she was arguing and cooperating at the same time? "Ditching the car should create the impression that you've already moved on."

"My car being here implies a connection," she pointed out.

"Connection to what? No one at the ranch has seen you. The assumption will be that you found another way out of town."

She spoke softly to the baby and then climbed into the passenger seat. As Jarvis drove across the grassy pastures to the bunkhouse, he was torn between emphasizing the remoteness of the new location as a safety feature and ignoring it to prevent undue worry if she did have a crisis. He kept his thoughts to himself and Mia seemed content with that.

The baby, too. "He got quiet fast," Jarvis observed.

She snorted, apparently unimpressed. "He loves car rides," she explained. "And he was up all night. They warned me it would happen."

"It?" he queried.

"The inconsolable baby. It's a whole thing, but like any new mom, I thought I could handle it."

He pulled to a stop at the bunkhouse and cut the engine. "You did handle it," he pointed out.

"Possibly at the expense of my sanity. A chunk of brain cells at the very least." She flicked a hand toward the view through the windshield. There was nothing to mar the view from here to the mountains. "Beautiful," she said. "I see why you like it out here. It's peaceful. Or it would be if I wasn't more removed from any kind of help than before.

"I'm sorry." She rubbed her eyes. "Forgive me for being cranky. Once I get some sleep, I'll figure out a way to handle my stepmom and stop imposing on you."

"I'm sure you will."

He unloaded her things while she gathered up her son. Inside, the bunkhouse was stripped to the bare essentials, but it was clean and dry. Here, in addition to basic conveniences, she had a table and chairs, plus she could choose from four bunks. He turned on the power and the water pump, made sure things were running as they should, then propped the stick against the wall by the door.

"You'll call if you have any trouble?" he asked.

She started to nod, but the motion was cut short by another yawn.

"Want me to stay and, ah, babysit while you take a shower?" he offered, trying not to think of what she'd look like under a hot spray of water. Unfortunately, memories of her poses in swimsuits flashed across his mind. He moved toward the baby, away from her before he did something stupid.

"I should be offended, but that sounds like heaven," she said, her mouth tilted into a grin.

"All right. Take your time." He had no idea what babysitting an infant required. Silas was currently dozing in his seat, and with a little luck Jarvis wouldn't have to do much of anything. If the baby did need something, he'd look it up online and figure it out.

Practical problem-solving was one of his favorite parts of his job. He'd never expected to enjoy working outdoors or all of the unpredictable moments among the daily routines of ranch life.

"You should go on to work after my shower," Mia said. "Silas and I can manage."

"You're sure?"

"We've been managing just fine for a couple of months now." Her smile was softer, filled with affection as she watched her son.

"What happened to his dad?" It was a nosy question, but he was more curious if there might be a better, more secure place for her and the baby to hide.

"Silas's father isn't part of our lives." Her head snapped up, her eyes flat, expression stern. "Go to work, Jarvis. You've helped enough today."

Okay, he'd crossed a line he hadn't even seen. He

was about to apologize when his cell phone buzzed on his hip.

She shot him an I-told-you-so look as he stepped outside to take the call.

"Where are you?" Asher didn't usually bark out demands, but he'd been under some serious stress since his father had been shot by a still-unknown assailant. That came on the heels of upheaval at the Colton Oil offices, as the board dealt with accusations that Ace Colton, then-CEO, was not a biological Colton and thus an imposter. Seemed the grass wasn't as green on the Colton Oil side of the family tree as Jarvis had always imagined.

"I'm out driving the access roads after all that rain." At least, he would be as soon as he drove in.

"Oh. Yeah, that was smart," Asher allowed. "Look, Selina's in my face, needing something installed at her place. Has to be today. Can you handle it?"

Just hearing Selina's name explained everything about the call and Asher's agitation. Selina Barnes Colton remained a thorny presence in everyone's life as the vice president and public relations director at Colton Oil. Payne's current wife, Genevieve, and all six of his children despised Selina, yet somehow she'd negotiated a chunk of the Triple R just a quarter mile from the mansion she'd considered her own for the duration of her marriage.

Jarvis credited Selina's attorney with her posh, post-divorce settlement, but Asher and his siblings were convinced Selina had some unsavory leverage over their dad. Whatever the actual cause, the effect was Asher having to juggle schedules when Selina made noise about needing something on her part of the property repaired or demanded help with one project or another.

The whole situation was an odd echo of Mia's trouble. It seemed like both Selina and Regina might be unfaithful second wives whom their husbands' offspring hated. Women who manipulated people to maintain control.

Since Jarvis had been on the ranch, he'd been to Selina's home to unclog a sink, rip up carpeting for a flooring change, and install new blinds in her home office and a guest room. In general, she annoyed most of the crew Asher sent to help her. She couldn't seem to be polite and came at the men with either overdone flirty innuendo or flat-out dismissal.

Unlike his peers, Jarvis didn't mind taking on her calls. He used those opportunities to chat with her about the history of the ranch. So far, her information hadn't changed his search parameters, but he was gaining insight into the side of the family he'd never met. Although his boss didn't know his real reasons for not complaining about Selina, Asher definitely appreciated having a cowboy who didn't gripe about being her on-call handyman.

"Sure thing," Jarvis said. "I'll go straight over." Well, straight there after a stop at the warming hut and his own room for a shower and change of clothes. He could flirt with Selina to get the cup of coffee his system was craving.

"Thanks. Nothing out your way needs attention?"

Only his personal quest. "Everything is clear out here."

"Great. Let me know when you're done with my former stepmother," Asher said.

Silas let out a cry that filtered outside.

"What's that?" Asher asked.

As a dad, Asher was naturally dialed in to that sound. He and Willow were blending into a family of four with their baby girls, Harper and Luna.

"Radio," Jarvis improvised. "One of those vasectomy commercials."

Asher chuckled. "Those always get on my nerves."

"Kids or commercials?" Jarvis joked, as if he had any clue about the perils or rewards of fatherhood.

"Can't speak for all kids, but my girls are worth it every single day," Asher said, proudly. "If you hear Selina say anything useful, you'll let me know?"

That was one of the first cousin-to-cousin rules of handling jobs at Selina's place. If she mentioned anything Asher could use to get her off the Triple R and out of his life, he wanted to hear it. "Always, boss."

"Thanks."

Mia had quieted Silas once again and she waved at him from the doorway. He promised he'd be back to check on her this evening, reminded her to call if she had any trouble and then went to deal with Selina.

It would be a day working from the truck rather than on horseback as he'd come to prefer, but every day on the ranch beat a day in the office. Convinced Mia's car was still hidden after the rain, he did what he could to cover the tire tracks to the bunkhouse before heading toward his place. He felt a bit more human after his lightning-quick shower, but he wasn't looking forward to Selina knowing he'd kept her waiting.

The woman was hot when he arrived, her toe tapping and her face sharp with a frown when she opened the door.

"Oh, Jarvis." Her entire demeanor seemed to soften without even moving a muscle. "*You* are always worth the wait." Her eyes cruised over his body, lingering on his chest and south of his belt before she lifted her gaze to his face once more. "The fresh-scrubbed look is good on you."

He wouldn't be surprised if she asked him to work shirtless one of these days.

"Thanks." He resisted the urge to curl his lip in distaste, or pluck his shirt from his chest. He only now regretted pulling his clothing on over still-damp skin. "I figured you'd prefer fresh scrubbed to muddy."

"Hmm." This time the long perusal of his body ended with a fast lick of her lips. "I suppose muddy could be appealing. In the right circumstances."

She was too obvious in her bids for attention, but Jarvis considered her mostly harmless. She flirted and talked a good game, but he doubted she'd back up that bold, sexy bluster by actually getting muddy in any way, shape or form with a simple cowboy.

Jarvis was well aware that she considered him eye candy, which might be flattering from another woman. From Selina, it felt sticky. From the start, he'd chosen to play along—with extreme caution—so she'd keep talking to him.

He smiled, employing the easygoing charm that had won over many a person in boardrooms and out here on the ranch. "What is it I can help with today?"

"You are such a treat." A catlike grin spread over her face, and her blue eyes sparkled. Her hair was down, the red-gold waves flowing over her shoulders. She stepped away from the door so he could walk inside. "The problem is back this way."

He followed her through the house. She was an attractive woman and her casual sundress played up her best features. Surely, she'd tempted many a man on or off the ranch into her bed. Jarvis focused on the newest additions to her luxurious decor rather than the woman herself. She was always changing something. Yeah, her attorney had been superb, but she still struck him as lonely. To his relief, today's trouble wasn't near her bedroom, but outside, where she kept making improvements to her deck and outdoor kitchen. Selina loved to entertain.

"I ordered new fixtures for the sinks and a better wine cooler. Take the old one if you want it."

What was he going to do with a wine cooler? He could hear the crap he'd take from the other ranch hands if he put it in his room. "We'll see," he said, eyeing the various boxes. The thing might be of some use to Mia out at the bunkhouse or even his sister, Bella.

"It impresses women when men are prepared," Selina said suggestively.

He arched an eyebrow. "Prepared to serve wine properly?"

"Boy Scouts have a stellar reputation for a reason," she demurred.

He laughed, unable to temper the reaction. She sucked in a breath. "What's so funny about that?"

"You'd be bored with the Boy Scout–type in about thirty seconds flat."

She folded her arms under her breasts, boosting them a little. He kept his eyes locked with hers, refusing to take the bait. She pouted. "Fine. You might be right." Sauntering closer, she dragged a finger across his shoulders. "Rugged and rough is *much* more to my liking."

Today, maybe. Selina wasn't the type that stayed content. Hell, she'd had it all with Payne and seemingly tossed it aside to chase younger men. Of course, she'd landed on her feet. Ignoring her attempts to distract him or bait him into something physical, he focused on the fixtures.

"I need to let Asher know I'll be here awhile." Looked like his search for confirmation of Isaiah's story would be pushed back another day.

"You do that," she said. "We can make a day of it."

"Sure." It would be a day of crawling around, squeezing under counters and twisting himself into tight spaces while Selina eyed him like a prize.

She drifted away on a cloud of expensive perfume and he shut off the water at the valve that served her outdoor entertaining space. At the breaker box, he cut the power to the outdoor appliances, just to be safe.

Normally, he had no opinion about how Selina lived. Her choices weren't his concern. But today it bothered him. She had so much luxurious space, all of it protected by a security system, big fences and a crowd of people who helped her even when they didn't enjoy the task. Mia, on the other hand, was barely making do with her son in a basic cabin. From his perspective, he was sure both women were lonely with their circumstances, but Selina struck him as sad underneath all of that. Mia was afraid of the threats, overwhelmed and uncertain, but somehow she gave off a ray of hope.

He shook off the weird thoughts. The talk-show shrink routine only proved he needed real sleep in his bed rather than the truck. And it wouldn't hurt to have something else to think about besides the mother and baby he'd left stranded on the opposite side of the ranch.

If only he could convince Mia to move to the main house until she sorted out the problem with her step-mom. Mia would rightfully throttle him if he exposed her that way. She'd been adamant that Regina was too close to both Genevieve Colton and Selina to take that chance. He couldn't argue it, having no real clue about the people the Colton Oil side of the family called friends.

Pushing all of that to the back of his mind, Jarvis set to work on the new plumbing fixtures. The sooner he knocked this out, the more daylight he'd have for his own agenda. To his surprise, Selina didn't hover over him. She took a couple of business calls from a lounger on the other side of the outdoor kitchen. Around noon she even offered to pick up lunch for both of them. He took her up on that since he'd missed breakfast.

But when she wanted him to linger over the food with her at the shaded table, he politely declined. Even though Asher would want him to chat her up, he was too tired and achy to guide the conversation without being obvious.

"Are you thinking you're too good for me, Jarvis?"

"Hardly," he said with a sincere smile this time. "We shouldn't leave your wine suffering at the wrong temperature."

He didn't have to like Selina to respect her talent for negotiation. Though the Coltons openly wished she'd leave the ranch and Colton Oil, she stuck hard and kept her head high despite her mistakes. Whether that was some unsavory blackmail or just her nature didn't make much difference to him. It took tenacity to pull off the life she'd carved out for herself.

"No, we wouldn't want the wine to suffer." This time when she chuckled, the sound seemed more genuine than calculating. Walking over to the brand-new faucet, she stroked the spigot with great affection. And just like that, Selina the seductress was back. "The oil-rubbed bronze is perfect," she mused, peering at him from under her lashes. "I should've gone with it from the beginning."

He wasn't about to fall into her games. "It fits the vibe you've got out here," he said, keeping his tone neutral.

She pursed her lips, as if deciding how best to come at him next, when her cell phone rang. Checking the screen, she gave him a flirty wave of her fingers and walked toward the house.

"Regina!" she gushed. "I was just thinking of you. Tell me everything new."

It was logical that Selina might know more than one Regina, but Jarvis didn't believe in coincidence. Did Selina suspect Mia was hiding on the ranch somewhere? Did Regina?

Mia's warning came back to him, complete with an icy trickle of dread down his spine. Selina and Regina were too alike not to be friends, or at least well-connected enemies. A moment ago, Jarvis had wanted to get out of Selina's reach as fast as possible; now he needed to drag things out just in case this conversation could be of help to Mia.

He turned the water on again and tested the seals and flow on each fixture. Taking far more time than the task required, he racked his brain for an excuse to get into the house and closer to Selina's office.

Gathering up trash and old fixtures, he caught a break to hear that she'd stopped in the kitchen. "What's the occasion?" Selina paused, listening. "Aren't you thoughtful? Norton will *love* that."

The comment dashed any hope that Selina wasn't speaking with Mia's stepmother. "Why isn't Mia helping? I know the baby is still so new—"

Selina went quiet. Regina must have interrupted.

"Well, I suppose the silver lining is you won't have to see her flaunting all that baby weight as if it's a badge of honor. That's just the worst." She added, "As if I'm in the wrong because I chose to take care of my body. After all those years modeling, I expected her to have more pride than that." Regina's reply brought out Selina's catty laughter.

Jarvis had a sister and, though his aunt and mother had died, he was aware of how some women could act toward one another. Mia's fuller figure was beautiful and real, whether or not she was still carrying baby weight. He bristled with an inexplicable urge to defend Mia. And if he did, she'd be in more trouble.

"Do you think her ex wrote that in to the prenup?" Selina queried under her breath. "What? He never wanted kids? So all those rumors about his brilliance are true," she muttered. "There's a man with my kind of priorities."

Grinding his teeth, he continued with his work. Two by two, he carried wine from the outside cooler into the kitchen, avoiding eye contact with Selina. She didn't seem the least bit perturbed that he could hear her end of the call. At least this uncomfortable scene would help him reassure Mia that her stepmother wasn't onto her current location.

When the wine was out of the way, he disconnected the old cooler and pulled it out of the space. While he was unboxing the new appliance, he heard Selina return, her call apparently over.

"Jarvis?"

He didn't turn around, his hands full as he carefully lifted the wine cooler out of the protective packaging. "Selina?" he mimicked her tone.

"Turns out I need a bit more help. From you."

"How's that?"

"My friend has an important gathering coming up. Important to her, anyway. I could use a date with a handsome cowboy. How about you?"

He pretended to read the installation manual. "Cowgirls are more my type," he replied.

With an amused giggle, she came around to help with the clingy packaging on the wine cooler. "What about *this* cowgirl? I need a date hot enough to make Regina Graves weep with envy."

He didn't think a woman who could threaten a baby could cry real tears. "That's quite a compliment," he said. "Who is Regina Graves?"

"Just another second wife, though she's still married to her musty old wallet," Selina said.

"You mean old man?"

"Semantics. I mean she's still earning her keep. It's a lot of work making a man believe you're in love with him. She's stuck and I'm free to date without any worries."

Jarvis barely kept his opinion locked down. "As long as your date makes her jealous."

"Especially on this occasion. Come on, Jarvis. You're a *man*." She licked her lips. "You don't need to understand the female mind in this instance. This can't be the first time someone asked you out because of that jawline or those shoulders. Not to mention…" Her gaze ventured south. She didn't need to finish the sentence.

"You don't think your friend is happy in the marriage?"

"How would I know? I don't even care." But the expression on her face said she knew all too well that love and devotion weren't Regina's motives for staying married. "What is wrong with you today? Have you met someone?"

"No," he replied. "I'm as free to date as you are."

"Then stop being a prude about this and say yes." Selina hopped up on the counter and crossed her slender legs at the knee. "Norton Graves has money growing out of his hairy ears and Regina loves to flaunt it. She's throwing a party next week and I could use a date. A *really hot* date. Say yes and I'll owe you."

Jarvis eyed her. It felt like a trap. The last time he'd seen Norton Graves, speaking at a luncheon before he'd left his career for ranching, the man's ears had been perfectly normal. Maybe Selina was right and guys didn't notice those details.

"Oh, don't get too excited there, cowboy. This is a one-night-only deal. I don't do relationships."

Jarvis did a mental eye roll to avoid getting lambasted. Again. He didn't want to go anywhere with Selina if he could prevent it. A night with her pawing at him and selling an attraction he didn't feel wasn't his idea of a good time. "I'll have to check my calendar," he said.

"Your calendar." Selina cackled. "Jarvis, you sound like a real Colton."

Thankfully, he wasn't in a position where she could see his face. He *was* a real Colton, even if Payne had refused to acknowledge the truth. In that moment, he decided he'd kick Selina out of her precious house if it did turn out Triple R belonged to him and his siblings.

He managed to make the connections without cussing her out or wrenching his arm out of the socket. Kneeling, he scooted the wine cooler back inch by inch into the space. Sitting back on his heels, he eyed the appliance and started to adjust it to level.

"Say something," Selina demanded. "Seriously, Jarvis. Don't be coy. You're the hottest thing out here. Help me out."

Thing. He took his time rooting around in his toolbox for the small level. He didn't do relationships, either, but he hoped like hell he'd never treated a woman with as much disregard as Selina did him. "Not sure I can swing it," he said. "I have a lot on my plate out here and a date goes over and above my usual tasks."

"This would be vaguely personal," she said. "You forget how much I know about this place. Asher gives you plenty of time off. I need to show up with the hottest man in town. Only the *best* eye candy is worth rubbing in Regina's face," Selina confessed.

"Sounds like some friend," he muttered. He set the level in place and then purposely missed the mark just to keep her talking.

"She's not all bad, but she is in a class by herself. Think about what you'll gain, rubbing elbows with wealthy businessmen who could help you get your career back on track."

"My career is on the perfect track," he said.

She swore. "What will it take to convince you to help me out?"

"When is it?" He made incremental adjustments until the wine cooler was perfectly level. Selina didn't tolerate anything less than perfection.

She gave him the date and time. "I'd need you to pick me up. And it'll be dressy."

"I'll check my calendar," he repeated.

She hopped down from the counter, arms crossed under her breasts. "While you're checking the calendar, I'll be checking with other available men."

He smiled, stretching his arms wide, giving her a good view and oozing the charm she expected from him. "You won't." Dropping his arms back to his sides, he pulled out his phone and checked the ranch schedule. "I'd hate for you to show up to such an important event with the second-best eye candy."

"Can you even do evening attire?" she demanded. "I can pop for a suit if you need it."

He rubbed his hand on his shirt, pulling the fabric tight. Predictably, her eyes glazed and her lips parted. He politely ignored her practiced response. "I know how to clean up when necessary."

She leaned back, her assessing gaze drifting across his body once more. "I bet you do. Put me out of my misery, cowboy. Just say yes."

He scanned the calendar and confirmed he was not on duty that evening. It would've been nice to discuss this with Mia before giving in to Selina's demand. Canceling on Selina would create more problems and make her a bigger nightmare than ever. Technically, he didn't

owe Mia anything, and maybe a little up-close recon of
Regina would help Mia decide what to do next.

"Invitations like this one aren't easy to get," she
pushed. Her hands on her hips now, she stared him
down.

"You're making it sound better and better," he
drawled. "Irresistible, really. You need a date, you've
got one." He ticked off the pertinent points on his fingers. "I'll dress appropriately. I will pick you up. I will
converse appropriately. I will *not* expect any relationship nonsense."

"Mmm-hmm." She tapped a fingertip to her lips.
"Do you have a gray suit?"

"Charcoal," he replied, more amused than offended
at this point.

"Good, good." she purred. "I can work with charcoal. Do you have a decent car?"

"Just my truck."

"You'll drive my sports car," she declared.

"That will be an experience," he admitted.

"But you can't put the top down on the way to the
party."

"Scout's honor," he agreed with a wink.

"And you won't drink." Her blue gaze turned hard
and serious. "I want to enjoy myself."

"All right." Maybe if she got tipsy he could squeeze
her for more details about the ranch history or whatever she might be using against Payne and his children.

He packed up his toolbox and then wedged the old
wine cooler into the new cooler's box to protect the
glass front. "I'll just pull my truck around to get all
this out of here."

She caught his elbow. "In a minute. At the party, if anyone asks, you are totally into me."

"Of course I am, sweetheart."

She tilted her head, a sneaky smile on her face. "You've done this before."

"Feigned avid interest in a pointless conversation? Yes. Yes, I have."

She smacked him lightly on the shoulder, then bit her lip. He guessed she thought the rehearsed expression was sexy and appealing. Maybe it was for other men. For him, Selina was too obvious for her own good. "Stop."

"You first," he said. "There's a lot of ranch to cover and I should get out there. Unless you have more rules and requirements? Have a little faith. Everyone there will see that you have me wrapped around your little finger."

"Do I?"

"Selina." He picked up his toolbox and treated her to one of those long, obnoxious looks. "We both know you'd toss me out the minute you believed that." She was pretty and she'd kept herself in shape, she just didn't spark his interest beyond a basic appreciation for the packaging. He winked at her. "Until next week."

"Fine." She sniffed. "How long until the new cooler is ready to go?"

"Give it two more hours," he suggested.

He walked away from her lovely, entertaining space, taking the long way rather than cutting through her house to get to his truck. He supposed his truck out front served as solid groundwork for their "date" next week. Anyone in or around the main house would notice his personal truck and wonder who'd stopped by.

She would definitely make up a detailed story that painted her in the best possible light. He didn't care. Let her say whatever made her happy. A happy Selina posed fewer problems for Asher and the rest of the crew.

Grimacing at the hours he'd spent with Selina, he sent a text update to Asher and then went out to see how he could best help the crew make the most of the day. Assuming they didn't run into any trouble, he might get some time for his search after all.

Chapter Four

Mia wasn't the least bit ashamed about the waves of gratitude that had been flowing through her all day. At this point, those buoyant feelings were probably the only thing keeping her upright. Silas had been fussy all day, despite the vast improvement in both weather and their accommodations.

The bunkhouse must have been remodeled and updated sometime in the past few years. The building was an excellent use of a simple rectangular layout, with four bunk beds at one end, a bathroom and kitchenette on the other end, and a square oak table in between. Big windows let in plenty of light and she even had a decent internet connection. Jarvis had been right on point about how much easier life was with running water and power. For Mia, this modest building might as well have been the luxurious sprawling country house she was supposed to be selling for her father.

Her shower earlier had cleared her mind and given her a wonderful boost, but she needed sleep. So far, Silas had only slept if she rocked him, despite being up all night long. Whenever she tried to put him down so she could nap, too, he wailed. And the wailing meant more worries, since her son's cries had exposed her original hiding place. Although Jarvis hadn't been joking about the remote location. Surrounded by acres of fallow fields and a clear view to the horizon, there was no chance of anyone surprising her out here.

Though the parenting books and classes had assured her this would happen, she fretted over every detail, worried he was running a fever or coping with colic. His temperature was normal and his food was staying down. His tummy felt normal rather than distended. She stripped him to his diaper and confirmed his clothing wasn't the problem. She changed her hold as she rocked him and tried the pacifier. Nothing helped.

Since she had electricity and her phone was charged up, she reached out to her pediatrician via online chat. The professionals concluded that her baby was perfectly healthy, just in a foul mood.

Well, that made two of them.

During the discussion, she was encouraged to let Silas cry a bit. In Mia's mind, two months seemed far too young to expect a baby to self-soothe, but she supposed the suggestion was more about giving her some space and a measure of peace than for her son.

Choosing to believe Jarvis's claim that they wouldn't be found, Mia buckled Silas into his car seat and stepped outside. She set her cell phone timer for ten minutes and focused on the stunning mountains in the distance while her son's miserable cries nearly broke her heart.

It was the worst ten minutes of her life. She rushed back to him and cuddled him close, murmuring nonsensical apologies. Neither she nor her son were any happier for the experiment, but no one could accuse her of not complying with professional guidance.

Swaying side to side with Silas in the crook of her arm, she picked up her phone to call Tamara. *No, no, no.* That call would leave Tamara in the awkward position of lying if Regina asked about Mia and Silas. Babies and mothers had been surviving moments like this since the beginning of time. It wasn't pretty or fun, but they would get through.

She paced outside, wishing for a cool breeze, but nature didn't cooperate, just gave her more of the still afternoon heat. If they'd been home, in her suite at her father's house, she would've had Silas's swing or bath seat. She would've had the option to relax outside in the glider swing under the shade tree, where she'd grown up chatting with her mother about anything and everything.

Everything but the emptiness that death would leave. She hadn't known to ask about that. After moving back in, that glider was where she'd first talked to Silas about the grandmother he would never know. That special place had been where she dreamed about a yard of her own with a swing set, sandbox and a baby pool for her son.

Her father had mentioned creating a space for his grandson with all of those things in his yard, whether or not she stayed. He'd wanted to have everything that would keep Silas happy when they visited. Thanks to Regina, that grand plan was wrecked. Mia had been shoved out of her father's life until she found a viable solution. Regina would never accept Mia's promise to keep quiet about what she'd seen, which meant Silas would never be safe at their home. Gone was her hope for family dinners and frequent visits with Grandpa, reminiscing over the past and imagining the future. It hurt her heart to think Silas would grow up without his grandpa and they'd never enjoy those strong family connections.

Rehashing all those unpleasant and bleak thoughts wouldn't do her any good. While Silas fussed, sweat dampening his downy-soft baby curls, she sang to him, praying that something would break this wretched cycle they seemed to be mired in.

"You're so tired, baby," she said, tears of exhaustion welling up in her eyes. "It's okay to sleep. We're safe." Was she convincing him or herself? It didn't make much difference. If he relaxed, she could do the same.

Growing desperate, she carried him inside and straight to the bathroom. Removing his onesie and her T-shirt and shorts, Mia turned on the shower. Picking up her son, she stepped under the spray, keeping the water lukewarm. The water put a halt to their combined tears as the fine spray hit her skin and misted around his tiny form. The sudden quiet was such a relief, even if he wasn't asleep.

The blissful reprieve lasted while she toweled them both off. Wrapped in a towel, she curled up on the bunk and fed him until he dozed off. Confident he was sleeping, she gently laid him down on a folded blanket on the floor and inched away, holding her breath.

His limbs twitched and he sighed, but he didn't cry. She counted it a victory when she was able to get her clothing on without interruption.

Though her eyelids were heavy and her energy gone, she resisted the urge to stretch out and sleep. She opened her laptop and used her mobile hot spot to connect to the internet, looking for any signs that her father might have reached out in concern, or that Regina had been slinging mud against her.

It didn't take long to find her stepmother's comments on Mia's most recent social media posts. There was the inquiry about getting back to work with a link to an article on working-mom solutions, as well as a gushing comment about seeing the "sweet grandbaby" soon. Though the wording was correct and polite, Mia read the underlying sneer behind them.

She noticed a picture of centerpieces on Regina's time line, along with a comment about an upcoming gathering to honor her "amazing husband" in which she expressed high hopes that the whole family would be there.

Mia choked on the water she was sipping, smothering the sounds so she wouldn't wake Silas. As if she'd bring her baby to an event hosted by that crocodile. Yes, she wanted desperately to see her father, to speak with him privately, but not with the threats against Silas ringing in her ears.

But then another dreadful thought crossed her mind. What if Regina meant to hurt Norton at the party? It would give her the perfect alibi: a hundred or so close friends milling about, all of them witnesses to the tragically premature death of her beloved, wealthy, investment-banker husband.

Mia rubbed her gritty eyes. She should go to the party, if only to protect her father. It wasn't exactly party-crashing after Regina's public comments on social media. If she didn't attend, she'd be setting herself up for criticism from everyone else in town, but if she did go, who would protect Silas?

There was the small problem that she didn't have

anything to wear. The dress she'd been wearing the day she'd caught Regina cheating wasn't dressy enough for the evening. She hadn't been thinking about formal wear when she'd packed in a rush to get her son to safety. Mia pushed to her feet and started to pace. Worrying about a dress wasn't the priority.

She'd never regretted moving back into the suite at her father's house more than she did right this minute. Going back meant leaving herself and her son vulnerable to attack. She couldn't watch Silas and Regina every single minute, not without help, anyway.

Her relationship with Regina had been fraught from their first introduction, but she'd never expected it to devolve into murderous threats. Mia had been a teenager and not the least bit interested in a replacement mother. Good thing, too. Regina hadn't been interested in anything resembling maternal affection. That rough start had grown over with thorny vines and choked with spiky weeds.

Their mutual dislike had escalated into cutting sarcasm through the years as Regina successfully pushed Mia out of the nest. Her concerns had been interpreted—thanks to Regina whispering in Norton's ear—as the antics of a spoiled girl who didn't want to share her daddy.

Looking back, Mia could see where she'd gone wrong with her constant griping about the unfairness of life in general and her stepmother in particular. By the time she'd learned to keep her thoughts to herself, Regina had complete control of Norton's affection and opinions. When Mia had discovered her college fund was empty and confronted her father and stepmother, it shouldn't have been a shock that her father believed his wife's lies over his daughter's truth.

Another battle lost to her father's blind love for the viper he'd married. She'd vowed that would be the last battle, choosing to make her own way, using what she knew and the natural abilities and strengths at her disposal.

Modeling had covered tuition and expenses. She'd built up her professional network and cultivated friendships outside of her father's sphere of influence and therefore out of Regina's grasping reach.

And now she was locked in another battle. Alone. Her father would never believe his wife had threatened his grandson. He'd been slowly convinced Mia was a perpetual problem, always in need of help, especially after the pregnancy ended her marriage. She never should've accepted his offer to move back in. Her father meant well and she'd been feeling vulnerable enough to go for it. Shame on her for believing things might be different now that she and Regina were adults. The house was big enough that they could have easily avoided each other.

Mia had been willing to let the past lie, but obviously Regina had felt threatened. In hindsight, Mia suspected that Regina had always worried about Mia catching her sleeping around.

Well, she'd done that.

Her mind spinning, Mia tried to push that disgusting picture out of her head. Knowing Regina's tendency to take what she wanted, whenever she wanted, Mia didn't believe that had been the first time. She doubted her stepmother had bothered to hide her affairs at the country house before Mia had moved back in. Not that it mattered.

She sat down again and closed the laptop, dropping her head to her folded arms on the table. Her thoughts were sluggish and she couldn't pin down the perfect way to tell on Regina without causing anyone else harm.

If she didn't tell…if she did…if she didn't…

The only thing that interrupted the futile cycle was Silas crying again.

Mia didn't bother checking the time. She simply gathered up her baby and moved through the motions of care, praying he'd eventually sleep off whatever was upsetting his system. As she tucked Silas into the sling that kept him close to her body, he subsided into general fussiness, which felt like a vast improvement over the constant crying. Her stomach growled and she was rooting through the grocery bag for a snack when she heard an engine rumbling closer.

Her immediate tension caused Silas to give a start, but he didn't wail. Maybe his throat was as tired as her ears. With one hand on the stick Jarvis had brought along from the warming hut, she peeked through the window and was immediately rewarded with a view of Jarvis swinging out of his truck. The man had an excellent, fantasy-inducing body. If she ever got to sleep again, she was sure her dreams would be memorable. Tantalizing. She soaked up the way he moved, his long stride and the easy smile on his face as he approached.

She opened the door for him, enjoying the sparkle of amusement in his deep brown eyes as he stopped at the threshold.

"Hey," he said.

"Hi." She'd never been shy a day in her life, yet Jarvis managed to scatter her thoughts with a smile and she wasn't sure sleep would fix it. Something about him just slid right past the defenses she'd built up against charming men. "Come on in."

He dipped his chin toward the baby squirming in the sling. "Did I catch you at a bad time? Is he hungry again?"

"I wish it was that simple." She suddenly felt disheveled and frumpy despite the shower and better conditions. He'd left her in a fully equipped cabin and she was more of a mess than she'd been this morning. "Our long night turned into a longer day." She swept her bangs to the side. "We're fine, really. It's just that nothing is making him happy," she said.

"He's not sick, is he?" Jarvis set a bag on the table, his amusement gone and the sparkle in his eyes replaced with concern. "Do you need a doctor? You should've called me."

"No, no. We're fine," she repeated. "But thank you." She went to rub the crick in her neck and discovered the clip holding her hair up had drooped to the side. No wonder he'd been amused when he walked up. She must look a mess. "I did an online chat with his pediatrician."

Silas stretched his limbs, one tiny foot kicking her diaphragm. The sling was great, until it felt like pregnancy again. She shifted him for her comfort and he started to cry again. She swore under her breath, immediately feeling guilty. She couldn't make that a habit or his first words would be embarrassing and completely inappropriate.

"Pardon me. As I said, we've just had one of those days."

"On top of a rough night," he observed.

"Parenting." She shrugged, bouncing gently in an effort to soothe her son. "It happens."

"Guess so." His mouth curved into a smile. "This gives me a new perspective. I suddenly have way more respect for how my parents handled this in triplicate."

She couldn't have heard him right. "Triplicate?"

"Yup. They wound up with two boys and a girl all at once without even trying."

"You're kidding. Wow." She patted Silas's back. She really couldn't imagine dealing with three of him. "I hope you tell your mom and dad they're incredible every time you see them."

"I wish I could. They were awesome." His gaze was on Silas and his voice went soft. "They died when we were ten."

"Jarvis, I'm so sorry. Losing my mother was devastating." To lose both parents at once was inconceivable.

"It was a long time ago," he muttered. "We got through."

She knew getting through wasn't always enough. Restless, Silas pushed against her again, bringing her full attention back to the present. "I really thought the separation thing would be a few years coming."

She unwound the sling and realized he needed a clean diaper. Taking care of that calmed him for a few minutes, but he resisted when she tried to hold him again so she laid him down on the blanket on the floor so he could stretch and kick and fuss to his heart's content.

"I brought you a hot sandwich and a salad," Jarvis said. "Have you eaten?"

She opened her mouth and snapped it closed again, uncertain. "I must have," she said. "I was about to have a snack when you pulled up."

"Have a meal instead." He placed a bottle of water next to the to-go containers.

Her backside had barely met the chair when Silas erupted again. She stood, but Jarvis waved her back into the chair. "I wanted to talk about something, but it can wait. You look like you could use a relief pitcher. Eat."

She wasn't sure she could manage a coherent conversation right now. As he approached Silas, she started to ask how much experience he had with babies and stopped herself. He was only helping out while she was right here in the room, not applying for a position as a nanny. He certainly couldn't do any worse than she'd done today.

Mia popped the lid off the salad container, watching as Jarvis crouched on one knee by her son, his strong, tanned hand looking enormous as he let Silas kick at his palm.

"Don't you like cabins, little man?" he asked. "Is it too quiet out here for you?"

Silas's fussing eased and his big eyes followed the sound of Jarvis's voice.

"I didn't think about that." Mia felt dumbstruck. Of course Silas was more accustomed to background noise in and around her father's house. Out here on the ranch, things were so still. "I've tried talking and—"

she gave in to a yawn "—and singing. It just hasn't been enough."

She wasn't enough. The thought steamrolled right over her and tears threatened to ruin the wonderful food Jarvis had brought. She stabbed her fork into the salad, refusing to give in to the nonsensical emotions. She'd feel better after some sleep. Assuming Silas would eventually allow that.

"Would you mind if I held him?" Jarvis asked. "I could take him for a walk and you could take a nap."

"Oh." It was a generous offer and yet she hesitated. She was supposed to be doing this parenting thing on her own. Every time he was nice to her, she was filled with a weird, indescribable blend of feeling grateful and inept. "That isn't necessary."

He was already picking up the sling. "I think it is." His brow furrowed as he studied how it should work and where it would adjust to his frame rather than hers.

"Here," she began, reaching across the table for the fabric. "But you shouldn't feel like you have to do anything more. You've done so much for us already."

"You're supposed to be eating," he scolded with an easy grin on his face. "I can do this. With an online assist."

She watched him as he scowled into his phone and smothered a laugh when she heard a tutorial video start to play. She'd had to watch that video herself a few times.

Not Jarvis. He got it in one. He had the sling on and the baby snuggled close, a pacifier in hand. "We'll take a walk," he announced. "You eat up and then take a nap."

He was doing what? "You're too hot." She felt the

heat of embarrassment climbing from her neck into her face, searing her cheeks. "I mean, the weather. It's too hot. Outside. You don't have to do this," she repeated.

Jarvis's gentle, knowing smile brought her rambling to a stop. "We won't go far."

"He might get hungry."

"Then you'll be right here. Take a nap, Mia."

"Do you know about—"

"Mia. Whatever I don't know, I'll look up." He raised his phone. "We'll manage. I promise."

Silas didn't fight Jarvis the way he'd shoved and kicked her. His eyes were wide as he quietly stared up at the cowboy, his mouth working on the pacifier. Oh, she would not be jealous that her son preferred a stranger over her on his worst day. She had to respect Silas's taste in strangers. Like her son, she felt better when she stared at Jarvis, too.

"It's weird," she admitted. "Taking a nap while you're out with him. I mean, I trust you."

"Mmm-hmm."

"But what if—"

"Try. Just try to sleep." He walked over to her, looking for all the world like he did this kind of thing all the time.

Maybe he did. She didn't know him. "Do you have kids?" she asked, horrified that she might be keeping him from his family.

"No. Quit stalling and finish eating so you can sleep." He patted Silas. "Tell your momma goodbye. We have man things to discuss."

She leaned in close to kiss her son's downy head and was met with the heady combination of Jarvis's warm and masculine scent mingling with the sweetness of her baby. That was dangerous territory. Edging away before she jumped him, she hoped her burst of hormones and attraction weren't too obvious. "Have a good time," she said.

"We will." Tipping his tan cowboy hat and giving her a sexy wink, Jarvis walked out. With her baby.

Instinctively, she jerked forward to follow. Scolding herself, she took another bite of salad and tried to appreciate the flavors. Jarvis had proven himself trustworthy time and again. If he'd shared her location, she would've heard about it by now. He wasn't running off with her child, her heart. He seemed genuinely respectful of her desire for secrecy. Another yawn seized her and she knew she'd be a fool to waste this opportunity. She needed rest more than food. After stowing the takeout containers in the small refrigerator, she flopped down on the bunk and pulled the edge of the sleeping bag over her legs.

JARVIS WALKED WELL away from the bunkhouse before he started talking to the baby. He didn't want Mia to have any reason to follow them or worry that he was in over his head. He was, but he would figure it out. Kids were *not* his thing and he'd never taken much interest, knowing they wouldn't be part of his future. He'd always resisted the burdens that came with choices like commitment and family. His siblings had recently opened themselves to that kind of thing, but Jarvis planned to keep holding out. Why give fate a chance to steal one more person he loved the way his parents and grandfather had been snatched away? It would be hard enough to cope when his siblings inevitably died.

Every family needed a fun-loving uncle. Maybe if

they'd had one, they wouldn't have been saddled with a kid-hating aunt. *Families* sounded stable and reliable, and he sincerely hoped that for his siblings, that would be how it turned out. Most of the time, family sucked. Being right here on this ranch was all the reminder he needed. Generations ago, two Coltons had screwed each other over, and Payne's side of the family prospered while Jarvis's had floundered.

He looked down at the baby and knew that if his brother or sister needed him to step up as a guardian, he would do it. And he'd do it with far more affection and attention than they'd received from Aunt Amelia. By all accounts, she'd been a pleasant, approachable woman until losing her husband. "That's my role," he said to the baby. "Fun uncle. I'm good with it. No sense doing something that would make me that kind of sad and bitter.

"You've been running your momma ragged, little man," he said to the infant. The dark circles under her eyes had been more pronounced than this morning and he was worried about her.

Tiny fingers curled into the fabric of his T-shirt and the baby's head rested heavy against his chest. He'd been as surprised as Mia by Silas's reaction to his voice. "Kids won't be in my future," he said. "Frankly, your efforts this past twenty-four hours aren't changing my mind."

Feeling rude, even though he knew the baby would never remember this conversation, he backtracked a bit. "Not that you aren't adorable in your way. Loud and opinionated can be good traits. Like, if you grow into a coach," he mused. "Or a stockbroker. Definitely need to be loud and decisive for that job."

The baby shifted and sighed, and Jarvis looked down to see he was fast asleep. His lashes were dark crescents on his chubby cheeks. "Way to go, little man."

Maybe if Mia and Silas both got some good rest at the same time, it would serve as a healthy reset. He wasn't sure how long Mia needed to stay, but he was determined she'd have the time and safe space that she needed.

He should tell Asher about Mia before the foreman found out about her presence and revealed it by accident. Jarvis was happy to cover her expenses if she did actually need money for a hotel or a rental car. She'd claimed money wasn't an issue, but she'd also implied her stepmom could track her down by following her credit card purchases. He was better off finding a solution for Mia off the ranch. There just wasn't a good way to inform Asher without breaking Mia's trust. The reverse was just as true. Asher wouldn't see this solely as an exercise in hospitality or charity. The man was compassionate, sure, but this was crossing a line.

Then again, maybe it wasn't Asher's decision, assuming Jarvis found Isaiah's mystery box soon and the contents of the box were accurate and useful. He hadn't spent a minute on his search today, despite having plenty of daylight after the work was done. He'd wanted to get out here to see Mia, and not with Selina's perfume clinging to his hair and clothing. So he'd squandered the daylight with a hot shower and some research into the Graves family before picking up food for Mia's dinner.

"Your grandpa Norton is a pretty big deal," he said to the sleeping baby. "Your momma, too. Your dad is smart as hell, but way too glossy. Just my opinion."

The pictures online of Mia with her husband at various events were almost blindingly beautiful. Tech mogul Roderick Hodges could've made a career modeling, as well. "Good genes, though," Jarvis admitted. "And he's wildly successful. Still, if your mom left him, you can be sure it was for the best." He wondered what it would take for Mia to tell him that story.

He'd skimmed through several early articles on Norton Graves. He'd read archived reports on the man's financial strategies, his interviews and theories on investing and even a graduation speech or two. Jarvis had found pictures of Norton with Dalinda, his first wife, who was from Jamaica. The biography claimed the two had fallen in love at first sight during a professional conference. Mia had inherited her mother's almond eyes, flawless skin, sumptuous curves and brilliant smile.

"A shame you won't know Mia's mom. As grandmas go, she probably would've been amazing."

From all accounts, they'd been a normal family until her death. There wasn't much in the way of personal news on Norton and Mia until she'd started modeling. Norton had done an excellent job protecting his daughter's privacy. Then as her career blossomed and her smile became known worldwide, reporters covering her industry and her father's looked for any crossover they could find. The media seemed to believe Norton had pulled strings to get her into the right agencies and on the right assignments, but no one found any evidence.

"I don't think so. Your momma's tough and determined enough to get what she wants when she wants it. Except maybe sleep," he said, patting the baby's back.

Silas snored lightly and Jarvis smiled at the sweet sound. It was more than a little disconcerting how right it felt to be walking over a field with a baby strapped to his chest.

"Right or wrong, this is a short-term gig," he said aloud. Reminding himself or informing the baby? "Families can be good when they work. For as long as they work." And when something broke down, families were an unending source of disappointment and pain. "The trouble with families is that people are involved." Regina was a prime example. "I hope for you and your mom it works, little man."

However Mia decided to proceed, Jarvis thought Regina should do hard time just for threatening harm to this innocent little boy. It infuriated him that the woman thought it was reasonable to put Mia and Silas in jeopardy for getting caught in her own mistakes. It was easy, out here with the sun sinking low on the horizon, to understand why Mia had chosen to hide rather than confront her stepmother head-on or give in to the woman's demands.

Pausing to soak up the stunning sunset in front of him, Jarvis swayed side to side, lost in his thoughts as the evening breeze stirred the gray-green grasses. He understood Mia's panicked reaction better with every encounter. His own bone-deep need to protect the baby and the mother were impossible to ignore. He could only imagine how much more intensely Mia felt about protecting her son.

When Jarvis and his siblings had been orphaned, they'd relied on each other to muddle through the grief and loss. Their parents hadn't had much in the way of money or assets, and the family court had dumped the three of them on the closest relative's doorstep.

Aunt Amelia wasn't cut out for mothering. Any maternal instinct was noticeably absent in the way she treated them like short adults. "We were left to handle ourselves," he said to Silas. "She was a wasp, impatient and sharp. Man, I couldn't wait to get out of school and out of that house."

And then she'd died. Suddenly. Proving that people were fragile and relationships were fleeting. They'd been twenty-one and it shouldn't have mattered overmuch to any of them. But Bella had cried and cried at the news. Spencer had been shell-shocked. Jarvis had dealt with the funeral arrangements, alternating between numb detachment and blazing fury over being abandoned again.

No more family for those "poor Colton triplets," as they'd been known in school and around the neighborhood. Oh, sure they'd had their grandpa, but Isaiah wasn't what anyone could call stable, dealing with alcoholism and early-onset dementia. Jarvis had cleaned out Amelia's house. He'd sold the place and split the money among the three of them.

He'd gone through the expected motions of life, finishing college, finding a great job and throwing himself into it. Dates, girlfriends, poker nights with friends and holidays with his siblings. All of it had been just a little out of sync until he'd come to the Triple R.

This felt right, with or without Isaiah's stories and the potential fortune at stake. He could breathe out here, heal. He could push himself when necessary and relax when it wasn't. Early on, all of those right feelings had made him mad, too. Resentful that Payne Colton's greed and pride had kept the triplets away from this amazing place.

Even with Mia's son in his arms, this twilight sky, the panoramic fields and the deep blue shadows of the mountains felt right.

The baby shifted but didn't wake. Jarvis stroked the vulnerable spine. He had the sickening feeling that Mia's will stated Silas should be raised by Norton if anything happened to her. Who else would it be since she was an only child? If the worst happened, would Regina step into the motherhood role or simply dispose of the inconvenient infant? A chill raised the hair on the back of his neck as he turned toward the bunkhouse.

"It's your momma's business, but I hope she's smarter than that." The woman needed a partner to help her with days like this one. Not him, obviously. His heart was too hard to take this on full time. He was done taking chances on people and leaving himself open to the inevitable pain. But capable as she was, motherhood was tough and Mia needed someone she could trust standing with *her*.

The idea of another man walking with Silas and partnering Mia put a bitter taste in Jarvis's mouth. Dumb but true. "A nanny," he said. "She needs a reliable, kind nanny."

He reached the bunkhouse as the sky deepened and the first evening star twinkled overhead. He paused, singing "Twinkle, Twinkle Little Star" to the baby even though Silas was sound asleep.

The light over the kitchenette was on and Jarvis was pleased to find Mia in her sleeping bag. She was curled on her side, one hand tucked under her chin, her breathing deep and even.

He debated unwinding the sling and decided not to mess up the one thing that was working. Since coming to the ranch, he'd pulled his share of all-nighters. Most of those had occurred during calving season, but there had been other reasons, as well.

He eased himself down into one of the chairs at the table and propped his legs on a second chair. Pulling out his phone, he opened the app he used to track his search for the Triple R ownership evidence Isaiah claimed was buried out here. He studied the landmarks he had pinned on his custom map, comparing those points to the log of coordinates where he'd searched already. It would be smart to get back and finish that attempt near the warming hut. First thing tomorrow, before he got busy with the normal ranch schedule, he promised himself.

The baby scooched around inside the sling and Jarvis held his breath. When the little guy sighed, working that pacifier, he relaxed again. If he could keep the kid asleep all night, it would be ideal for Mia.

He stared at the dark curls covering Silas's head. How old were babies when they started sleeping through the night? Asher didn't complain of short nights or interrupted sleep these days, so his girls must sleep all night most of the time.

He searched the topic on his phone and found answers with a wide enough age range to be annoying rather than helpful. As a milestone, sleeping all night seemed to involve some mysterious baby X factor that was unique to each individual child. How did parents manage this stuff?

He went back to looking up Regina Graves. Most of the news he found related directly to her marriage to

Norton. Doing the math and skimming the old publicity photos, he figured Mia must have been a teenager when her father remarried. Though she smiled in her father's wedding photos, her eyes were flat and a little sad.

That led him to the pictures online of Mia's modeling career and eventual wedding. On that happy day, she wore ivory lace that flattered her skin, her eyes sparkled and her smile was the brightest he'd ever seen as she linked hands with her groom, Roderick. Jarvis studied the man again. Her ex was well over six feet tall and powerfully built. For a man known to push the envelope with computers and tech, his thick blond hair, blue eyes and chiseled features were Hollywood worthy.

Jarvis studied the baby resting contentedly in the sling. Silas didn't resemble his father at all, only Mia. Maybe Jarvis was biased, but he hoped it stayed that way. For everyone involved.

The baby snuffled, hiking up his hips and rubbing his face on Jarvis's chest. The pacifier came loose and Jarvis started singing, his voice low and gentle as he nudged the pacifier back in place.

It worked for a few minutes, then he squirmed again. Jarvis stood up and carefully unwrapped the sling, still singing. Every minute he could give Mia had to help her. Nestled in the crook of his arm, Silas went back to sleep. Jarvis kept singing and swaying.

MIA CAME AWAKE to the mellow sound of a baritone voice singing softly. It was "Home on the Range," she realized as the melody registered in her sleepy mind. Feeling refreshed, she let herself be lulled by Jarvis's efforts to keep her son quiet.

It was the sweetest sound and she didn't want to move and spoil the moment. From under her lashes, she watched him sway gently, silhouetted by the pale light over the sink. She'd never seen a more devoted picture of fatherhood, unless she thought of her own father. She tried to imagine Roderick tending to his son this way and the pieces wouldn't fit.

There was a picture similar to this one in her baby album. Her mom had caught her dad in the act of singing her to sleep one night. Dalinda had been adamant about creating and keeping memories. After her death, Mia was doubly grateful for her commitment. The album of her first year was in her father's study at home and she'd planned to share it with Silas one day, to use it as a model for his baby book. Would she ever see that precious scrapbook again?

Right now she used an online journal to keep up with Silas's baby milestones. The program allowed her to share the online pages with friends and relatives and she could order prints of the pages. But her recent days had been so bad that she hadn't wanted to revisit them—until this moment, as she watched Jarvis with her son.

Stretching slowly so the mattress wouldn't squeak in the frame, she eased up to a sitting position. Jarvis didn't stop singing until he reached the end of his verse. When he finally looked up, the intensity of his gaze stole her breath.

Her body heated in an instant and hormones she barely recognized sat up and begged. For Jarvis. A taste, a kiss, a touch. Any tangible connection he'd allow, she'd gladly accept. What would those hard-working hands feel like on her skin? Her fingertips positively itched to feel the rasp of the whiskers on his square jaw.

She tried to smile, focusing on other reactions and signals. She needed the bathroom and based on the full-ness in her breasts, her son would soon need to nurse. Much safer to address those needs instead of this sud-den longing for a man who was simply kind enough to help a stranger.

She hurried to the bathroom and took care of herself, splashing water on her face to cool down her heated cheeks. Silas was fussing again when she emerged, but it wasn't anything like it had been.

Or maybe it was just as bad, but sleep had blunted the sharp edge.

Jarvis was on the floor again, changing her son's diaper, a more bizarre sight than watching him sing a lullaby. He glanced at her and a grin spread over his handsome features. "Feeling better?"

"Much. Thanks to you." She picked up Silas and started to nurse while Jarvis disposed of the diaper and washed his hands.

It should feel awkward, but didn't. She blamed the illusion of normalcy on the late hour. Since giving birth, she'd discovered that two in the morning gave her a false sense of being separate and distant from real-world constraints. She could think and say things in this hour that no one else would ever hear. It was liberating. Especially after nearly six solid hours of uninterrupted sleep.

"How did you get him to sleep for so long?"

Jarvis shrugged. "Ask him. I didn't do much at all."

"You sang to him."

He tapped his phone. "Just applying advice I found online. Every cowboy knows that song."

She shook her head at his deflection. "*Thank you*, Jarvis. You have no idea how much I needed the break." She brushed fingertips over her son's head. "We both needed this. You're a natural."

"That's, *um*... No. I don't think that fits."

Maybe this rare hour was only soothing and restorative for her. "Easy, cowboy. It's a compliment, not a commitment."

He sat down across from her, his lips tilted sheepishly as he kept his gaze averted. "Noted. Do you want me to stay?"

Yes. "Since you're the hero of the hour, you can do as you please," she said. "Just be warned, he might not go another six hours."

He scrubbed at his face. "I'll stay. If I go back now, it's likely to raise more questions than if I'm out all night," he explained.

She'd visited the Triple R several times for various events and never once given a thought to where or how the crew lived. "You live on the ranch?"

He nodded, a challenge glinting in his gaze. "Is that a problem?"

"Are you kidding?" Even if it was, why did her opinion matter? "I just never thought about that aspect of the operation at a ranch this size."

"No one does. Not even me. Living here isn't required, but I like it. Plus, it's convenient."

"I bet." She paused to burp Silas. "Thanks again. I feel like a new woman."

"Happy to help." His gaze warmed and his smile sent tingles all through her system.

Shocked by her raw responses, she averted her gaze.

"How can I repay you? There has to be something I can do."

"Do you rope cattle or ride fences?" he joked.

"I can *walk* fences," she volunteered quickly. "I do have a wealth of skills beyond mothering." That might be overstating it, but she was a quick learner and she enjoyed learning new things.

"If only we needed a swimsuit model."

She rolled her eyes. "You looked me up."

"Didn't have to," he said. "We studied your career in my business classes."

"You what? That's…" She shook her head. "No. No way. How old are you?"

"Relax." He chuckled. "I'm thirty-one. It was right after your first swimsuit-edition cover. We were studying how you'd branded yourself."

"It wasn't easy." She looked at Silas. "Dad wasn't amused by my decision. Furious is more accurate. He didn't want me 'flaunting myself,' as he put it, but I needed the money to get through school."

"Your dad didn't help with your education?"

"It would be more accurate to say that my stepmother helped herself to my college fund. She had a better story than the truth when I discovered the problem."

"Your dad believed Regina?"

"Yes." Jarvis's dumbfounded expression was such a comfort. For him to side with her without needing any proof was a balm to her battered heart. Silas, his tummy full, was starting to doze off again. That was miraculous. She wanted to gush and thank Jarvis all over again, but she thought that might embarrass him, so she kept the words inside. "They say love is blind. In Dad's case, they're right."

She missed the rocking chair from the nursery, but she managed to mimic the gentle motion. It soothed her as much as her son as her mind drifted back to those grim days. "I can't say there's a single day that I ever liked my stepmom." She could talk about it now without too much animosity or grief. "From the start, she struck me as fake."

"Spoiler alert, it seems like you were right."

"Well, she's been good to my dad and I can't deny that he's happier. He was crushed when Mom died."

"If Regina's been good to your dad, why do you think she'd follow through on the threat to hurt him?"

Mia snorted softly. "The woman is after his money. Any thoughtful gesture or kind effort she's made has carried her closer to gaining control of his fortune and more influence in his professional circles."

"But she was never in banking. Not like your dad."

Mia glanced up from her son's sweet face to catch the furrowed brow on Jarvis's face. "Someone's been doing his homework."

"Protecting the ranch, remember?"

She started to laugh, caught herself before she woke the baby. When she had Silas wrapped snug and settled into his car seat, she rocked it a bit with her toe. "You've been researching all of us."

"Only to a point."

She didn't know why it was funny. It should be offensive or off-putting at least. Instead, she wanted to give him a high five. Or a hug. A kiss. Please, yes, a kiss. Her gaze dropped to his lips and she pressed her own together—hard—to stop her runaway thoughts about how he would taste and feel.

"Regina is ruthless. Manipulative. She says one thing and does another all the time."

"With your college fund."

She nodded. "And her marriage vows. I'm not sure she expected to deal with Dad for decades. As far as I know, she only has control of her accounts, not his. And I'm pretty sure she hasn't convinced him to cut me out of the will, though she is his primary beneficiary. After this incident, though, if she can keep me away and spin it right, there's no reason to keep him around."

"Mia."

The tenderness in his voice nearly broke her. Serious talks in the wee hours were perilous. Worse were the questions she burned to ask *him* about his past, his choices, and if he might be willing to have an affair with her. Nothing permanent. No obligations.

"I really should get some sleep before he wakes up again," she said.

"Yeah. I'll be out of here by sunrise." He waited for her to crawl into the bunk, with Silas in his seat tucked between her and the wall. Then he turned out the light and stretched out on the bunk opposite hers.

For the longest time, she listened to his breath, imagining how it would be to have all that strength wrapped around her. Sleeping alone had been the biggest adjustment when she'd left Roderick. It had been such a strange sensation not having his solid body to curl into, to reach for in the night.

Thank goodness the bunks were narrow or she might have embarrassed herself by asking Jarvis to spoon her. Her imagination took over and she shifted restlessly, willing herself to sleep.

"Mia?"

"Mmm?" It was nice to know he wasn't asleep, either. Could it be because he wanted her, too?

"Why did you marry Roderick?"

Her sex-fantasy bubble burst. "Love." That had only been part of the equation. "Love and money," she admitted. She rolled over to face him, her back pressed close to the hard side of the car seat. "I'm not ashamed of that."

"I wouldn't say you should be."

"We had an understanding about life and goals. He was a good match for me in several areas—we were both ambitious. And he was hot," she joked.

"Obviously." Jarvis chuckled softly. "You were a stunning couple."

She groaned. "I hate the internet." She didn't, really. It was one more tool she'd used to her advantage even after her prime modeling years. "I mean, thanks."

His bunk creaked as he shook with smothered laughter. "You should sleep," he whispered when he caught his breath.

"Same goes, my friend," she replied. "Thank you for everything today," she said quietly. "If we're not up when you leave, have a good day tomorrow."

"You, too. Remember to call me if there's trouble."

"There won't be," she said. She was too cozy, too safe here in this moment for any trouble to touch her.

"I'll bring out a truck and some dinner tomorrow night."

"Mmm. Sounds good."

She shouldn't let him keep helping her, but she enjoyed his company. He gave her something wonderful to anticipate, a happy thought that shot like a sunbeam through the clouds of uncertainty and fear in her mind.

Chapter Five

When his phone beeped with the morning alarm, Jarvis rolled out of the bunk, more rested than he expected after the short night. As quietly and quickly as possible, he made use of the tidy bathroom and dressed again in the same clothes from yesterday.

The baby and Mia slept through it all. Her dark hair spilled across the pillow and one hand was tucked next to her son's knee while he slept in the car seat. He hoped they had a much better day today.

It was all he could do not to kiss her goodbye before leaving the bunkhouse in search of strong coffee. If she needed to stay on, needed more time to make a plan, it would be smart to keep an overnight bag here. Not that he was so eager to move in, but so it was less obvious he was spending nights away from the ranch.

Early sunlight washed over the paddocks near the main stable and filled him up with positive energy. Maybe that energized feeling was more about Mia than the clear day, but either way, he'd take it. Gladly. He picked up his task list for the day, more than a little relieved there weren't any work orders at Selina's place.

He needed to find a way to talk to Mia about the party. Selina had texted him a couple of pictures late last night in various dresses. He wasn't sure what he was supposed to do with the information and he responded as vaguely as possible. Whatever she wore, he'd be in his best suit. Coordinating colors seemed more suited to a high school prom than an adult occasion, but maybe her social set put more stock into that kind of thing.

He'd worked through the various chores inside the barn and moved on to cleaning and repairing cattle trailers when Asher found him. Even with his hat shading his face, Jarvis could see the Triple R foreman was in a somber mood.

"Walk with me?" Asher asked.

He could've made it an order, but he hadn't. Curious, Jarvis turned off the hose he'd been using and fell into step beside him. "What's up?"

Asher paused, watching a few horses in the close paddock, then moved out farther still. Whatever he had to say, he clearly didn't want to be overheard. A slippery coil of dread settled at the base of Jarvis's gut.

"Word is you haven't been in your room the past couple of nights."

Jarvis didn't try to deny it. "That's true." He rubbed a smear of dirt from his hands before looking Asher in the eyes. "When you hired me, you didn't say anything about bed checks."

Asher swore. "That's not what this is."

Jarvis waited.

Leaning his forearms on the top rail of the fence, Asher hooked one booted foot on the lower rail. "You can have a place in town, you know that. But if you're planning to walk off the job, tell me straight up."

Jarvis relaxed. "I don't have any plans to leave,"

Jarvis said. "I like it out here." He couldn't leave until he found Isaiah's evidence. If that find went his way, he was definitely staying. Forever.

"Then where have you been?"

"Why does it matter? If there's a problem, say so. Do I need an alibi or an attorney?"

Asher winced. "Depends on where you've been."

He knew Asher wasn't kidding. "I've got nothing to hide." Nothing but a frightened woman and baby who were in serious danger if Regina found them. "What's your real question?"

"Are you sleeping with Selina?"

"No." Jarvis wouldn't have been more shocked if his boss had thrown a sucker punch. Still, Asher looked downright sick to his stomach. Pretty much how Jarvis felt when Selina flirted too hard. He shook his head, trying to clear the random images. "No," he said again. "I only go over there when you tell me I have to."

"The rumor mill is that you're taking her to some fancy party next week."

"Well, yeah." Jarvis searched for the right explanation. "I was going to run it by you." He could hardly tell his boss he was going so he could do some recon for Mia and possibly warn Norton about Regina. "She took a call from a friend yesterday and then pretty much harangued me into being her date. I can't say I'm looking forward to it."

"Then why did you agree?"

That was an easier question than where he'd spent his last two nights. "Hell, I don't know." That was complete honesty. "Mainly, I agreed to shut her up. You know how she is. I'm not going along so I can schmooze around for a new job, though she did toss that out as a carrot. She doesn't believe I prefer the ranch over an office."

Asher nodded as if that made total sense to him. "Do you prefer the ranch? I'm worried you're bored."

"Not a bit," Jarvis said. "This is the best work I've had, barring the days when Selina snaps her fingers."

"So you're not into her?"

Jarvis just stared down that question.

"Good." Asher rubbed his forehead. "All right." He took a deep breath, his gaze on the horses ambling across the paddock. "Now I need to ask a favor."

Again, Jarvis waited. It was a tactic he'd learned in the business world, but even among less-than-chatty cowboys, silence often proved the most effective way to get information.

"When you're out with her," Asher began, "would you please keep an eye on her? I've seen her at parties and she likes to indulge. The more expensive the champagne or the more open the bar, the happier she is."

"Regardless of whether or not I like her, it's not my nature to ditch a date when she's drunk."

"I'm asking more than that, man." He tipped back his hat. "I need you to stick close. Let her flirt and let her ramble. She doesn't censor herself when she's drinking. If she gets to talking, if you can keep her talking, I want to know if she says anything about shooting Payne."

Jarvis whistled. "You think *she's* the shooter?" This just got more and more interesting.

"Doubtful. No one knows who shot my dad. Yet. We will find out, one way or another." He glared out across the landscape. "I'm not sure she's capable of pulling the trigger, but she might hire it done. I can't see how taking him out helps her, but then again, I'm not a criminal."

Jarvis reeled. As far as he'd heard, there were still no leads about the attack on Payne Colton. He figured there were plenty of suspects. The man had money and land, but he hadn't won any popularity contests in the area.

"The woman got a house and a seat on the Colton Oil board," Asher said, his voice a low growl. "Whether or not she's the shooter, she must have been blackmailing him. That's the only way to explain how he caved to her demands when they divorced. Maybe he threatened to stop cooperating."

Jarvis didn't know Payne the way Asher did, hadn't seen the fallout of what sounded like a rocky marriage on the best of days. "I'll stay alert."

"Thanks. Just stick close. Pay attention to who she talks to and listen for anything helpful. Maybe she'll get tipsy and start bragging."

He thought he and his siblings had been treated poorly by Payne, but the longer he worked here with his cousin the less he envied the way Payne's children had been raised and all the advantages they'd enjoyed. Those benefits clearly had come at a price.

"Can't be easy to be Payne's son," Jarvis said.

"Can't say it is. I know my dad's a jerk, but whatever his opinion, you're a cousin to me. I'm asking as family, to protect family."

How strange to hear those words from one of the Colton Oil Coltons. Jarvis had groomed himself to dislike them nearly all of his life, considering them the snooty side of the family tree, too aloof to bother with him. But as his own family died out, snipping his roots out from under him, a small, childlike piece of his heart had longed for a connection.

Ridiculous. That piece of him needed to sit down and shut up. The last thing any piece of him needed was another emotional beatdown. He could help Asher, but he had his own reasons for wanting Selina to open up. To that end, he'd make sure she had a drink in her hand all night long.

"I'm a good listener," he said. "Per her orders, I'm driving, so I have even more reason to stay sober. You'll get a full report."

"Great." Asher relaxed, removing his hat and combing a hand through his hair. "I appreciate it more than I can say."

"Best save that appreciation until I actually have something." The men started back toward the barns. "Would you have asked me for this if I'd said I was involved with her?"

Asher laughed and clapped him on the shoulder. "Not a chance," he admitted. A grin creased his face. "If I thought you were seriously into her I would've fired you."

Jarvis believed him. "I would've deserved it," he said. Asher had made it clear from the start he expected loyalty to run alongside hard work.

A strange morning, complicated by a lack of sleep, but he got through the rest of his assignments with willpower and focus.

Once he was done, everything extra came down on him like a ton of bricks. He'd needed to speak with Mia about the Graves party and he'd been half tempted to give her his real reasons. Now he had the extra excuse of helping Asher. If he was lucky, she would immediately trust him not to reveal her hiding place.

Before he headed out to continue his search for Isaiah's mystery box, Jarvis took some time and chatted with a few of the other hands. He'd thought he'd made some friends, but it seemed he'd held back just enough to be considered gossip fodder. Maybe if he cultivated those relationships, the rumors about him and Selina would slow down.

When he finally got back to the location near the warming hut, his focus was divided between his search and Mia's continued safety. It troubled him that she'd had to rely on an online chat instead of taking her baby to the doctor. Yesterday hadn't been anything serious, but it wasn't fair to make her wait for him if a real problem did crop up.

He needed to figure out a way to get Mia a vehicle, something she could use if there was an emergency. Moving her car to the bunkhouse was one option, but doing that meant Regina might spot her easily if the woman visited the Triple R or if Mia had to drive into town.

He could probably give her access to a ranch truck, but most of those were equipped with a GPS tracker. He didn't want anyone revealing her hiding place because they were confused about a vehicle left sitting at a remote bunkhouse near currently unused grazing fields.

For the first time, Jarvis regretted the immense size of Rattlesnake Ridge Ranch. It wasn't as simple as driving a truck out to her and hiking back.

Not in the afternoon heat, anyway. He supposed he could handle the vehicle swap at night. If he picked her up at the bunkhouse and she rode to the ranch with him, she could drive a ranch truck back to her hiding place.

That still didn't leave him with an explanation for Asher about the location of that truck. He let transportation issues simmer in the back of his mind, returning to the place he'd been digging when he'd first heard Silas's cries.

He grimaced at the hole he'd left behind. After his previous attempts to find the evidence supposedly buried on this ranch, he'd carefully covered his trail. Here, in a hurry to find the crying baby, he'd made a glaring error. Anyone who happened upon this would wonder who was digging and why. Those were questions he wasn't ready to answer.

As with all of his previous sites, this one, too, was a big fat no-go. When he'd finished filling in this hole, he leaned on his shovel and stared out across the grazing land. "Maybe Granddad's brain was playing tricks on him. Could be he was making stuff up or getting old stories confused. Everyone else thinks so." It felt a whole lot better when he had these one-sided conversations with his horse. Thankfully, no one was out here to witness his lack of common sense as he addressed his truck.

He tossed the shovel into the bed and settled behind the wheel. Turning on the engine, he cranked the air-conditioning as cold as it would go. Making the note on his search app, he put the truck in gear and headed back toward his assigned room.

He showered off the workday, put on clean jeans and a better shirt and opted for tennis shoes rather than boots tonight. He packed up a few things, just in case he didn't make it back, and then went to join the majority of the crew for supper. With rumors flying, it was better if he met those head-on rather than let them fester. Personal lives were always juicy gossip in a small town and this wasn't the first time Jarvis had been a prime target. Just the first time here at the Triple R.

Over the meal, he fielded questions about what Selina had needed and what she'd been saying about him. Amid the heartfelt thanks tossed at him from the men who appreciated him "taking care of her," he realized he'd given her carte blanche to say anything about their status as a couple. She sure was taking him up on that, based on the nonsense flying around about their intense affair and his "new" prospects in Mustang Valley. The woman was a mess in Jarvis's mind, but he couldn't call her a liar without losing a valuable opportunity to help Asher and Mia.

As soon as he was able, he extricated himself from the conversation and an invitation to go out for a beer. He wanted to get some hot food out to Mia as soon as possible. He didn't think she'd heard his promise to bring a meal back tonight and the shock on her face when he pulled up to the bunkhouse confirmed it.

"I wasn't expecting you back tonight." She'd brought a chair outside and was sitting with Silas resting on her thighs. She wore shorts and a loose top with a scoop neck. Her feet were bare.

She had pretty feet, which had to be the first time he'd ever had *that* thought. Her toenails were polished with a soft pink color that emphasized the warm color in her darker skin. He ached all over, wanting to kiss her, to have that privilege.

"I picked up a burger for you. Cheese, bacon, pickles and mayo. You can dress it your way."

The wariness fell from her gaze, replaced by anticipation. "Please don't tell me you learned that online."

"No. I figured you needed something fresh and hearty, so I took a chance." He reached into the truck for the drink carrier. "And something sweet sounded good, too."

"Burgers and milkshakes?"

He nodded. "Your choice of chocolate or strawberry. Unless you're allergic or something."

"No allergies. Oh, I could kiss you." She waved him closer. "One perk of pregnancy was not obsessing over every calorie."

He traded the burger bag for the baby, pleased beyond reason when the little guy gazed up at him with wide, dark eyes. "I take it today was a better day?"

"Absolutely a perfect day." She unwrapped a straw and stuck it into the top of the chocolate shake. "Thanks to you." She repeated the process with the strawberry shake, handing it to him.

Jarvis shifted the baby easily and took a long pull of the cold, creamy treat. "You want me to take another walk?"

"Stay." She smiled up at him and something went loose and gooey in his chest. "I could use some adult time and age-appropriate conversation."

He could think of a thousand inappropriate ways to be an adult with Mia. But he did need to speak with her about Selina, the party and her plans... She moaned as she bit into the burger and his thoughts simply vaporized.

"Jarvis." She licked a smudge of mayo from her thumb. "I don't know how you knew, but this was exactly the right thing."

"Glad to help." He cleared his throat, swaying a bit with Silas. "I said I'd bring you some transportation, too. Y'know, in case you or the baby have some trouble and I can't be here quickly."

Her gaze scanned the area, tracking back toward the warming hut. "There isn't really a good place to hide my car."

"I had the same thought. I was thinking I'd leave you my truck and keys."

"What? No. That's silly. I can't take your truck."

He leaned against one of the support posts for the roof that covered the narrow porch. "I don't like the idea of you being stranded out here. It doesn't have to be an argument," he added when her gaze narrowed.

She took another bite of the burger and closed her eyes while she chewed. Swallowed. She swiped a bit of sauce from her lip with her tongue and he nearly lost track of the entire reason he was out here.

"I want you to be safe. And to have options," he said, his voice rough. "The ranch trucks have GPS and someone might wonder why a truck is out here by itself."

"GPS?"

"It's a big ranch."

"True." She grinned. "Lucky for me."

"In my truck, you can get away if you need to, go to town or whatever."

Her dark eyebrows drew together. "Town feels like a risk no matter what vehicle I'm driving, but you can't baby me forever."

A voice in his head wanted to promise her that very thing.

What a bizarre idea, that Jarvis Colton would baby

Mia Graves. Except he wanted to bring her surprise milkshakes and help with *her* baby, and otherwise spoil her the way she deserved. They could share meals and laughter and talk each other to sleep at night. He'd be honored to shelter her from a wicked stepmother and help her restore her relationship with her dad.

All of that was way outside the realm of reality— *his* reality. He was a single ranch hand, and he liked it that way.

"It's better to have the option," he pressed. Giving her the option to leave was the strongest argument he had. He couldn't guarantee he'd be close if something did happen to her or the baby.

"I'd rather come up with a true exit strategy."

No. Thankfully, he kept the reaction locked down. He was just getting to know her. To like her. He wasn't ready for her to make an exit. Where was all this ridiculous need coming from? It felt bigger than infatuation, but this was hardly the time or place to start dating. Besides, the sooner she was out of here, the sooner he could get back to his search. Turned out a working ranch didn't leave quite enough time for two secret side projects, and he wouldn't abandon his grandfather's last dream.

"About that," he said when she finished eating. The baby was dozing in his arms, looking like an angel. "Something came up and maybe I can help you brainstorm a way out of your predicament." *Predicament* made her situation sound almost palatable.

She froze, staring up at him. "What came up?"

"Your stepmother is hosting a party and I've been invited. Aggressively invited." He'd thought this would be fine, that he could explain without hurting her, but the crushed look on her face stopped him short.

Her gaze darted all around, as if expecting her step-mom to jump out and attack her son. She crossed the porch and plucked Silas right out of his arms, holding the baby close to her heart.

"Regina invited you to a party?" Her lips parted and then closed into a flat line. "You said you didn't know her."

"I don't." His arms empty, he didn't know what to do with his hands. He shoved them into his pockets. "She didn't invite me, Selina did. Aggressively, like I said. When she gets her teeth into an idea, it's hard to distract her. You told me those two run in the same circles. Selina got a call from Regina. About the party."

Mia's dark eyes narrowed, making him feel smaller than a bug under a microscope. "Go on."

"Part of the gig at the Triple R is jumping whenever Selina snaps her fingers. Drives Asher nuts," he added. "The rest of the guys, too. She's a huge flirt and some-times gets a little too familiar."

"What?"

"Doesn't matter. My point is Asher sent me to her place to install new fixtures in her outdoor kitchen."

"Why does she even live on the Triple R?"

"The views and proximity to the Colton Oil offices," Jarvis replied. "That's what she tells us, anyway."

"The views." Her tone was snarly and her gaze raked over him rather than the nearby mountains. "She has no right to touch you or anyone without permission."

She studied her son as if imagining him subjected to Selina's unwelcome advances. It was a strange glimpse into that theory that mothers always saw their children as babies. Not that he had any experience of an adult relationship with a mother figure, having lost his own mom, Christy Colton, when he was still a baby-faced kid.

"She got off the phone with Regina and came at me, pretty much demanding I take her to the party."

"Why you?"

He didn't blame her for being suspicious. "She wants eye candy—her words—to flaunt in Regina's face. For friends, they seem to be ultracompetitive in a nasty way."

"They are." Mia rolled her eyes. "That actually makes sense."

"I only said yes to get close to your dad. I could warn him, or try to catch Regina making a threat." And if he was super lucky, Selina would spill more details about the generations of history of the landownership or how he might get his hands on the original deeds from the late 1800s.

"You can't confront her," Mia protested. "You're just as likely to put yourself and us in danger if you do that."

Was she kidding? "Didn't you hear me? I can get a message to your dad. She'd never know. Someone has to stand up for you. You're out here alone and scared and—"

"I'm *not* helpless," she snapped, cutting him off. "I'll leave the ranch tomorrow morning. Tonight, if you drive me back to my car."

He groaned and pushed a hand through his hair. At least the stick was out of her reach while she was looking so murderous. "I don't want to drive you away, I want to *help*." Hadn't that been obvious from the start?

"Confronting Regina is the opposite of helpful," she

said, keeping her voice low for the baby's sake. "I did my own due diligence on you today, Jarvis Colton."

"What are you talking about?" He crossed his arms over his chest.

"I assumed with a name like Colton you might have a share in the ranch. Especially from the way you talk about it."

His blood turned cold. "That matters to you?" Of course it did.

She came from money and surely expected the people around her to be in the same league. By all reports, she'd earned a fortune herself during her modeling years. Just last night, she'd openly confessed that she'd appreciated her ex-husband's financial success, which had added to her net worth by marriage. Naturally, a man like him, a typical working cowboy with a middle-class bank balance, wasn't good enough.

"I couldn't figure out why I've never heard of you or seen you with your cousins," she said, dodging his question.

Their blood relation was not even close enough for the triplets to be called distant cousins, according to Payne.

"Why would you have heard of me?" Her stratospheric social circle wasn't even within sight of his. He resented the old hurt and sense of inadequacy that came bubbling to the surface. He'd really thought he was past this.

"Mustang Valley is a relatively small town." She peered at him through her lashes. "It's not like being a Smith with an address in Los Angeles or New York City."

"I'll have to take your word." He wasn't well traveled; aside from a wild weekend in Cabo San Lucas, he hadn't been anywhere more exotic than Las Vegas.

"We're only a couple of years apart."

"Make your point, Mia." He couldn't take much more. Wanting a woman who was making it crystal clear she'd never have lowered herself to speak with him under normal circumstances. He'd been infatuated, instantly attracted and she'd merely been in need. He was dangerously close to beating himself with that stick she kept by the door. He'd liked the woman he'd met in the warming hut, but maybe that just wasn't the real Mia Graves.

She settled back on the chair, the baby resting on her shoulder. "Why did you change careers so drastically?"

"It was time for a change." He forced the words through clenched teeth and gracelessly changed the subject. "Once it's dark, I'll hike back to your car and use that for as long as you choose to stay here."

"Why, Jarvis?"

"Because you need transportation," he said, purposely misunderstanding her question. He didn't owe her his life story or detailed explanations. Maybe once people saw him in Mia's car, Regina would be pushed to do something to incriminate herself.

Mia glared at him. He didn't think she realized how sexy that expression was. She definitely didn't know how it heated his blood. "You'll have the truck whether you like it or not," he added. "It's the smart move."

She patted the baby's back gently while she sipped at her milkshake. "What about Selina? You can't take her to a party at my father's house in my car."

"She told me I'm driving her car."

"Told you…" Mia cocked her head, then burst into

merry laughter. The baby flailed his hands happily in response. They were the cutest pair. And cute had never been one of his goals or interests.

"I won't go if it bothers you," he said. Irritated as he was, he wouldn't like himself if he purposely did something to upset her.

"I'd think it would bother you to be objectified and used," she said.

"Says the supermodel."

"*Former* less-than-super model," she corrected him. "Who knows what she's talking about."

"I don't care what Selina or Regina or anyone else thinks of me. If I go, I'll be *in* the house. I can talk to your stepmom, search for something useful, warn your dad. Whatever you need."

"And if Regina catches you, you're in danger."

"I'm not as fragile as I look," he joked. Humor was his safe zone during sticky conversations. Better to joke than let out any ugly or real feelings. "Take your time and think about it. I can cancel."

"Not if you want any peace," Mia pointed out.

"Let me worry about it." He picked up his milkshake and turned to watch the horizon. "I can handle Selina better than most."

"I BET YOU CAN," Mia quipped. "She'd probably enjoy it if you handled her." In Selina's shoes, Mia would delight in being handled by Jarvis. Good grief, she had to get a handle on these wayward thoughts and hormones. She hadn't felt this kind of wild, uncontrollable attraction in…ever.

He shot her another annoyed glance, as if he had hard things to say and he didn't think she could bear to hear them. She'd offended him somehow. Unable to pinpoint her error, she didn't know exactly how to smooth it over. She really should let him be the one to worry about that shark in designer clothing. There were more important people for her to worry about. She finished off her milkshake and tried to find a lighter topic of conversation while Silas dozed in her lap.

The weather was trite and she didn't know enough about cattle to carry that subject. "You should go to the party," she said, cycling back to pertinent matters. "I'll think about it and let you know where to look for anything incriminating in the house. Though, if Selina's agenda is to rub you in Regina's face, she likely won't let go of you all night."

"Not fragile." He knocked his fist lightly to his chest and her eyes drank in the motion.

No, the man didn't look the least bit fragile. He was as firm and sturdy as the ground beneath them. Of course, the ground itself had proven vulnerable during the earthquake a few months ago. A philosopher might find some correlation there, that the world and everyone in it was subject to life-altering change at any moment. Completely breakable under the right pressure and circumstance.

She was tired of feeling weak and unsettled. Tired of Regina applying pressure that forced this awkward circumstance. Mia would much rather find a way to explore Jarvis's considerable strength and the tenderness underneath it. Every kindness he showed her, every time he held her son, she felt drawn in, as if he pulled her by an invisible string. Worse, she liked the sensation.

Because it was new, or because it was him? The

two were inextricably intertwined. Jarvis was new in her life but what he made her feel was tantalizing, uncharted terrain. She wanted to dig in and find the source of the hot sizzle in her bloodstream when she merely *thought* about him. Her marriage hadn't been passionless, but it hadn't had *this*. Jarvis wasn't out here with her because it made him look better. He wasn't looking for an inside track to her father. He looked at *her*, at her son, with a fresh sincerity she hadn't realized her life had been missing.

"More than searching for dirt on Regina, I'd feel better if you can confirm that my dad's all right."

"Consider it done," he promised. As he moved closer, the last rays of sunlight set the sky on fire behind him. "Do you want me to give him the video?"

She couldn't even imagine how that would be possible. Regina knew how to keep her father isolated, even in a crowded room. Always at his ear, hovering while whispering endearments, hanging on his arm and his every word. "We have time to think about it," she said, avoiding that ugly minefield for tonight.

"You really miss your dad."

How did Jarvis, basically a stranger, see right through her? She smiled down at her baby, too raw to look at the man crouched at her side. "I've missed him for years. Having a child of my own only makes it harder to understand why he chooses her over me every time. It wasn't like this with my mom. They were a team, sure, they were the authority, but I was part of it. Included, even when I didn't get my way. I admit I struggled with the adjustment when he brought Regina home. I was a brat."

"You were a kid," Jarvis soothed.

"A bratty kid," she said, compromising. "Yes, it hurt seeing another woman where my mom used to be. Worse was that he wouldn't talk to me like a miniature adult anymore. I didn't want to break them up. Not really. I was fighting against being cut out." She sniffled, tracing the shape of her son's tiny fist. "And it happened, anyway. Fighting so hard only brought it on faster. This entire situation is just the latest battle in a war for my father's attention and affection."

"Based on what I've heard from you and Selina, Regina is warring with you for Norton's influence and money," Jarvis said. "And she fights dirty."

"You're right," Mia allowed. "Maybe that's why I keep losing ground." She shook her head, embarrassment creeping in. "I didn't mean to dump all of that on you. Sorry. And I thought pregnancy hormones were bad," she joked. "I'm learning motherhood is full of pitfalls." She stroked Silas's perfect ear. "I look at him and can't imagine putting him second to anyone."

"Because you're a good mother," Jarvis said, his tone gentle. He brushed a tear from her cheek.

"My dad was a good father," she countered. His tune had changed when Regina showed up and twisted all of her childish mistakes into character flaws that disappointed him. "He provided and nurtured. He gave me a head for business and urged me to use it."

"You did that."

She sniffled again. "Pardon me." She blinked rapidly, willing this meltdown to stop before she lost all control.

Jarvis walked into the bunkhouse, returning with a packet of tissues from the diaper bag.

"Thanks." She blotted her eyes and runny nose,

wishing she could recapture the cool, self-assured inner strength she'd enjoyed before her pregnancy. "I'm not always such a mess."

To her relief, he didn't offer an opinion on that. How could he? They'd known each other for only a few strange days.

"There has to be a way to make Regina pay for this mess she created," he said. "Between the two of us, we'll figure it out."

She believed him and couldn't decide if that belief was rooted more in fantasy or desperation. "Why did you walk away from your career to come work here?"

Jarvis's chest rose and fell on a deep sigh. Sitting down, he leaned back against the pillar and stretched out his long legs, crossing them at the ankles.

It wasn't a particularly sexy pose, but to her he was temptation personified. She could hardly blame Selina for insisting on a date. Mia had found Jarvis's headshot as well as pictures of him in a suit for a community fund-raiser kickoff in town. Selina had chosen superb eye candy for Regina's party.

"Several reasons, starting with a need for change," he was saying. "I was doing well enough, but it was the same old thing day after day. Meetings and conference calls, maintaining an image that didn't feel right."

The words sounded rehearsed and she wasn't buying it. "You could've done anything, but you came to this specific ranch. A Colton ranch," she said, pointedly.

"True. And I leaned on the connection, used my last name to win over Asher. Payne likes to pretend the three of us aren't actually related to him and his kids. His children aren't as bad, though."

"That's silly. You are related." His gaze locked with

hers. Oops. She hadn't meant to reveal just how personal her search had become. "Small town," she said as breezily as possible. "Both your family and his have deep roots. Any other conclusion is impractical."

"Well, Payne's an arrogant jerk," Jarvis said.

The cavalier response wasn't as convincing as he probably intended. This issue of family mattered to him. "Being excluded hurts," she said.

"What hurt more was being dumped with an aunt who didn't want anything to do with us."

"So you came here to get under Payne's skin?"

"In a way." He slid one palm across the other as if testing the calluses. "Not that he's noticed me. I showed up here to prove Payne doesn't know everything about me or my siblings, and discovered that I enjoy the work."

"I get that," she said.

"You do?"

His furrowed brow was as appealing as everything else. "Sure. I went into modeling because I needed a speedy fix for my financial crisis and discovered I enjoyed it. No, no," she said when he opened his mouth. "You won't divert me this time. You might love the work, but there's more to it."

He chuckled and the sound made her want to stretch and purr. Did he know how he affected her? How could he not? She assumed he'd seen his reflection recently. His body was formed by the work he did, rather than hours in a climate-controlled gym with precise exercises and supervision. The resulting differences had never been so clear to her.

And she really had no business comparing Jarvis to her ex-husband.

"Mia?"

She blinked and heat washed over her face, down her throat as she got caught staring at him.

"If you're tired, go in and rest," he suggested.

"I'm fine. Adult conversation, remember? Keep talking. I've been open with you. Give me whatever you're holding back."

He only smiled, the expression slow and indulgent. She pressed her knees together against the quivering response at her core and shifted her attention to the gentle slope of Silas's nose.

"How about a story?" he asked.

"As long as it's real."

"I can only tell you what's real to me," he replied. "My grandpa used to tell us that we should be as wealthy as Payne and his kids. He told me that back in the 1800s, his grandfather's brother, on the Colton Oil side of the family tree, stole the ranch from our side of the family."

"Your grandfather, Isaiah Colton, told you this?"

His casual expression turned razor sharp. "I'm starting to hate the internet too," he groused. "What do you know about it?"

She motioned for him to keep talking. "Tell me more."

He raked a hand through his thick hair. "No one in the family believed Isaiah's tall tales. He talked about gunfights and feuds that started generations ago between Colton brothers. He claimed that trickled down and is the reason Payne pretends we aren't related."

"Why didn't anyone believe him?"

"It was Isaiah. He was half-drunk more often than he was stone-cold sober. I loved those stories of generations long gone. Stories about poker games, cattle rustling and shoot-outs as the area was settled, stolen and settled again. It was a lark, really. But when the dementia set in near the end of his life, he got agitated and vocal about it. And detailed. He talked to me more, insisting that I listen to what he called the facts. Granddad was convinced the Triple R belonged to us and he wanted me to find the proof and take it back."

She was on the edge of her seat, literally, leaning forward to hear more. "Have you verified his story?"

"I've done some research into dementia and confabulation. It's entirely possible he's twisted up old Western movie plots and family rifts."

"But you became a cowboy, anyway."

"I did. With dementia, sometimes the oldest memories are the truest. And his details, Mia—they convinced me to try. That's why I'm here. Near the end of his life, he told me the proof of rightful ownership of the Triple R is buried here on the ranch.

"The legend, according to Isaiah, goes that his granddad, Herman Colton, lost a chunk of prime acreage in a poker game. Herman swore to anyone who would listen that he was cheated in that game. Enough people believed him that his brother, Eugene, agreed to buy back the land for him. Isaiah told me the brothers struck the deal, but then for some reason Eugene refused to sign the acreage over to Herman. He kept it in the family, passing it down the line."

"Kept it and kept adding to it," she said.

"Yes. Isaiah said Herman had a signed letter of the agreement between him and Eugene, proof of the poker game stakes, and even a confession from the man who cheated to win."

"Herman is the one who tossed the land into the pot."

"Haven't you ever done anything impulsive?" he challenged.

"Sure." She'd been having plenty of impulsive thoughts about Jarvis, but she wasn't about to drive her only ally away by jumping him.

"Herman's fault." He thunked his head back against the post. "I don't blame you for thinking it. Growing up, I heard ghost stories of how Herman cursed our branch of the family tree. It wasn't until he was dying that Isaiah gave me actionable details."

"Such as?"

"He described a metal box with Herman's initials scratched into the top of it. Told me that inside the box, in addition to the proof about who should own the land, there was more family history Payne couldn't ignore. One way or another, Payne would have to acknowledge us. Herman buried that box on the land that he felt was rightfully his and urged his sons to take it back once Eugene was dead."

"Why wait?"

"Granddad said Herman spent years searching for the card cheat, waiting to get a confession out of him. Distracted, he relied on his family to manage the smaller plot of land, while he burned through any ready cash following a gambler around the territories. Eventually, one bad season followed by another forced them to sell out."

"To Eugene's sons?" she asked, certain of the answer.

He nodded. "Got it in one."

"Wow." The story was preposterous and plausible at the same time. In his shoes, she, too, would have been hard-pressed to let it go as an old man's rambling. "Takes courage to follow through the way you have. Does either Asher or Payne know what you're up to?"

"No." His chin came up, as if he dared her to contradict the tale or threaten to blow his cowboy cover. "I'm aware dementia can do strange things to the mind," he admitted softly. "But Isaiah talked about landmarks. So many details…" Jarvis's voice trailed off as his gaze drifted toward the darkening mountain range. "On a spread of this size and searching by myself, I have to be realistic that even if the story is true, I might never find one small box."

A fresh excitement twinkled through her system, like the stars popping into view overhead. She loved learning new things. "That's why you were out there the day you found me," she said.

"You mean, the day you were channeling Babe Ruth?" He grinned. "I was out there riding fence first and searching second. Asher's a good man and a fair boss. If he was a jerk like his dad I might shirk the workload, but I respect him too much."

"So you'll work here until you find Herman's box and can stake your claim?" She looked out over the acreage shrouded in darkness. Landmarks or not, there was too much ground for one man to cover.

"In a perfect world, yes. It would be a blast to march into Payne's office, looking for his wife, Genevieve, and demand a fair current price on the land."

"That's a deal I could broker for you," she teased. "You'd be rich in an instant."

He snorted. "Rich divided three ways, plus your commission." He winked. "At this point it would be just as satisfying to see Spencer and Bella react. They'd be shocked to learn that I bought into this family myth. Truth is, I feel better about the work I do here, rich or not, than I ever did at the office."

"You loved your grandpa," she whispered. "I want Silas to know his grandpa, to make lasting memories. Regina is bent on preventing that." Her dad was all Silas had. Roderick's parents had shown zero interest in being part of their grandson's life. Anger rose up high and fast, unhindered by the choking fear of her stepmother's threats. Something about Jarvis being around gave her hope and courage that she could find a solution Regina wouldn't slither out of.

Silas started squirming and fretting, and she checked his diaper. "It's that time again," she brushed her nose to her son's. "We'll be back."

But Jarvis followed her, pausing just inside the doorway. She heard him laugh and glanced over to find him eyeing the heavy stick she kept propped by the door.

"Always prepared," he observed.

"Mothers and the Boy Scouts," she said. Once Silas was in a clean diaper, she curled into a corner of the bunk, giving him a chance to nurse while she mulled over Jarvis's story. It made her happy that he'd shared it, that he trusted her not to betray him. It felt good to be on even ground with their shared secrets and concerns. "Have you done any research into the records of sale for this property?"

"I did visit the records office," he replied. "The documents on file match what everyone has accepted as truth. Per those official documents, Payne's side of the Colton family tree bought the land generations back and built a thriving cattle operation."

"Mmm. Okay." Her mind was spinning, happily distracted by his search over her own problems. "You didn't find the box out by the warming hut, so where will you look next? How do you decide where to search?"

"I've been working off the landmarks Isaiah described and I keep track of the locations with a geo-caching type of app."

That sounded fascinating. "Do you think I could help?"

"Why would you want to?" he asked.

She shrugged, hoping the nonchalance would hide her intense curiosity about the quest. More than anything, she wanted to thank him for helping her. Well, that was a lie. She wanted to keep seeing him. "It's better than my current agenda of convincing potential clients to list their property for sale with a shiny new real-estate agent they can't meet in person."

"Yet," he said. "We'll figure out a way around your stepmom. I didn't anticipate any help with the search, but if you feel like it, I'll gladly accept."

"Good." Her spirit soared. "Tell me more about the landmarks."

He pulled out his phone. "I'll just send you everything I have. What's your email?"

She gave him the information. A moment later, her phone chimed with the incoming message. "This will be fun," she said, mostly to the baby. Her phone chimed again and she did a double take, checking the alert on the screen. The first message wasn't from Jarvis at all. In fact, it looked like an email from her ex-husband. "What the hell?"

Jarvis was beside her in an instant. "More trouble?"

"I—I don't know yet," she admitted. She wouldn't deal with anything negative while nursing her son. The first part of protecting Silas was putting his needs first. "It's from my ex. He hasn't contacted me since the divorce was finalized."

"Not even when Silas was born?"

"Of course not," she said.

"But you said he's the father."

"He is." She deliberately kept her tone bright to remind Jarvis this wasn't the time for a stressful conversation.

He held up a hand and backed away. "I get it. All of that can wait."

She shot him a grateful smile. "He'll be out soon. We might even get through a second night in a row."

Jarvis sat down on the bunk across from her, an odd expression on his face. She wasn't sure she wanted to know what was going through his head. He didn't avoid looking at her as she fed her son, but he didn't ogle her or stare in an awkward way.

At last her baby's bottomless pit of a stomach was content and quiet. Once he was tucked into the car seat that currently served double duty as his bed, she picked up her phone and headed to the table. The email from Roderick was as succinct as it was jarring. Her knees went weak and she wobbled into the first available support, which happened to be Jarvis.

His arms came around her and he eased her into a chair at the table. Her fingers trembled as she read through the full message again. "I can't believe this."

Thankfully, Jarvis took the phone and read the message himself. "He's asking for a custody hearing?"

She pressed a hand to her stomach, wishing now she'd skipped the milkshake. "He relinquished his rights before I delivered. The divorce settlement covered everything." She swallowed a panicked sob. This couldn't be happening. "He got everything he wanted. So did I."

"Meaning?"

"Roderick wanted complete and total freedom. Forever. No visitation, no obligation to be a father. He agreed to set up a fund for Silas's college expenses and he had to pay me half of the value for our house. The alimony payments were calculated and once we agreed on a number, he paid me in full so he didn't have to think about me ever again."

Jarvis touched her gently, his hand warm at the nape of her neck, his fingers circling gently over the knotted muscles. "I don't want to be a dad, but I can't imagine walking away from my wife if we got pregnant. I didn't know my parents for long, but I remember how in love they were. Committed to each other and us as a family, through thick and thin."

"My husband was furious when I told him I was pregnant."

Jarvis's hands stilled. "Why would he demand a custody hearing now?"

"Because the universe is laughing at me? Maybe his mom decided she was ready to be a grandmother after all." She curled over, resting her head on her hands on the tabletop. Jarvis just kept kneading her neck. The man was a saint. "Mia Graves, so sure she could be mother of the year all by herself."

Behind her, Jarvis snickered.

"Don't laugh at me. There's a mug and everything."

"Sweetheart, you're the best mom I've seen in ages."

She opened her mouth to argue and a low moan came out instead. Jarvis cleared his throat and she knew she should move out of his reach. But it felt so damned good to be touched this way. He was only being a friend—a caregiver, really, but she wasn't strong enough to resist this.

"Your hands are miraculous." It had been so long since anyone had touched her like a woman; medical professionals didn't count.

"This says you have to appear tomorrow. Your husband has serious clout to get a hearing in family court so fast," he said.

"Ex-husband," she corrected.

"Right." His fingers changed directions, spearing into her hair and massaging her scalp. She could happily melt into a puddle of not caring about anything outside of this bunkhouse.

"This doesn't make any sense," she said. "What could have changed that he wants to exert a paternal claim now?"

"Usually, that kind of pull is reserved for emergencies," he added. "When we were orphaned, it took a week for them to get everyone into the court at the same time."

His voice was as soothing as his hands. Floating somewhere just shy of bliss, she let go, listening and surrendering.

"We stayed with Isaiah that week, but he couldn't run herd on the three of us and he didn't have the money to hire help. The court decided to dump us on our aunt. Amelia complained bitterly from that day forward about the burden of three children she never wanted."

"Have things improved with her since you're all grown up?" Mia asked.

"She died when we were twenty-one."

She sat up now, twisting to catch his hand in hers. "I'm sorry."

He frowned at their joined hands. "Don't be. The four of us did little more than survive those years. My siblings and I were as relieved to cut loose at eighteen as she was to see us go. Why was your ex mad about the pregnancy?"

"He never wanted kids. We agreed not to have children before we married, so he felt betrayed. He reminded me he married a model and expected me to stay in photogenic form."

"So he married you because you were hot, too." Jarvis's eyebrows jumped up and down in a comical innuendo. "Can't fault him for that."

The man could make her laugh, even while her ears burned at the compliment. "And my money," she agreed. Reaching for a bottle of water, she took a long drink. She crossed to the bag of supplies on the counter and pulled out her vitamins. Silas needed her to stay healthy and strong. And calm. "Our marriage wasn't as cold as it sounds. We did care about each other." She paused for another sip of water. "I thought it was love. A good and solid love that would last."

"Until you got pregnant."

"Yes." Her gaze went to Silas. "We were both shocked, but I saw it as a miracle and he saw it as a problem. So we parted ways. If it wasn't amicable, it was civil."

"You miss him."

She sighed in defeat. "Not as much as I should."

"Come sit down." Jarvis pulled out the chair for her

again. When she sat, he started massaging her shoulders. "Read the message again."

Her laptop was closer, so she used that instead, regretting the loss when his hands fell away for a moment. He stood behind her, somehow without looming, as she opened the email. "Hang on." She looked closer. "This isn't his primary email address. There's a dot here when it should be all one word."

"Then let's assume that link to the court calendar isn't valid, either."

She used the track pad to hover the cursor over the link without clicking it. "One way to check." Opening a new tab on her browser, she entered the family court into the search bar. As she compared the links, it was clear someone was trying to fool her.

It was chilling that anyone would attempt this. Not anyone. "Regina," she said with a hiss as a new wave of fury blasted through her system. She pushed back from the table, pacing back and forth across the bunkhouse. "I don't know how she did it, but it has to be her."

"Agreed."

"I would've gone," she said as disappointment in herself chased the temper. "I would've rushed Silas right into her trap."

"What happens to Silas if, um, if something were to happen to you?"

She met his gaze and saw a flash of the wounded little boy he'd once been. "My will stipulates management of his college fund to his legal guardian along with his daily expenses. Naturally, I left him a trust fund, too, that he can access when he's twenty-one."

"Who's the guardian?"

"Melody Williams, my best friend from college.

She loves kids and we have similar values and phi-
losophies," she added. "She was my labor coach and
she stayed with me at the house for the first couple of
weeks. She's done video chats with us since she had
to go back home."

Jarvis frowned. "Why hide in the warming hut instead of with her?"

"I couldn't put her in the line of fire too," she countered.

"Fair point." Jarvis held his hands up in surrender.
"I'm staying again tonight."

Guilt weighed her down, sapping the benefits of the
massage. "You should be in your own bed."

"I'll sleep there all I want later," he said.

"Spoken like a man without kids."

He smiled at her and tugged her up from the chair.
"Tomorrow, I'll scoot out of here early and take your
car into town. Maybe I'll even drive by the courthouse."

"You shouldn't do that." If Regina did see him, she'd
harass him at the very least.

"Of course I should. My brother's a cop and I haven't
dropped in on him in a while. Trust me." He wrapped
one loose tendril of hair around his fingertip. "Please?"

"One condition," she said. He smiled and she momentarily lost her train of thought. "Let me help you
figure out where to search for Herman's box of proof."

She didn't like how he dismissed her suggestion
with an eye roll. "You've done more for me in the past
few days than anyone has done in years. It'll be fun
for me, I promise."

"Fine," he relented. "As long as you're discreet."

She leaned back. "Please. I'm a model. Discretion is

my middle name. The things I could tell you about…
Well, never mind."

He grinned. "You are a tease."

His playful tone made her want to be. "I've been
called worse."

"Tell me a secret. Not about any one model. I mean
a trade secret."

"Hmm." She tapped a finger to her lips and her
mouth went dry as his gaze locked onto that spot. A
delicious heat shimmered through her bloodstream.
Would a kiss be such a big mistake? "In the preshoot
prep, nearly every model looks like the girl next door.
Plain. Mundane."

"Like I'd fall for that one," he said, his lips tilted
into a grin. His hands slid to her elbows, holding her
in place. "Nothing about you is mundane or plain."

His fingers gripped firmly, drawing them together.
Her breasts brushed up against his chest. She wanted
to plaster herself to him, to discover exactly how firm
those muscles were.

"Please kiss me." The words fell from her lips and
she couldn't muster any shame. He was the most genuine person she'd met in ages. Since her father had
written her off as too spoiled to try to mend fences.

Jarvis tempted her, roused a desire she hadn't known
existed. Oh, she'd wanted her husband, had enjoyed a
healthy sex life in those early years. But longing? She
wasn't sure she'd ever felt this intense pull. More than
a little afraid she'd break down and beg, she felt her
heart race as he leaned close.

At last his lips brushed over hers. Featherlight and
full of promises, with a hint of challenge. She kissed
him back, let herself sink into his scent and taste as her

hands molded his shoulders, stroked up the column of his throat. She laced her fingers behind his neck and held on, letting the heat, the sweet, sizzling contact, burn away every unpleasantness.

His hands came around her, gliding up her spine, down to her hips, urging her closer still. The kiss filled her with a lightness, an unrivaled joy. Here in his embrace, she found a piece of herself she hadn't known was missing.

That discovery rocked her emotionally, left her gasping as she pulled back. For a brief eternity they stood there, staring at each other. Her heart pounded so loudly in her ears she couldn't think.

"I, ah, I won't stay," he said into the charged silence.

She wanted to argue, but she was too fizzy from the aftershocks of that kiss. "Probably for the best," she managed.

He stepped back, his fingers still twined with hers. The next step parted them completely. She locked her knees, braced one hand on the chair for balance.

"Text me if you need anything from town."

She nodded. If she tried to talk, she'd beg him to stay, beg him for more than a kiss.

She wasn't sure how long she stood there, lips tingling, body humming, wishing for him to stride back in and overwhelm her again.

That was her first postdivorce kiss. While she was pregnant with Silas, rebound dating hadn't been a priority. Did every woman have that bone-melting reaction? She was probably just dumping every random emotion on Jarvis's broad shoulders.

Those shoulders could take it.

She moved to turn out the lights and crawl into her

bed when she saw the glint of keys on the table. He had left her his truck. Which meant he was crossing serious acreage on foot, in the dark. She dashed off a quick text message.

Let me know when you're home safe.

The reply came back within a few seconds.

I'm safe. Go to sleep.

Suspicious, she went to the window. Sure enough, Jarvis was in his truck, the glow from his cell phone highlighting his handsome face.

Relieved that he wasn't crossing the ranch alone in the dark, she went to bed without inviting him back inside. She curled into her sleeping bag, hoping to dream of Jarvis and his talented hands and mouth.

Chapter Six

Jarvis left Mia's hideout in the soft gray before dawn. The landscape blurred as he jogged toward the warming hut where her car was hidden. This might have been the worst idea he'd ever had.

Second worst, if he counted that kiss.

No. No, that was all wrong. That kiss didn't belong in a negative category of any kind. It had been the *best* kiss of his life and though he'd slept lightly, Mia had been the star of his dreams.

Kissing her was better in real life than any fantasy he'd had in college. No matter how he tried to scold himself for crossing that line, he didn't regret it. Her big brown eyes had been glazed over with longing when he walked out, beautiful and tempting. He wasn't sure where he'd found the willpower to sleep outside when he could've slept with her.

The most important factor, far more important than slaking his desire, was that he wanted to help her. And as long as she needed his help, he should probably keep his hands and his lips to himself. Neither of them needed more complications right now.

When he reached the old warming hut, he dug her car out from under the various layers hiding the vehicle, grateful when it started immediately. He was already second-guessing his plan to drive it to town later this morning, but it would definitely get him to work on time.

In his room, he showered and changed and started plowing through the day's task list. As time for the false court appearance neared, Jarvis tracked down Asher and asked for a couple hours off for an errand in town. He also offered to bring anything back for the ranch.

Armed with a short list for a stop at the feedstore, he swapped his dusty T-shirt and boots for a button-down shirt, his good belt and a clean pair of boots. He headed out through the back gate, just to avoid anyone near the main house who might recognize Mia's car.

The ten-mile drive into Mustang Valley was un-eventful, not that he'd expected trouble. Regina had no reason to think Mia was on the Triple R. Jarvis parked behind the courthouse with thirty minutes to spare be-fore the fake hearing, so he decided to drop in on his brother at the police station.

Spencer was just walking out and did a double take when he saw Jarvis. "Look who came home from the range." He gave Jarvis a one-armed hug. "Bella and I were about to grab lunch down at Bubba's Diner. She'll be happy to see you."

"I need to take a rain check," Jarvis said. He sud-denly didn't know how to explain himself. He'd wanted to ask Spencer for advice, maybe cajole him into hang-ing around the courthouse for an hour or so. He had no idea what to do if he was right and Regina showed up with the intention of trapping Mia and Silas.

"A rain check?" Spencer froze. "What's going on

with you? Did you—" His cell phone rang from his pocket, cutting off the query. "It's the US Marshals office. Let me take this."

Jarvis was grateful for the reprieve. He wasn't in the mood for another lecture on what Spencer and Bella called his delusions of cowboy glory. Without Mia's permission, he couldn't give any details about why he was in town. So he stood there, listening to his brother's end of the call.

"No record at all?" Spencer scowled at the street in general while he listened. "What about the other name, Luella Smith?" A pause. "Yes, I know what witness protection means. And I'm sure you know what interagency cooperation means."

Jarvis tried not to listen too closely while he watched for any sign of Regina.

His brother shook his head, frustration stamped on his face as he ended the call. He shoved his phone into his pocket. "Don't repeat this," he said, donning his sunglasses. "I'm working to verify what I suspect is a bogus line Micheline Anderson fed me."

Jarvis recognized the name. Anderson had founded the Affirmation Alliance Group and transformed a ranch near town into a retreat with a self-help focus. Rumors were swelling that the AAG was actually a cult, bilking members out of their money instead of offering a beneficial service. So far Spencer hadn't found anything definitive, but for Jarvis, his brother's suspicions was more than enough confirmation.

Spencer nodded, his brow puckered over the sunglasses. "She's doing all the right things and the group has been a big help in the community, especially after the earthquake. But I have a bad feeling."

"Then something's wrong," Jarvis said. His brother's instincts were as dependable as Boris, his chocolate Lab K-9 partner. "Did you learn anything helpful?" he asked.

Spencer knew Jarvis would never blab about anything. Though the parts of the conversation he'd overheard raised questions, he wouldn't press. The triplets shared a unique and innate trust. One more reason why he felt awkward keeping Mia's dilemma to himself.

"I hope so," Spencer replied. "Time will tell. Positive thinking is great, but I still can't make the pieces of the AAG fit together into a wholly legitimate business model." He clapped Jarvis on the shoulder. "Come on. Bella will chew me out if I'm late, unless you distract her. Get her talking about wedding stuff."

Jarvis chuckled. "Not this time. I have my own crazy to-do list today."

Spencer eyed him with an expression Jarvis figured he'd learned at the police academy. "Asher sure is leaning on you."

"I'm reliable," Jarvis said with a smile and a wave. He jogged backward a few paces. "Tell Bella I'll call."

He circled around to the side door of the courthouse, wondering what in the hell he'd say if he ran into Regina. Nothing, obviously. Although he could recognize her from local publicity as Norton's wife and the videos Mia had shared, Jarvis was a stranger to her. And what were the odds she was even here? From what Mia had shared, he supposed Regina was bold enough to ambush Mia directly, but he didn't know.

His stomach knotted. In about a week he was going to walk into a party hosted by the very woman he was spying on today. Suddenly, this felt like the dumbest

idea in the world. If she noticed him here and then recognized him at her party, it would be a short leap for
her to guess Mia was hiding at the Triple R.

His bravado drained away, leaving him with a void
that quickly filled with uncertainty. This wasn't some
lark. A woman's life was on the line, and the future of
her baby, too. But he was here and committed to the
effort. He had to follow through.

He took the stairs to the second floor toward the
courtroom specified in the email. There was no sign
of Mia's ex, or anyone else. The hallways were way
too quiet for any court to be in session. The pervasive
hush was worse than in a library. He turned a corner,
following the only sound—a low, impatient voice. Her
body was silhouetted against the light pouring through
the window at the other end of the hall, making it impossible to verify that it was Regina.

Sitting on a bench near an open office door, Jarvis pulled out his phone, pretending to text while the
woman fumed aloud in hushed tones as she paced the
width of the hallway.

"Keep looking," she said. "Yes, I'm sure that's her
car. I told you she is *not* up here." She paused, rushed
back to the window, her high heels clicking across
the marble floor. "What do you mean, it's not there?
There's a bracket thing. In the back seat."

She'd snarled those last words and Jarvis knew
he was watching and listening to Regina. As they'd
thought, this custody hearing was a trap for Mia. He
kept his head down, angling his hat to hide his face.
Not that Regina would've registered anything outside
of her current tantrum.

"She didn't just disappear."

Oh, but she had, he thought once the sound of her heels faded. He walked toward the window where Regina had been and looked down at the parking lot. He couldn't see anyone showing too much interest in Mia's car. But the rear tire was flat on the driver's side. A hot spike of temper slammed through him. Regina was showing every sign of being too desperate. Spencer would call this "escalating."

Pressing the panic button on Mia's key fob, he was quickly rewarded as Regina's glossy updo rushed into view. Following her movements, he identified the person who was most likely helping her by the car while Regina had been on the lookout up here.

Though Jarvis wasn't eager to take another look at the indiscretion Mia had caught on video, he would have to so they could verify if the man down in the parking lot was the same man Regina had been with at the country house. In the meantime, he had to do something about Mia's car. And he needed a lift back to the ranch, by way of the feedstore. Thankfully, he knew exactly where to find his sister and brother.

He hurried down the street to the diner, pleased to find Bella and Spencer still at lunch at a table near the window. He ordered a sandwich to go so he wouldn't delay their meal and then sweet-talked his sister into driving him back out to the Triple R.

"Only if you're buying," Bella said, though she couldn't suppress her smile.

"Deal," Jarvis agreed.

"What happened to your truck?" Spencer asked.

"I was borrowing a friend's car, but it has a flat. The garage is taking care of that and I'll get a ride into town after work to pick it up." He was sure one of his siblings would call him out on the fib, but Spencer was distracted by someone or something outside.

Bella and Jarvis exchanged a look. When Spencer was in cop mode it was hard to break through with normal conversation. While they waited for his sandwich, he dutifully admired her sparkling engagement ring and urged her to fill him in on her fiancé, Holden, and the initial wedding plans.

"It's still weird to think of you getting married." He raised his chin toward Spencer. "Both of you."

Spencer continued to be preoccupied, but Bella wiggled her eyebrows. "Maybe we'll rub off on you."

Jarvis laughed. "Not a chance. Cowboys don't get married, we just ride off into the sunset with the woman of the moment."

Bella elbowed him, hard. "Have you seen Ainsley around the ranch?"

"Not much," he said. "It's a working ranch. I'm not there to plan a family reunion."

Bella slumped in her seat, deflated, and he felt like a jerk. His sister had always longed to be closer to their Colton Oil cousins and had recently bonded with Marlowe over her newborn. Payne's dismissive remarks about their parents and grandparents never seemed to faze her. Probably because she'd been saddled with two ornery brothers and a fractured home life. He could tell her the grass wasn't really greener on the Colton Oil side of the family tree, but why wreck her fantasy of having cousins who'd always cared? "Marlowe, Ainsley and Asher are all right," he said. "They've never treated me like a leech. Maybe you should reach out."

"Are you well?" She pressed the back of her hand to his forehead and he swatted it away. "Sorry," she said, though she clearly wasn't. "You're not sounding like you."

Admittedly, Mia was rubbing off on him more than his siblings. Watching her cope with an unthinkable scenario on her own made him face uncomfortable facts. Bella and Spencer had partners and love now, and assuming all went well, they had someone to lean on in tough times. Despite all they'd been through, it would be natural and right for their spouses to come before him. It didn't mean he wanted a wife and kids, just that he should probably cultivate friendships with people other than his sister and brother. Eventually. Today his plate was full enough.

On a low grumble, Spencer shoved out of the booth. "Excuse me a second."

"And that's lunch," Bella said, shaking her head. "Remember to leave a good tip." She patted Jarvis's cheek and followed Spencer.

Jarvis took care of the bill, tipping well like his sister would do, and then grabbed his take-out bag. Bella had followed Spencer, standing a few paces away while he spoke with Micheline and her assistant, Leigh Dennings. The pair were finishing lunch at an outdoor table at the bistro across the street. Considering the phone call he'd overheard, he assumed spotting the women had diverted Spencer's attention.

"What do we do?" Bella asked under her breath.

"What we do best." He winked at her. "Stick together." He strode right into the conversation, greeting both Micheline and Leigh with his best smile as he propped a hip on the railing that framed the outdoor seating area. His sister followed suit and soon the five of them were conversing.

"Jarvis Colton." Leigh sighed. "I haven't seen you around town lately," she said. A blush flowed over her cheeks at the admission and Jarvis heard his sister snort. Leigh and Bella had competed in the Ms. Mustang Valley pageant recently while Bella was researching a story on pageant culture. Leigh, as the winner, still seemed to shine with the victory.

"I've been busy on the Triple R," he explained. "The cowboy life works better for me."

She fanned herself. "It does work. You look great."

Jarvis inched closer to Bella, using her as a conversational shield. On his other side, Spencer angled himself to block Micheline from the chatter, though Jarvis could still hear them clearly enough.

"I've made some calls, Micheline. You probably won't be surprised that the US Marshals Service doesn't have any record of you or Luella Smith as protected witnesses," Spencer said.

Jarvis struggled not to react to that while he kept up the conversation with Leigh and Bella. During his investigation, Spencer had learned that the person "Micheline Anderson" had only begun to exist at the same time that Luella Smith, the woman who switched her baby for the real Ace Colton, disappeared.

"Well, of course they wouldn't tell you anything," Micheline said after the waitress picked up the bill and her credit card. "That would defeat the purpose. Not that any of it pertains to me, though I appreciate your thorough concern."

Jarvis caught Spencer's scowl and knew Micheline had struck a nerve. He continued to distract Leigh, with Bella's help, even as he listened to his brother. "I'd like it if you would make time to speak with me."

"For private coaching, just call Leigh and set up an appointment," Micheline said, her tone warm and smooth as honey as she handed him a business card. "We'll be happy to help you find your most productive mind-set."

Spencer accepted the card, responding in kind. "A few minutes at the station would put my mind at ease about recent events that intersect with you and the AAG."

"This is bordering on harassment, Sergeant Colton," she added with more bite than barbed wire. She signed the receipt and shoved her copy into her purse. "If you'll excuse us." Micheline stood and urged Leigh to do the same. "We must be going."

"Where to?" Spencer asked.

Leigh hefted a full tote over her shoulder. "Micheline is delivering our popular *Be Your Best Self* seminar to the local chapter of the Arizona Insurance Council," Leigh gushed. "Those events are life and career changing."

Jarvis could only marvel at the pride rolling off the young assistant. Her cow-eyed devotion was a bit unnerving.

"It was a pleasure to see you, Jarvis." Leigh fluttered her fingers and scampered away.

Behind him, he heard Bella snickering. "Stop," he muttered under his breath.

"Hey, Micheline!" Spencer called out. Both women turned. "Is AAG a cult?"

Jarvis whistled softly. His brother was clearly frustrated with Micheline's convenient answers for everything. The investigation must be taking some worrisome turns to push him to such an aggressive tactic.

Leigh gasped and pressed her fingers to her mouth. Micheline smiled, the expression brittle and cold. "Of course not, Sergeant. Good day." She turned on her heel and marched down the block, Leigh trailing after her.

"You okay?" Bella asked.

"I don't know," Spencer said, his gaze still locked on the two women. "I'm missing something."

"You'll figure it out," Jarvis assured him. "You always do."

ALL DAY LONG Mia had ridden the high of that kiss, reliving the feel and taste of Jarvis's mouth. Her dreams had been delightful, if a bit unsatisfying. It was a shock how one intense embrace could give her this renewed sense of self as a woman apart from motherhood.

She'd gone out to offer him breakfast and found the truck empty. But the text message that came through informing her he'd picked up her car reassured her that he hadn't walked all the way back to the ranch.

The second text message he'd sent was no comfort at all.

Custody hearing was a trap. Your car has been towed due to a flat tire. More later.

She'd thanked him by text and spent the next hour stewing over what to do about Regina before taking Silas out for a long walk to clear her head.

As much as she enjoyed the ranch, she couldn't stay out here indefinitely. She was basically squatting on Colton property—not a great look for an aspiring real-estate agent. More than that, she was already too fond of Jarvis.

Fond. What a flimsy word for all the things he made her feel.

He'd taken care of her without undermining or minimizing her concerns. He'd given her a peaceful sense of safety and security she hadn't experienced in years. She'd always seen herself as the bold one, going out and striving for her goals. She'd never realized how much she enjoyed solitude or how much she missed it after Regina had stormed into her life.

Self-assessment could be a pain.

She rubbed Silas's back as she walked along, her stride parallel with the mountain range in the distance. Emotionally, in her heart, she'd been a mother the moment the pregnancy test showed positive. Roderick had asked her to end the pregnancy. Ending the marriage had been the only solution.

Divorce had meant facing more disappointment in her father's eyes, but once she started to show, his excitement over being a grandfather had eclipsed everything else. Silas's arrival had rebuilt a bridge that Regina had nearly destroyed with her manipulative nature. Mia had never expected to be in this position a second time, isolated from family and a trustworthy support network. Of course, with Regina around, anything was possible.

Once more, Mia debated putting the video out there. Sending it directly to her father would cut him to the core. If he even saw it. Mia had no doubt Regina was screening Norton's email. Through the years, several emails and text messages to her father had gone missing before he'd read them, causing all sorts of communication issues that made Mia look like a problem child.

The family court email only proved Regina must

have had skills or expert help to twist Mia's next attempt at making contact into whatever form suited her
stepmother. Silas was safe in her arms, but her father
was not. Until she was sure her father could be protected, she couldn't expose Regina's infidelity to the
world. They were still at an impasse.

Returning to the bunkhouse, Mia tucked her sleeping son into his car seat and then opened her laptop.
She started a file, writing down everything she recalled from her conversation with Jarvis, eager to explore how she might help *him*. She found it sweet and
a bit curious that he believed so strongly in the validity
of his grandfather's stories. If she could help him sort
out his search, it would make her feel like the scales
were closer to even.

She started with the easy stuff, details he probably
already had, locating online birth records for Jarvis and
his siblings. From there, she easily traced his family
tree to Isaiah. The further back she went, the closer to
Isaiah's grandfather, Herman Colton, the murkier the
official documentation got. Fortunately, the publica-
tions in and around Mustang Valley had been scanned
and enhanced online. In those websites, she searched
for family notes and random articles about the people
of the era. Some mentioned Herman's brother Eugene;
others called the two men cousins.

Which was it? Jarvis would need to know. A tighter
family relationship might give him a better chance to
make a claim to the ranch, no matter what evidence
Herman had buried out here. Her real-estate classes
covered a bit about inheriting and selling properties,
but he would definitely need an attorney if he planned
to go up against Payne and his family.

After the next predictable interruption from Silas, she started to backtrack through the land sale records. She worked her way from the most current tax records until she reached older documents that had been scanned into the system. It would be nice to see these in person, but she did her best to decipher the increasingly faded handwriting and drawings of the land parcels involved on each deed.

She came across a registered deed of sale between Herman Colton and a T. Ainsley. Payne's first wife had been Tessa Ainsley. It was entirely possible the Ainsley on the deed was one of *her* ancestors. Wouldn't that be something, for Payne to have married a descendant of the family who'd had ownership of the property generations ago?

The sale covered more than half of Herman's acreage and all of his livestock at the time. Maybe dementia ran in the family and Herman had forgotten or been confused. That didn't explain the poker game or the deal between Herman and Eugene. Maybe Eugene had forged Herman's signature. She pressed her fingers to her temples. Anything was possible while this part of the country was being settled and developed.

Mia took a screenshot to share with Jarvis later and leaned back in her chair. Without knowing which year the poker game occurred, she couldn't be sure if this information validated Isaiah's story or affirmed Payne's ownership of the land. Assuming the registered sale was legitimate, she might have just eliminated any reason for Jarvis to keep looking for confirmation of his grandfather's story. Would he give up?

She didn't think so. His dark eyes had been bright with curiosity and intent as he told her the story. She'd been honored that he shared it with her. Jarvis didn't seem the type to open up with just anyone.

"And who would I tell anyway?" she said to Silas, brushing her nose to his.

She kept digging. Eugene and Herman had started with parcels that had shared a border, each man expanding as successful seasons allowed. It would be interesting if she could track down the livestock records, as well.

With the original property borders in mind, and the information Jarvis had shared, she shifted her focus one more time to try to narrow down his search parameters. Naturally, he'd been working off Isaiah's story, supposedly passed down from Herman himself. She thought that was odd, in and of itself.

By the time Jarvis sent a text that he was on his way over with dinner, she had what she thought were two excellent target areas.

Surely, a possible treasure hunt was why she was so excited when she heard a truck approaching. Yeah, right. Why did she even try to lie to herself? Jarvis was the reason butterflies were performing complicated aerial maneuvers in her stomach.

"How's it going?" he asked, striding up to the bunkhouse, a big smile on his face.

She'd known her car had been the only casualty at the courthouse, and still a rush of relief poured through her that Regina hadn't hurt him. His presence filled her with a beautiful happiness. His scent wound around her, mingling with something savory in the bag he carried. Even Silas kicked his legs happily, his face turning toward Jarvis's voice.

"We've been productive," she said.

"No nasty texts or emails?"

"All clear on that front."

"That's good." He paused and she wished he'd kiss her. "If a little surprising," he said as he unpacked the food.

She agreed. After Jarvis foiled Regina's plans at the courthouse, she'd expected a barrage of threats, either directly from Regina or from her fake family court template.

"Where'd you get the truck?" she asked.

"It's a loaner from the ranch."

"But you said—"

Jarvis smiled and tickled Silas's bare foot. "This one is so low-tech no one cares where it is. It was never GPS tagged." His eyes met hers. "I triple-checked."

She peered past him through the open doorway. The truck was in rough shape, with a dent behind the passenger door and spots of rust around the wheel wells. "You'll leave me that one?" she asked.

"No. Keep my truck for now. There will be fewer questions if I'm using the old model." At the table he unpacked the meal. "The garage called to let me know the tire was replaced today, but they can hold on to the car for you. I wish we could've taken it to the police station for evidence collection."

"You brought enough food for an army," she observed. There was no sense repeating herself about why they shouldn't involve the police yet. Until she had something more substantial than the classic bitter-step-daughter story, she would keep the threats under wraps.

Jarvis pegged his hat on a hook by the door. "I wanted to eat with you tonight. Unless you need me on sway duty."

It took her a second to register the meaning, and then she laughed. "We're all set here. He just ate."

Jarvis's warm gaze drifted over her and a slow smile curled his sinfully sexy mouth. "Then we should catch up."

He'd brought barbecue and corn bread, along with fresh salad and steamed veggies. "I wasn't sure what you liked, so I loaded up a bit of everything."

"It's perfect. Now stop stalling and tell me all about what happened at the courthouse."

His brow furrowed. "I'm glad you didn't go." He shoved his fork into the pile of shredded meat but didn't lift the bite to his mouth. "Whatever she had in mind, I doubt it was pleasant." He paused long enough to gulp down a bite of the barbecue. "She was waiting for you outside the courtroom, at the window that overlooks the parking lot. Someone else was down there, keeping her informed." He pulled his phone from his back pocket. "I think this is the guy."

Mia wiped her fingers on a napkin and picked up the device. She enlarged the picture as far as it would go. "That looks a lot like the man she was with at the country house."

"Thought it might be," Jarvis muttered. "Assuming he was invited, we can't go after him for trespassing."

"Correct." She poked at her salad. "You're sure she didn't see you?"

He spread his arms wide and grinned. "She was looking for you and the baby, not a random cowboy. She completely ignored my existence."

She appreciated the way he made her laugh, despite the fear rattling her nerves. "This really is above and beyond the call of cowboy assistance."

"I'm not so sure," he said.

Seeing the kissable smirk on his lips made it tough to stay on her side of the table. When would she find her perspective? She couldn't keep turning one errant kiss into something significant. He'd initially helped her for the sake of the ranch and now he felt obligated to see it through. It didn't exactly make for a level playing field.

"Maybe you should bail on the party," she suggested.

"No." He shook his head. "I'm more curious than ever, and you want an eyes-on report about your dad."

"If she gets suspicious, you could be in trouble. I should go and force her hand."

"Judging by what I saw today, that woman was born calculating and mean," he stated. "Her suspicions are the least of my worries. I promise I'll look good enough that Selina won't let me out of her sight and so different from a working cowboy that Regina will have no idea that she passed me in the courthouse today."

He looked pretty damn hot right now, but she kept the observation to herself. She had to believe in him. "I added the video file to my cloud folder at my attorney's office." She hadn't meant to bring that up, but someone trustworthy should know. "Along with the fake custody email that came through last night."

"Does your attorney check that folder? Will he take action?"

"Only if I request it. I just wanted you to know so if something happens…"

"Nothing will happen." His voice rumbled through the cabin like thunder. "At the party I'll speak with your dad and make sure he's feeling well and sounds like himself. If I can gather any more information, I'll do that, too. Then we'll make a plan to get you out of here and safely back to your life."

She was sure he didn't mean to hurt her feelings, but she felt as if he was pushing her away, nudging her along like a willful steer. Chances were good she was too sensitive and too lonely out here to accurately interpret what Jarvis did or didn't mean by every other word. He'd helped her and she'd done something to help him, as well.

"Speaking of plans," she began, pausing to snag another piece of the corn bread. "I worked my way through the land records and have some suggestions about where you might want to search."

"Tell me you found a land survey with an *X* on it, signed by Herman."

She laughed. "If it were that easy, you'd have found it without my help." She told him her theories on the landmarks and how they might have changed through the years. As well as where the original boundary had probably been.

He drummed his fingers on the table, repeating the pattern when Silas turned toward the sound. She melted a little at the effortless way he engaged with her baby. A string of "if onlys" raced through her mind and she yanked herself back to reality. Jarvis wasn't her Mr. Right just because he was within reach and kissed her senseless. He wasn't going to fall in love with her because they'd traded secrets and family drama.

Determined to be as good a friend to him as he'd been to her, she told him about the registered sale between Herman and T. Ainsley.

"How can both be true?" he wondered. "If Herman sold the land, why pass on the story about it being stolen?"

"Bad blood between the brothers? Signatures were hardly verified back then the way they are now."

"A forgery?" A frown creased his brow. "Yeah, I guess that's possible."

He went quiet, lost in his thoughts while she cleaned up the remnants of their dinner and bagged the trash.

"I'll keep looking."

She startled at the sound of his voice and they both chuckled. "I thought you'd say that. I'm glad." She wanted to ask if he'd keep kissing her, too, but her typical bravery failed her.

"It's always been a bit of wild-goose chase, but if I stop now I'll have to find something else to keep my shoulders in shape."

His shoulders looked perfect to her.

"Will you be okay out here tonight?"

"Of course."

He studied her face, and then shocked her by reaching out and nudging her chin up. "No circles under your eyes." She might believe it was a clinical assessment if not for the heat in his gaze. "And it looks like you got some sun today."

She should move out of his reach, but her body refused to cooperate. "We went for a walk, not far, but fresh air helps him nap."

"I could stay." He released her chin. "You might need a break overnight."

If he stayed, she'd want to spend every spare minute awake, in his arms, learning what pleased him and savoring every pleasure his sexy mouth and strong hands could create. "It sounds almost like you enjoy being with my son."

"He's cute." Jarvis hooked his thumbs in his pockets. "I enjoy you more," he said, his voice loaded with charm. "You're beautiful, Mia." He touched his lips to hers in a soft, fleeting kiss that left her feeling cheated.

She caught his shirt and drew him close. "Want to give that one more try?"

"I want to do more than try," he confessed, his rasping tone scraping away any pretense. He covered her mouth with his, his tongue sliding with hers in a hot caress that shot tingles straight to her toes, hitting all points in between.

It had been years since she'd felt an all-consuming desire like this. She and Roderick had fallen into a nice and predictable pattern. Enjoyable enough. Or so she'd thought.

She let herself loose, willing to cede control to Jarvis while her knees trembled and her heart raced. This was something altogether new and exciting. She dropped her head back as his lips traced her jaw, kissing, nipping and soothing a path down her throat.

"Mia," he whispered her name against the pulse throbbing at the base of her neck and she shivered. "You feel… I want… This is crazy."

"The best kind," she agreed. "Don't stop." Her breasts ached as desire arced through her like an electrical current. She pressed closer to the hard wall of his chest and moaned at the contact, relishing the sweet friction.

His hands molded to her hips, eased higher over her rib cage. One of his hot palms cupped her breast, stroking and teasing her through her T-shirt and bra. It was enough to bring her right to the edge.

"Please, Jarvis." She kissed him again and worked his shirt free of his jeans. Her reward was the incomparable feel of warm skin and crisp hair over slabs of mouthwatering muscle.

He trapped her hand, his breathing ragged as he retreated. "We can't."

She opened her eyes to find him watching her too closely. She arched an eyebrow in query.

"We shouldn't," he amended. "Seriously." He looked around, his gaze as hot and bewildered as she felt. That was a small consolation that she wasn't in this alone, but it steadied her.

"The baby," he said desperately.

"Is asleep," she pointed out. She reached up and smoothed a hand over his cheek, loving the feel of his whiskers against her palm. She loved every nuance and discovery Jarvis allowed. He had so many textures and layers beneath that rough-and-ready exterior. "And he's too young to remember anything he might see."

She clamped her lips shut and didn't protest when he stepped back. Pride would not allow her to beg for the connection or passion he wasn't ready to give.

"Mia." He pushed a hand through his hair, his chest expanding on a deep inhale. "I want you, but I don't think it's smart. For you."

"Uh-huh." She crossed her arms, reflexively preventing her heart from leaping into his hands. "Do you always lie to yourself?"

"Hang on." He scowled at her. "I'm not *lying* to anyone. Being with me isn't a smart move. It would be fun, unforgettable, no doubt. But I don't buy into the whole family dynamic. You do. I—I'm more like your ex."

Please. He could toss out all the excuses he wanted; she'd seen his reaction when she told him about Roderick's response to her pregnancy. "You think having a baby ruined my body?"

"What?" His gaze raked over her, leaving her feeling scalded. "Hell no."

"Then you're nothing like my ex." She recognized fear and uncertainty, having seen it often enough in the mirror lately. "I didn't ask you for a ring or even a promise, Jarvis." She had no idea how she was keeping her cool. "To be blunt, I'm attracted to you. I'm woman enough to say I'd like to follow that attraction to its logical conclusion. Just healthy sex, no strings."

He didn't need to know her emotions were surging all over the place. That was her problem, her responsibility. She could keep her mushy feelings well away from the need blazing between them. It was entirely possible this blaze would burn that emotion to cinders, anyway.

"That sounds cold." He stalked over to the door but didn't leave. On an oath, he turned back and she saw his arousal straining against the fly of his jeans. There was nothing emotional about her response to that view. Her mouth watered and heat pooled between her thighs.

"You wanted poetry?" she asked. "Being coy has never been my strong suit."

"I'm just a messed-up cowboy." He pushed a hand through his hair. "You're a model."

"I'm a woman. If you're messed up, I'm a wreck," she said. "But I'm honest. I want you."

"You deserve the best, Mia." He sounded so sincere.

"You deserve rings and promises from a man who believes family is a functional institution."

The pain underscoring his words was like a knife in her chest. "What do you mean?"

"I barely remember what a healthy family looks like. The three of us were dumped on an aunt who was forced to step up because that's what 'family' does. She didn't want to call us hers any more than Payne Colton wants to claim us. Family is obligation and responsibility and I can't—I can't give you that."

"Jarvis. Whatever you're thinking, stop and hear me." She took a cautious step closer. "When you kiss me, I feel like *me* again. When you touch me, I don't feel afraid or frumpy. That's a gift, a treasure. And right now, that's plenty. It's probably all I can handle. I'm not going to fall in love over a kiss and demand an exclusive, permanent relationship."

She was fairly sure that *was* a lie. She had the sense that Jarvis would be easy to love, either on the rebound or for forever. Thank goodness she'd learned to control her facial expressions during her modeling career.

He dropped his head back, staring at the ceiling. "I didn't mean to insult you or overreact or whatever the hell it is I'm doing."

She moved around the table and pulled a bottle of water from the refrigerator. "Stay if you want. I won't attack you in your sleep."

"Same."

She heard his boots against the floor as he walked away from the door. "I feel weird kissing you, knowing I'm going out with Selina in a few days."

That admission might be closer to the real issue, but she sensed there was more, something twisted up with his pessimistic views about family. She hadn't expected dating as a single mother to be easy. Hadn't anticipated that she would be this intensely attracted to any man so soon. Maybe Jarvis could help her more by giving her a reality check about her hopes for her future.

"Not that it means anything." He slid into a chair at the table. "She was very clear that my only purpose is to look good and be into her, so she can make Regina jealous. As if I'd be tempted to stick around." His nose wrinkled and his lip curled as if he'd tasted something sour.

Mia laughed at his absurd expression and the baby jerked in his sleep but relaxed again. She sat opposite him, doing her best not to stare. "Your charm and flirtation skills must be off the charts."

"I have my strengths." He winked and her belly quivered.

"You do," she agreed. It was a challenge to sit and talk when only minutes ago he had her body throbbing and speechless, but this seemed to be what he needed. And she wasn't ready to be alone.

"Being around Selina is like trying to walk a rattlesnake." His amusement turned somber. "There's a woman who made the right choice by not having kids."

"It must have been terrifying for you when your parents died," she murmured. "I'm sorry." She stretched out a hand, offering comfort without pushing it on him.

He lifted his gaze, his dark eyes shaded by his furrowed brow. "I don't remember anyone saying that," he said. He touched his fingers to hers. "I'm sure they did. They must have?"

"Probably," she said. "I remember hearing it. I can't imagine how you and your brother and sister suffered.

My world wasn't ripped apart like yours. I still had Dad. I didn't have to move." She laced her fingers through his. "Losing someone you love is always devastating, no matter when it happens. I wasn't sure Dad would ever smile again after Mom died. There was an invisible cloud that followed me around everywhere, a shroud over everything. Sunlight, bright colors, flavors and feelings, all of it was dim for a long time. Grief takes time to wade through and the effects linger."

She hoped not forever. Jarvis was too good a person to spend his life afraid of living deeply and completely. She understood abandonment, even if her experiences differed from his. Her dad had essentially walked away from her, withdrawing his support and confidence in her. At the first curveball, her husband had chosen his idea of the perfect couple over adapting along with her and becoming a family.

"My brother and sister are moving on," Jarvis said. "It's good. They'll both be married soon." He withdrew his hand, leaning back in the chair. "Probably with kids."

"And you'll be the cowboy uncle."

"Absolutely." A hint of a grin tilted his mouth. "All of the fun, none of the pressure. The traditional path isn't the right fit for me."

"Isn't searching for proof of Isaiah's stories a way of moving on?" she pressed. She refused to mention that kissing her could qualify, too.

"The search started as a weird way to connect with our past and, if Isaiah's information is right, the result might be a better future for the three of us."

She sipped her water. "In my book that sounds like

a man who knows exactly how to value, work for and honor his family."

He shrugged off the compliment. "At this point, I think I'm just too stubborn to quit."

"Stubborn doesn't have to be a weakness. Being willing to fight and adapt is also a good family trait. Your list of strengths is getting longer."

"Stop it," he said without any real heat.

"Why?" She turned the ring on her thumb. "Families are as different as the people who make them up. I had family with Mom and Dad. I had a family of friends in college. Now, with Silas, I have a new family. Just because it doesn't resemble some gooey holiday commercial doesn't make it less valid."

"I hear you, Mia. But I just can't give anyone that much power to hurt me again. I've dealt with enough pain for one lifetime. And the flip side is I don't want to risk hurting anyone, either. Not the way I was hurt as a kid."

Her heart ached for him, for cutting himself off from the world. Loneliness was a pain unto itself. She wished she could make him see that. Taking a deep breath, she gave him her award-winning smile. "That's understandable. Trust me when I say I'm not looking forward to the moments when Silas and I hurt each other. Life won't be perfect. One of us already shows signs of a strong and unquenchable temper."

Jarvis laughed. "At least one of you."

She ignored the jab. "You're talking to a woman who's cleared her own path more than once. Going it alone is exhausting," she admitted. "Without you, I probably would've given in to Regina or flat-out run away and changed my name by now."

"Not likely, with your famously beautiful face."

She soaked up the sweet words, the heat in his eyes as he said them. "I can do wonders with makeup," she teased. "Yes, the person you love most is also the person who can hurt you the deepest. I still want to have love in my life."

"After what happened with your husband, I'd think you'd be done taking those chances."

"I'm not. The fact that it was easy to walk away from Roderick only confirmed that what we had wasn't as deep as it should've been. And when I said that, I was actually thinking of my dad."

"The man who put his new wife ahead of his daughter." He shook his head. "Doesn't that prove the wisdom of keeping part of yourself protected from that kind of rejection?"

She wondered if he heard the brokenhearted little boy in his voice. "At the risk of sounding like a shrink, I'll remind you that the loss of your parents when you were so young had a lasting impact. Compounding that when you lost your aunt—"

He shoved roughly to his feet, the chair scraping across the plank floor. "Her death wasn't the same at all."

"The same or different, it was another loss," she soothed.

"More like a burden lifted." He scrubbed at his face. "She didn't want us, we didn't want to be with her. More family dysfunction." He sighed. "How did we get on this topic, anyway?"

"You stopped kissing me."

"Well, call me a fool," he said with a wry grin.

"I'm not asking for more than you want to give," she

reminded him. "I'm only suggesting you allow yourself to think about what you need to take."

"From you?"

She rolled her eyes. "From anyone, Jarvis. You're a good man. One of the best men I've met. You said all that about what I deserve, but you deserve happiness, too. Peace. Family. Love. However, *you* choose to define any of those things."

"Right." He grabbed his hat. "I'll be back tomorrow. Text me if something comes up or you're low on anything."

"I will. Thanks." It took every ounce of willpower to stay in her chair, to keep her mouth shut.

He paused, the door halfway open. "I'm not angry."

"Me, neither." Halfway in love with a man who didn't believe in the concept, but not angry. "See you tomorrow."

With a curt nod, he was gone. A moment later the truck engine rumbled and faded as he drove away. Obviously, she'd said too much. She didn't regret it and wouldn't retract a word. The world needed more good men like Jarvis, and he needed more good from the world.

Chapter Seven

The intense conversation with Mia simmered in the back of Jarvis's mind for days. He'd been annoyed as hell that first night. Had even considered not going back. Couldn't do it. She needed someone keeping an eye out for her, even in the updated bunkhouse. It wasn't safe for her to go into town, not while Regina still held so much leverage.

So he manned up and went back day after day, determined to keep his distance physically and emotionally. It wasn't easy; the woman left him wanting, but he managed. They found a routine and kept conversations on the lighter end of the spectrum or locked onto his search pattern. There were more kisses, yet by some tacit agreement they kept those lighter, too. He made sure she had what she needed, including a few minutes to herself every time he stopped by.

Still, her challenge haunted him, forced him to think about things he'd always pushed down or ignored. How did he define happiness? He was completely at peace and content with his opinions on family and love and his future role as the fun-loving uncle. But happiness? That should probably involve more than a career, more than time with his siblings.

Spencer and Bella were happier with their new-found soul mates than he'd ever seen them. After all they'd lost, that kind of leap into commitment and love seemed like too big a risk. One of them had to stay sane and logical. If he was okay as the family backstop, why did it matter what Mia thought about his choices?

He was still searching for a good answer for that.

He did enjoy spending time with her son far more than he wanted to admit even to himself. He wouldn't call himself attached; he was just more curious about how the baby soaked up the sights, sounds and smells each day. Jarvis had come by on his horse one afternoon and he swore the little guy smiled when Mia guided his tiny hand through the mane.

All of those relaxed and easy moments made tonight more difficult. Putting on a suit and heading out to a party with a different woman felt all kinds of wrong. Selina and Mia might run in the same social circles, but they were on opposite ends of the personality scale, in Jarvis's opinion. Selina was cold and sleek and calculating, and Mia was everything warm and kind and beautiful. Both women had tremendous strength, but he preferred Mia's easygoing glow over Selina's sharp edges and pushy manner.

He couldn't accurately term the time he spent with Mia as dating, but it was definitely more fun than the myriad roles he had to play tonight. Spying for Asher. Bolstering Selina's pride. Assessing Norton's health for Mia. Not to mention the variations on those themes that included giving Norton a message or finding something incriminating on Regina. He didn't want to let Asher or Mia down, and disappointing Selina would backfire in the worst way on the ranch.

Per Selina's last text message, he parked behind her house so the ranch truck wouldn't mar her home's perfect curb appeal or alter the impression that someone wealthy was escorting her to Regina's event. Smoothing his tie and checking his cuff links, he strolled up the walkway, admiring the flawless landscaping the ranch crew maintained for her. He rang the bell and waited, trying not to wish the evening over before it began.

Selina opened the door and he was momentarily struck mute. Her dress hugged her body like a second gleaming skin. Gold sparkled in the black fabric, catching the light and winking in and out as she moved. Gold bangles slithered up and down her wrist as she invited him in.

"You look great," he said, choosing a bland compliment.

Her gaze narrowed. "My, my." She walked a circle around him and he sympathized with a fresh side of beef in a butcher shop. "You do clean up nicely, cowboy."

"Thanks." He gave her a slower appraisal this time, adding enough heat until her eyes twinkled.

"That's what I'm after," she said with a sassy giggle.

He had to admit she was an attractive woman, even if she wasn't his type. Thanks to Mia, he found himself wondering if Selina believed in family. Probably not, considering she might have cheated on Payne, clearly resented his kids and had carved out a chunk of his estate for herself in the divorce.

"This is going to be epic."

"I'm glad you approve." He knew she believed his sole purpose this evening was to send Regina into a fit of jealousy. He'd play his part, hopeful that an "epic" distraction would be enough for her to slip up about the situation with Mia.

"We'll be the talk of the party." She tossed him a set of keys. "You aren't going to wimp out over a little gossip, are you?"

He smiled. "It'll be a pleasure."

She sucked in a tiny breath and petted his shoulder. "Keep that up and you might get to hang around more often."

He guided her fingers down to curl around his elbow and escorted her out to the sleek sports car waiting in her driveway. "I didn't know you had a Jaguar."

"One more perk of being a Colton ex-wife," she said, her tone low and sly. "Coma or not, Payne will never say no to me."

After opening the door and helping her into the passenger seat, he rounded the hood and sank into the supple leather upholstery. He rested his hands on the steering wheel, admiring the gleaming walnut accents, before adjusting the seat and mirrors to suit him.

Selina snickered. "When we get to the party, can you aim a little of that passionate infatuation my way?" She put the address into the car's navigation app and sat back again.

"I promise." He glanced over. "When I was in college, we used to daydream about status cars. Some of the guys went out and took test drives."

"Not you?"

"Not me." While the test drives motivated others, Jarvis knew that getting a taste of what he couldn't yet afford would've only frustrated him. "I had plenty of time for that once the money was in the bank to back it up."

"Oh, that's right. I forgot you put yourself through college and landed a real job before you signed on here," she said. "Are you really thrilled about riding a horse these days instead of driving a Jaguar?"

A few weeks ago, he might have bristled or felt defensive at the sly dig. After finding Mia and especially after their talk, he chose to take the comment at face value. "They're both temperamental," he joked. "Turns out the ranch is an excellent fit for me. I get to drive a horse *and* a Jag."

"Just for tonight," she reminded him, coolly. Her perfectly manicured nails dug into the small purse on her lap. "Listen. Even if Payne survives, I'm sure he won't ever admit that your tenacity and independence impressed him."

That hit harder than the reminders that they were from two different worlds. "I don't know why." He cleared his throat. "We were just three orphans who coincidentally shared his last name and hometown."

Selina scoffed. "Whatever he says, I think he's always been impressed by you."

He shot her a quick look. That was a surprising reveal and he wasn't sure what she gained by sharing it. Selina was impossible to figure out. He pulled away from the Triple R, taking the turn with care and minding the speed limit.

"Oh, open her up," Selina said. "I'll cover any speeding ticket."

She didn't have to tell him twice. He forgot the strife and ghosts lurking in his family tree and drove toward a less-traveled stretch of road where he could let the Jag loose. The engine responded with a throaty growl and they were suddenly flying low through the twilight, the speedometer edging toward ninety, then ninety-five, miles per hour.

Selina made a sound that landed somewhere between a squeal and a laugh. Jarvis didn't take his eyes off the road, even as he eased off the accelerator and brought the car back to a normal, law-abiding speed.

"That was exhilarating!"

He glanced over and caught Selina's wide grin and bright eyes. She had color in her cheeks that made her look remarkably youthful and carefree. Right now, it was easy to see why Payne had fallen for her, and possibly, why he'd been convinced to keep her close both at Colton Oil and at the Triple R.

Darkness swept over the valley as they drove to the exclusive gated neighborhood where the Graves family lived. The pale stucco homes and red tile roofs were set well apart from each other and the landscaping, highlighted by low lights and streetlamps, seemed to be coordinated from the entrance to each individual drive.

Mia had grown up here. It was impossible not to picture her as a little girl learning to ride a bike or as a teen lounging away the summers with a pack of friends around a backyard pool. He'd done those things, too, but across town, and on a much more modest scale.

When they reached the Graves' driveway, Selina flipped down the visor mirror to check her makeup. "Jarvis, I think your burst of speed was more effective than an hour with concealer and highlighter." Her cheeks were still rosy and her eyes bright. She added a bit of gloss to her lips and then gave him a nod.

On that cue he steeled himself to run the gauntlet

with the various items on his agenda. He came around to her side and opened her door, extending a hand. She emerged with such perfect grace he assumed she'd practiced the maneuver. Or maybe it was one of those things that society women instinctively knew how to accomplish. His mind inevitably drifted to Mia, recalling paparazzi photos that documented her vehicle exits through her modeling years. Beautiful, enticing photos of long, shapely legs and that stunning smile that made anyone she looked at feel like the only relevant person on the planet.

Selina slipped her hand around his elbow, bringing him back to the moment. Her fingers clutched his arm through his suit coat, tightening with every step they took toward the house. She didn't lean too close, but she made it clear she wanted him to stick with her. He played along, stealing glances and smiling as if they shared a secret, all the while imagining Mia beside him.

Norton and Regina Graves were not waiting to greet them. The doors of the magnificent home had been thrown wide open, light spilling out over the walkway. Two men in catering uniforms stood sentry, checking identification and invitations.

"My place at the ranch has more square footage," Selina said quietly as they stepped into the foyer. "But Regina upgraded with more marble when she remodeled and brought Norton's decor into the current era."

Jarvis bent his head to her ear. "Bigger is better," he said, knowing it would make her smile.

"And younger is a plus, too," she replied, her eyes twinkling as she caressed his biceps. "Let's go raise some eyebrows, cowboy."

He recognized many of the faces as he worked the room as Selina's oversize accessory. She surprised him by making genuine introductions while they chatted with industry leaders from across the Southwest. He'd expected to be dismissed breezily if not outright ignored.

She paused between conversations, angling her body closer. Her fingertips stroked his lapel. "Here we go," she said for his ears only.

Regina glided up, a glass of champagne in her hand. She wore her hair up, but that was the only similarity to the first time he'd seen her at the courthouse. Tonight the dress and heels, along with the jewelry, made a clear statement that she was the trophy wife every man should want.

"Selina!" she gushed. "I'm so glad you've made it." She turned a bold smile on Jarvis. "Is this the nephew I've heard so much about?"

"No, no." Selina laughed easily, but he felt the bite of tension as she slid her arm around his waist. "This is Jarvis Colton, the man who has simply made the last few months a *delight*. Jarvis, this is Regina Graves, our hostess and Norton's wife."

Jarvis glided his hand down Selina's back in a gently familiar and possessive move. In the past the gesture might have felt gallant or warm. Tonight he just felt sticky. "You have a lovely home, Mrs. Graves."

"Thank you." Her gaze narrowed, her lips tilting as she assessed him.

"Where is Norton?" Selina made a show of looking around while pressing close to Jarvis's side. "We haven't had a chance to say hello to the guest of honor."

"He's out on the deck with a cigar and a few close

friends," Regina said, the insult clear though she'd delivered it with a sugary smile. "Do enjoy yourselves until he returns."

With a lingering gaze for Jarvis, she walked off. He wanted a shower.

"Oh, well done," Selina said under her breath. "She's fuming."

"Happy to help," Jarvis said, moving his hand along her spine again.

He let Selina guide him to and fro through the house, until the conversations blurred together. Per Asher's request, he kept Selina sipping on champagne. Not enough to allow her to wreck her own agenda, but enough that she might feel talkative while he drove her home.

Selina couldn't be persuaded to interrupt the cigar smokers on the deck, so Jarvis had to bide his time until he could get a good look at Norton. Hopefully, hanging with his "close friends" meant he was safe. Unless Regina had tampered with the man's cigars. He wouldn't put anything past her.

Selina shooed Jarvis away once she was immersed in a conversation with several women. He seized the opportunity, selecting a sparkling water and giving himself a tour of the grand house. With luck, he might get to Norton's office or even upstairs before anyone noticed.

Everywhere he looked, he was greeted by high-end luxury. The furnishings were perfect, the colors and textures and accent pieces creating a flawlessly coordinated effect. He was sure every piece was comfortable, but nothing was comforting.

As he wandered through, he realized the decor was

light on family memorabilia. Even his aunt had framed their school pictures each year. He assumed the house had been staged for the party and the personal items removed for safekeeping, until he found photos of Regina and Norton on a mantel and more candid shots of the couple framed and featured on a bookshelf. Notably absent were any photos of Mia or Silas. Hearing a slow click of high heels on the tile floor, he paused to admire the selection of books.

"Here you are," Regina purred at his shoulder.

Jarvis stepped out of her reach, barely suppressing a shudder.

"You've wandered a bit from the party." She closed the distance again, her perfume snaking around him. "Is the crowd too much?"

"I do enjoy the quiet," he replied. "I hope it's not a problem."

"No, of course not." She watched him with a shrewd gaze. "You're welcome to make yourself at home."

Ugh. She was testing him. He was torn between calling her bluff and calling her out. Embarrassing Selina would wreck his chances of gleaning any information for Asher. And Regina didn't strike him as a woman to succumb to an ultimatum from a stranger. He'd believed Mia before that Regina would strike if pressed. Now he could see it in her eyes. She was wondering how to steal him from Selina.

"Norton has quite a collection here," he said, gesturing to the bookshelf.

"How do you know the collection isn't mine?" she countered. "Maybe we share it."

The emphasis she placed on "share" made his skin crawl. He evaded her next attempt to touch him. "Classic philosophy and modern business must lead to fascinating conversations with your husband." Jarvis spotted a man Selina had introduced earlier and made his escape. "If you'll excuse me. Please, give Norton my best."

He figured Selina would give a cheer when she heard about it, but he wasn't sure one shower would be enough to erase the ick-factor. He spoke with a few more people as he made his way toward the back of the house. Being familiar with Norton's career and having a thorough understanding of industry and business ventures in the region gave him a leg up on the typical eye candy. He used it to his advantage, gathering snippets of conversations and comments to share with Mia later.

Jarvis learned Norton had been golfing twice since she'd gone into hiding. He hadn't missed any meetings and no one voiced any concerns about his health or behavior. All of that should ease Mia's concerns.

What he found more distressing was the lack of concern for Mia or her baby. She was Norton's only child and had been visible and influential as a model and as Roderick's wife. No one seemed to miss her. In fact, any sign that Mia had ever lived here or had any relationship with her father was gone. He assumed Regina was behind that, clearing out anything that diverted Norton's focus on his wife. Rounding a corner, Jarvis came up short as he found himself in front of a painting of Norton and a young Mia. They looked happy and connected, and her natural beauty was already shining. He wondered if Regina had tried to remove it entirely or if she hadn't yet dared.

Norton walked up right then, his eyebrows lifting when he saw Jarvis.

Jarvis offered his hand and his name. "I've followed your career for some time, Mr. Graves."

Norton met his handshake with a firm grip. "A pleasure to meet you, Mr. Colton. Hope you've followed my advice, as well."

"Naturally. And I'm better off because of it," Jarvis admitted. "Is this your daughter?"

Norton faced the painting, his hands clasped behind his back and a frown pleating his gray eyebrows. "Mia, yes. I miss the girl she was back then."

"She's off with a family of her own these days?" Jarvis queried.

"Family? No." Norton's mouth firmed. "Not anymore. Her mother and I had such hopes for that girl. She squeaked through college, refusing to apply herself to her studies. Then she married an upstart tech genius from New York City." He sighed. "His business flourished, but the marriage failed, as I warned her it would. Now she's all but disappeared, taking my grandson with her."

That was far more than Jarvis had expected. He felt like Norton had siphoned all the air from the room. "I—I'm sorry, sir."

"I'd hoped, despite Mia being beyond reach, that her son would mark a fresh start for us, but she seems determined to disappoint me." He rocked back on his heels. "I really thought that would pass once she was out of her teens and twenties. Sometimes common sense skips a generation."

"I've never thought of it that way." Jarvis didn't know what else to say. He wanted to leap to Mia's defense, was in fact trying to come up with some way to clue Norton in that his daughter was in trouble. He was about to tactlessly blurt out the message from Mia when Regina appeared.

"There you are, my love." She slid up close and rubbed his shoulder. "This isn't the time for melancholy."

"Oh, I know." He gave her a tired smile. "The young man here asked about Mia."

"Jasper, is that right?" Regina said with a bored expression.

"It's Jarvis, ma'am." He corrected her politely and nearly blew it with a laugh when he saw the "ma'am" register on her face.

"Jarvis," she repeated, her tone chilly. "Mia was a lovely girl and we miss her terribly. I've tried to shield Norton from the worst of her carelessness." She caught her husband's hand between her own. "Children are forever hurting their parents. Something I'm sure she'll learn soon enough." To Norton she said, "You'll have another chance, dear. I'm sure it's only a matter of time before she comes to the door groveling for help again."

"Tried to help her launch a business," Norton grumbled.

"Of course you did. That's who you are."

"Such a disappointment." His face crumpled. "I don't understand it."

"She's selfish, Norton. And self-absorbed. On the bright side, you'll always have me, my love." She kissed her husband. Not anything brief or classy or even affectionate. No, she took the time to fuse her mouth to his in an intimate display that made Jarvis's stomach curdle. "Now, happy thoughts. I came looking for you because the mayor just walked in. You should say hello."

When he was out of earshot, her sharp gaze locked

onto Jarvis. "I'll thank you not to upset my husband further this evening."

"Not my intention at all. I was merely admiring the painting." He smiled when Selina found him and hurried over. "Enjoying yourself?" He drew her close to his side.

"It's a fabulous night." She grinned up at him. The expression softened when she saw the painting over his shoulder. "I'm surprised this survived the remodeling, Regina."

"It will go to storage soon enough," the woman snapped. "Mia ran off," she said, her voice just loud enough to carry. "He just needs time to accept it. Norton is heartbroken. I always knew she was a lost cause, but the baby—" she pressed her hands over her heart "—he was crazy over that little boy."

"That's terrible." Selina didn't sound too broken up about it.

"Eventually, he'll come around," Regina continued. "After the way she left…" Regina shook her head sadly. "Some scruffy, gold-digging boyfriend had been by a few times. Only when Norton was at work, of course. Then poof, without a word, she's moved out and taken the baby. But not before stealing all the cash from my purse and clearing out a fund Norton set up for the little tyke. She hasn't spoken to either of us since. He's heartbroken," she repeated, her gaze drifting to her husband across the room. "I haven't told him I've started searching for the child. I documented everything and I'm sure we can get custody of the baby when the time comes."

Jarvis had never wanted to strike a woman until this very moment. Regina and her lies brought out the worst in him. He focused on Selina and this time he used her for support.

"Good luck with that," Selina said. "It's been a lovely party, Regina, but we should be going." She batted her lashes at Jarvis. "We both have to be up early tomorrow."

"Of course." Regina's smile didn't reach her eyes and her mouth was pinched at the corners. "We'll have to make time for lunch soon."

"Definitely. Just call." Selina extricated them from the conversation and aimed straight for the door. "Having ungrateful, greedy stepchildren is the worst. I almost feel sorry for her."

Jarvis made a sound of agreement, but his temper was about to boil over. Regina was a world-class liar and he hated that it was on him to inform Mia of how misinformed her father was. He'd leave out as much as he could and she'd be happy to hear her dad appeared healthy.

For how long?

"Do you think she meant it, about suing for custody?" he asked, driving away from the Graves home. He hadn't meant to bring it up, especially not with Selina, but it bothered him.

"Not a chance," Selina waved that off. "Regina is making the right noises to appease that old coot. She loves to flaunt her money and pretend she has all the power."

Jarvis agreed with that assessment one hundred percent.

"There was a time when I felt sorry for Mia. She and Norton were close before he met Regina."

"You don't feel sorry for her now?"

"Are you kidding? She landed on her feet. Her husband was sinfully rich and even better looking." Selina slid the bangles up and down her arm. "People don't realize how quickly things can change. I used to have more money than Regina. Back when I was Mrs. Payne Colton."

Jarvis snapped out of his Mia worries. This was exactly the opening Asher had hoped for. "From where I stand, it seems you landed on your feet, too."

"Of course it looks that way, to you. And I do have some pull, although being his ex-wife means more trade-offs." She reached over and squeezed his thigh, just above his knee. "These days Regina might have the bigger bank account, but I can be seen out and about with whomever I please. She's stuck fawning over that love-blind old man."

Jarvis stopped her wandering hand before it crept too much higher on his leg. With a giggle, Selina subsided. "I hope she's being smart about things."

"What things?"

"Well, if Norton catches on to her antics and affairs, she's doomed. And if she's been spending as wildly as she seems to be, life after divorce will be a bear. Voice of experience."

"Was the adjustment difficult?" He really didn't care, but he needed to keep her talking.

"In some ways." Selina yawned. "But I'm set for life. A beautiful home, an excellent salary and benefits, plus all the help I need is just a finger-snap away." She snapped and then stroked his knee again. "Payne used to complain and taught his kids to resent me, but he really should've been more discreet."

"About what?"

"Oh, everything and nothing," she said. "His secrets and misdeeds are my gold mine."

Asher would go nuts when he heard this.

"I'll let you in on a secret, cowboy." She reached out and petted his shoulder this time. "A smart woman is always paying attention. Don't you ever underestimate a pretty face." She sank back into her seat once more, and before Jarvis could prod more out of her, she was out.

"Great."

Parking in front of her house, Jarvis roused Selina enough to get her inside. He didn't venture any farther than the foyer, though he'd done enough errands here that he knew the layout well enough. Once she was steady on her feet, he pressed the Jag keys into her hand and urged her to lock the door behind him.

Back outside, he couldn't get away fast enough. He rumbled across the sleeping ranch in the older pickup and parked near his room. He wanted out of the suit and into a shower.

Jarvis had once found Selina calculating and clingy. Tonight he'd gone a few rounds with the new champion of manipulation, Regina. Knowing Mia was eager for news on her dad, he planned to text her as soon as he was back in his room.

Walking to his door, he nearly jumped out of his skin when the shadows moved. "Asher. You nearly gave me a heart attack."

"You've never been jumpy," his boss replied. "Did something happen?"

It took a moment for the genuine concern to sink in. He'd only spent a few hours with high society, but he wasn't cut out for that level of sniping and veiled threats. He'd made the right choice coming to work at the Triple R. "Dodging Selina's wandering hands makes me jumpy," he admitted.

"Was she chatty?"

"A little." He unlocked his door and invited Asher in. "She let me drive the Jag."

"Lucky you."

He smiled and tugged his tie from his collar. "I'll say. That was the bright spot and it was so early on I nearly forgot it." He shrugged out of his coat and draped it over the chair.

Each room in this bunkhouse was a small apartment, furnished with a bed, dresser, small table, two chairs and a private bathroom. Each man on the crew who stayed in these quarters could add what he wanted to the setup. Jarvis hadn't added much beyond a good television. He'd put most of his belongings in storage since hiring on here.

Asher braced his hands on the other chair, impatient now. "Don't keep me in suspense."

"You were right to think blackmail. She definitely knows something damaging about Payne," Jarvis reported. "She warned me not to underestimate a pretty face, that smart women are observant."

"She didn't tell you what it was?"

"No. Said he wasn't discreet and that his secrets and misdeeds were her gold mine."

Asher swore. "She was the one who slept around. All of the financials from their marriage look clean."

"I'd say it's more than that." Jarvis held up his hands. "Gut instinct, that's all," he added. "I wanted to ask more, but she fell asleep."

Asher swore softly. "It was too much to hope for a

written confession. And confirmation that she does have legitimate leverage is helpful. I know it couldn't have been an easy night." He popped Jarvis lightly on the shoulder. "Thanks for going the extra mile. Take tomorrow off."

That startled him. "You sure?"

"I am."

"Thanks," Jarvis said with feeling.

Once Asher was gone, Jarvis sent Mia a text to confirm her father was healthy, promising to explain everything tomorrow.

He waited, but she didn't reply immediately. She was probably asleep or dealing with the baby. Desperate to wash off the clinging scents of heavy perfume and cigar smoke, he went to take a shower. He'd check for a reply once he was clean.

His short shower went long and when he finally felt like his skin was his own, he turned off the tap and toweled off. With the towel wrapped around his hips, he picked up his phone. Still no reply from Mia.

With Regina's nonsense ringing in his ears, his gut clamored for him to get out there and check on her. It was nearly one in the morning and startling her at this hour was crazy. Rude.

He needed to go to bed and he sure as hell didn't need to interrupt her sleep. Even if he wasn't on the schedule tomorrow, his body was used to ranch hours and he would be up with the sun, anyway. He could check on Mia then. Maybe take her some breakfast.

He was about to toss the towel on the rack and climb into bed when his phone buzzed. The screen showed a text message from Mia.

Are you still awake?

He sent back an affirmative reply immediately.

Can we come in?

He stared down at his phone, momentarily dumb-struck. What was she doing here? If anyone saw her, she'd have to leave before word got back to Regina.

A soft knock at the door followed and he rushed across the room to invite her in. She stood there, her hair loose around her shoulders, both hands gripping the handle of the car seat. Silas was sound asleep.

The threat of disaster crashed over him and he pulled her inside, reaching around her to close and lock the door. "Mia. You shouldn't have come," he said, his voice a low growl.

"I know. I—" Her gaze dipped, then came back up to his face. "I was worried about Dad." Her eyes cruised over his mouth and lower again. "Thanks for the text…"

He would've sworn she was touching him, the way his skin tingled under her gaze, but her hands were locked onto the handle of the car seat. If she kept look-ing at him like that, he was going to want a lot more than kisses. He already did.

Chapter Eight

Mia stared at Jarvis. He didn't even have to touch her and she was speechless. She knew coming here was a huge risk, but she'd thought the danger revolved around Regina finding her hiding place.

No. Not even close.

In this tidy room filled with Jarvis—his tempting scent, his presence, his heated gaze—she was risking much more. Personal humiliation was only the start. Jarvis stood before her, essentially naked. If she gave one small tug of the towel, she could enjoy the full view. She wasn't as ashamed as she should be that her fingers itched to do just that.

Thank goodness her hands were busy with the car seat. Car seat. Her son. A cowboy who claimed he didn't want a family. Those should be all the reasons she needed to behave herself.

"You're sure Dad's okay?" she managed.

He reached over and took the car seat out of her hands, setting it gently on the floor. Silas didn't even twitch. "Norton is fine. I heard his friends talking about recent golf outings and meetings over a few lunches or drinks and cigars after work. No one expressed any concerns about his health or well-being."

"Okay. Good." Since he'd relieved her of the car seat she didn't know what to do with her hands. Weaving her fingers together, she tried to keep her gaze away from his body. She'd known Jarvis was in shape, but to see most of his potent build on display was messing with her head.

While working as a model, her sense of modesty had died a quick death. Behind the scenes at photo shoots and fashion shows, all kinds of things happened and all types of bodies were on display, by accident or design. She'd been up close and personal with many men the world considered perfectly photogenic, including her husband.

Jarvis had just elevated the standards of perfection for her. He was sculpted from hard work and the demands of an active ranch. His muscles had purpose from those wide, ripped shoulders down to his strong forearms and calloused hands. Hands that had stirred up cravings she'd convinced herself she could live without. At least, she'd planned to forgo those physical needs until she found someone willing to stick around and be her partner through this thing called life.

Right this minute, she didn't care how temporary Jarvis might be. She wanted him.

"You really shouldn't be here," he said.

There was something akin to guilt in his eyes. Her presence rattled him. She shouldn't take any delight in that, but she did. She glanced toward the bathroom and saw the light through the bottom of the door. Did he have company? The bed was neatly made, but maybe they hadn't gotten that far yet. "You, um. Oh, crap. I didn't mean to interrupt."

"What? No. No." He shoved a hand through his damp hair. "I'm alone. Check if you want."

She shook her head. "I trust you." Even if she didn't, it would be petty to check. They didn't have any kind of understanding. Not to mention how foolish it would be to expose herself to someone who might know Regina.

He cocked an eyebrow and as if he'd read her mind, he went over and shoved the bathroom door open. "Alone," he repeated. "The party was..." He spread his arms wide. If he didn't dress soon, her self-control would spontaneously combust.

"Pants." Her voice was as rough as sandpaper. "Please."

She focused on her sleeping son. There was the perspective she needed. When he grew up, she wouldn't want women marching into his room to ogle him.

"Right. Just a sec." A drawer opened and closed behind her, followed by the rustling of more movement. "Dressed," he said. "Sorry about that."

"I'm the one who should apologize," she began. Her thoughts vaporized. His version of dressed didn't do anything to quash her desire. He was in a soft T-shirt and loose gym shorts that were just as enticing as the towel had been.

"Mia, sit down." He pulled out a chair for her and sat in one across from her. "I was planning to come out first thing tomorrow to tell you everything."

That had been the agreement and she'd been too impatient to stick to the plan. "I expected you to be out late, but no one is up at this hour." And she'd wanted to see him.

"Asher was."

True. "I saw him walk back toward the house. He didn't see me."

Jarvis scowled, clearly unhappy with her decision. "And if Silas had cried?" He closed his eyes, pinched the bridge of his nose. "Forget it. Mia, your dad looks healthy. I wouldn't call him happy, but he doesn't look weak or sick. He's upset about your disappearance and he misses you and Silas, but there's no sign that Regina is causing him any physical harm."

To her amazement, the surge of relief still ran second to her sizzling attraction for the man sitting across from her. He was helping her because being kind was part of his nature. Whether they indulged in hot kisses or not, he didn't change his stance on being involved with her and Silas beyond this crisis.

"My mind has been reeling all night, playing through worst-case scenarios," she confessed. "I know you didn't dare send a message while you were there."

"I reached out to you as soon as I could."

"I know. I knew you would." She rubbed at her temples, wishing she'd had the courage to kiss him when he'd been standing there in that towel, fresh from the shower. This was all on her, her fears and issues. She was a hypocrite, caving to fear and worry after everything she'd said to him about loss and grief and moving on to live again. "Call me paranoid. I couldn't shake the feeling that Regina had gotten to you." It had consumed her, pushed her to be reckless. If she'd lost Jarvis to her stepmother's games, she'd truly be alone in this mess. "And then you didn't act very excited about me dropping in."

"I'm not. Under normal circumstances it would be great, but taking this kind of chance, when Regina is actively searching for you, makes me worry. You were right that she's dangerous. I saw that tonight. The woman lies as easily as she breathes."

Mia closed her eyes. Jarvis had seen through the woman who consistently fooled everyone else. "What did she say?"

"Nothing that matters." His lip curled and he squinted one eye in an expression of extreme distaste. "The worst was watching her kiss your dad." He groaned. "Like they were alone. It was…"

"Awkward?"

He nodded. "And gross. I wanted to bleach my eyes." He blinked as if he could erase the images from his mind. "She is spreading rumors about you and how you left. I'm not sure who believes her."

Only one person mattered. "Dad believes her." She could see it in Jarvis's dark eyes. "Love is blind," she muttered. "I really should be used to this by now. I've been an idiot thinking anything would change."

"Has your dad sent any more texts?" Jarvis asked.

"No. He made some crack about being disappointed in me, didn't he?"

She could tell by the furrow between his eyebrows that she was right about that, too. "You don't have to protect me. He's been disappointed with me pretty much from the moment he met Regina."

"How did she get in his head so fast?" Jarvis asked. "I saw the painting of the two of you. You were close."

"That's why it hurts. It's like he just forgot everything he knew about me, everything we'd been through. Looking back, the timing was the biggest factor, I think. I was a teenager, poised for a normal rebellion, anyway. She made the most of it. He was lonely and she was perfect for him."

"She wasn't perfect for him if she didn't like you."

Mia's heart twirled in her chest. How did he always know exactly what to say? "She really doesn't like the idea of losing money if Silas and I are around to claim any inheritance. Catching her with another man at the country house is just an excuse for the timing." A shiver caught her as she watched Silas sleep. Her son was utterly defenseless.

"So catching her might have upped her time line," he said. "Didn't they have a prenup?"

She shook her head. "Dad's will was amended to provide for her and she simpered and cooed that it was the perfect solution. Convinced him she was there for him, not the cash."

"He believed her?"

"He always does. She came to the marriage with a pretty hefty net worth. He had no reason to think she wasn't sincere." Silas shifted in his sleep and Jarvis reached over, rocking the car seat gently. "But she is greedy. She wants it all. However she gets us out of his life, she can then rework the will in her favor. And make herself a wealthy widow."

"Selina told me tonight that no man should under-estimate a pretty face."

"She's not wrong." Mia grinned, thinking of Regina and Selina's long and strained friendship. "Were you everything Selina hoped for tonight? Tell me Regina was jealous."

"Yeah." He swallowed and shifted in the chair. "It worked."

"Has Selina booked you for an encore performance?" It wasn't easy to hide the jealousy creeping into her voice. If only she and Jarvis had met in a normal fashion, they might've had a chance.

"No." He stood. "Let's get you out of here before someone notices my truck is back. I'll follow you."

"You don't need to do that," she protested. "I know the way."

"I won't let you drive across the ranch alone again." He went to his dresser. "Don't argue," he said, returning to the table. He pulled on socks and running shoes. Hands braced on his knees, he looked at her. "Should I plan to stay over?"

"I, um." What a good question.

"Let's keep it simple. Yes or no, Mia."

There was nothing simple about his question or the answer she wanted to give. She watched him, wary as he moved in, resting a hand on the back of her chair, his gaze dark. He wasn't looming over her, but she felt surrounded, anyway. She breathed him in.

"Yes."

He caught her reply with a kiss, his lips tantalizing and teasing. There was none of the usual urgency this time. All that longing and need that had been ready to combust settled into a warm thrum low in her belly. The sense of incredible pleasure just waiting for the right moment rolled through her. His bed was only a few paces away, her son sound asleep.

He eased back without a word, his dark gaze unfathomable. She pressed her hands between her knees to keep from grabbing him and holding on for dear life. He made quick work of shoving clothing into a backpack and shrugging it over a shoulder. With a pair of boots in one hand, he plucked up the car seat as if it weighed mere ounces and declared himself ready to go.

She was ready, too. For far more than the drive across the ranch.

On the short drive out to the bunkhouse he'd turned into her safe haven, Mia thought of all the things she should say when they arrived. She should thank him for going with Selina tonight and checking in on her father.

He hadn't wanted to mingle with strangers tonight, but he had. For her. He was the first person in years to do something for her without expecting anything in return. Even her marriage had turned into a series of bargains and deals.

Silas stirred when they reached the refurbished bunkhouse and Jarvis volunteered to walk with him before he woke up all the way. The man looked damn perfect when he wasn't holding Silas, but when he did, white picket fences, Sunday dinners and holidays with Jarvis danced across her vision.

Technically, she didn't *need* a life partner; she wanted one. And now any future applicant for the role would have to measure up to the high standards Jarvis had set. It really was a shame she hadn't met him before marrying Roderick.

"What will you do with your day off tomorrow?" she said once Silas was out. She and Jarvis were stretched out on opposite bunks, but she was too wired to sleep.

"Dig," he said, grinning. "I'm planning to follow more of the research you came up with." His voice was a soft rumble through the dark space. "Maybe tomorrow will be the day we prove Isaiah wasn't hallucinating."

"I hope the family legend is true."

"If it is and I turn out to be the crazy rich owner of Triple R land, should I watch out for your pretty face?"

She laughed uncontrollably. The idea of her trapping him was so ridiculous. Her heart might be harboring fantasies, but she wasn't foolish enough to think they could come true. Jarvis had his own life, his own goals. She was a detour for him at best, no matter how those kisses made her feel.

As her giggles continued, he tugged her out of her bunk and over to his. "You'll wake the baby, shaking the bed that way." His breath was warm against the shell of her ear.

The contact quashed her humor instantly. She tried to hold herself away from him, but he wouldn't have it. Lying on his side, he pillowed her head on his biceps and pulled her back against his chest. With his muscled arm across her waist, his hips were snug against her bottom.

It was the coziest she'd been in ages. "You're better than a pregnancy pillow," she whispered.

"I don't want to know what that means," he said. "Go to sleep."

How could she possibly *sleep* when he surrounded her this way? "And if I can't?"

"Then odds are good we will definitely wake the baby." He nuzzled the back of her neck with his lips, soft, feathery touches that set her on fire.

"It'll be your fault," she teased. "You dragged me over here." She traced the bones and tendons in the hand that kept her snug against him.

"I dragged you over here to sleep." His thumb caressed the curve of her breast. "We can talk in the morning."

She wanted to talk now. Questions and wishes and

what-ifs bounced around like popcorn through her mind. She knew what she wanted and knew that she was overthinking his every action, hopeful that he was changing his mind about what he wanted. From her, from life. From them.

Please, let there be a them.

Could there be anything here but wishful thinking on her side? He kept showing her this incredible tenderness and a protectiveness she could get used to. She never thought protectiveness would be a turn-on, but it ranked high on her list right now. Easy enough to explain that away because Regina threatened everything Mia held dear.

If her stepmother found out about Jarvis helping her, he would become a target. The idea made her queasy.

Shifting to talk with him, she realized his breath was deep and even and his hand was slack on her belly. He really was sleeping as soundly as the baby. The awareness delighted her. He trusted her. Resting her palm over his hand she held him close as an unprecedented contentment lulled her.

She'd always found the saying "home is where the heart is" trite. Here, in this modest bunkhouse surrounded by grassland, she was living it. Jarvis felt like home, the home she'd treasured before her mother had died. Back when the Graves family was strong and solid, and the house a haven where she was welcome to be herself.

If there was one thing she categorically resented about Regina, it was the way she'd razed all those memories in favor of the "right" colors and "refreshing," updated style.

Mia dashed away a tear.

There had to be a way to knock the blinders from her father's eyes. Only when he saw Regina for the snake she was would Norton and Silas have a chance to know each other. Only then would their broken communication and crushed expectations have enough room to heal.

Chapter Nine

Jarvis stopped digging long enough to swipe the sweat off his forehead. He was a fool for continuing this search on such a hot day. Opening another bottle of water, he considered calling it a day. Isaiah had waited years to tell him the whole story, assuming it was true. Another few months wouldn't change anything.

The day after the party, he'd eliminated one long stretch of possibilities that fitted Isaiah's story and the deed records for parcels less than a mile away from the warming hut. In the days since, he'd searched areas based on Mia's research and recommendations, hoping to find something conclusive. It was frustrating to know he could miss the box by only a few yards. Unless he brought out heavy equipment to turn over every square inch, he would have to settle for one average hole at a time.

From his back pocket, his phone chimed and he smiled when he recognized Mia's number. He slid the icon and said hello.

"Hi."

Her voice trembled on the single syllable and he froze. "What's wrong?" He tucked the phone between his chin and shoulder and started filling in the hole.

He'd brought the horse this afternoon, enjoying the slower pace and the quiet solitude. Now he regretted the decision. It would take him forever to reach her if she was in trouble.

"I'm okay," she said in a rush. "There's another text from my dad a-and I'm letting it upset me. Sorry for bugging you."

"You never bug me," he said. It was more than reflex; it was the truth. He'd have to wrestle with that later. "Was it another demand to come home?"

"Yeah."

A few days after the party, Norton had reached out to Mia, surprising them both. Jarvis wanted to be encouraged, but he was guarded. When he was talking to Norton that night, it had seemed as if Mia's dad had all but given up on seeing his daughter and grandson again. They suspected Regina was behind the new text messages somehow, but they weren't sure how to respond.

No matter how he much he assured her of Spencer's discretion, Mia wasn't ready for him to share any of this with his brother. She was too fearful her dad would pay the price.

"No email, not a phone call?"

"No." She sighed. "I'm being silly and impractical to take it at face value."

"You're being a hopeful daughter," he said. In the background he heard Silas gurgling. "How's the little man today?"

"Goofy." This time he heard a smile in her voice.

Since the night of the party, when she'd let him hold her while they slept, he was getting better and better at reading her, in person and over the phone.

He spent most of his nights with her on that narrow bunk. On the rare occasions when he couldn't get out to her, he missed her and the baby more than he was ready to admit.

Sleeping beside her didn't eliminate the clawing desperation to make love with her, but it was better than not touching her at all. Although she'd made her willingness to get physical with him clear, he resisted taking that leap while her life was still in turmoil.

"How goes the search?" she asked.

"I came up empty here," he said. "It's too hot anyway, though it might be worth a closer look tomorrow. You'll be okay a while? I need to get back, stable Duke and clean up. I'll be there as soon as possible with dinner."

"I'll be fine," she replied. "Thanks, Jarvis. I really appreciate you."

Appreciation was safe. Smart. So why did he want her to say something more meaningful? He hadn't said anything of the kind to her. "Text me if something sounds good."

"Okay."

After ending the call, he stowed the shovel and climbed back into the saddle. He urged the horse into an easy canter, eager to see Mia's face. And the text message. When he reached the stable, he forced himself to take his time with Duke. Routine tasks kept him grounded. Always had. He'd been one of the weird kids who liked doing dishes and vacuuming because it gave his mind time to wander. It really shouldn't have surprised him that this straightforward life as a cowboy would fit so well.

Not easy, not simple, but straightforward.

Mia was tied to all of it. And she shouldn't be. She kept researching the questions in the Colton family tree and land records while he dug up small pockets of the Triple R. She wasn't doing anything he couldn't have done alone, but it was going a whole lot faster with her as his partner. They had a system, a friendship with the promise of heat, more than a relationship.

He reminded himself of that fact every single day. He wasn't relationship material, though this time with her and the baby eroded his confidence in that theory. Her sunny outlook and persistent hope in the face of her stepmother's manipulations made him reconsider options he'd sworn off years ago. Her philosophy challenged him and made it increasingly difficult to remember why he shouldn't follow the example his siblings set, taking chances on love and life.

The difference, he reminded himself, was crystal clear. Eventually, Mia would go back to her life and raise her son. They wouldn't need him to bring her groceries and supplies or watch their backs. Eventually, a woman like Mia would find the right man, a man who believed in love and plans, and all the possibilities of the future rather than all the pitfalls.

As nice as he felt with her, he knew himself. He enjoyed her and this interlude in part *because* it couldn't be permanent. Women from Mia's background didn't look for the long-term gig with cowboys who were raised on the lower end of middle class. She came from money, was used to luxury.

Sure he'd made a name for himself in business for a time, but he'd tossed that reputation aside for a quest to prove his Colton name was as valuable as those who sat around the Colton Oil boardroom.

As he took the older truck into town, he was grateful it was still here. Since coming to the ranch, he'd become fascinated with broken things, things that could be fixed with time and patience and elbow grease. He'd assumed an operation with Payne Colton at the helm wouldn't bother with repairs, tossing out anything that didn't function and replacing it with something new. But he'd discovered that Asher had an eye for profit that included being practical and he didn't throw money or men around without careful thought and planning.

Driving toward Lucia's Italian Café to pick up a pizza, he thought about taking Mia on a real date. Mustang Valley was a step down from parties in New York City or Paris. Still, he'd enjoy going out, just the two of them, or going somewhere with Silas. Dancing could be fun. Or maybe a baseball game, in honor of how they'd met, he mused as he parked and headed for the café.

Distracted, he didn't notice Regina walking over until she was practically on top of him.

She raked him with a hungry look that chilled his skin. "Jasper, isn't it?"

"Jarvis," he corrected again, smiling politely. He wouldn't let her feel like she had any advantage. "Nice to see you again."

"You're certainly casual this evening. How…rugged."

"Everyone needs a bit of downtime," he replied diplomatically.

She emitted a tiny, brittle laugh. "I suppose so." Something was off. She didn't appear as polished as she'd been at the party. "Is Selina meeting you? I'd love to say hello."

"Not tonight," he said. "I'll pass that on when I see her."

Regina's delicate eyebrows arched. "So the two of you aren't exclusive." She inched close enough that the skirt of her dress brushed around his jeans. "That's fascinating."

"I'm flattered you think so." He didn't add any of the warmth or charm that consistently amused Selina. "Give my best to your husband."

She blocked him when he moved toward the pickup counter. "Norton mentioned you," she said, her gaze searching him for any reaction. "After the party," she clarified. "He was sure he'd met you before."

"I have one of those faces," he said.

"No." She tilted her head, studying him. "You really don't."

"My brother is on the police force here in town," he said. "People confuse us all the time." It wasn't true, but she didn't know that. This time he managed to sidle past her to the counter.

Regina hemmed him in. "Maybe I should speak with your brother."

"About what?"

"Our missing daughter." She enunciated each word.

He swallowed the urge to correct her. Regina had no right to claim any piece of Mia. "You mentioned her at the party. Still no word?"

She clutched the pendant on her necklace. "It's tragic the way he misses her and our grandson. I'm sure she's just acting out, but with every day that passes, Norton worries that she's actually gotten herself into trouble."

The kid at the counter called his name. "I'm sure Spencer can help. Good luck," he said, using the bulky pizza box to give him some distance as he scooted around her. "No one in town wants to see Norton unhappy."

It was the only warning he dared to give her, since he was supposed to be just Selina's current fling. Dressed as he was tonight, she'd probably figured out he worked at the Triple R. How else would Selina have met him? There was no reason for her to think Mia was hiding at the ranch, but he sure didn't want Regina coming by and poking around.

Jarvis hated making Mia wait, but he refused to take a chance on Regina having him followed. He carried the pizza into his room and dropped it on the table. He wanted to call, but he sent a text so no one could possibly overhear him.

He was officially paranoid.

Got hung up. Will be there in a bit.

Her reply came back immediately.

Can't wait.

Pacing like a wildcat, he forced himself to sit down and think it through. What did he know and what could help Mia?

There was no reason for Regina to assume he had any connection to Mia. Regina had been at Lucia's without Norton, making this a prime opportunity for Mia to reach out to her father. He sent her another quick text suggesting she call her dad, explaining why.

If they could just find a way to get Norton somewhere safe long enough to trap Regina with that disgusting video, this entire mess could be over. Then Mia could explain everything to his brother and Spencer could take it from there.

He really wanted this to be done—for her.

MIA STARED AT the text message, her earlier worry replaced by hope. Jarvis wanted her to call her dad while Regina was too far away to interfere. What would she even say to him?

It didn't matter—she had to act. She dialed quickly, swearing when it went straight to Norton's voice mail. She didn't dare leave a message, certain her stepmother had a way to review those as well. Instead, on a hunch, she dialed her dad's office.

"Norton Graves."

Her knees went weak at the sound of his voice. "Dad. Hi."

"Mia? Where are you?"

His shock shamed her. She should have done this weeks ago. "I'm, um, away," she said. "Visiting friends in Tahoe." She didn't have any friends in Tahoe that Regina could hurt.

"Without listing the country house? Mia." She could picture him turning toward the panoramic view outside his window, his gray eyebrows pulled into a disapproving scowl. "That's disappointing."

Of course it was. "I did meet with the buyer I mentioned. No offer yet. Then I had a problem with my phone and didn't see your messages until today," she improvised, babbling. "I didn't mean to worry you."

"Messages? Honestly, Mia, you've been so flighty I didn't bother reaching out."

A chill slid over her skin. So all of those messages were more traps set by Regina.

"As Regina reminded me," Norton continued, "you should be focused on the baby. Our contract with you expires at the end of next month, anyway. I'll just relist it with someone who has the time and focus."

"Dad." Tears clogged her throat.

"Enough business. We both know things don't always work out. You'll land on your feet. Tell me about my grandson."

She shared the latest milestones, including how Silas was smiling often, enjoying time on his belly, and babbling. "You'll see it all for yourself soon," she promised.

"I want to believe—" Another voice interrupted and she heard him give her name. "Mia? Regina just brought over dinner. We'll have to finish this later."

"Sure," she managed. "We love you," she added only to see her screen flashing that the call ended.

Her nerves rattling, she berated herself for failing. That had been her chance to explain it all and she'd blown it. It was like getting tossed back in time to her teenage self. No authority, no influence with the one adult in her life who mattered.

She sat down at the computer, hoping Jarvis would be here soon. It was time for her to either give up and leave Mustang Valley or call Regina's bluff. With Silas still sleeping and no sign of Jarvis, she reviewed the notes she'd made since catching Regina at the country house.

She'd carefully documented every threat, direct or implied, against her, her son and her father. She'd downloaded her call and message logs as a precaution, taking screenshots as well. Over the past weeks, she'd spent hours poring over Regina's social media posts, looking for any pictures of the man she'd been cheating with, the same man Jarvis had seen at the courthouse.

Jarvis had urged her time and again to speak at length with his brother and let the police set up a secret meeting with her dad. It was time to use that connection and create an advantage. With her report complete, she uploaded it to a cloud file until she and Jarvis could decide how to proceed.

They'd been out here, playing an odd version of house and becoming something more than friends and not quite lovers. Eventually, someone else from the Triple R crew would wander out this way, and then where would she go?

She didn't want to *go* anywhere. Since leaving Roderick, she'd planned on creating a real home for her and Silas. A home close enough to her friends and father, right here in Mustang Valley. Free to be the mother and professional woman she'd always envisioned. She wanted to zip into town for business meetings or playdates, or even enjoy a butterfly-inducing date with a certain sexy cowboy. Whatever simmered between them should have a chance to grow once she was out from under this mess with her stepmother.

She'd find a way to triumph over Regina's plans. Silas deserved all the love, family and roots she could give him.

At last she heard the truck. Her heart skipped ahead and her stomach rumbled. She was hungry for dinner, but hungrier for the man delivering it. Pausing just long enough to be sure it was Jarvis, she dashed outside and gave him a hug.

"Did it go well?" he asked, his arms coming around her.

"No." She pressed her cheek to his solid chest, taking the comfort he offered. "He's still effectively brainwashed, but hearing his voice helped me. Thank you."

He smoothed a hand over her hair, then tipped up her chin and gave her a soft kiss. The tears she'd held back escaped now as his tenderness surrounded her. She forced herself to smile before she turned into a watering pot. "You smell like pizza."

He grinned. "Lucia's. Sorry I didn't get it to you hot."

She released him long enough to take the pizza from the car. "Smells heavenly, hot or cold. Let's eat."

"One thing," he said, following her into the bunkhouse. "Those texts weren't from your dad, were they?"

She shook her head, temper and sadness battling within her heart. "I knew it and still it's a gut punch."

"I'm sorry, sweetheart."

The apology and endearment, though he'd said it before, washed over her like a cool breeze. She tried not to read too much into it but might as well have been trying to hold back a sunrise. There were so few things in recent weeks that made her smile and gave her joy. She wouldn't ignore a single one of those gifts.

They ate their fill of pizza while she told him about the call and the file she'd compiled and uploaded.

"So the messages were definitely a setup," he said, clearing the table. He returned to his chair and reached over, covering her hands with his. "That can't be easy to digest. What if I went to your dad's office to speak with him? Or asked Spencer to deliver him a message?"

"A policeman walking into an investment-banking firm doesn't send the right message. And Regina is mean, but not stupid. If you walked in there, she'd storm the ranch just like you were worried about at first."

"Fair." He stretched his neck. "If you trust someone else, I'll go to them."

"I'll think about it," she said. Silas stirred and she opened her laptop. "Go ahead and take a look at the file. Make sure there isn't something else your brother might need."

"He's the cop, not me." He read through the file, swearing occasionally under his breath while she fed her son. "These threats need to be on an official record somewhere," he said at last. "If you're ready, why don't I take this to my brother and let him decide what comes next. I visit him often enough at the station that it's not suspicious."

"Okay."

"Okay?" Jarvis echoed. "Just like that?"

"Isn't it past time?" She sighed. "Hearing Dad's voice flipped a switch for me. As things stand right now, I lose him either way. By hiding or pushing Regina to do her worst. It's a huge risk, and it scares the hell out of me, but I'd rather lose him while trying to win, than just roll over."

Once Silas had a full tummy, he didn't want to settle down. He kept turning toward Jarvis's voice as they talked, smiling and babbling and making Mia wish for so many impossible things.

Jarvis had found her while looking for his roots.

He didn't have family in mind for his future. She respected that, she did, but Silas was the next generation and that meant making plans and building up hope for the days and years ahead.

Her internal debate must have translated to Silas. Her son was happy enough but clearly had no intention of going back to sleep. "At least he isn't screaming this time," she said. "But it promises to be a long night."

"We could take him for a drive," Jarvis suggested.

She glanced over and noticed he was serious. "Where?"

He hitched a shoulder. "Around the back roads. Don't babies like that kind of thing?"

"They do." Her foolish heart fluttered. Had Jarvis been reading up on baby care, or did he remember that about Silas in particular? "He fell asleep when I drove to see you after Regina's party."

"Then let's go."

They took his truck because the car seat bracket was already installed. He drove because he knew both the truck and the area better than she did. That left her free to pop Silas's pacifier back into his mouth whenever he spit it out.

"Far cry from Selina's Jag," he said as they reached the paved road that bordered this side of the ranch. "She let me open it up on this road."

"How fun for you."

"It was. I got it to ninety-five before I brought myself back down to earth. Selina giggled like a teenager."

"I bet. Have you always wanted a sports car?"

"I used to dream of driving a Mercedes," he said. "That daydream is a rite of passage for business majors."

"One quick drag at ninety-five cured you?" She

studied his handsome profile, wondering what he wasn't saying.

His lips tilted up on one side. "I wouldn't say that. The truck is comfortable. It suits me better right now."

"Well, I'm sure you look just as good driving the truck as you did driving Selina's car." She admired his capable hands on the wheel, wished she had the guts to ask him to put those hands on her.

At last Silas fell asleep and they turned back toward the bunkhouse. "Oh, look, a shooting star." She leaned forward, pointing through the windshield.

He craned his neck and then sat back in the seat, a smile on his face. "Better make a wish."

She didn't tell him she already had.

Back on Triple R land, he drove on past the bunkhouse. The tires bumped over the ground, but he kept on going until at last he stopped and cut the truck lights. Looking proud of himself, he rolled down the windows, allowing the cooler night air to flow through the truck.

"What are we doing?" she asked.

"It's a surprise." He hopped out of the car and pulled a blanket from behind his seat. "Come on." That sexy, irrepressible grin flashed. "If Silas wakes up, we'll drive some more."

He managed to lower the tailgate in near silence and she gawked while he spread out a blanket over the truck bed. Then he walked back to where she waited and extended a hand.

She placed her palm in his and his fingers curled around her as he assisted her up. Into the truck bed and his strong embrace. His arms banded around her, his fingers locked together at the base of her spine, just above the curve of her backside.

His lips touched hers softly, the urgency building with each heartbeat, each dreamy touch as her lips parted and his tongue twined with hers. A wicked, eager thrill rushed over her, from her scalp to her toes and she moaned against his mouth, wanting so much more than she had a right to ask for.

She longed for a deeper connection, more than these tantalizing kisses. Sex. Affection. Love.

He'd demonstrated such warm affection for her and she could probably persuade him to have sex with her, though she knew it wouldn't feel complete without love. Maybe that made her old-fashioned, but she had endured enough disappointment. She eased away, resting her head on his shoulder and her hand over his thudding heart.

He gave her a squeeze. "Let's watch the stars," he said.

She peeked through the window, confirming that Silas was still asleep, then she and Jarvis stretched out side by side in the pickup bed.

As stars shot through the dark velvet sky, Mia's thoughts meandered through the past and present. Her husband hadn't loved her enough to adjust and adapt when she got pregnant. And here she was with Jarvis, who demonstrated wonderful care for her and Silas, yet claimed he wasn't cut out for family life.

She watched another star fall and made another wish, this time for one more season of the type of happiness she'd known before her mother had died.

"Did you make a wish?" he asked.

"I can't seem to stop," she admitted. "You?"

"Not really. I stopped making wishes when I was a kid."

"After your parents died?" She shifted to her side so she could see him as well as another section of the starry sky over his shoulder.

"I think it was later," he said, his wistful tone breaking her heart. "Our aunt couldn't seem to give us anything beyond the basics of food, shelter and clothing."

"I'm sorry for your loss, Jarvis."

"Life can play dirty," he said. "Then and now, I think we were all grateful to stay together. That singular factor saved us more than anything else."

They were quiet then, content to rest with only the sounds of Silas's soft snores and the occasional hoot of an owl.

"It's peaceful out here," she said softly, not wanting to shatter the spell. "It makes me feel small and gives me hope at the same time."

"Hope to go home?"

"Well, yes. You know I want my life back." They watched another streak of starlight. "I also hope to find someone to love and build a family with. I've always craved that special bond my mom and dad shared. They were so in love."

"Love?" He shifted to stare at her, incredulous. "You still believe in love after everything you've been though?"

"Yes. Every time I look at Silas," she said with confidence.

"Oh, sure. That's different."

Was he almost agreeing with her? Hope flared that he might defeat the grip of his past. "How can love be different from love?"

He immediately pulled back, from her or the conversation, far enough that the cool air moved between them. It was mere inches, but it felt like a canyon holding them apart while she waited for his answer.

"You know what I mean."

She was so tempted to comfort him, to gloss it over. If she did, the opportunity might never come around again. Boldly, she said, "I'd like to."

He sighed, surprising her by pulling her close. "Aside from my brother and sister, love has let me down every time," he admitted. "Mom and Dad loved us and it didn't save them."

"Everyone dies." She watched another star fall. "*Not* loving someone won't keep you safe, either."

"I don't understand you. You elevate optimism to an art form."

"How can I not?" Snuggling into his warmth, she searched for the right words. "I've seen true love firsthand. So have you. Granted, I settled for an illusion of the real thing. Roderick loved the image of us. He didn't love *me*. Love is adaptable. Steadfast and devoted, in any facet or form, love sticks."

He shifted again but didn't release her. Maybe she was getting through. If she could do nothing else for him, she'd give him a chance to heal from his devastating losses. "Whatever you call it, loyalty or responsibility or commitment, you show love, Jarvis. It might not be the romantic facet of love, but love is there, in your choices and your actions."

His body tensed. "I really want to disagree with you."

She tapped her shoe to his boot. "Why argue when we could enjoy the stars?"

Giving her shoulder a squeeze, he relaxed and they watched the sky until her eyelids were drooping. "You should take us back," she said, sitting up a bit. "We all need some rest."

"In a minute." He laced his fingers with hers, his face tipped up to the sky.

"Do you know your constellations?" she asked.

"That's Cowboy 101," he said.

"Really?"

"No." He bent his head and kissed her. "But these views are a big perk on night shifts."

"You love being a cowboy."

"Does that bother you?" he asked.

"No." She'd spent her life around powerful businessmen and been groomed and educated so she could hold her own in any setting, social or professional. Her time around barns had included the glossy, luxury side of ranch operations, not the more functional side. She liked what Jarvis did, the obvious pride he took in his work, and the honest-work scent of sunshine and sweat that lingered on his skin after a long day outside. "Does it bother you?"

"Not a bit. I don't have any desire to go back to an office, whether or not I find evidence that this ranch belongs to my side of the family."

"So you'll work for Asher forever?"

"Not forever." He took his eyes off the sky and shot her a confident look. "I'm still learning. He's an excellent manager on all fronts."

"That shouldn't come as a surprise," she said. "He has a tremendous reputation."

"We didn't exactly run in the same circles, Mia. We still don't. Not yet, anyway." He pushed a hand through his hair, mussing the dark locks. "More than once I've thought, if this place is mine, I'd find a way to keep him. If it's not and I buy my own ranch, I might lure him away."

His low laugh rolled over her, as warm as melted chocolate and equally as tempting. What would that sound feel like under her hands? Her mouth watered and she yanked her wayward thoughts back into line.

"I could broker a land deal for you," she teased. Being here, feeling safe with him was such a treat. But a life in hiding couldn't last. Silas would need his regular checkups. Regina might as well stake out the pediatrician's office if she wanted to catch Mia and make good on her threats.

Mia watched the shadowy scenery on the drive back to the bunkhouse. She could make a new life elsewhere, but with Regina's threats looming over her head, worry would be a constant companion. That was no life for her son and she couldn't bear the thought of leaving her father to cope with Regina's devious nature alone. The woman was greedy and Mia had no doubt she'd continue to take whatever she wanted, whenever she chose—even Norton's life.

Tomorrow, she'd allow Jarvis to bring everything to his brother on her behalf.

JARVIS RESTED QUIETLY in the bunk. Mia's sweet curves were pressed up against him and she was out. Looked like fresh air and car rides were effective sleep-enhancers for mothers, too.

Unfortunately, he couldn't stop thinking about her persistent faith in love.

After everything she'd been through, she wasn't

just wishing for love; she was determined to create it, to celebrate it as though it was a reliable emotion. She wouldn't find or create love with him, obviously.

He was temporary.

That rankled more than it should, considering he wasn't in the market for a family, anyway.

He'd been telling himself this was about protecting the ranch, protecting his potential legacy and treating Mia as he would want someone to treat his sister. But he didn't feel anything brotherly toward the woman in his arms. No, he felt invested. Attached.

That attachment went beyond uncomfortable and straight into dangerous. To her. The only love he trusted, the only relationships that hadn't ended in disaster, were those with his brother and sister. And even that dynamic had changed since they were both engaged and planning weddings now. Those right and true relationships nudged Jarvis a bit more to the fringe.

He wasn't resentful, exactly. He was experiencing what might be best described as envy nipping at his heels. And bafflement. How could Spencer and Bella take the chance? What did they have that Jarvis lacked?

Oh, he could go and ask. His siblings would listen, try to help. Even if they could help him figure out the mess in his own head, he wasn't in the mood for lectures on his choices about business, ranching or women.

He breathed in the soft clove fragrance of Mia's shampoo, and pushed the envy and pointless questions aside. There would be plenty of time to sort out his issues once Mia and Silas were safe and gone.

Chapter Ten

Mia read the text message from her father and pocketed her phone while she considered her reply. She'd brought Silas outside for an early morning walk while she tried not to think about Jarvis going to share the ugliest parts of her life with his brother later today. This time, she thought the sweet request for an update on the baby was probably from Norton and not one of Regina's tricks. She couldn't imagine her stepmother being kind even as a ploy.

Only last month, she'd walked with Silas through the neighborhood where she'd grown up, or through the park in town, her son in his stroller. Today she carried him in the sling, not straying too far from the remote Triple R bunkhouse, not another person in sight.

The warm sunlight painted the grassy pastures and highlighted the mountains in the distance, framed by the cloudless, blue sky. The picturesque setting made her feel like everything would eventually work out.

With a baby nearly three months old, she'd expected to be taking meetings and calls and building up a solid network for her new real-estate career by now. Instead she was still out here, hiding from her stepmother's threats.

Although she'd used her time to keep up with properties and trends in the area, she'd had far more fun helping Jarvis with his history and search. It was an easier task because she didn't have a stake in whatever he found. The deeds, acreage claims, and sales from Herman and Eugene's generation were convoluted. With luck, if Jarvis found the box, those conflicting documents might be explained.

He'd absolutely won her over with his determination to keep searching, even after she'd found documents on file that Eugene and his descendants came by the property legally, negotiating back and forth with T. Ainsley. For a man who claimed he didn't believe in family, Jarvis was going all out to prove there was merit behind his grandfather's stories. She hoped that whatever he found would be exactly what he needed for his heart and his future in ranching.

Her phone chimed again. Another text, this time a direct request for an update on the progress on the listing. Why had her father told her he wasn't going to talk business if he didn't mean it? And why had she lied about working with a buyer?

"Mommy never should've lied," she said to Silas. "Let this be a lesson—mommies and daddies always find out the truth."

Daddies. Oh, how she wanted a daddy for her son someday. When she thought of Silas calling a man daddy, having a father figure to emulate, Jarvis's face came to mind. It was ridiculous, putting that face to her fantasy, yet she couldn't seem to remove his dark eyes, square jaw and lopsided grin from the picture.

She might've lied to her dad about the buyer, but she couldn't lie to herself about Jarvis. Her heart was firmly planted in his reluctant hands and it might as well stay there for now. As long as he didn't have any idea and she didn't blurt out that she was in love with him, her heart would be safe enough.

She rubbed her nose to Silas's and then faced her phone. What could she tell her dad that would appease him and not be a lie? She quickly let him know that the first offer was lower than his bare minimum. As in zero at the moment. She followed that with a query about why he was in such a hurry to liquidate the property.

Countless happy memories with her parents and later friends had been made at that house. After Regina's intrusive entrance into her life, the country home and the surrounding property remained the site of fond moments with her dad, hosting clients and family friends.

She couldn't imagine a reason—other than a wife who loved to shop and redecorate—why her father would need a quick influx of cash. Her hands went cold. This must be Regina's doing. She could easily picture her stepmother hovering over his shoulder and pestering him to push her. Just to flush her out of hiding.

Would the woman never be satisfied? Of course not. Regina thrived on control, from the suits and ties her father wore to the office, to the amount he spent on his weekend golf trips, all the way down to Christmas gifts.

His reply came back that his only concern was for her and the baby. Well, that made two of them. The somewhat comforting message was trumped by the next.

You can't be in business if you aren't doing business.

She couldn't argue with that, so she didn't reply.

Come on back, Mia. We'll have lunch at the club and talk things out in person.

If only she could be sure Regina wouldn't be there, ready to poison her salad or snatch Silas. She turned off her phone and kept walking.

Her father had been an integral part of her life. Being separated from him and keeping her son away made her heart ache. Norton, who managed fortunes during the day, had helped her with homework and even coached her youth soccer teams when she was young.

Until Regina had changed everything.

"Maybe I didn't want to share," she admitted to her drowsy son. "Maybe your grandpa could've listened to my concerns or done a better job of protecting our relationship." And maybe they were both human. Her father, her hero, had put more stock in the sniping observations of his new wife than the daughter he supposedly treasured. Mia, frustrated, had only made things worse.

"I won't be perfect," she murmured, "Obviously," she added, her gaze drifting to the mountain range in the distance. A perfect mother would surely know how to get out of this mess. "I do promise to listen, to consider what's best for *you* in every decision we face." She hoped she could keep that promise.

"It takes two people to wreck a good relationship," she told Silas. Looking into his sweet face now, it was impossible to think of a day when they would argue, when hurtful words might fly fast and mean, undermining trust.

She wondered if the lunch invitation was worth the

risk. If she went, she could talk with her dad about the house and the baby. They could walk the office space he'd recommended to her last month. They could cover everything except his wife's cheating. The temptation to accept filled her and she was doubly grateful she'd turned off the phone.

She finished her walk with Silas, passing Jarvis's truck. Inexplicably antsy, it was all she could do to settle the baby in his seat for the rest of his morning nap, rather than drive out to where she expected Jarvis to be searching today.

He hadn't seemed to mind when she'd met up a time or two before, but Mia really needed to exert some force on her future. She sat down at the table and opened her laptop. Her dad made a good point. She wouldn't have a business if she didn't *conduct* business. She did have connections with people familiar with the country house. An additional advantage was her knowledge of the people most likely to have the interest as well as the means to invest in the property.

She drafted an email with one target in mind, adding a few pictures she knew would entice. If she brokered a private sale, it would give the lies she'd told her father credence. Not only that, but the commission would be a financial cushion she could use to relocate.

Roderick had joked about buying the country house on his very first visit. More than once, while they dated, she'd been sure he stayed with her simply for the long weekends they spent out there.

Once she'd hit Send, detailing the ideal offer, she fixed herself a cup of tea. She should've done this first. If she had, she never would've found Regina with another man. Instead she'd been determined to prove she had skills, not just connections; that she was beautiful, but had a brain, too. Of course, she hadn't been eager to speak with her ex about anything. Now she was desperate.

Weary of her own problems, she turned her attention back to Jarvis's search and refused to watch the clock. With the names from the land deeds, she continued to wade through history, pleased to discover more records about when various parcels of the current ranch were purchased from the government or landowners who'd given up on taming the territory.

Jarvis worked his way through his daily assignments, not looking forward to going to Selina's house again. He knew Asher passed those calls to him, hoping the woman would open up more about the leverage she had on Payne. He wanted to help his cousin, but Jarvis couldn't bring himself to flirt with the woman anymore. One night playing the role of sexy accessory had been more than enough.

After spending time with Mia, Selina's presence felt even more cloying. According to Asher, Selina had a problem with the lighting on her patio. He hoped it was something simple as he cantered across the ranch from the stables to her house on Duke.

"Jarvis!" Selina called as he looped the reins over the fence rail edging her patio. "You always know just how to dress. Can I get you a drink, cowboy?"

It was the opening Asher would expect him to sidle right through. He gave her his best smile and tipped his hat. "Better if we wait until I know what the trouble is," he said.

"The trouble is you won't drink with me." She

winked and then gave him what he assumed was supposed to be a sexy pout. She touched him as if she had
the right, her glossy, hot-pink fingernails tracking the
line of his forearm. Her eyes were clear, despite the
drink in her hand. Too bad. If she was drunk, it might
be easier to distract her away from him.

He turned his thoughts to Mia, but that only made
it worse. He'd rather be with her than anywhere else
and he was stuck in the female equivalent of a tar pit.

"What do you need, Selina?" He didn't have much
time before he was supposed to meet Spencer at the
police station and he didn't want to be late. Mia needed
him to have that meeting so she could get back to her
life. "Asher mentioned something about a lighting
issue?"

"Did someone put a burr under your saddle, cowboy?" She walked around him and made a humming
noise as she eyed his backside. "Nothing obvious. Want
me to take a closer look?"

He moved out of reach before she sank those hot-
pink claws into his backside.

"You're no fun today."

"Lots of work on the schedule." He hoped to get
through it all before his meeting in town so he'd still
have some time to poke around a new site for Herman's box.

Selina sipped whatever was in her glass and arched
a perfect eyebrow. What had Payne ever seen in her?
From one moment to the next, her entire body language
changed. The overblown flirt was gone and a sensible
woman in her place.

"It is the lighting." She flipped the switch near the

outdoor kitchen. "That section in the middle is broken or whatever." She gestured with her glass.

Why did people want to ruin a gorgeous view of a starry sky with strands of white lights? "I'll take care of it. Do you have a ladder?"

"I thought you came fully equipped," she said.

He laughed, despite himself. "Stepladder, Selina." They kept basic tools here for times just like this one.

She made a moody noise and cocked a hip. He didn't take the bait. With a shake of her head, she set her glass on the nearest table and sauntered toward the storage closet cleverly built into one of the stone pillars that framed the outdoor kitchen.

"You're seeing someone new?" she asked, opening the door and holding it for him.

The question set his teeth on edge. "I've been working too hard to see much of anyone," he replied.

"Oh, that's not what I've heard at all."

He ignored her, more than happy to use the stepladder as a shield between them.

"I heard some new cowgirl has you wrapped around her little finger." She crooked her own pinkie and wiggled it at him.

Cowgirl, no. Mia was more like a big-league hitter. He grinned, thinking of Mia and the stick she'd been all too willing to employ.

Her lips formed a surprised O. "It's true." She lifted her glass. "Cheers and congratulations to the happy couple."

Jarvis climbed the stepladder to look over the wiring for this section of the string lights. "You don't sound all that sincere," he commented absently.

"I'd be less disappointed if you tell me it's a nonexclusive kind of thing."

It wasn't. Well, technically it wasn't anything. But if it became something, he wouldn't be sharing Mia with anyone. He just shook his head.

"Come on, Jarvis," she cajoled. "I could use a little romantic excitement, even if it is vicarious."

He tested each bulb within reach, pausing to look down at her. She was staring at his crotch. *Ew.* "Are you running low on gossip fuel?" He climbed down, moved the ladder and climbed up again.

"Knowledge is power," she said, examining her nails now. "I shared my secrets with you."

"Did you?"

"Didn't I?" She swirled the golden liquid in her glass.

So that was the reason she'd called. She was worried she'd said too much after the party. Being Selina, she would assume that he'd do what she'd done and use any secrets to her advantage. Or maybe she really was more worried about sharing juicy gossip with her friends at the next Sunday brunch.

He moved the ladder again and waited until she met his gaze. "You didn't."

What might have been relief flashed across her flawless features. "Tell me your secret, anyway." She leaned in on the other side of the ladder. "I know you can't possibly be serious about this cowboy nonsense."

He gave her an innocent smile. "A real man doesn't joke about boots and belt buckles. Besides, being a cowboy means helpin' purdy ladies like you." He laid it on thick, hamming it up and earning her spiky laughter.

He found the problem at last. Where the nonfunctioning section connected to the previous strand, the plug had been loosened just enough to break the connection. He made the fix and verified everything worked properly again. He supposed he'd let her get away with the fake call, but it put him on edge.

"All better." He folded the ladder, keeping it between them. "Anything else, Selina?"

Color flared on her cheeks and her gaze roamed over his face. "You know how to make a woman feel special," she said. "I enjoyed our evening at Norton and Regina's party."

Just hearing Regina's name made him angry. He smothered the reaction, not willing to give Selina any reason to ask more questions. Crossing his wrists over the top of the folded stepladder, he just waited for her to spell out what she wanted. She watched his hands and licked her lips. The woman was an operator who believed he would just fall in line for the chance to land in her bed.

Asher, knowing nothing about his feeling for Mia, would want Jarvis to dive in. Although he admired his boss man, respected him and sympathized with him, he couldn't even pretend it was an option. No matter what kind of blight she was to the family, there were lines Jarvis wouldn't cross. "There is someone," he said. "Just met her last weekend."

She stroked one perfectly manicured fingertip over his banged-up knuckles. "Then it's not serious."

Jarvis chuckled at the blatant invitation. "Serious enough." He eased just out of her reach. "Any other *maintenance* concerns?"

Her lips curved into what might be the first genuine smile he'd seen. "Not today. Thank you, Jarvis."

"You're welcome." He stowed the stepladder and headed out with a tip of his hat.

"Whoever she is, she's a lucky woman," Selina called after him. She strolled over, shading her eyes as she looked up at him sitting in the saddle.

He winked. "I'll tell her you said so." He cantered away, grateful for the wind on his face and the raw power of the horse under him.

Selina was treacherous with a hefty streak of pathetic. He supposed if he found something that negated the deed of sale, he could make Asher's day by ousting the woman. Somehow, he didn't think it was exactly the solution his boss was hoping for.

When the house was well out of sight, he slowed his horse and took the time to update the task schedule. A couple of items had been added to his list, including another pass over the fence near the warming hut where Mia had first hidden. He made a note to handle that task.

Thinking about the timing and knowing his brother, he looped Duke's reins around the nearest paddock fence while he went into his room to call Spencer.

"Catch any criminals today?" he asked when Spencer picked up.

"Better than wrangling steaks in progress," his brother replied.

Jarvis opened his laptop and then accessed the cloud file Mia had prepared. "The cattle are far more personable than your criminals."

"Probably true. You calling to bail on our meeting?"

"Sort of." Jarvis sighed. "There's a lot going on out here today. I'm sending you some information. If you want me to come in after you read it, I will."

"You're making me nervous."

"Not intentionally." He was nervous as a cat after bumping into Regina in town. "I'd rather not come to the station. Read what I'm sending and then give me a call about how you want to handle it."

"What kind of trouble are you in?"

The worst kind, he thought. He was in over his head over a woman, ready to do anything to make sure Mia and Silas came out of this on top. "Read the info. I've gotta get back to work."

Outside, he scratched Duke behind the ears and gave him a carrot before swinging up into the saddle. They headed out to the fence line on the to-do list, passing the various pastures and buildings. Other than the Colton mansion near the front gate and the necessary updates, he didn't think the ranch had changed much since Herman was burying the box that was probably long gone.

The voices of his siblings echoed in his head, scolding him for taking such a wild detour from his business career. He couldn't explain his faith in Isaiah's tales to himself; how was he supposed to explain it to them?

Besides, he expected them to accept and understand him, especially during times like this one, when he didn't fully understand himself. That was the perk of sharing a womb. Or it should've been. Had been in the past. Since losing their parents, the triplets had dealt with life as a team, supporting each other always and reflecting insights back at one another when needed.

He was probably overdue for a sounding board or reflection session. But it would only help if he bothered to listen. They'd tried to corner him on his motives when he'd taken the Triple R job. He'd dumped his original career to become a cowboy, dealing with animals, sunburn, cuts and calluses, and Selina, just for a chance to prove their granddad was more than an aging, confused drunk.

Maybe Spencer and Bella didn't remember Isaiah the same way Jarvis did. His siblings had been aggravated when they'd been moved abruptly from Isaiah's house to Aunt Amelia's place in town. Deep down, it had been easy to keep Isaiah's secret when he knew his siblings wouldn't give any credence to the tales. Arguably, the man had done his best and come up short. Even back then, as a kid, Jarvis had understood that they needed something their grandfather couldn't give, especially not while grieving his son and daughter-in-law. Not that Amelia had managed much better, but the court had seen her as the stable option.

Admittedly, his case of hero worship for their granddad had only intensified with his work on the ranch. Not so much due to the search as the work itself. Was it weird to hit his thirties before having the epiphany that he was born to be a cowboy?

Weird or not, it was his life. Checking the app for the precise location, he found it was not far from Mia's current hideout, and it took serious willpower to veer away from the bunkhouse. He would visit later, hopefully after following up with Spencer. Just the thought of seeing her sent a surge of happiness through his veins. He really needed to get this infatuation under control.

Turning, his gaze caught on something out of place closer to the road. Most likely a trick of the light, but he knew every inch of this ranch and, from visiting Mia every day, this section specifically. He walked the horse over to where the dirt had been kicked up and rutted out around the scrubby growth between the ranch and the road.

The herds hadn't been in this area. Good news was if they'd been pushed up this way, the fence was still intact. He slid down from the saddle and walked Duke forward slowly. Even from several paces away, he could see snapped twigs and the brush pressed back, not unlike the damage he'd seen when Mia had hidden her car near the warming hut.

His blood went cold when he spotted a clear boot print in the soil. The tread was thick cut, more like a military or tactical boot than the gear worn by the crew. He held his foot near the mark and judged it of a similar size. He followed the trail of those distinct footprints where they joined the tire tracks.

It was possible someone had been drunk, driven off the road and had ambled about until they came to their senses. He'd believe it if the trail meandered or had been muddled. It didn't. One set of boot prints led toward the fence, took a brief stroll along the fence line and then turned back to the tire tracks.

He didn't like it, not this close to Mia's hiding place. Not right on top of his run-in with Regina and Mia's uncomfortable call with her father. Had someone been looking for her? He took pictures with his cell phone of the boot prints and the tire tracks and the damaged vegetation.

Questions and options raced through his mind. Call in his brother, notify his boss, ask Selina to invite Regina over for a chat so he could get his hands around that devious woman's throat.

He started with the most crucial piece and sent Mia a text message to confirm she was all right. He waited for a reply, and his heart pounded as he pulled himself back into the saddle. Duke sidestepped, sensing his distress. He took a deep breath, willing himself to calm down for the horse. For the next calls he'd have to make to Spencer and Asher.

He was about to blow up Mia's secret, force her to hide elsewhere, all because Regina was a greedy, dangerous person who would go to any lengths to keep her power, money and status.

Impatient and increasingly unsettled, he called Mia, riding toward the bunkhouse while the call went through.

"Jarvis?"

Her voice hit him like a ray of morning sunlight, and the sharpest of his worry evaporated like dew. "Yes." He forced a smile onto his face, into his voice. "I was close and wanted to check in."

"That's thoughtful. I—I'm good."

The catch in her voice sent him right back into worry mode. "You've had trouble today? Where are you?"

"No trouble," she replied. He didn't quite believe her. "We're at the bunkhouse. I've got my hands full with Silas," she said. "Did you meet with your brother?"

"I spoke with him and he's going over your information now." He didn't mention his side trip to Selina's house. "I just needed to hear your voice."

"Oh, good." She sounded delighted by that admission. "Wait. Did something happen?"

"Not really." He wanted to tell her everything and press her for what was on her mind, too. But he didn't have facts and he wouldn't upset her without reason.

"I'll be at today's dig site soon. Do you need me to bring anything along with dinner tonight?"

"That's more than enough."

Now that she sounded more relaxed, he felt better, too. Ending the call, he forwarded the pictures he'd taken to Spencer, with a request to factor them in with the information from Mia. With no damage to the fences, he wouldn't tell Asher yet.

As if on cue, his phone rang and Asher's picture filled his screen. He kept Duke at a slow walk as he answered the call.

"I saw you finished at Selina's place," the foreman said.

"It was a loose wire on those string lights on her deck," Jarvis replied. "Did she complain about me?"

"Should she?" Asher countered, laughing. "You know I'm more curious if she said anything helpful."

"No clear admission of anything. My take is that she was fishing to find out if she'd told me something important when she was so tipsy after the party."

"You couldn't use that?"

Jarvis watched the terrain for landmarks. "No. If I had guessed and been wrong, she would've known I was lying. Better to keep her off balance."

"Probably right. Where are you now?"

"I rode off into the sunset to give Selina something to ponder," Jarvis joked. Asher howled with laughter. "Have you heard about anyone interested on the northern property line? It looks like someone pulled off the road and was poking around."

"No one should be out there," Asher said. "Probably a drunk driver."

"I looked around and came to the same conclusion,"

Jarvis said. "The fence is fine," he added. "I took some photos, just in case, but I didn't see any damage worth reporting."

"Well, that's a plus. Keep me posted."

"Will do," Jarvis promised.

Hours later, Jarvis knocked on the door of Mia's bunkhouse. It was well past dark and his shoulders ached after another fruitless attempt to find a small metal box on the massive ranch. At least dinner would be amazing. Fried chicken, corn on the cob, green beans, biscuits and berry cobbler had been on the menu tonight for the crew. Although he hadn't expected to be on the cleanup crew, a mishap with a kitchen knife meant he had to fill in.

"Sorry I'm late," he said when she opened the door.

She treated him to that beautiful, open smile that made him feel downright heroic. "Smells delicious," she said, eyeing the bag in his hands. "You're forgiven. Get in here."

"Grab a plate." She did while he unpacked the bag, opening the various containers for her. "How was Silas today?"

"He had a great day. Fresh air and sunshine, a full tummy, playtime and good naps."

"Living his best life," Jarvis observed.

"He is." She ate while he amused the baby.

The little guy was taking in everything with those big brown eyes. Although Jarvis knew Mia's ex was part of the baby's DNA, whenever he looked at the baby he only saw Mia's features. If the genetics held, the little boy would be breaking hearts by preschool.

He and the baby smiled and played. He tried not to dwell on how natural it felt to chatter along with the baby while he waited for Mia to open up about what was bugging her. It was something to do with her son, if he read her correctly.

"Thanks for feeding me." She blotted her lush lips with a napkin. "Did you see Regina in town?" That she'd felt the need to ask was a huge clue to the issue on her mind.

"No. But I've been away from civilization most of the day. I had to handle the meeting with Spencer over the phone."

"Oh."

"Regina might be manipulating your father's phone and emails, but she can't possibly have access to the MVPD."

"True. I'm just…"

He picked up the baby and moved to the table. "Just?"

"Tired and paranoid. And sad. Dad texted me this morning, but it probably wasn't him. So I was careful."

"I don't think it will take Spencer long to get back to us."

A faint smile touched her lips. "Were you able to search at all?"

"I found another place the box is not," he said.

"Good." She took a bite of the cobbler and closed her eyes. "This is epic." She handed him a fork. "There's enough to share."

One more boundary he plowed right through for Mia. They polished off the sweet dessert and she reached for her laptop. "I think I have a better idea. Come over here."

As he sat down, he caught her minimizing a map

of residential Las Vegas and a tab with home listings in Denver. "Are you thinking of moving?"

"Yes. Call it plan B. Or G, or whatever letter I'm up to by now. We can talk about it after you see what I found for you today."

His stomach cramped. His search seemed less important lately. He had all his life to find that box. Mia's situation was more urgent. She couldn't stay out here indefinitely and was clearly making plans to move on.

Without him.

Why the hell did that hurt?

Yes. She was thinking of moving. Said it as if that was the most obvious solution. It was. She couldn't live in secret out here forever. He looked down into Silas's face, his ears ringing and his heart hammering that his time with this little guy was limited.

"Jarvis. You're not listening."

"Sorry." He focused on the map of the ranch filling her screen and the point where her finger hovered. "Your son is a terrible distraction."

Her expression softened. "I know."

An unsettling feeling of rightness sifted over him. This woman, with that warm, uninhibited love shining in her eyes and her child in his arms, was right. For him. He could almost hear the click as everything snapped into place. He hadn't counted on this at all.

Was her love worth the effort and risk theory rubbing off on him? He'd initially blamed her philosophy about life and living on motherhood and a daughter's tender heart and devotion. He had no idea how to explain the reaction rocketing through him.

He felt Silas getting sleepy and he stood up, swaying gently with the baby. "Why add this spot to the search?" he asked, the unfamiliar emotions making his voice rough.

"I made a few calls this afternoon. Many of the public records have been scanned in and I was able to access them online. I'd rather be there in person, but…" Her voice trailed off and she stroked a curl of hair over Silas's ear.

"Anyway," she cleared her throat. "I took a closer look at which acreage was acquired when." She zoomed in. "We're here," she pointed. "And this sector northwest of us is a prime spot to look." She tipped her face up, smile blooming. "I think it's *the* spot."

In his arms, Silas gurgled. "He seems to agree," Jarvis joked. "Tell me more."

"Either Herman or Eugene Colton picked up this strip of land just a few years before the date on that deed of sale that shows Herman sold the property to Ainsley."

She clicked and opened a new window on her screen and a spreadsheet opened. "This is hardly proof of anything, but this is the list of when which parcels changed hands. Between Herman and Eugene and the Ainsley family, the acreage that melded into the Triple R was in flux for a long time."

"But we're not sure that first deed of sale between Herman and Ainsley was legit." He said it out of habit as much as belief. He still had faith in his grandfather's story, but that properly filed deed of sale would be hard to overcome. "It doesn't make sense that Herman would sell the land *and* keep searching for the card cheat while telling anyone who'd listen that the property was rightfully his."

"I know." She looked at him, sadness filling her lovely eyes. "You may never know exactly what happened."

Well, he had no chance of separating fact from legend without the box. "So that's the spot?"

Her teeth nipped her lower lip and her mouth quirked to one side. "All it needs is an *X*," she said with confidence.

"Can I take a look?"

She scooted over and he handed her the baby, before taking the seat she'd been using. He scrolled in and out on the image as he read through the documentation of this particular acreage. "This is even farther out than I expected."

"We know the land and landmarks can change over time."

He nodded. "Weather, usage, roads and development. Earthquakes."

She rested a hand on his shoulder. "You won't offend me if you disagree."

He gave in and leaned into her comforting touch. "It's worth a look." He smiled, pulled out his cell phone and noted the position. He added a star to it, his reminder that the location was her suggestion. It was strange having help in this endeavor, a quest he'd relegated to white-whale status.

"I guess I have my marching orders," he said. Sitting back in the chair, he moved the cursor over the Las Vegas tab, but he didn't open it. "So tell me why you're thinking of moving away."

"An email came through earlier. It was an update on the college fund my dad and I set up for Silas. Someone closed the account. The money is gone."

He knew Mia was thinking about her stepmother's previous theft. "Who has access?" he asked.

"Only my father and me," she said. "It has to be Regina. Either she convinced him to move the money or she managed to fake the signatures. Again."

It was exactly what he'd been thinking. "Convincing your dad to move the money seems like a hard sell. Even if he's upset with you, he wants what's best for your son."

She gave a low growl of frustration. The sound was far from intimate, but it slid under his skin, anyway. Made him wonder what kind of pleasured sounds he could draw out of her.

"Did you try to call?"

"As soon as I saw the email," she said. "My calls went straight to voice mail. I sent text messages, but he hasn't answered. Regina hasn't answered for him, either."

He knew she was thinking the worst, that Regina had finally attacked her father to draw her out. "Wouldn't closing or moving an account like that have to be done in person?"

"It can be done online," she said. "I don't care about the money. That account was entirely a gift for Silas from Dad."

The baby had dozed off in her arms and he hoped her distress wouldn't wake him. One thing that struck him time and again was how down-to-earth Mia remained. Practical, kind and genuine.

"Online or in person, there has to be a record, whether it's security cameras or electronic documentation. This is something Spencer can dig into. Let me loop him in," Jarvis urged. "Your dad handles accounts for many high-profile people and businesses. If he's being coerced, people need to know."

"That's true. Do it."

He sent the information on to Spencer, then studied her profile. While talking about his search, she'd been animated and confident. Now she looked more defeated. "What's also true is that moving away won't guarantee your dad's safety. Regina is greedy and conniving. That won't change no matter what you do."

He ignored the small voice in his head that whispered he was being selfish by urging her to stay. She needed a life, a full and vibrant life, and once Regina was under control, she could have it right here in Mustang Valley, where he could still see her around town. It wasn't like they were destined for wedded bliss. He wasn't the man who could keep her and Silas happy and content in the long term.

Carefully, so he wouldn't wake the baby, he pushed back from the table. He stretched his arms overhead, then arched his back, easing the aches that affirmed an honest day's work on the ranch.

"You really do love being a cowboy." Her soft smile lit up her face and ignited something deep in his chest.

"You're right." Could she love him as a cowboy? He swallowed the question before it embarrassed them both. "I don't see it changing."

An operation this size always needed something, and each day was a slight variation on the last. Yet it was the constancy amid all of it that appealed. And like a fool, he kept wondering if she could be happy with an average cowboy rather than a slick, wealthy businessman. Even if his old career miraculously put him in the same financial league as Mia, he couldn't go back to that life, not even for her.

"Will you stay again tonight?" She peered up at him through her lashes.

"Sure." Of course he'd stay. It wasn't just about keeping watch. He was too attached to her and her son. The smart move would be creating some distance before he spouted promises he couldn't keep. "And with a little luck, tomorrow night I'll be here with dinner and Herman's box in hand," he said lightly.

With Silas down for the night, they talked of other things, lighter topics until they were ready for bed, as well. Mia was a woman who deserved promises and a man who would keep them. Jarvis came from a long line of men who drank heavily and died early, leaving the people who dared to love them behind. He wasn't an alcoholic, but that wasn't enough to convince him he'd be different in the long run.

His siblings, the only two constants in his life, had found the courage to fall in love. That was great and fine for them. Jarvis couldn't muster up the same faith in a happy ending for himself.

"Jarvis?" She twisted around to face him in the bunk. "Will you be here for coffee?"

"I'll probably need to get out of here early." His mouth touched hers almost against his will. He needed that sweet taste of her to carry him through the night. She was warm, her lush lips tempting. His self-control fraying, he pulled her close, his fingertips caressing her generous curves.

"I want you," she whispered. The invitation fluttered against his throat. Butterfly wings carrying world-altering cargo. "I don't want to wait anymore."

The idea of spending the night with her body tangled with his hit him like a kick in the chest. With another woman, child or not, he might jump at the chance. He'd been the rebound guy before and been fine with it.

An easy, compatible one-night stand wouldn't be enough. Instinctively, he knew Mia wouldn't be out of his system with just one night. That was why he'd been avoiding anything more than hot kisses and sizzling caresses. He feared she was an addiction as detrimental to him as alcohol and bitterness had been to his grandfathers.

"We shouldn't," he said. "I want to," he insisted as her disappointment sagged against him.

"Because of the baby?" Her fingertips dragged down his chest and lower until he trapped her hand under his.

"Because of everything." An owl called and Jarvis listened. There was no reason to think Mia was in danger, and yet he remained alert.

"I understand." Her words brushed against his throat.

He was glad one of them did. "Get some rest." He brushed a kiss to her lips and heard himself make her a promise. "When this is over, if you still want me, I'm all yours."

"I'll hold you to that."

He was already hers. And he was increasingly convinced that nothing would alter that fact.

Chapter Eleven

Mia wondered how Jarvis was doing. She'd hoped to say good morning, share that magical first cup of coffee with him this morning, but he'd been gone before Silas had woken her.

As the day wore on with no contact from him, she started doubting herself for being direct last night. But she did want him, had wanted him from that very first kiss. One way or another, her time here would end. It was selfish and possibly arrogant to think making love with Jarvis would somehow bind him to her when she and Silas came out of hiding.

Needs and temptation aside, it wasn't fair to push him when she didn't know where she would end up. But it would've been amazing. Would *be* amazing, she reminded herself. She just had to be patient because Jarvis would keep his word about being all hers when this was over.

Mia looked at the calendar displayed on her computer screen and wondered exactly when "over" would get here.

Regina was still out there, still pushing and working the rumor mill to undermine Mia's credibility and her relationship with her dad. Nearly a month had passed and nothing outside of this bunkhouse felt safe.

It was an illusion. Temporary. Just because she didn't know what would crop up next, didn't mean she could keep leaning on Jarvis's kindness and kisses. When she'd divorced, she expected it would take years to find a man worthy of her affection and her son's trust. Finding them, Jarvis had changed everything from her relationship time line to uncovering a well of desire she'd never known before.

She shook off the wayward thoughts. There were far more important things to think about than the day she would finally get intimate with Jarvis.

Aggravated and restless, Mia opened the front door of the bunkhouse, making sure the sunlight wouldn't disrupt Silas's nap. The fresh air and open country should feel full of promise. This rugged land was beautiful, but it was time to make a move. She had a son to raise, a career to launch. It was impractical to think she could move out of town and stay safe. At some point, someone would recognize her and Regina would start her threats all over again.

Jarvis had asked her to give Spencer time. And why not? It wasn't like she had anywhere to be. Maybe once he verified the information in the file, he'd have a suggestion about how she should proceed.

Her phone vibrated in her pocket and she checked the alert on her screen. It was a text from her father. At least from his number, she thought grimly.

Mia, I need to see you.

What's wrong, Dad?

I'm afraid Regina has done something unforgivable.

Mia's heart soared with hope, even as logic insisted it was most likely another one of Regina's traps.

Are you in town?

She hesitated, wishing she could be sure it was really her father sending these messages.

Yes. Call me.

I can't. I'm so sick my throat's raw. I think Regina put something in my breakfast.

What? Her heart slammed against her rib cage. Another text came through before she could ask any questions or suggest he call an ambulance.

Honey, have you been hiding from my wife?

Could her dad have finally figured out he'd married a crocodile in designer clothing?

Please meet me at the house. Regina will be away for another hour. Bring the baby and let's talk this out. If you have evidence against Regina bring that, too.

That last line gave her a moment's pause. But if Spencer had reached out about the college fund, it made sense. This was an opportunity to gain an advantage.

Dad, where did we spend my eighth birthday?

In Disneyland. You went nuts for the princess parade. Hurry, honey. I need you.

OMW

Mia closed her laptop, her latest search unfinished. She shoved supplies into the diaper bag and called Jarvis. He didn't answer. She'd try again from the car and apologize when she got back. She couldn't *not* go to her father.

Moving as quickly as possible, she buckled Silas in to the car seat. Looping the diaper bag and her purse over her arm, she headed for the truck. Mia drove toward the house as fast as she dared, eyeing the clock. He hadn't given her much time. She'd known Regina was bad news from day one and finally—finally—her father's eyes had been opened to his wife's true nature. Using the hands-free option, she called Jarvis again and left a message this time.

"We'll take Grandpa to the hospital," she told Silas. She would insist on a full blood workup, an analysis of what had made him sick and a plan to flush it out of his system. The police could meet them there and take his statement. Jarvis's brother could smooth the way for that solution.

Oh, the idea of reclaiming her stable, loving relationship with her dad put a smile on her face as she parked the truck in the driveway. With Silas in his car seat, her purse and diaper bag over her shoulder, she rushed to the front door. Her father had left it unlocked; she didn't even need to use her code. That shouldn't have been such a high point, but it was. She and her father had been at odds for so long.

"Regina," she said, stopping short in the foyer. "How nice to see you."

"Is it?" She sneered. The woman who'd been a thorn in Mia's side for too many years, who'd effectively wedged her out of her father's life, aimed a gun at her. "Welcome home."

Dread flared along her spine, turned her palms damp with nervous sweat. "What are you doing?" She tucked the carrier behind her back to shelter Silas. "Where's Dad?"

"Upstairs, asleep. He's not as young as he used to be."

"He called me," she began. Her voice faltered when Regina laughed. "No, my dear, he sent you a text message." Keeping the gun steady in one hand, she held up a device and wagged it side to side. "Look familiar?"

Mia's stomach cramped. Both the phone and the gun her father kept in a lockbox in the bedroom were familiar. She'd known better and made a serious miscalculation, anyway. "What have you done?"

"Only what's necessary to protect my husband and his interests."

"*Your* interests, more like."

She shrugged one shoulder. "Your father and I are more frequently on the same page when it comes to you." She leaned a bit to the side. "And your brat."

"How did you answer the Disney question so well?" She had to keep Regina talking. She had to buy time for Jarvis to see that she'd called or for the housekeeper to come home or another miracle. Any miracle that would prevent Regina from killing her and Silas.

"Since you had the baby, your father will not shut up about your childhood. He pores over those scrapbooks every night." Her heart pounded in her chest. She absolutely believed Regina would pull that trigger. And she'd get away with it because Mia had walked right into the trap with her son. So many violent, furious thoughts ran through her head that she was tongue-tied.

"You were invited here for one purpose, Mia." Regina stared at her over the barrel of the gun. "Give me that damned video and anything else you think you've got on me."

"I don't have the video."

Regina rolled her eyes. "Cooperation is your only play," Regina snapped. "You've lost. You'll hand over your phone and give me all the links to where you've stashed copies. Do it now and I'll spare your son."

"No. I don't believe you." It wouldn't be that easy. "You've threatened him too often already."

Regina's eyes went wide and she gave a little scream but the gun remained on Mia. "All the more reason to cooperate. You have no power here. Give me all of your supposed evidence and your father won't die today."

Mia forced herself to speak her worst fear. "You've killed him already."

"Oh, Mia. You've thought the worst of me from the start. I *love* him. I'd never hurt him."

"Save it," Mia snapped. "You're an evil, manipulative excuse for a human being."

Regina lowered the gun slightly, her mouth agape. "I can't decide if you're too stupid or too brave. If I'm so terrible, you should damn well cooperate with me."

"Never." Mia held her ground. "You've done enough damage to this family."

"You selfish *tramp*!" Regina screamed. Her lips twisted into a grotesque snarl. "After everything I've put up with since marrying Norton. You have *no* power here. No room to negotiate."

She stalked across the room, the gun a very real threat between them. "You always do everything Daddy says. I know you brought that video with you. Along with anything else you think will turn him against me."

Mia took brief comfort in Regina's use of present tense when speaking about Norton. Maybe he was still alive.

Her comfort shifted to alarm as Regina stalked closer and, using the threat of the gun, forced her out of the foyer toward the front room, shoving her to the floor. The car seat landed with a thump and Mia sheltered Silas as best she could.

Grabbing Mia's purse, Regina stepped back, dumping out the contents. "Why do people hail mothers as saints?" she muttered. "This is a mess." She snatched Mia's phone and then glared into Mia's face. "*You* are a mess. What is the code?"

Mia gave it to her. She'd used a new phone, one strictly for business when she'd caught Regina with another man at the country house. And, just as Regina assumed, she'd stored the incriminating video on the cloud. Two separate servers, in fact, with one copy in the hands of the police. She was tempted to tell Regina all of that, but she'd made enough mistakes today.

Regina swore when she didn't find the video. "Where is it?"

"You have the wrong phone," Mia said calmly.

Regina's face contorted with rage. "I've always hated you. You're nothing but a leech."

Mia ignored the familiar rant, her mind on how to

escape without jeopardizing Silas. "Give me that video and I'll make sure Norton doesn't mix up his medications again."

"I don't believe you," Mia said. "I'm not handing anything over to you until I see my father."

Regina cursed a blue streak. "Fine. I'll indulge you one more time." She gestured with the barrel of the gun. "The last time," she added. "Go on upstairs and see him for yourself."

Mia moved as slowly as she dared, not wanting to aggravate Regina any more than necessary, yet buying as much time as possible.

Surely, Jarvis had seen her text by now or picked up her message. Yes, he'd be furious that she'd fallen for Regina's trap, but when she didn't call, he'd follow up. He'd find her.

She had to believe in him. That faith was the only thing keeping her heart beating in her chest. Fear for Silas was a beast, clawing at her gut. She had to find a way to prove she wasn't merely a spoiled brat and that Regina was the monster.

JARVIS'S SHOVEL SLICED into the earth and metal clanged hard against metal. The vibration ringing up his arms froze him in place. His breath stalled, trapped in his chest, until it exploded on an exhale.

"I'll be damned." Mia was right.

Of course she was. She'd thrown herself into his search, pulling strings and piecing together leads that he hadn't considered. Maybe she should give up real estate for treasure hunting.

Dropping the shovel, he fell to his knees and scraped dirt away from the top of an old metal box. He eased the box from its resting place and stared at it as shock and potential rippled through his system. Pulling a bandanna from his back pocket, he poured water on the fabric and rubbed the top of the box clean. His heart pounded as the *H.C.* scratched into the surface was revealed. "Just like Isaiah said."

His grandfather's story flitted through his mind. "You weren't crazy, Granddad." And by default, Jarvis wasn't, either.

Herman Colton had dug into this earth generations ago, and buried this box for his sons and their sons. Could there really be evidence inside that this massive, thriving enterprise belonged to Jarvis and his siblings now?

A chill ran through him and Jarvis sat down hard, suddenly afraid to open it. This could change everything. Or nothing. His sister and brother weren't into the Triple R. Jarvis was currently the only cowboy in the immediate family.

He tried to imagine Asher's face, hearing that Jarvis was the new owner. Jarvis didn't want to be the boss. He couldn't work this place any better than Asher. Hell, he wasn't ready to take sole responsibility of an operation this size. He scrubbed at his face as hope and fear zinged through him in equal measure.

The contents, assuming they confirmed Isaiah's story, would put the long-ignored Colton triplets on the map. A complete reversal of fortune. Their parents would have flipped out.

It was dumb to sit here wondering after investing so much time in the search. The answers were at his fingertips now. His hands shook as he reached for the lock and he pulled back. Mia should see this. She'd suggested this place, and finding the box was as much her victory as his.

If there were documents inside, it was probably better to open this in the presence of a lawyer. And somewhere other than outside under the bright sunshine, where the breeze might carry off something important.

Carefully setting aside the box, he picked up the shovel and filled in the hole. With the location marked on the app, just in case someone challenged his claim, he secured the box behind his saddle and rode for the bunkhouse.

"Mia!" he called as he pulled Duke to a stop. He tempered his excitement and lowered his voice, worried about waking Silas from a nap. It was such a "honey, I'm home" kind of moment, but he didn't care. Didn't even feel awkward about it.

"Mia, you were right," he said softly as he opened the door. He stopped and stared around the space. She wasn't here. The baby wasn't here. The blanket where he napped was near the bed. Her computer was on the table, closed.

His blood ran cold. Had Regina found her? He tore around to the back. The truck was gone. That didn't necessarily mean she'd left on her own. Maybe she'd gone for a drive so Silas would sleep. She might even be scoping out another likely search site.

That worried him. He saw a missed call from her number, but no voice mail. Sometimes those alerts were slow out here. He sent her a text that he'd found the box. With luck, that would bring her back sooner rather than later.

Unable to stand it any longer, he broke the lock and opened the box. There were letters and some old, grainy photographs and a Bible. The writing had faded with time, but most of it was still legible. His hands trembled when he realized he held the original deed for a chunk of Triple R land.

He read a letter from Herman and could almost smell the liquor on his ancestor's breath. It rambled on and on, not bothering to be tactful at all or hide his contempt for Eugene's poor character. Herman alleged that not only had Eugene reneged on the plan to reclaim property lost in the card game, he had also forged Herman's signature on a second sale of land to T. Ainsley. It was a slice of his family history, possibly true, but not likely to hold up in court against the documentation Mia had found on file.

The surge of relief startled him.

Jarvis carefully opened the old Bible, mindful of the cracked leather cover. He squinted at the births and deaths listed on the fragile front pages. Tucked inside was a piece of paper. Unfolding it, he smiled at a Colton family tree.

Herman and Eugene weren't brothers at all. The men had been cousins, he noted, tracking the names and marriages, the children that followed. The revelations in the collection of letters, the names and important dates of people he'd never known left ripples across his soul, changing his mind about the kind of family he came from.

He tucked everything back into the box. He wasn't comfortable leaving it out here unattended. Where were Mia and Silas? She hadn't replied to his text and he was getting restless. Had the baby gotten sick?

He tried to call her and got a service error. Better to stow the box in his room until he figured out what had happened to Mia. He and Duke weren't far from the main stable when his phone chirped from his shirt pocket. A voice-mail alert showed up from Mia's number. He scrambled to listen to the message.

"Hi. Dad thinks Regina poisoned him. Had to go. I'll call when I know more."

Jarvis swore, urging Duke into a gallop, his heart thundering with the worst-case scenarios. Regina was behind this. Had to be. Every minute gave that witch an advantage, but he couldn't ride hard and talk on the phone at the same time.

Reaching the stable, he handed off Duke to Jimmy with his apologies. Box under his arm, he called Spencer as he ran for the old ranch truck. "I think Mia's in trouble," he said without preamble. "Can you meet me at Norton Graves's place?"

"What kind of trouble?" his brother queried.

"You've been through the file I sent? You saw the threats her stepmom made?"

"Yes. In fact, I called Regina this morning and asked her to come in and talk."

Jarvis swore. That was the catalyst. "Supposedly, Mia's dad asked her to come over with the baby. I don't have evidence yet of a crime in progress, but it smells like a setup." Would that be enough for Spencer?

"On my way."

"Thanks."

At his truck, Jarvis placed Herman's box under the dash on the passenger side and tossed a towel over it. Then he drove as fast as the old engine would go to Norton's house, using his speakerphone option to call Mia. She didn't pick up, so he called again. And again.

As dread pooled in his gut, he kept trying her phone, praying the next time she'd answer.

Every minute felt like an hour. Though he tried to put his churning emotions into context, he knew he wouldn't calm down until he saw Mia and Silas healthy and whole.

"SEE. I TOLD you he was fine," Regina said.

Mia watched her father's chest rise and fall. "What did you give him?"

"Nothing fatal." Regina's smile could curdle milk. "This time."

"How do you expect to get away with this?" Mia demanded. If she could keep her talking she could find an opening. Where was Jarvis?

"You've been gone, out of sight, no contact for weeks. Your poor father has nearly worried himself to death." She cackled. "He'll be so disappointed to hear you relocated and refused to visit. Don't worry, I'll be here to soothe him through your heartless betrayal."

So the woman planned to impersonate her as she'd impersonated Norton. If Regina had her way, Mia wouldn't leave this house alive. She had to *do* something or Regina would get away with murder. Hers, her father's and, probably, her son's.

Staring into Regina's pitiless eyes, Mia felt her blood ignite. No way would she let this woman walk off as the sole beneficiary of the Graves estate, playing the part of a grieving widow.

"Go." Regina waved the gun, motioning Mia out of the bedroom.

She backed up, deliberately bumping her shoulder and then the baby carrier into the door frame. Silas started to fuss. Setting the carrier down, she made an issue of rubbing her shoulder while soothing her son.

"You're as clumsy as a cow," Regina snapped. "Worse than before you were pregnant. Trust me, a bullet will hurt more than a door frame. Pick up the brat and *move*."

Mia braced for the worst as she twisted around, but instead of picking up Silas, she grabbed a stone bust from the pedestal in the hallway. Only Regina would consider this cheap knockoff an artistic statement.

Swiveling around, she threw the bust at Regina. The woman screamed, squeezing the trigger as Mia wheeled back and tried to duck. The bullet hit the ceiling and dust rained down on them as Mia launched herself at Regina. But something caught her at the waist and hauled her back out into the hallway. Did Regina have help?

With a scream, she clawed at the thick forearm, desperate to escape with her baby.

Someone else shoved past her, shouting at Regina.

"Easy, Mia. Mia! It's me."

"Jarvis?" She slumped to her knees and he followed her to the floor. "What are you doing here?"

"Keeping Silas's mother out of jail."

Indignant, she looked around. "Where is he?"

"Spencer put him in the bathroom."

Despite the sounds of an ongoing fight in her father's bedroom, Mia jumped up and darted through the closed bathroom door across the hall. Jarvis's voice followed her, warning her to wait, but she couldn't possibly. Silas was awake and gurgling happily, flapping his arms. The car seat, safely in the center of the bath-tub, rocked with his motions.

"Oh, my baby." She couldn't help herself—she had to hold him. Lifting him from the seat, she cradled his head to her shoulder, kissing his chubby cheek. "It's all over now, my sweetheart."

"He's okay?"

"Perfect." She twisted to find Jarvis staring at her. "It's over, right?"

He nodded.

"Thank you." She realized what a fool she'd been rushing out here alone. As her errors stuttered through her mind, she realized how she'd played right into Regina's plans. If Jarvis hadn't shown up, with police backup, there was no telling how badly this might have ended.

"Jarvis—"

He cut her off with a sharp look. "Why would you do this? You could've been killed." His face was pale and she knew she had to find a way to reassure him. "I—I was only thinking of my dad. He asked for my help."

Jarvis folded his arms. "You called but didn't wait. You didn't give me much chance to help you."

"And yet you showed up in time. Thank you," she said again.

But timing wasn't the point. She saw the pain in his eyes and realized how her lapse in judgment, how putting herself and the baby at risk, hurt him. This man had gone above and beyond for her and she'd returned his kindnesses by being cruel, forcing him to worry that another person he cared for would be injured. Or worse.

"I'm sorry, Jarvis." He turned away, as if he couldn't bear to look at her. "You would've told me it was a trap."

"It *was!*" He hitched a shoulder, shuffling his feet. His brother called for him and he stepped into the hallway. A moment later he returned. "Regina's in cuffs," he told her, his voice flat. "I've called an ambulance."

Of course he had.

"They should be here any minute. Wait in the bedroom with your dad. All three of you are safe now." He held her gaze for a long moment, then his eyes shifted to her son, lingered there. "I'll see you around, Mia. Be well."

She stood there, feelings and words a logjam in her throat. He couldn't be walking away. Yet, this wasn't the time or place to demand he uphold his promise.

As she rushed into her father's bedroom, gratitude and relief soared through her. He wasn't awake, but he was alive. A chair and table had been upended, items and pictures from the top of his dresser scattered and broken. A framed picture of Silas and Mia was distorted by shattered glass.

Still, her father slept on, oblivious to the chaos Regina had staged. Jarvis had been right. There was no telling what might have happened if he and his brother hadn't shown up in time. Guilt blotted out the relief and tears threatened. She'd ruined everything, damaged something beautiful between her and Jarvis.

When the paramedics arrived, she stepped aside,

watched with a new fear as they gathered the pill bottles from the nightstand and transferred her father from the bed to the stretcher, wheeling him away.

Chapter Twelve

Jarvis listened to the updates on Spencer's police scanner as Regina fumed in the back seat. She tossed out threats even after Spencer read her her rights.

The ambulance was transporting Norton Graves to Mustang Valley General Hospital. He was sure Mia was with them. At the very least, she was following. Maybe he'd see her again when she returned the truck. A pulse of heat zipped through his veins at the idea. He was a fool.

Seeing her again wouldn't change the facts. She was more than a beautiful woman he'd fallen for. She and Silas were a ready-made family he wasn't convinced he could have.

"How do you do it?" he asked Spencer when Regina had been hauled deeper into the police station for processing.

"Do what?"

"Love. Your relationship with Katrina." He shoved his hands into his pockets. "You put your life on the line in this job."

"Not too often," Spencer said. "Is there a question in there?"

"*Everyone* left us," Jarvis said. "Everyone has let us down. What made you take that kind of chance?"

"Mom and Dad didn't exactly choose that car wreck," Spencer said. "Aunt Amelia did her best by us, considering she wound up with three kids when she didn't want any."

Jarvis slumped into a chair near his brother's desk, one normally reserved for criminals in processing. He should be happy Mia and Silas were out of danger, but he kept thinking about that expectant look on her face. Thinking about the promise he'd made that he had to break. Anything else would be emotional suicide.

"I've let her down," he muttered.

"Mia?"

Jarvis nodded. To be fair, she'd let him down, too, when she rushed into danger. "I can't be what she needs."

"Why the hell not?" Spencer demanded.

"Come on." He stood up, restless. "She has a kid. Me and fatherhood? That's a joke."

Spencer leaned back in his chair, fingers drumming on the armrests. "Is it? Do you love her?"

"How would I know?"

Spencer glared at him. "Only you can answer that." From the back, they heard Regina shouting. "Get out of here," he said. "I'll keep you posted." He clapped Jarvis on the shoulder as he walked by. "You do the same."

Twitchy as the adrenaline faded, Jarvis didn't know what to do with himself. He wasn't ready to go back to the ranch and talk with Asher. Spencer didn't need him here and neither did Mia. She was set now that her stepmother was in custody and she had her father back.

Family sucked, he thought. Always had. He walked

out of the police station, guilt digging into the back of the neck. Mia and Silas were a family and they didn't suck at all.

No, Mia and Silas were a sweet temptation he'd never expected to crave.

Jarvis slid into the driver's seat of the old pickup and tried to imagine how he'd fill his time without them. The idea left him hollow. He'd found evidence that his family, several messy generations ago, had tried their best with various degrees of success. All the way down to his parents.

Lost in his wandering thoughts, Jarvis drove through town, a little surprised to find himself at his aunt's old house. They'd sold it right after she died. He wouldn't find absolution here. He drove on to the cemetery where his parents, Amelia and his grand-dad were buried.

Herman's box had slipped out from under the towel, like some ghostly challenge. Jarvis owed it to Isaiah to let someone know the old man had been right about the family legend, even if those folks weren't around anymore.

With the box under his arm, he walked out toward their graves, staring down at the headstones. "I found it," he said to the hushed cemetery. "The old family legend is true. Isaiah wasn't just drunk or confused." He sat down, resting the box on his crossed legs. "I found the box Herman buried."

He looked to Amelia's headstone. "I was helping a friend with a baby the other day," he said. "I had to look up what to do on Google." He thought he had a better perspective now, being furious with Mia and still desperate to hold her and tell her it would all work out.

"I'm sorry we were so mad at you. A friend made me realize we were all grieving. Thanks for being a safe person to be mad at."

The admission lifted a weight from his shoulders, relieving a pressure he'd lived with for too long.

"Thank you. All of you." He toyed with the broken latch on the box. "I should've said that a long time ago and a lot more often."

With a sigh, he flipped open the lid and pulled out the old Bible. "I figured we could go through this together. I'll fill in Spencer and Bella later. Turns out Herman Colton and Eugene Colton were cousins, not brothers. Payne can't deny we're all related, but we're not as close as Isaiah thought."

Jarvis gingerly leafed through the fragile documents in the box. "The original deed is here, in Herman's name. He was spitting mad about Eugene being a thief, but it wasn't true. All of that land around the Triple R changed hands as fortunes changed. I'll show this to Asher, but it's only a matter of curiosity. Nothing in here disputes Payne's ownership. Which is fine. I couldn't take on all that by myself."

He was talking to gravestones and yet it felt right. A normal, peaceful interlude underscored by an intense sense of connection. "After Mom and Dad died, I felt cut off from everything but Spencer and Bella. This helps." His ancestors were far from perfect, but they'd cared and they'd done their best for those who came after them. "Maybe my generation can overcome some of Payne's nonsense." He'd never wanted the family ties just to make a claim on Payne's precious fortune. He'd simply been looking for roots. Now he'd found them.

With questions answered, by this box and the records Mia had uncovered, the bitterness faded.

Contrary to his siblings' concerns, he'd never felt like he'd given up anything by leaving the office for the ranch. He'd simply changed his direction to make something better happen. Something he'd hoped would change the conversation around his siblings.

The search itself, along with what he'd found in this box, had unlocked something inside him. Something fresh and hopeful that wanted to flourish.

"Thanks," he said again to the gravestones. "I'll come back again soon." And next time he hoped to have his family with him. It would take a bit of planning, but it would be worth it.

Mia's eyes were gritty from fighting bursts of tears for hours. She'd love to blame it all on hormones, but she had to accept responsibility. She was crying out all the stress of the past month. Weeks of wondering how to protect her son and her father had taken a toll. Without Jarvis… She started tearing up again.

She'd lost him and she hadn't been prepared for that price. Here they were, both safe. Her son snoozed in her arms while her father rested under the capable observation of nurses as the heavy sedatives Regina had dosed him with wore off.

Two of the three most important men in her life, she thought wryly, swaying side to side gently to keep Silas asleep. His car seat was handy, but she wasn't ready to let go.

She rapidly blinked away another wave of emotion. Why did she keep falling in love with men who wanted nothing to do with fatherhood? The pain cut deeply and a night without Jarvis hadn't eased the sting of reality. If time healed all wounds, getting over him would take years.

It might be better, just her and Silas. If she'd learned anything from her time with Jarvis, it was that giving her son a solid foundation of love and being valued was essential for his future.

She could do that. Clearly, she had to do that.

"Mia? Is that you?"

She turned at the rasping sound of her father's voice and hurried to his bedside. "Yes, Dad." She gripped his hand. "I'm here. We're here," she added.

"Oh, honey." He squeezed his eyes closed. "Honey, I'm so sorry I didn't believe you about Regina."

"Love does that," she said. "And you loved her." She loved Jarvis and a piece of her always would, whether or not they ever managed to reconcile. It was the most challenging thing to accept. The heart was stubborn.

"I love you, too. Loved you first." He coughed. "Love blinded me to her faults." Another cough interrupted him.

"Rest now," she soothed. "Don't stress about it. We're all fine now."

"I'll make it up to you," he said. He shifted, fiddling with the bed controls so he was sitting up. He patted her hand and beamed at Silas. "Can I hold my grandson?"

"Of course." She could see the regrets swirling in his gaze. "He's overdue for grandpa time."

"Because I'm an old fool," he crooned to the baby. "No more. Your momma is a smart woman. The sooner you learn that, the happier you'll be." He lifted his face to meet her gaze. "You come first, Mia. Take the country house, for as long as you need it."

As much as she appreciated the gesture, she couldn't erase the image of her stepmother's infidelity. Her dad still didn't know about that. "What if we sell it and donate the proceeds to charity?" she suggested. Single mothers, victims of crimes, an orphanage were just a few options that came to mind. There were countless places that money could make a difference and then she'd never have to step foot on the property again.

He lifted an eyebrow. "You loved that place."

"It's time for a change," she hedged.

"A fresh start is a good idea for both of us." He smiled down at the baby. "All of us. But where does that leave us? I can't bear the idea of going back to the house where she…where she abused both of us."

"Well, it's technically a crime scene at the moment," she said. "I know of a property between the Rattlesnake Ridge Ranch and town. It's not as grand as the house in the neighborhood or even the country house. But it's closer to your office and it could work for the three of us while we sort things out."

A week ago, in a dreamy, love-induced haze, she'd put in an offer, hoping to tempt Jarvis to build a life there with her. Close enough to the Triple R to keep him in the job he loved, close enough to town to make her real-estate career viable. Though Jarvis might never call it home, it was still perfect for her and Silas and her dad for as long as he wanted to stay.

A nurse walked in, all smiles. "Now, this is what I like to see." She took Norton's vital signs while he bragged on his tiny grandson. "You have a lovely family, Mr. Graves. The doctor will be around soon."

She'd barely stepped out before a volunteer knocked on the open door. "Is there a Silas Graves here?"

Mia bristled, moving between her father's bed and the doorway. "Silas is my son. He isn't a patient."

The volunteer looked down at a card he held. "We actually have deliveries for Silas Graves, Norton Graves and Mia Graves."

Wary, Mia planted her hands on her hips. "Deliveries from whom?"

"This card doesn't say."

"Then we can't…" Her voice trailed off as Jarvis filled the doorway.

"Can't what?" he asked.

She stared, utterly dumbstruck. She hadn't expected to face him this soon. Wasn't she allowed some time to pull the ragged pieces of her heart together? There should be rules about this kind of thing. She should definitely be allowed a shower and fresh clothes before facing him.

"I'll take it from here," he said to the volunteer. "Can you please bring in the cart?"

With a nod, the volunteer stepped aside and pushed a cart into the room behind Jarvis.

"How are you feeling, sir?" he asked Norton, striding right past her to the bed.

"Grateful to be alive," her father replied. "Thanks to you and your brother."

"Your daughter had it under control," Jarvis said. "We just batted cleanup."

He caught her eye across the bed and she felt the heat in her cheeks, remembering their first meeting when she'd been nearly knocked his head off with that stick.

"She's my pride and joy," Norton said. "Even when I'm a fool. And she has excellent intuition."

Mia blinked. It was the first time she'd heard that kind of compliment out of her father since before he'd married Regina.

"I agree." Jarvis grinned. "I brought a few things, just to brighten the room until they kick you out."

She noticed several items on the cart. Flowers, a few wrapped boxes and a portable crib on the bottom shelf. What did this mean? Hope bloomed, bright as the lilies in the floral arrangement. Tears stung her nose and she sniffed them away. Whatever he was about, she would survive this and cry about it later, when she didn't have an audience.

"Mr. Graves, these are for you." He set the vase of colorful flowers on the counter where Norton could see them easily.

Her father's brow furrowed. "Thanks."

"You're welcome." Jarvis turned back to the cart. "This is for the precious guy in your arms."

"We won't need the crib," she snapped ungraciously. "I think they'll discharge him today."

But it wasn't the crib he'd pulled from the cart, but a deep square box. "Go ahead and open it," he said, putting the box in her arms.

Her knees were jelly and she sank into the chair before they failed her. She heard the voices, but not the words as Jarvis and her father chatted.

She opened the box and stared at the contents. A small baseball cap and the smallest baseball mitt she'd ever seen were nested in with a soft, squishy ball stitched like a baseball.

"Jarvis?"

"Just thinking ahead. If he inherits your batting stance, you should get him started early."

It should've been funny, a flashback to their first meeting. Maybe she'd find the humor and kindness behind the gesture later. But he'd said *you*, not *we*. Why was he crushing her heart this way?

"This one is for you." He set the box of tiny baseball gear aside and rested a longer box across her knees.

"A bat? You're definitely ahead of yourself." Would she even share these things with her son? Silas was too young to remember this month, so full of upheaval, and she wasn't sure she'd ever be strong enough to share even the happier stories with him.

"Just open it."

She didn't know what to make of the quirk of his lips. Avoiding his gaze, she slid the ribbon off and raised the lid. She frowned at the contents. It wasn't the baseball bat she'd expected. It was a length of hickory, polished to a gleam and cushioned in a bed of midnight blue velvet. There was a sheer ribbon tied around one end of the stick. A sparkle in the center of the bow caught her eye. It couldn't be…but it sure looked like a diamond engagement ring.

"What's that?" Her father leaned over Silas for a peek.

"Nothing. It's a long story," she answered, scrambling to put the lid back on the box. She couldn't make sense of what was happening.

"Let's put the right ending on that story." Jarvis dropped to one knee in front of her. "I love you, Mia. You and Silas. You've changed me, shown me what lasting love looks like. Will you marry me and be my family? Will you let me love you both for the rest of our days?"

"Say yes!" her father encouraged.

"What happened to trusting my judgment and intuition?" she asked, shooting her dad a look. To Jarvis she said, "I'm more of a package deal now than I was before. You said—"

"I've said a lot of stupid things. It was all fear talking."

"Fear?"

He nodded. "All my life I've lost the people I love most. Love felt more like a curse or a burden, until you."

She remembered how he'd resisted her attempts to give him some perspective.

"I was out there searching for my past and when I stumbled onto you and Silas I found my future. Marry me, Mia. Let's build the family we both deserve."

"Oh, Jarvis, yes." Her heart swelled with joy. "I love you, too. I was afraid to admit it and run you off."

The smile that creased his face melted away every cold spot inside her. Hope and love gleamed in his brown eyes. He glided his thumb over her cheek, wiping away a tear. It seemed she was crying in front of everyone after all.

At least this time, for the first time since Silas was born, she was weeping tears of joy.

JARVIS COULD HARDLY believe his proposal had worked out. Soon he would have a wife, and with a little paperwork, Silas would legally be his, too. It had all come together and he was the happiest man on the planet. Every time Silas fussed or cried, he jumped in, eager to provide whatever his little guy needed. He'd have to curb that tendency in time, but at this stage there was no such thing as too much love. He'd never thought he had so much love inside him, ready to pour out over the people who mattered.

This evening, after another long day of work, he'd hustled back home—his *new* home—to pick up his fiancée. Norton had moved with them to the property Mia had found and was babysitting so Jarvis and Mia could go over to the Triple R for dinner with his siblings and Colton cousins.

As he pulled through the main gate and followed the drive toward Ainsley's wing of the Colton mansion, it felt remarkably normal to be here as family rather than just as an employee. Not family like Mia and Silas, but family with shared history. Roots he would be sure to nurture for the next generation.

"Are you okay with this?" she asked.

"Perfect," he replied honestly. "Since finding Herman's box, I'm more at peace with all of it than ever before. You gave me that, Mia. Thank you." He held her hand as they walked up to a sprawling deck where Ainsley was setting out a charcuterie board on a long table.

"Welcome, welcome." She invited them up to join her on the expansive deck. "You're the first to arrive. It's a gorgeous evening," she said, grinning. "The two of you look so happy."

The two of them. It was a heady sensation going from solo to a family. He had a fiancée and a son to raise and, hopefully, more children in the years ahead. He and Mia were creating something that would stand the test of time, no matter what life threw at them.

He turned as another car pulled up, and grinned as Spencer got out. Mia gave his hand a squeeze. It was a wonderful reminder that he had love beyond his brother and sister now. Now. Forever.

"Katrina's on her way," Spencer said as he joined them. "I couldn't wait to tell you the good news. Regina pleaded guilty to everything."

Mia relaxed against Jarvis and he slipped an arm around her waist. "Everything?"

His brother nodded. "Threats, extortion, drugging Norton, all of it. She even gave us the name of the man she'd been with in the video. Same guy knifed Mia's tire at the courthouse and came poking around the ranch, too."

Mia gaped at Jarvis. "He what?"

"I spotted tracks at the warming hut and didn't see the sense in alarming you." He bore up under the hard glare, lifting her hand to his lips. "It's the last secret I'll keep from you."

She and Ainsley traded a skeptical glance. "This calls for champagne," Ainsley said brightly. "Four glasses?"

"I'll have to take a rain check," Spencer replied. "I can't stay."

"That's a shame," Ainsley said. "Join us for the toast at least. Have you heard anything more about Ace's situation?"

Jarvis had heard bits and pieces of the accusations that the former Colton Oil CEO had been switched at birth with another baby at Mustang Valley General. Spencer hadn't discussed every detail of the investigation with him, but his cousins had started opening up since he'd shared the contents of Herman's box with Asher.

"I have a working theory," Spencer said. "It's taking time to come together."

The four of them settled around a heavy ironwork

table and Ainsley filled three champagne glasses and poured water for Spencer. They toasted to newfound family.

"I'm tracking down verification," Spencer continued. "Everything in my gut says Micheline Anderson *is* Luella Smith, the other mother at the hospital the night Ace was born. I'm sure she switched the babies."

Ainsley studied the bubbles in her glass. "If you're right, where is the real Ace Colton?"

"That's the question, isn't it?" Spencer shook his head. "Micheline's Affirmation Alliance Group feels like a cult to me. She swears it isn't and I can't prove it, yet, but the woman might not be as benign as we thought."

"How will you be sure one way or another?" Mia asked.

"Time," he said again. "I'll keep asking questions and we'll follow every thread until we have the facts."

"You're not the only one with a gut instinct," Ainsley said. "I have a terrible feeling that Micheline is our Ace's biological mother." She sipped her champagne. "This is such a complicated mess."

"It is," Spencer agreed. "If you'll excuse me, I have to get back to the station."

"Don't worry." Jarvis lifted his chin toward the car as his brother drove away. "With Spencer on the case and all of us invested in finding the truth, he'll figure it out."

"Maybe," Ainsley said, thoughtfully.

Jarvis knew Ainsley by reputation more than personal experience, but he couldn't help worrying that she might do something rash in an effort to find something to help her family.

His family, too.

Fortunately Katrina, Bella and Holden, Bella's fiancé, arrived, followed by Asher and Willow. It was a fabulous evening of good food and laughter, and the relaxed kind of family dinner he'd never expected to enjoy quite so much.

On the way home, he voiced his concerns about Ainsley to Mia. It was amazing to have someone to talk with about anything and everything. She listened attentively, assuring Jarvis that his rapidly expanding family would find a way to work together to get to the bottom of the Ace Colton mystery and all the other recent troubles.

After kissing Silas goodnight, they retired to their bedroom and, in the luxury of their king-size bed, Jarvis made up for all those nights when he hadn't done anything more than kiss her. When they were both sated, he pulled her close, as he'd done night after night on that narrow bunk, and reveled in the bliss of having a family of his own.

* * * * *

COMING SOON!

We really hope you enjoyed reading this book. If you're looking for more romance, be sure to head to the shops when new books are available on

Thursday 2nd April

To see which titles are coming soon, please visit

millsandboon.co.uk/nextmonth

LET'S TALK

Romance

For exclusive extracts, competitions
and special offers, find us online:

facebook.com/millsandboon

@MillsandBoon

@MillsandBoonUK

Get in touch on 01413 063232

For all the latest titles coming soon, visit
millsandboon.co.uk/nextmonth

 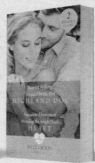 

JOIN US ON SOCIAL MEDIA!

Stay up to date with our latest releases, author news and gossip, special offers and discounts, and all the behind-the-scenes action from Mills & Boon...

 millsandboon

 millsandboonuk

 millsandboon

It might just be true love...

MILLS & BOON
MEDICAL
Pulse-Racing Passion

Set your pulse racing with dedicated, delectable doctors in the high-pressure world of medicine, where emotions run high and passion, comfort and love are the best medicine.